LADY OF SHADOWS

LADY OF DARKNESS
BOOK TWO

MELISSA K. ROEHRICH

ALSO BY MELISSA K. ROEHRICH

Lady of Darkness Series
Lady of Darkness
Lady of Shadows
Lady of Ashes
Lady of Embers
Book 5- Coming Spring 2023!

ISBN: 979-8-9852991-0-6 (*paperback*)
979-8-9852991-4-4 (*hardcover*)

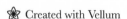 Created with Vellum

For Lindsey Leigh, Megan Bollman,
and Chelsay Tysver–
Thank you for helping me battle my shadows and find their beauty when the
stars went out.

Chateau

Solembra

Fiera
Moutains

Fire
Court

Tana River

To
Avonleya
<---

Windonelle

Baylorin

Water
Court

White
Halls

Wind
Court

Shira Cliffs

larion

orest

Dresden
Forest

on

Toreall

Witch
Kingdoms

Earth
Court

ck
lls

on

Jonaraja
Forest

Night
Children

Shifters

ra

A Lady of Darkness Reference Guide

Having a little trouble remembering all the people, gods, and who fits where?
With this quick and easy reference guide, you'll have all the information
you need at your fingertips.

ᏀhᏋ ᏀWO BIG OnᏋs

Scarlett Monrhoe: Scar-let Mon-roe
Our heroine, Death's Maiden,
Princess of the Western Courts

Sorin Aditya: Sore-in Ah-deet-yah
Your new book boyfriend,
Prince of the Fire Court,
formerly known as Ryker Renwell

BAᎩLORᏌn CᏲARACᏀᏋRs

Callan Solgard: Cal-in Soul-guard
Crown Prince of Windonelle

Cassius Redding: Cas-ee-us Red-ing
A member of the Assassin Fellowship,
Scarlett's personal guard,
Commander in Windonelle army

Nuri Halloway: Noor-ee Hal-o-way
Death's Shadow, Night Child

Juliette: Jewel-ee-et
Death Incarnate, Witch

Mikale Lairwood: Mi-kay-l Lār-wood
Dirty bastard, Successor Hand to the King

Veda Lairwood: Vā-duh Lār-wood
Mikale's sister, Conniving bitch

Tava Tyndell: Tā-vah Tin-del
Daughter of Lord Tyndell

Drake Tyndell: Dr-ache Tin-del
Son of Lord Tyndell

Lord Balam Tondel: Lord Bay-lum Tin-del
Leads the Windonelle armies

Alaric: Ah-lār-ick
Assassin Lord

Sloan: Sl-own
One of Prince Callan's personal guards

Finn: Fin
One of Prince Callan's personal guards

PLACᏋs

Baylorin: Bay-lore-in
Rydeon: Ride-ee-on
Solembra: Soul-em-bruh
Xylon Forest: Zy-lon For-est
Jonaraja Forest: Jon-uh-raj-uh Fore-est
Avonleya: Av-on-lay-uh

Windonelle: Win-dun-el
Toreall: Tore-ee-all
Threlarion: Thruh-lair-ee-on
Dresden Forest: Drez-den For-est
Shira Forest: Sheer-uh For-est
Maara: Mar-uh

A Lady of Darkness Reference Guide

FAE CHARACTERS

Talwyn Semiria: Tal-win Si-meer-ee-uh
Fae Queen

Eliné Semiria: Ell-ee-nay Si-meer-ee-uh
Former Queen of the Western Courts

Henna Semiria: Hen-uh Si-meer-ee-uh
Former Queen of the Eastern Courts

FIRE COURT

Cyrus: Sigh-russ
Second-in-Command of the Fire Court

Rayner: Rā-nir
Third-in-Command of the Fire Court

Eliza: Ee-lie-za
General of the Fire Court

Beatrix: Bee-a-trix
Fire Court Healer

WATER COURT

Briar Drayce: Br-eye-er Dr-ace
Prince of the Water Court

Sawyer Drayce: Soy-ur Dr-ace
Second-in-Command of the Water Court

Neve: Neh-vā
Third-in-Command of the Water Court

Nakoa: Nuh-kō-ah
Commander of Water Court armies

EARTH COURT

Azrael Luan: Az-ree-ehl Lou-on
Prince of the Earth Court

WIND COURT

Ashtine: Ash-tin
Princess of the Wind Court

OTHER CHARCTERS OF NOTE

Deimas: Day-i-mas
Former King of Mortal Lands

Esmeray: Ez-mer-ā
Former Queen of Mortal Lands

Hazel Hecate: Hay-zl Heh-ka-tay
High Witch

Rosalyn: Roz-uh-lyn
Night Child Contessa

Stellan: Stel-on
Shifter Alpha

Arianna: Are-ee-on-uh
Shifter Beta

A Lady of Darkness Reference Guide

ᏝᎻᎬ GODS

Anala: Ah-nall-ah
Goddess of Sun/Day/Fire

Saylah: Say-luh
Goddess of Shadows/Night

Celeste: Sell-esst
Goddess of the Moon/Sky

Sefarina: Sef-uh-ree-nuh
Goddess of Wind

Silas: Sigh-lus
God of Earth/Land/Forests

Anahita: Ah-nuh-hee-tuh
God of Sea/Water/Ice

Reselda: Ruh-zel-duh
Goddess of Healing/Health

Falein: Fae-leen
Goddess of Wisdom/Cleverness

Arius: Ar-ee-us
God of Death/Darkness

Serafina: Sair-uh-fee-nuh
Goddess of Dreams/Stars

Temural: Tem-oor-all
God of the Wild/Untamed/Adventure

Sargon: Sar-gone
God of War/Protection/Courage

ᏝᎻᎬ SPIRIT ANIMALS

Amaré: Ah-mār-ā
Phoenix, Bonded to Sorin

Shirina: Shi-ree-nuh
Panther, Bonded to Scarlett

Maliq: Mal-eek
Wolf, Bonded to Talwyn

Nasima: Naw-seem-uh
Silver Hawk, bonded to Ashtine

Rinji: Rin-gee
Red Stag, bonded to Azrael

Abrax: Uh-brax
Water horse, bonded to Briar

Celene: Suh-leen
White Fox

Paja: Paw-juh
Golden Owl, previously bonded to Eliné

Ejder: Edge-der
Dragon

Kilo: Kee-low
White Python

Altaria: All-tar-ee-uh
Black eagle

Ranvir: Ran-ver
Dragon

THE DARKNESS

S carlett couldn't tell what was real and what was a dream. She remembered riding with Sorin, racing for the border. She remembered fighting and cutting down Night Children. She remembered Callan and Finn and Sloan and Eliza. She remembered fiery pain in her side.

She remembered vomiting over and over. She remembered fire and water and ice and ash. She remembered pain. So much pain. Her entire body ached. Her ribs throbbed in agony where they had once been broken. Maybe they were broken again. She didn't know.

There were times she could swear she saw a black panther lying at the foot of the bed. There were times white light seemed to encompass her. There were times the beautiful man was there, watching her. There were times she was sparring with Nuri. There were times she was sitting on a bed talking with Juliette. There were times she was walking along the beach with Cassius. There were times Mikale was kissing her, and there were times it was Callan whose lips were pressed to hers. There were times she was lying with her head in Sorin's lap, each reading a book, content to just be.

Sorin.

Sorin with his arm wrapped around her waist while they rode.

Sorin kissing her by a stream. Sorin telling her that her mother had been a Fae Queen, that she was a Fae Princess. Sorin, the Prince of Fire. Sorin, who called her Love. Sorin, who had saved her only to break her.

Was any of it real?

She didn't know. She wasn't entirely sure she cared anymore.

The only constant was the shadows. Shadows that kept her company. Shadows that twisted around her, keeping out the others. Keeping out the crushing darkness. Odd, she thought, that shadows were creatures of darkness but kept the dark from encompassing her wholly. Every once in a while, a light would try to break through, but the shadows were impenetrable. Shadows that protected her. Shadows that sang to her. Shadows that soothed her.

Now she found herself in a thick forest, and the beautiful man was here. His silver hair was the color of her own as he walked silently beside her. She was barefoot, but pine needles did not prick her feet. Sunlight streamed through the trees, illuminating a well-worn path.

The man stopped as they entered a clearing, so she did too. The air was still here. Not a leaf moved on the trees around the clearing.

"Close your eyes, Lady of Darkness." The man's voice was smooth and cool. A chill went down her spine. She hadn't heard his voice since he'd bid her to rise when she had been in Mikale's grasp.

Real? Dream? Did it matter?

Scarlett closed her eyes and images flashed through her mind.

Veda stabbing Cassius. Nuri bleeding out. Mikale taking her in an old office. A prince sleeping before a fire. Plunging a dagger into Juliette's heart. A friend stroking her hair to help her sleep. A dark shadow leaping the rooftops with her. Golden eyes staring into hers. A star going out. A Prince of Fire.

She gasped, her eyes snapping open, her hands clutching at her chest.

"Shh," the man murmured, and for the first time ever, Scarlett glimpsed a flash of sadness on his face. "Not yet, Lady. Close your eyes."

Scarlett shook her head. If she closed her eyes, those images that haunted her, that dragged her down into the depths of her darkness, that pulled her under, would come for her again.

"Do it," he whispered, bending down to speak into her ear. "See who answers your call."

Dream. This was a dream. It was too bizarre not to be.

Maybe it had all been a dream. Maybe she would wake up on the cold stone floor in the Lairwood House. Maybe Mikale would still have her...

She sighed and closed her eyes. She wasn't sure how long she stood there until she felt a soft wind rustle her unbound hair. The cloak she was wearing shifted in the breeze, and she felt her shadows almost vibrating with excitement.

She's coming, she's coming, she's coming, they whispered to her soul.

Scarlett felt the man beside her stir. He had moved behind her and rested his hands on her shoulders. He squeezed them gently, tenderly. "Open your eyes, Lady of Darkness. See who answers to you."

Scarlett slowly opened her eyes and before her stood a panther. She was sleek and beautiful and her muscles shifted under her gleaming coat of shadow and darkness and night.

"Shirina," the man whispered reverently into her ear. "Lady Saylah's servant."

Saylah. The goddess of shadows and night. The goddess who was often whispered of along with her brother, Temural, the god of wildness and untamed adventure, and their parents Arius, the god of death and darkness, and Serafina, the goddess of dreams and stars.

The panther's silver eyes mirrored Scarlett's as it let out a loud growl. Scarlett jumped back, but the beautiful man steadied her. "Do not fear her, Lady of Darkness. She will guide you. She will protect you. A creature of untamed shadows."

The panther slunk forward and brushed against Scarlett's side. Scarlett tentatively reached a hand out and ran it along her back, feeling those powerful muscles under her fingers.

"It will be time to wake soon," the man said quietly. "It will soon be time to face the shadows."

"I'm not ready," Scarlett whispered.

"One never is." His cool, low voice sent shivers up her spine every time he spoke.

"Who are you?" Scarlett whispered, as she sank to her knees. Shirina laid down beside her and rested her giant head in her lap.

The man sank down to the ground next to her, propping an arm onto his bent knee. From the trees, a giant eagle swooped down and came to rest on the same arm. He gently stroked the bird's head.

"Go and face your shadows. Then it will be time for us to meet," he said, his voice impossibly gentle.

"I don't want to go back." She dug her fingers into the panther's silky fur as tears slid down her cheeks. "It hurts. It just... I am not strong enough."

The beautiful man beside her was quiet for so long she thought he had gone back to just being a silent presence, but then he spoke. "True strength, Lady of Darkness, is being brave in the hard seasons. True strength is getting back up one more time. True strength is believing you were made for such a time as this and fighting against all odds. True strength is having hope even when the stars go out."

The panther had rolled to its side and was practically sprawled across her lap now, purring deeply. The eagle on the man's shoulder ruffled its feathers slightly.

"Are you real?" Scarlett finally asked after several more minutes of silence. "Or are you just a dream?"

"Are reality and dreams mutually exclusive?"

Scarlett turned to look at the beautiful man, and a faint cool smile played on his lips. The eagle suddenly let out a screech and soared into the sky. The man stood and extended a hand to Scarlett. "Get up, Lady of Darkness. Hope is for the dreamers."

With a final stroke of her hand down the panther's sleek fur, Scarlett placed her hand in the man's and rose to face the shadows.

PART ONE

THE SHADOWS

CHAPTER 1
SORIN

For the first twelve hours he was home, the Prince of the Fire Court did not leave his private bedroom. Beatrix had to summon additional Healers to help keep Scarlett comfortable and asleep. She vomited often as her body detoxed and went through withdrawal from the tonic. Sorin and Briar were exhausted from having to counter her magic as it surfaced over and over again. Finally, the vomiting ceased. Finally, a slight color returned to her cheeks. Finally, flames and ice stopped appearing. Finally, she slept.

Shadows still swirled around her, but they seemed to have lessened. Then again, maybe he was just hoping they had lessened. They wouldn't let anyone touch her. Anyone who tried was burned by them. The Healers had gotten creative, using old spells to keep her asleep rather than relying solely on their healing magic. He forced his way past them a few times to try and comfort her in any way possible, but her darkness only allowed it for a few minutes at a time before he was forced back out.

When Scarlett hadn't so much as sighed in her sleep in the last hour, he slipped from the room and found Prince Briar Drayce sprawled on the couch in his sitting room, his eyes closed. He opened one eye when he heard Sorin's approach. Sorin flopped into one of the chairs and groaned.

"Well, that was delightful," Briar drawled, thick with sarcasm.

Sorin grunted in reply, closing his own eyes. He hadn't been this drained since before he went to the human kingdoms. He wasn't sure he could summon enough flame to light a candle at this point. He had been drained when they arrived, and every time he managed to fill a little of his magic reserves, it was immediately depleted once more.

"So you're back," Briar said after several minutes of silence.

Sorin grunted in reply again.

"Did you lose the ability to speak in the mortal lands?"

Sorin threw him a vulgar gesture and heard him bark his laughter.

After a few more minutes of silence, Briar tried again. "You're back for good?"

"I'm back for good," Sorin replied, opening his eyes. Briar was still sprawled on the couch, ice crackling at his fingertips. "How do you have any magic left?"

"I haven't spent the last three years in magic deprived king-doms?" Briar offered.

"Valid point."

"So the female?"

"The female."

"She's strong."

"She is."

"She's Fae."

"She is."

"I'm going to need a little more here, Sorin," Briar said, annoy-ance creeping into his tone. "You bring power like that into our Courts, I'm going to need some sort of explanation as to who she is."

"She's my twin flame."

"You're kidding." Briar sat up, the crackling ice disappearing.

"Nope."

"You're sure?"

Sorin held up his left hand to show him the Mark that adorned it, closing his eyes again. Briar swore under his breath. "She doesn't bear a companion Mark."

"No, she doesn't."

"Normally both parties choose the Mark," Briar proceeded cautiously.

"She is not normal," Sorin replied simply.

"Clearly." When silence filled the space again, Briar said, "Sorin, who is she?"

Sorin opened his eyes and found his friend watching him carefully. He snapped a shield into place around his quarters. Briar straightened at the action, and Sorin felt an icy shield snap into place as well. After another minute, he took a deep breath before saying, "She is Eliné's daughter."

"Bullshit," Briar exclaimed. "How is that even possible?"

"I have no idea."

"How can you be sure?"

"I can't, but she has this," he held up his right hand that was still adorned by the Semiria ring. He heard Briar swear again. "She also clearly has both fire and water magic. Something unique to Eliné."

"Who is her father?"

"I have no idea," Sorin answered. "She doesn't either. Scarlett didn't even know she was Fae, let alone that her mother was a queen."

"Who?"

"Scarlett," Sorin answered. When Briar continued with the confused look, he added, "The female in my bed."

"Ah," Briar said, understanding passing over his face. "So…you brought her here?"

"Where else was I supposed to take her? This is where she belongs. This is her home."

"Talwyn will be livid," Briar warned, the ice returning to his fingertips.

"Hence the extra shields," Sorin muttered.

"Shadows dance around her," Briar remarked casually.

"That they do."

"Who are the others? That Cyrus and Rayner escorted to the guest wing?"

"A mortal prince who is in love with the female in my bed and his personal guards," Sorin answered, his head falling into his hands.

"Because we didn't have enough drama with Talwyn and Azrael, you decided to bring more?" Briar asked.

Sorin lifted his head from his hands to find Briar smirking at him.

"I am glad you find this so entertaining," Sorin ground out.

"Is there anything else I should know?" Briar asked.

"Yes, but it can wait until tomorrow. I will tell you everything then. I need to sleep. I haven't had a proper night's sleep in three years," Sorin answered, swiping a hand down his face.

"It shows," Briar quipped.

Sorin glared at his friend, throwing him another vulgar gesture.

"Send word if you need me," Briar said, standing from the couch, and stretching his arms above his head. "Although maybe use a fire message rather than your damn bird."

Sorin chuckled and stood himself, facing Briar. "Thank you."

Briar clasped him on the shoulder. "Welcome home, Aditya. It's good to have you back."

"It's good to be back," Sorin admitted. Then he added, "I'm locking them out until she wakes up. They will not be happy."

"I will take care of it," Briar said as a portal of water appeared.

"And make sure they don't torture the mortals too much," Sorin said with a grimace. Cyrus was going to be outraged to learn he had to babysit humans for a time.

"Done," Briar said. He stepped through the water portal, and it snapped shut behind him.

Sorin took a deep breath and took it all in. He was finally home. His magic, although nearly depleted, simmered in his veins. He walked to his bedroom, found Scarlett hadn't moved, and continued on to the bathing room. His bathtub was more of a bathing pool. It was ten feet long and three feet deep. It was already full, and he had just enough magic left to heat the water. As he passed a hand over the top of the water, steam began to rise. He was still in his fighting leathers from their two-day trek to the border. Those events seemed as though they'd happened weeks ago. He peeled his sweat-laden clothes from himself and eased into the pool. Benches lined the edges of the tub, and he collapsed onto one.

A half hour later, he was so relaxed he could hardly keep his eyes open. He slid on loose pants and walked out to his room.

And stopped short.

Lying at the foot of the bed was a panther as dark as the shadows that swirled around Scarlett. The panther lifted its head as Sorin came into the room, a low growl escaping from it.

"Shirina," he breathed, bowing low. The goddess Saylah's spirit animal had not been seen in... Sorin actually had no idea when the goddess' panther had last been seen.

The panther cocked its head to the side, her silver eyes glowing as they studied him. Then, with a slight nod of her head, she settled back down, closing her eyes. Sorin slowly made his way to Scarlett, giving the panther a wide berth. She had shifted slightly in her sleep, and the color had left her cheeks. He grimaced as he pushed through the biting shadows to feel her forehead and found it icy to the touch.

"Shit," he muttered under his breath.

As if in answer, there was a soft knocking on the bedroom door. He turned to find Beatrix standing in the doorway. She was older, her hair with more grey than not, but being an immortal, she did not look her age. She looked past him to Scarlett, and a frown formed.

"You must be exhausted," Sorin said quietly.

"As are you, Prince," she replied with a curt nod of her head.

Beatrix came to Sorin's side, unfazed by the panther sleeping at the foot of the bed, and held her hands over Scarlett. White light flowed from them as she passed them over her body. The light pushed through the shadows, and he could see the effort Beatrix was having to exert to do so. She paused for a moment and reached for the bowl on the nightstand—just in time for Scarlett to lurch forward and vomit. His very soul ached for her. His twin flame.

11

Sorin reached into the shadows once more and held her hair back. When she was done, she settled back into the pillows. Her eyes were half open, but they locked onto Sorin. She studied him, her eyes seeming to search his. Beatrix muttered a spell low under her breath, and her eyes fluttered shut once more.

"She should sleep for a few hours again," Beatrix said, pulling Sorin from his thoughts.

"Good," Sorin mustered, not taking his eyes from Scarlett, an idea forming in his mind.

"Summon me if needed. Do not let her get up if she wakes," Beatrix warned.

"If she wakes?" Sorin repeated, his eyes snapping to the Healer. "I thought you were keeping her asleep until the withdrawal is over."

"I am trying, Sorin," Beatrix replied. "She is strong. I cannot say how long I can keep her in this state."

Sorin nodded in understanding, his eyes going back to Scarlett. If he could communicate down the twin flame connection…

He felt a delicate hand on his arm, and he turned to find kind, violet eyes studying him with tender understanding.

"Do not go into her mind right now, Sorin," Beatrix said softly. "Her mind and body and soul are in great turmoil. You must not add to it."

"But I could help her through it," Sorin argued, his eyes returning to the female in his bed.

"No," Beatrix answered, shaking her head. "You do not know what you will discover there. It would be a great breach of trust. She has not yet accepted the bond. And with her magic? I do not know if you would come back. She could unknowingly trap you there."

Sorin did not respond. The twin flame connection would give him access to everything she was feeling and experiencing right now. If he could go in for just a moment, see where she was struggling, he could take a little of the burden.

"Sorin Aditya," Beatrix said, her voice more authoritative and commanding than it had been a moment ago. He turned again to look at her and found her violet eyes severe with disapproval. "I may be a dominant Healer, but I can still access the crafts of my sisters. She will change the course of history."

"No," Sorin interrupted. "I know Talwyn wants to use her. She cannot have her."

"We will need her, Sorin. *And* you," the Healer continued. "We will need what you two will become together, as well as what she will become on her own. Until she can control her magic and we know the extent of her power, you must act with diligence."

"I hear you, Beatrix," Sorin conceded. "Thank you. For everything."

Beatrix gave a slight nod of her head as she began walking to the bedroom door. "Summon me immediately if she wakes or if something appears wrong."

"I will."

When Beatrix had left, Sorin grabbed an extra blanket from the chaise lounge near the balcony doors and settled into one of the overstuffed chairs. The panther, seeming to accept that someone else was now present to watch over Scarlett, leapt to the floor, stretched with a wide yawn, and vanished in a flash of silver light. Sorin was asleep within minutes.

CHAPTER 2
CALLAN

C rown Prince Callan paced around the spacious guest
quarters he had been provided. His personal guards and
friends, Finn and Sloan, occupied the quarters with him.
It was a three-bedroom suite, complete with a sitting room and a
game room. Each bedroom had its own bathing chamber and
dressing room.

"You're acting like a caged mountain cat," Finn muttered from
where he was stretched out on the sofa with a book in his hands.
Sloan was sitting at the dining table, finishing his breakfast.

"We have been here five days, and no one has given me any
update on her," Callan growled. The last time Callan had seen
Scarlett she had been bleeding out on a couch after being stabbed in
the side.

Until her shadows had exploded, sending everyone in the room
flying into tables and walls. Then he'd been ushered out by two
others that hardly spoke to him. They'd been dumped here and had
been all but ignored since.

"I really don't think she is yours to worry about anymore," Sloan
said gruffly from his place at the table.

"You wouldn't care," Callan snapped. "You never liked her."

14

"You're right. I never liked the assassin that managed to elude us at every turn, sneaking into your rooms and bed," Sloan agreed, taking a bite of his toasted bread and marmalade.

"If you had bothered to try to talk to her rather than snap at her at every turn, maybe you would have," Callan answered. "She and Finn get along just fine."

"Do not bring me into this," Finn said from the couch, turning the page of his book.

Callan resumed his pacing. This was ridiculous. They'd been allowed out of their quarters, of course. They weren't prisoners, but they weren't exactly allowed to go where they liked either. In fact, they weren't allowed in any part of the western side of the palace.

They had been shown very little of the Prince of Fire's palace. They had seen a dining room, the eastern gardens, and the great hall. The basics of any palace. He had thought his castle was grand, but this put it to shame. A river ran through the middle of the building. A godsdamned river.

The guest quarters were on the eastern side of the river. They had seen the bridges that crossed to the western part, but they had been stopped when they had made to cross them. Apparently, the private wing of the palace lay on that side, and he could only assume that was where Sorin had her.

This was absurd. He was a crowned prince. He would not be denied information he desired.

He strode for the main door, and Finn and Sloan shot to their feet behind him.

"Where are you going?" Finn sighed, sliding his feet into boots.

"To get information," Callan answered, flinging the door open. He heard Sloan and Finn cussing behind him. He didn't bother to wait as he strode down the hallway. He knew the way to the main foyer well enough by now. He rounded a corner and heard a clipped, cultured, feminine voice from behind them.

"My, my. Where are our guests off to in such a hurry?"

Callan turned to find a woman—no, a female—striding towards them down the hallway. Eliza. The female had traveled with them from Baylorin, apparently having been harboring a secret identity while there, just like the Fire Prince had.

Eliza's hair was a brilliant shade of red-gold, and it hung in sweeping curls down her back. Tattoos that had not been there before whorled around her chest and down her bare arms beneath the sleeveless tunic she was wearing. Apparently, their absence was part of some glamour that was put on them in the mortal kingdoms. Callan didn't quite understand it all. Weapons adorned her no matter where you looked. Her gray eyes studied him as she drew nearer. She was beautiful, yes, but also terrifying. He had rarely seen her since they'd arrived, and when he did, it was quick, short conversations as she was passing by.

Callan straightened as she stopped in front of him. "I am going to see how Scarlett is doing."

"You can certainly *try* to go and see her," she said with a smirk. Challenge gleamed in her eyes, and he saw Finn and Sloan casually put their hands on their weapons.

"You would keep her from me?"

"I would do no such thing. By all means," she said, gesturing with her hand. "Go ahead."

"All right," Callan said with uncertainty, glancing to Finn and Sloan. "Thank you." He began walking, and the female fell into step beside him. She was silent as she walked with them. Awkwardly silent. "So you are his general? It is not a fake title like *his* was?"

"That I am," she answered. Short. Direct.

"I cannot help but feel you are leading me to a trap," Callan said cautiously while they descended some stairs.

"I am leading you nowhere," she answered. "I am following you."

They were on the main floor of the palace now, and a bridge was ahead. There was a bridge on every level of the palace. They were made of some sort of glass from what he could gather, but he hadn't been able to study them further as he had never been allowed onto one other than when they were escorted to their quarters the first night.

The guard at the bridge straightened and saluted, but Eliza

strode right past him. Callan hesitated beside the guard, who didn't so much as acknowledge them.

"You do know this is actually a trap, right?" Sloan muttered from behind him.

"Not if she is going to let us cross this blasted bridge," Callan retorted.

She had paused halfway across the bridge, looking over her shoulder to see if they were following. "Well, he certainly has no information for you," Eliza said, nodding to the guard.

So Callan took a step. They crossed the entire bridge without incident, and he held in his sigh of relief. But now that they were on the other side, he paused, unsure of which way to go.

"Lead the way," she said, gesturing with her hand again.

"I... This was a trick all along," Callan sputtered, glaring at her.

"I have not deceived you at all," she retorted, crossing her arms. "Did I not say you could try to go see her? Pick a direction."

"Fine," he said through clenched teeth and started forward. She fell into step beside him once more. They had climbed a set of stairs and started down a hallway when a male stepped from smoke and ashes before them. Rayner. This one was Rayner. He would never forget the terrifying male with eyes that swirled like smoke.

"How did they get here?" he asked in that dangerously quiet voice of his.

"They crossed the bridge," Eliza said with a smirk.

"I can see this," Rayner replied, his swirling eyes sliding to her. "Why were they not stopped?"

"I suppose because I was with them," she answered with a shrug.

"Look, I am just trying to inquire about Scarlett," Callan said, trying to maintain politeness and keep the agitation from his voice.

"Who?" came a male voice from behind him.

"Shit," Sloan muttered. "Where do they keep coming from?"

The other male who had escorted them from what he assumed was Sorin's chambers that day was now standing at the top of the stairs they had just climbed. He had golden eyes that were nearly identical to Sorin's.

17

"Scarlett Monrhoe," Callan said with a sigh. When the male gave him the same quizzical look, he added, "The woman that came here with Sorin."

"What are they doing here, Eliza?" the male asked, ignoring him now and looking at the female.

"They crossed the bridge," she answered again.

"Then they should cross it back to the other side," he said pointedly to them.

"No," Callan ground out. "Not until I am told how she is faring."

The three Fae exchanged a look.

"I do not think it is any of your concern," the male said. What had his name been again?

"It most certainly is my concern. She is my…" he trailed off. What was she?

A prince holds her heart. Nuri's words from that day in the tavern clanged through him. He had arrogantly thought she'd meant him, but then he'd learned that Sorin was actually a prince. *The* Fire Prince.

But she had been his once, hadn't she? His Wraith of Shadows. Did shadows still trail her wherever she went? Did they still swarm her and flit around her?

"She is your what, Princeling?" Eliza taunted.

"She is a friend who saved my life, and I wish to know how she is doing. I wish to see her," Callan finally answered, trying to sound like the prince he was.

The Fae exchanged a look again.

"I told him he could try to go see her," Eliza supplied with a shrug.

"Oh, for fuck's sake," the other male said, running a hand down his face. "You're like a damn cat playing with its dinner."

"Cyrus," Rayner chided quietly, "we have guests in our company."

Cyrus waved his hand dismissively. "If his Highness has not heard language before then he is more pampered than I originally thought." Cyrus rubbed his thumb and forefinger across his brows as if he had a headache. He turned and faced them once more. "You will not get to her. Even if you manage to find the door to the Prince's rooms, you shall not get close to it. There are wards preventing anyone from entering. Not only that, there are *more* wards that will keep you from even getting to his hallway."

"But you—"

"And," Cyrus said, cutting him off, "on top of all of that, there are spells that misdirect your path. You will never find his door without an escort directly to it."

Callan stared at him in disbelief. That type of security was... unbelievable. Sorin must have hated life in the mortal lands.

"You see, Princeling," Eliza said to him, her voice going cold. Gone was the boredom she had been portraying. No, before him stood a General who commanded armies and protected an entire Court. "No one gets to our Prince without our knowing. No one gets to his door without going through one of us first. And if you get through one, there are two more to work around." Flames danced in her eyes, and fire appeared at Cyrus's fingertips.

"Can you find out for me then?" Callan asked, pushing down the fear that was threatening to buckle his knees.

"No," Cyrus answered. "We cannot."

"Why not?" Finn said from behind Callan, stepping to his side.

Again the Fae exchanged a look.

"We do not know if we are free to divulge such information," Rayner said in his soft, grave voice.

"Can you not ask him?" Finn asked.

"Did you not listen?" Cyrus snapped. "The wards are preventing anyone from entering."

"But...even you?" Callan said with realization.

"Yes," Cyrus retorted through clenched teeth. His tone said it all. He was not happy about being separated from his prince. Finn and Sloan often threw fits when he insisted on being left alone. Now a full-fledged, fire-wielding Fae stood before him, furious about being kept from his prince.

"No one gets in? What if something happens?" Callan balked.

There was a sound of rushing water and another male stepped from a swirling vortex of the same.

"I would know if something happens," the male said. He had seen this male briefly before. He had arrived right before Scarlett had lost control. He felt Finn and Sloan tense behind him. At least the three Fae he already knew stood between them and the newcomer. The male's face was hard, but his eyes twinkled. His build was nearly identical to Sorin, but his eyes were the icy blue of Scarlett's. His tunic was the turquoise of the sea, and his pants were light gray as he stood before them.

"But he said no one is allowed in," Callan argued.

"He means they are not allowed in right now, and he is pissy about it," the male said with a glare at Cyrus.

"He has never locked us out of his rooms, Drayce," Cyrus said sharply. "Not until he returned with *her*." The new male merely blinked at him.

"This should not be this difficult," Sloan growled from behind Callan. Callan turned to look at him with surprise, and so did all the Fae in the hallway. "All my prince wants to know is if the woman is all right."

"She sleeps, Prince Callan," the male said. "That is all I can say."

"She has been sleeping since she arrived here? Did she have her tonic? She has not woken at all? What of her wound?" He nearly fell to his knees with relief that someone had finally told him something.

"Our best Healer is watching over and treating her, and Sorin has not left his rooms once. She is constantly watched and monitored," he answered. "Now, it would indeed be best if you crossed back to the eastern side of the palace. I will escort you myself."

Rayner disappeared into smoke and ashes, and Cyrus stalked off, cussing under his breath. Eliza fell into step beside their company once more.

"Do the shadows still follow her?" Callan asked, as they descended the step.

The male's jaw clenched. "Yes. We are working on that."

"Who are you? I thought Cyrus was his Second."

"He is."

"And Rayner is his Third."

"Yes."

They had come to the bridge and stopped beside it. "Then who are you to be allowed in, and they are not?"

A smile pulled at the corner of the male's mouth, and Callan had the distinct feeling that this male found mischief and roguery amusing. Eliza had already started across the bridge. "I am Briar Drayce," he said, motioning them to begin crossing. "Prince of the Water Court, and I will warn you only once, mortal prince: Should you cross these bridges again without permission, you will find Sorin's Inner Court not nearly as pleasant about it."

"They weren't exactly pleasant today," Callan replied, stepping onto the bridge.

"Indeed," was all Briar said before he turned and headed down a hallway.

They reached the other side of the bridge to find Eliza waiting for them. "Come," was all she said, and she started off towards the stairs. Callan looked to Finn and Sloan, who only shrugged, so they followed her.

She led them down to a subterranean level of the palace and then down several hallways until they had to be at the back of the palace. As she turned down yet another hall, the sound of weapons clanging and men grunting grew louder, and they finally came to a stop in front of a large room.

It was a training room. Various rings were full of males and females sparring with all sorts of weapons.

"What are we doing here?" Callan asked.

"Your two guards look ready to kill someone," Eliza said with a knowing look. "You all need to work off some aggression." She signaled one of the males to come over. "Go train," she said with a jerk of her chin to Finn and Sloan. They indeed looked relieved to have something to do. "Teach them a few things," she said to the soldier, "but don't kill them. They're mortals."

"Yes, General," the soldier said and jerked his chin at them. Finn and Sloan began to follow.

"You do not spar?" Callan asked Eliza as she turned to leave.

"Do you wish to spar with me?" she asked, raising a brow.

"No," he replied quickly.

"Wise answer," was all she said before she turned and walked back the way they had come.

Callan watched her go, then entered the training room. Someone put a sword in his hand, and he stepped into a ring with Finn.

CHAPTER 3
SCARLETT

S carlett woke in a large bedroom chamber. She'd been here before, but she had no idea if that had been a dream or real. She glanced to the foot of the bed, half expecting to see the panther there. She wore no clothing, and the sheets were soft and luxurious against her bare skin. She slowly looked around the room, taking it in. The room was warm. There was a fire crackling in the hearth with two overstuffed chairs flanking it. Two bookshelves that reached nearly to the high ceiling, crammed with books, stood to either side of the fireplace. To the right of the massive bed there was a desk that was neatly organized. A chaise lounge sat near a window to the right of the fireplace under some windows. To the left of the fireplace was a great set of double doors leading out to a balcony.

Scarlett rose from the bed and grabbed a blanket from one of the overstuffed chairs. The scents of cedar and ash enveloped her as the shadows curled around her arms. She wrapped the blanket around her naked body and went to the doors. With a push, they opened and she stepped out onto the balcony. The view was breathtaking. They were high in the mountains. Snow-capped peaks filled her vision for miles. Trees spanned the mountainsides, and though it was obviously cold outside, the balcony was as warm as the interior of the room.

Scarlett walked to the balcony railing and looked over. She was in some sort of castle or palace or tower, high above the ground. Her breath hitched as it brought back another room high above the ground where she had been locked away. Her shadows stroked soothingly down her arms. She forced herself to breathe in and out. In and out. That was over. That had been real, right? Sorin had come for her.

Or was that the dream?

Scarlett turned and went back inside, closing the doors behind her. She passed a room that clearly led to a bathing chamber of some sort. Next to it was another doorway that led to a walk-in closet that rivaled her own back at the Tyndell Manor. In fact, it was larger than her own, but only half full. She ran her hand along the various tunics and shirts that hung in the closet, the same familiar scent clinging to them. A large oak dresser stood on the opposite wall. An assortment of daggers lay scattered across it, and there were swords discarded nearby on the floor. All of them had the same black metal blades that Sorin's weapons had been adorned with.

Scarlett turned back to the clothing and pulled down a deep red button-up shirt. It was huge on her, hanging down nearly to her knees. She buttoned it except for the top button, discarding the blanket onto the floor. She found a belt among the daggers and cinched it around her waist, adding one of the daggers to it. As she turned to leave the closet, she noticed the full-length mirror in the corner and froze.

She looked the same, yet different. The shadows were adorning her, of course, but there was more. She brought her face close to the mirror, studying her reflection. Her silver hair was almost…silkier, shimmering like starlight. Maybe this was a dream after all. Her ears were slightly elongated, coming to points at the ends. She could've sworn she was a few inches taller somehow. Everything about her seemed longer, more graceful.

Scarlett left the closet, her footsteps completely silent on the marble floor. The door to the chambers was half open, and she slipped through to find herself in living quarters. It was larger than the bedroom chambers. A large brick red sofa occupied the center with an overstuffed chair on each side, forming a U-shape around the fireplace on the opposite wall. On the far right was a grand piano, polished and gleaming. There were three doors along the far wall leading somewhere. But on the far left and directly in front of her was a long dining table with platters of breakfast foods lining the length of it.

Scarlett's stomach grumbled, and she took slow steps towards the food. Real or dream? She still hadn't decided. She cautiously took a piece of melon and popped it in her mouth. The juice exploded. She must have been starving, because it tasted better than any melon she'd ever had. She took a few more bites of fruit and picked up a cherry pastry. She was halfway through the pastry when the main door opened.

"Sorin, your Inner Court are some of the whiniest bunch of—" a man started, but stopped short at the sight of Scarlett.

Scarlett turned to study him. She'd decided after the first bite of pastry this was likely a dream, so rather than reach for her dagger, she took another bite of the cherry treat, waiting to see how this particular scene would play out. Would she even remember it? It had been a rather dull dream so far.

The man had shoulder length hair that was so blonde it was nearly white, as if he spent every day in the sun. His eyes were the bluest she'd ever seen and reminded her of her own. He was muscled and built just like Sorin. He wore pants that hugged all the right areas and a loose fitting tunic that still managed to show off his chest.

"Scarlett," he said cautiously, "you are awake."

Scarlett cocked her head to the side. He knew her? She put the last of the pastry in her mouth, watching him.

"Does Sorin know you are awake?" the man asked, taking a tentative step into the room.

Scarlett took a step back, and as she did, a ring of fire encircled the man. Her shadows swelled, reaching tendrils of darkness to him.

He swore and a thin shield of water appeared between him and the fire. Scarlett merely raised her eyebrows. Water. Not fire?

"Scarlett, please," the man said. "I am a friend. I swear it."

Scarlett just stared at him. She picked up a pear from the table and took a bite, leaning against the table as she continued watching him.

"Sorin!" the man called.

Scarlett's head snapped to one of the doors along the opposite wall. She heard his muffled voice yell something about being there in a moment.

"Aditya, now!" the man called again. Scarlett turned her attention back to him. Sweat was forming along his brow.

"Coming," came an exasperated huff and then, "Ho-ly hell."

Sorin appeared at the doorway of the middle room. He held an open book in his hand, which he promptly closed and set on a low table near him. He wore loose-fitting pants for lounging and a button-down shirt that was open and unbuttoned. His features had changed like her own, and there were some tattoos that hadn't been there before.

Scarlett merely took another bite of her pear. Maybe it wasn't a dream? She really couldn't tell.

"Scarlett," Sorin said slowly.

She again said nothing. Just watched him, as if she were watching a play at the theater.

"Sorin," came the man's voice. "A little assistance here?"

Sorin's eyes stayed fixed on Scarlett. He closed his fist, and the ring of flames guttered and died. The man's shield of water disappeared immediately, and he seemed to be panting slightly, like he'd just exerted himself.

Sorin took a step towards Scarlett and a thin shield of flame formed around her, her shadows coiling to strike. Sorin's mouth twitched into a slight smile.

"Sorin, she has been sleeping for days. Her magic is fully replenished. Do not antagonize her."

"I am well aware, Briar," Sorin replied, slowly continuing towards Scarlett, the small smile still in place.

A flame leapt from Scarlett's shield straight to Sorin, but he merely caught it in his hand, tossed it back and forth like a ball a few times, and then closed his fist around it, extinguishing the flame. She straightened and turned to look at the other man, but Sorin said in a low, commanding tone, "Here, Scarlett. Keep your eyes right here."

Her eyes locked back onto his, and her pear thudded to the ground. Sorin. He was real. He was here with her. He had come for her. He had taken her from Mikale. He had not left her alone.

He was the godsdamned Prince of Fire. He had known her mother. He was responsible for her mother's death. He had kept secrets from her. So many secrets.

Sorin stood right before her shield now. He placed a hand on it, as if placing his hand on a window. "Hey, Love."

Scarlett narrowed her eyes at him. "Hello, *Prince*." Hatred and venom dripped from that one title. They stared at each other for a long moment, then she said, "Is this real, or is this a dream?"

Sorin's smile faded and a look of concern passed across his features. "This is real, Scarlett."

"You came for me?"

"I will always come for you."

He stilled as her shadows reached out for him, swirling around his legs, his arms, his torso, searching him. She could feel him beneath her own hands as they moved, as if they were an extension of her own being.

Slowly, Scarlett brought her hand to the shield and placed her palm against his. The flames flickered a few times, then disappeared entirely. They stood there, palm to palm, eyes locked on each other. He certainly *felt* real, but so had so much else in her dreams.

When Sorin reached to bring a hand to her cheek, she stepped back, out of reach. "This is real?"

"This is real, Scarlett. It is not a dream," Sorin answered gently.

"Callan, Finn, and Sloan? They are here. That was real?"

Sorin's jaw tightened. "Yes, they are here."

"Eliza. Is she real, or was she a dream?"

"Eliza is a very real person."

"Cassius. Is Cassius here? I want to see him."

"No, Scarlett," he said gently, shaking this head. "Cassius and Nuri are back in Baylorin, safe and protecting the children."

Scarlett fell silent, tendrils of her shadows reaching out to the prince once more. Sorin didn't move as they swirled over his chest, stroked down his cheek, coiled around his throat.

"Do you want me to summon Beatrix?" the man asked quietly.

Shadows pounced on the man, and he winced as they wound around his wrists.

"Here, Love," Sorin said, his voice low. "Stay with me."

"Sorin," the man said, his voice low and urgent. "She cannot control it."

"She will not learn if she is asleep," Sorin argued.

"We cannot keep doing this. She needs to ease into it. Train her in the courtyards, not in your drawing room," the man countered.

"I will not shove her into a cage to be tamed," Sorin snarled, his voice going steely.

"She is standing right here," Scarlett snapped. They both whipped their heads to her, and she scowled at them.

"The choice is yours, Scarlett," Sorin said. "I can summon Beatrix, our Healer, to help you sleep through more of this, or you can try it on your own."

"I do not need to sleep any more," she sighed, her shadows reeling back to her. "What I need is a bath."

"I agree," Sorin answered. Scarlett leveled an unimpressed stare at him, and he shrugged. Then he leaned forward until his face was inches from hers. Her breath caught at his closeness. She thought he was going to kiss her, and she readied to punch him right in the godsdamn face, but then he whispered, "You smell." She brought her fist up to do just that, but he caught her wrist with a smirk. "A necessary touch. To protect myself."

"You are still an ass," she replied with a roll of her eyes, jerking her arm back and out of his grip. The man behind them barked a laugh, and she turned to face him. "Who the hell are you?"

The man straightened at being directly addressed. "This is Briar.

You sort of met him when you first arrived," Sorin cut in. "He was here anyway."

Scarlett studied the man a moment more before saying, "Have you known Sorin long?"

"Since we were children," Briar answered, curiosity lining his face and glimmering in his blue eyes. "We were practically raised together."

"Did you also know my mother?" She heard Sorin suck in a breath beside her.

"Scarlett, let's go discuss this in another——"

Scarlett held up a hand to silence him, and her shadows twined around his throat. Her eyes remained on Briar.

"I served in her Inner Court alongside Sorin, yes," he answered.

"And has he always been a secret-keeping bastard?" Scarlett asked, now leveling a cool stare at Sorin. She could have sworn he winced slightly.

"A secret-keeper only when necessary," Briar answered. "But he has always been a bastard," he added with a wink.

"Thank you for that," Sorin interjected with a roll of his eyes.

Scarlett's full attention turned back to him. "All I want you to do is tell me real or dream. I don't want your ability to conveniently leave out important information to get in the way. Do you think you can do that?" When Sorin nodded, she continued. "You came for me, and we fled Baylorin."

"Real," Sorin answered.

"Lord Tyndell is working with Mikale. They know I am Fae and knew my mother."

"Real."

"Callan and I kissing on the journey here?"

"Gods, I hope that was a fucking dream," Sorin muttered.

"Me and you kissing on the journey here?"

"Real, Scarlett. That... By the stream was very, very real," he whispered.

"The Fae Queen is searching for a weapon. You figured out *I* was this weapon and kept it from me."

"Scarlett, that's not——"

Her shadows tightened around him. "Real or dream?" she hissed.

"Real."

"My mother… She was a Fae Queen."

"Real."

"I was stabbed."

Sorin shuddered imperceptibly. "I thought you were going to die."

"The man with the black eagle and the…" She looked down at her forearm where the three stars were inked on her skin. She had wanted to ask about the panther, but didn't want to appear as if she'd completely lost her mind. She was sure she sounded half-insane.

Sorin's brows bunched. "That was a dream, Scarlett," he said softly.

The tenderness in his voice made her heart squeeze in her chest. She brought her eyes back to his. "You are the Prince of the Fire Court and are responsible for my mother's death."

Briar sucked in a breath. "Scarlett, he is not—"

"It's fine, Briar," Sorin cut in. "I can handle it. I can handle what she needs to say to me."

Scarlett fought back the tears stinging the back of her eyes. "Real or dream?" she demanded.

Sorin swallowed. "Real, Scarlett. That is real."

Scarlett jerked back a step from him. *Real.* That had been real. He had been her mother's closest confidant. He had been her Cassius. And he was responsible for her death.

Breathe, her shadows whispered to her, curling around her ear. *Breathe, Lady of Darkness.*

She met Sorin's eyes once more and a cruel smile twisted onto her lips as she said in a low, icy voice, "You have much to explain."

"I wanted to tell you in Baylorin, Scarlett. I wanted to tell you so many things," he started.

Scarlett ignored his last words, walking past him toward the bedroom, her shadows like a fog behind her. Too much. This was too much right now. She needed a moment to breathe.

30

"She is remarkably similar to Eliné and yet not," she heard Briar whisper, awe in his voice.

"She is no Eliné, I assure you," Sorin replied. "She has endured more than Eliné ever did." Her fury weakened a touch at his words, until he added, "She is also a much bigger pain in my ass."

In a flash, she had pulled the dagger from her belt and flung it across the room. It flew by Sorin's face, slicing a shallow gash along his cheekbone, and embedded in the still half open entry door. Brair's eyes were wide, but Sorin merely smirked at her. "You missed." With a mocking sigh, he added, "I suppose we could continue your training now that you've gotten your beauty sleep."

Scarlett narrowed her eyes at him. She could swear her veins were crackling with icy fire. "You and I both know I missed on purpose. If I wanted you dead, my beloved darkness would ensure that was the case." As if in emphasis, those shadows rose up behind her in a swirling mass of dark fog that had Briar's eyes widening even more as he stepped back from her.

"So you do not hate me enough to want me dead then?" Sorin asked.

"Oh no, Sorin," she purred, slowly closing the distance between them. The corner of her mouth kicked up into a smirk when she heard his heart rate jump. "I definitely want you dead." She brought her hand up and ran her finger lightly along his face, brushing back a lock of his dark hair. His eyes darkened a shade at the touch. She ran her thumb sensuously over his bottom lip as she said softly, "I just haven't decided how thoroughly I want to break you before I end your life. Where can I bathe?"

He held her stare as she registered a shift in his ash and cedar scent. Something heady and lush. But then he stepped back from her.

"Right this way, Love," Sorin replied, strolling past her as if the shadows and her words were nothing, his hands sliding into the pockets of his loose pants.

"Your arrogance is truly astounding," Scarlett said, rolling her eyes.

"Right back at you, Princess," Sorin answered without even looking back at her.

"Fucking prick," she muttered, throwing him a vulgar gesture as she followed him into the bedroom. Briar's laughter carried to her as the door clicked shut behind them.

CHAPTER 4
SORIN

I t took every ounce of Sorin's self-control not to look over his shoulder as he led Scarlett through his bedroom to his private bath. The desire coursing through his veins from her fingers on his skin…gods. If Briar hadn't been in that room, he would have been all over her. He would have risked that wrath and that darkness. She was a storm he didn't know that he'd survive.

The giant tub was finishing filling as they entered. He had almost dropped to his knees when he had come out of the study to find her up and walking about. Her magic was still out of control. The shadows still wreathed her, but she was awake and color had returned to her face. He walked to the edge of the tub, stopping beside a low table with various towels and soaps. He finally turned to Scarlett.

She stood at the edge of the tub near the steps. She still wore his shirt and some primal part of him gave an internal satisfied smirk to see her in it, covered in his scent. He had inwardly flinched when she'd stepped away from his touch in the sitting room. Her shadows had not burned him today, though, not like they had apparently bit at Briar. They had coiled around him tentatively, as if feeling him out, trying to decide how they felt about him. She was different, yet the same. She had been beautiful before, but in her Fae form, she was stunning. She toed the water and jerked her foot back.

"It's freezing," she scowled.

Sorin simply waved a hand over the water and steam instantly began wafting from the surface. "Show off," he heard her mutter under her breath as she unfastened the belt around her waist.

When she started with the buttons of the shirt, he cleared his throat and started for the door. "Enjoy your bath," he said, his voice husky.

She cocked her head to the side as she said, "You have questions to answer."

He paused. "I will answer every single one when you are ready, Scarlett."

"Then I am ready now."

His throat went dry as the shirt slid to a pile on the floor, and she stepped into the enormous tub. He could swear those shadows receded, taunting him with the view of her naked body. She had always had little regard for propriety. He'd learned that quickly enough. He would never forget the morning she had spoken to him on the stairs in little more than a silk bathrobe. Her words from moments ago floated back to him. *I just haven't decided how thoroughly I want to break you...*

This would certainly be a good fucking start to that, and she knew it. She had always known how to use every weapon available to her.

He walked back to the edge of the tub as she went under the water. He could see her drift a little ways underneath before she came back to the surface.

"You have tattoos now," she said, lifting her long hair between her fingers as it floated around her in the water. Her voice was different than it had been in the sitting room, almost far away sounding, like she was in some kind of trance.

Sorin leaned against the wall near the tub, trying to keep his eyes on her face. "The cost of the glamour to keep my Fae form hidden was that my Marks were also hidden and nullified."

Scarlett merely nodded. He had seen a little of the real Scarlett break through in their light bantering in the drawing room, but she had retreated back into some sort of shell. The place she went to survive. He didn't know if he should speak or remain silent. He chose the latter. She reached for some soap and washed her long hair, and when she surfaced from rinsing it out, she said in that same unsure voice, "This is not a dream." Not a question, but a statement, as through trying to reassure herself.

"This is real, Scarlett," he answered.

"How do I know? There was so much that seemed real before…" she trailed off, biting her bottom lip.

"Love, look at me." Sorin waited until she brought those icy blue eyes to his own. "This. Is. Real. You are safe."

"Safe? With you?" She tilted her head to the side, seeming amused. "Such an interesting word choice, Prince, but you've always been a master of wordplay, haven't you?"

"Scarlett." Her name was a plea on his lips.

She said nothing. Just slid under the water again, a few bubbles rising to the surface when she let out air before coming up again.

"I have so many things to say to you. So many things to scream at you. I can hardly stand to be in the same room with you," she said quietly. Sorin felt as if her shadows were tightening around his throat again. That's how much of an effort breathing became at her words. "And yet I again find myself without a choice because you are the only person who can give me any answers…providing you don't *withhold* information."

The venom and hatred in her tone was palpable, but gods, watching the water move around her, seeing her breasts, her bare body. He could hardly focus.

He swallowed hard. "Can we please discuss this anywhere else?"

"Why?"

"Because watching you in the water with nothing on is not easy, and you know that."

A sensuous smile formed on Scarlett's mouth. "You do not wish to join me?" she asked, tilting her head to the side again.

"That is all I wish to do. I wish to enter that tub and show you exactly how sorry I am. To make you believe that I would never intentionally hurt you," he ground out. "But not when you...have just woken up."

"Why was I naked when I woke up?"

"You burned through all your clothing. Repeatedly. When your shadows would allow anyone to try and clothe you that is."

She nodded slightly, then she went under the water again, for much longer this time. He could see her, sitting on the bottom of the giant tub, her eyes closed. One minute. Two. Three. He was about to jump in after her when she pushed to the surface, gasping for breath.

"Scarlett, please get out," he rasped. He was about to jump in anyway at this point, but she moved to the steps. She climbed out, water dripping down her bare skin. He grabbed a towel from the low table and walked the few feet to her, wrapping it around her shoulders.

He paused when she met his stare and held it. "Say it, Scarlett. I can take it."

Instead, she stepped back from him, gripping the towel around herself. "Do you have any other clothes besides shirts for big muscled Fae?"

Sorin huffed a soft laugh. "Yes, Love, they're out on the bed for you."

"Don't call me that," she said as she left the bathing room.

He gave her plenty of time to get dressed before he finally walked out to his own bedroom. He found her on the balcony in a red, long-sleeve top that exposed her midriff when paired with the loose black pants that hung low on her hips. There wasn't even a scar where she had been stabbed with a shirastone dagger. She seemed to be gripping the railing, her knuckles white, and her shadows had thickened again.

She looked over her shoulder as he approached, then back out to the Fiera Mountains that stretched before them. "How is it so warm out here?"

"I am the Prince of Fire. I can keep my home plenty warm," he answered, leaning against the doorway. She stiffened at the mention of his title, and when she didn't speak again, he asked, "You are suddenly afraid of heights?"

Scarlett seemed to realize she had a death grip on the railing and lowered her hands, fisting them at her sides. "The last time I was in such a high room, I was not permitted to leave."

Realization slammed into him. Sorin closed the distance between them in a heartbeat. He took her face between his hands and said, "Scarlett Monrhoe, you are allowed to leave this room, these chambers, this palace, whenever your heart desires. In fact, once you have learned to wield your magic, you can leave these lands whenever you desire. You are no one's object to be kept in a room."

Those icy blue eyes locked onto his. "You're touching me," she whispered.

"It's a necessity," he answered.

A single tear slid down her cheek, and Sorin gently wiped it away with his thumb. She leaned forward, her forehead resting against his shoulder, and he brought his arms around her. With a thought, her wet hair was dry, and he stroked it, breathing her in. Her shadows swirled around him tentatively. He'd been watching her sleep for days, grateful she'd been asleep for what her body went through to overcome the withdrawal of that drugging tonic. But what had she endured in her dreams? What had occurred to make her question reality so much?

"I hate that you made me hate you."

"I hate that I did that too," he managed around the lump in his throat.

"I wish I didn't hate you because I need you, and I can't have you," she whispered, and she pushed herself away from him.

He'd been wrong.

He couldn't take it as he watched her walk away from him and back into the bedroom.

SCARLETT

Scarlett settled into one of the overstuffed armchairs near the fireplace in Sorin's bedroom. The fire crackled in the hearth. She pulled her knees into her chest, hugging them close. The shadows caressed her face, her arms. She was safe. This was real. She wasn't going to marry Mikale. She wasn't locked high in a room.

She could see it all. That bronze and black room with the uncomfortable bed. The look of triumph on Mikale's face every time he entered. His viciousness each time he forced her tonic down her throat. Plunging a dagger into Juliette's heart. Veda stabbing Cassius. Nuri bleeding out. Mikale taking her in an old office. Mikale—

"I didn't know if you were hungry," Sorin said, coming in from the great room and pulling her from her thoughts. She jumped, and he gave her an apologetic look. He carried two plates piled high with fruit, roasted chicken, bread, and cheese.

"Thank you," she said quietly as he set the plates on an end table near her chair. She didn't even glance at the food. Sorin sat in the chair opposite her, his unbuttoned shirt falling open to reveal his toned body and those tattoos once more. "So you've always had those?"

Sorin followed her gaze to his chest where a Mark adorned the upper left side. "I always had most of them, yes," he replied. "They were hidden by the glamour."

Scarlett gave a slight nod of her head. "And that one?" she asked, nodding towards his left hand.

"That one is new, but a tale for another time," Sorin answered, studying the Mark that flowed along the back of his hand and down two fingers. Scarlett gave him a scrutinizing look, and she could have sworn he squirmed a little. "I swear to you, Scarlett. The Mark has a meaning, and I will share it with you, but there are some other things we need to discuss first."

Scarlett looked away from him to the windows. "You live in the mountains."

"Yes, but when fire runs in your veins you don't mind the cold," he shrugged.

"I didn't mean it was a bad thing. They're beautiful." Scarlett still hugged her legs to her chest and rested her chin on her knees. "How long did I sleep?"

"Five days."

Five days? Holy gods. And yet she found herself utterly exhausted. She found herself wishing she could just crawl back into bed. She didn't have to feel when she slept. She didn't have to deal with all of this.

She took a deep breath before she said, "If you aren't planning to…use me or turn me over to the Fae Queen, why didn't you tell me about my mother sooner? When you figured it out?"

"Because I didn't quite believe it. I still don't know how it is possible. I told you that Queen Henna went to fight Esmeray because the Western Fae Queen didn't have an heir. When Esmeray learned that Queen Henna had a daughter a few years after she had killed her, she came back once more and killed Queen Eliné's husband to ensure an heir would not be born in her line either. As far as I knew, she had never had another companion she would have considered having a child with, and I did not scent a child on her the last time I saw her," Sorin replied.

"You can scent that on someone?" Scarlett asked, her brows rising in surprise.

Sorin's head tilted to the side. "You will quickly find that you can scent emotions and…other things with your heightened Fae senses."

Not sure what to exactly think of that, Scarlett asked instead, "So you can't be sure your Queen Eliné was my mother then. Maybe my mother just had the same name."

"Scarlett." His tone was impossibly gentle and overly patient, like he knew she didn't want to hear or believe any of this. "Only the Fae Queens exhibit more than one power. Even if a Fae child has parents from different Courts, they will still only possess one power. Eliné's gifts were water and fire. Just like yours."

"That makes me what, then? A princess of the Fae lands somehow?"

"That is currently up for debate," Sorin answered. "You are a princess of the realm, yes, but you could also rule."

She finally turned to look at him. "How could I possibly rule a land I know nothing about?"

"It is your birthright," Sorin replied simply.

"I grew up in a world where birthright and privilege decided how you were treated in life," Scarlett answered bitterly. "That is not a world I would wish to be a part of any longer."

Sorin tilted his head, a contemplative look in his eyes. "Those are the words of a wise ruler, Princess."

"Stop calling me that," she snapped, hugging her knees closer. "It is not my desire to rule anyone. I know what it is like to have masters. I do not wish to be anyone's."

"The queen will be happy to hear that," Sorin retorted, resentment cutting into his tone.

"The Fae Queen?"

"Yes."

"You can say her name here?"

"Yes."

"I'm really not in the mood to have to pry things out of you," Scarlett said, exasperation heavy in her voice.

"Talwyn. Her name is Talwyn Semiria. She would also be your cousin, I suppose."

Gods, she had a cousin. A blooded family member. Who wanted to use her somehow for revenge for the death of her mother and father and aunt, apparently. But the death of her aunt would be...

"Sorin?"

"Yeah, Love?"

She winced at the pet name. "If you were so close to my mother, why the fuck did you have her killed?"

CHAPTER 5
SCARLETT

S he wasn't sure if Sorin was breathing when she met his gaze. He just stared at her, a mixture of horror and regret in his eyes. "Why? You act as if you cared for her. You say she was your closest friend. So why would you have her killed?"

"Gods, Scarlett." He ran a hand over his face. "I did not have Eliné killed."

"You've said yourself that the Fire Prince was responsible for her death. That sounds like you killed her to me," Scarlett bit back, her shadows darkening around her.

"I am responsible, yes, but I did not order her killed," Sorin replied.

"That doesn't make any sense."

Sorin pressed his thumb and forefinger to his brows. "Your mother left the Black Halls in the middle of the night. She left nothing behind indicating where she had gone or why. No clues and no way of tracking her down. Talwyn was still young by Fae standards. She had assumed her throne by this point, but Eliné was still highly involved in the affairs of the Eastern Courts. She was still heavily guiding her. When she left... Things slowly deteriorated between the Western Courts and the Fae Queen.

"We searched. For years, we searched for her. Many gave up hope, but I didn't. Talwyn didn't. We both believed she was still alive, and ten years after she left, we got a random tip that she was alive and being held just over the border of the Fire Court. That she had been there the whole time, right under our noses. We planned a rescue mission. It was a small group of my own most trusted and best warriors and two of Talwyn's. My Second was wary though. He thought it was a trap and that the information had been too easy to find—"

"Oh my gods," Scarlett whispered, lifting her head from her knees. "That story you told me, of the time you made a bad call, that was an attempt to come for my mother?"

The grief and pain that filled Sorin's eyes was gut-wrenching. "Yes, it was," he said quietly. "And because of our actions, *my* actions that day, whoever knew your mother's true identity had her killed. I don't know who had her killed or why us attempting to come for her suddenly made them decide it was too much of a risk to let her remain living, but my actions that day caused the order to be given. I am responsible for your mother's death."

When she had been told years ago by the Assassin Lord that the Prince of Fire had been responsible for her mother's death, she had naturally assumed the Prince had hired Dracon to kill her. But if Sorin hadn't been the one to do so, who did? Then her mind drifted to what her payment would have been if she'd completed her last assignment and killed Sorin. The Assassin Lord had said he knew how to find the Prince of Fire and would aid her in ending him.

"Oh my gods," she whispered again, her hand coming to her mouth.

"Scarlett?" Sorin asked cautiously, and her shadows receded.

Her eyes snapped back to his. She realized she had dropped her feet to the floor and her other hand was gripping the arm of the chair. Frost was slowly creeping along the fabric. She quickly released the chair, bringing both her hands to her lap. "The Assassin Lord knows who you are."

"What?" Shock filled his features, but he shook his head. "No, that's impossible. Do you remember what I told you right before we came to the border? Our identities have been kept a secret in the mortal lands. There are so many enchantments in place. There was no way I could have even told you I was the Fire Prince, Scarlett."

"He knows, Sorin. I don't know how he knows, but he does." Sorin started to argue again, but she pressed on. "My task was to kill you. Not Ryker Renwell. Sorin Aditya. He knew your name, and my payment for the job was information he had. Information including that he knew how to find you and that he would aid me in killing you; but if I had completed the task, both of those things would have already been accomplished."

"I don't know, Scarlett. I don't know how he would have learned any of that." She could hear the doubt in his tone, see it in his eyes.

She shook her head in frustration, launching to her feet and beginning to pace. "You don't understand, Sorin. My mother was very close to the Assassin Lord. There may be a Black Syndicate Council, but the Assassin Lord and my mother were the king and queen of the Syndicate. He may not have known how to get to you, but that is why you were my assignment. He also believes you were responsible for my mother's death. He knew with that kind of motivation I would have gone to the ends of the world to find you."

"But Lord Tyndell said he was the one who put the hit on me," Sorin said, his eyes tracking her as she paced.

"Alaric would have seen it as an opportunity. A chance to get rid of you without having to show how invested he was in the mission," she answered, waving her hand dismissively.

"Alaric?"

Scarlett stopped pacing, her eyes widening. Holy fucking hell. The beating she would endure in the Syndicate for uttering his name aloud would leave her unable to get out of bed for a week.

"Scarlett, he can't touch you here," Sorin said slowly, cautiously. "No one lays a hand on you here. No one."

A breath she didn't realize she'd been holding whooshed from her lungs. "Games, Sorin. The Assassin Lord likes to play games. My last assignment was a giant game to get me to come back home."

"This is your home, Scarlett. You belong here," Sorin said softly.

Scarlett was quiet for a long moment before bringing her eyes to Sorin's. "I do not belong here."

"You're Fae. You're a princess, a Fae Queen. You're with— Of course you belong here. This is where you were always meant to be," Sorin replied.

And his response was so simple, so matter-of-fact, so *decided*, that Scarlett wanted to scream.

"Don't you get it?" she asked, her voice rising. She ran her hands through her hair. "I do not want this! You took me from the only place I've ever known. You took me from one world where I was expected to be one thing to another world where even greater expectations are shoved on me. I do not want this! I do not want to be a princess. I do not want to rule. I do not need another master or cage, no matter how pretty it looks."

Sorin stood now, coming toe-to-toe with her. Her shadows lashed at him, but he did not back down. "Don't *you* get it, Scarlett? This is your escape. This is your chance to *do* something. This is your chance to make your own choices. This is your chance to be free."

"I do not want it!"

"You do not want it?" He huffed a laugh of disbelief. "I offer you freedom and you turn it down? You *want* that cage, don't you, Scarlett? You *want* to—"

But he was cut off.

He was cut off by a powerful surge of water that came straight from Scarlett's palms as she reached up to shove him. He flew across the room, surprise on his face. He hit the wall with a sickening thud, sliding down to the floor. He leaned against the wall, rubbing the back of his head.

Scarlett stood frozen to the spot.

Breathe, her shadows whispered to her. *Breathe.*

She closed her eyes. When had her life become such a gods-damn mess? Every time she turned around, something else was added to the storm. Every time she took a breath, another wave crashed into her, pushing her under. Shoving her down into the darkness.

There were hands on her shoulders gently brushing down her arms. He did it again and again. Finally, she opened her eyes and met his.

"Hey, Love." When she didn't say anything, when she didn't move, he said softly, "Come here."

Sorin tugged her gently, a little hesitant at first, but when she didn't resist, he pulled her into his arms. Her whole body relaxed into him. The power she could feel roiling in her veins, her gut, quieted. Even her shadows seemed to dim. She leaned into him, her head on his shoulder. She felt him press a kiss to her temple.

She didn't know when or how he did it, but she found herself sitting in his lap as he sat back in his armchair by the fire. They sat in silence for long minutes, and all Scarlett could think about was how impossibly she needed someone who had lied to her over and over again. He could wrap it up as nicely as he wanted by saying he withheld information, but he had lied to her. About her mother. About who he was. About who she was.

"Does she know?" she asked quietly.

"Does who know what?"

"Does Talwyn know what I am? That I'm her cousin? That I'm here?"

Sorin's hand had been gently stroking her hair and continued to do so as he answered. "She knows your power is here. When this kind of power enters our lands, we know it. Does she know who wields that power? Likely not yet. Does she know you are her cousin? No. I do not think she could possibly know that."

"But you must answer to her. She will wonder why you have returned without completing your task. She will wonder why you have returned without her weapon."

Sorin rubbed a thumb gently along her cheekbone. Her shadows trailed it. "She told me to return home weeks ago. That day you saw us in the woods."

"You defied her?"

"I told you. Talwyn and I do not always...agree on matters. My allegiance, Scarlett Monrhoe, is to you, as it was to your mother. I told you I would not leave you alone, so I did not return without you. If you do not want to rule or be queen, that is fine. The choice is always yours, but I will always stand in your court. Always."

"What if I do not want a court? What if I do not want to stay here?"

"Then it will be just you and me."

"You and me? There is no you and me. There's you and there's me," Scarlett replied.

"You know that's not true, Scarlett," he said, his voice low. "That hasn't been true for quite some time now."

Her heart hammered in her chest. His hand still stroked her hair and his other arm was wrapped around her waist, holding her close to him. "You're touching me," she said from where her head rested against his chest.

"If I could lie to you, I'd tell you it was a necessity, but it's not. I just wanted to hold you," he answered.

"And if I told you I wanted you to touch me more?" she whispered. She started tracing one of those tattoos on his chest with her finger, slowly following the swirls and whorls of it.

His hand stilled on her hair. After an extended silence, he pushed out a long breath. "I would kick myself for it, but I would gently remind you that you hate me."

Scarlett lifted her head from his chest. His eyes were on her, a mixture of agony and desire glimmering in them. She shifted slightly, and his hand skimmed over the bare skin on the small of her back. She tilted her head to the side so that her mouth was perfectly lined up with his, and he sucked in a breath.

"Scarlett, what are you doing?" She could hear the restraint in his voice.

"I'm going to kiss you," she breathed as she slowly brought her lips closer. "Are you going to stop me?"

"I should."

But when her lips met his, he didn't. No, when her lips met his, that hand that had been stroking her hair slipped into it, fisting and tilting her head back to where he wanted it so he could deepen that kiss. The hand on her lower back slid to her hip where his thumb began making small circles. When Scarlett opened her mouth to him, he groaned, and the sound rumbled through her as his tongue swept in, and she tasted his cloves and honey flavor. Again, that lush smokey smell mixed with his ash and cedar scent.

She pulled back, breathless. "You said Fae can scent emotions and other things."

"I did." His voice was gruff, and he was breathing as fast as she was.

Then the scent that sometimes mixed with his was…arousal. A slow grin formed on her mouth. "That could be a useful tool, Prince," she crooned.

Sorin closed his eyes, sighing in relief. "Gods, I never thought I would be so glad to hear your wicked tongue."

Scarlett pushed herself from his lap. "So do I have shoes here or am I required to walk around barefoot in such a fine palace?"

"I have more clothing and options coming for you, but for now, I believe Camilla left a pair of silk slippers by the main door for you," Sorin answered, getting to his own feet. "What would you like to do, Princess?"

Scarlett scowled at him. "I was going to say I wanted you to show me around a little, but now I want to learn how to control this damn magic so that I can knock you on your ass on purpose when you call me such things."

"Is that so?" he asked, raising an eyebrow, an amused twinkle entering his eyes.

"Yes," she answered, turning to walk to the sitting room.

"If that is what it takes to get you to start acknowledging and wanting to master your magic, I will call you Princess all day long," he taunted, striding past her to open the door. When he reached for the handle, though, she spotted the tattoo on his left hand again. It snaked down his thumb and forefinger, and it seemed incomplete somehow, like he'd had to leave in the middle of it.

"You never told me the story of this," she said, reaching out and running her fingers along the dark lines etched into his skin.

Sorin stilled, watching her trace them. "It is a Fae Marking, a tradition of ours."

"It seems unfinished," she replied, leaning forward to study it more.

"I suppose it does."

"Why?" she asked, her eyes flitting up to his.

"Because I do not know how it will look in the end."

Scarlett's nose scrunched in confusion. "Aren't you its creator? Don't you get to decide how it will look in the end?"

"Yes, but it's not the end yet, is it?"

Scarlett rolled her eyes. "These Fae customs are extremely profound."

Sorin only leaned forward and pressed a quick kiss to her brow. "Let me show you your home, Love."

Sorin

Sorin led Scarlett through the various halls and chambers of his Fiera Palace. He showed her the meeting rooms where they met for councils, and the offices where he normally worked. Although, he admitted, a large majority of his work was done in his chambers at night. He showed her the grand hall where they held festivities and balls. He took her out to the grounds and showed her the soldiers' quarters where some of his men stayed. He took her to the training rings and the stables. He took her through the gardens and the kitchens. He took in her delight that the flowers still bloomed way up in the mountains and stared at her in wonder as she greeted each servant and asked their name. He had no doubt she would remember each and every one.

"This is the guest wing," he explained, leading her down a hall in the eastern side of the palace.

"The rooms are huge," Scarlett exclaimed as they passed by one with an open door. She paused at the threshold. "May I?"

"Of course," Sorin replied, gesturing for her to enter. She

turned slowly in place, taking in the sitting room, game room off to the left, and the door leading back to the bedroom.

"You certainly know how to treat guests," she said, her hands going to her hips. He tried not to notice how her fingers grazed the strip of midriff her top left exposed or how his hand had been on that skin while she sat in his lap kissing him earlier. He tried to forget that he had turned her down when he'd wanted to carry her to his bed and touch her anywhere she asked. Gods, she had figured out the scent of his arousal faster than he'd expected. Not that he should really be surprised by that, he supposed, but if his mind lingered on that idea too long…

"Can I have this one?" she asked, jerking him from those thoughts.

"Can you what?" He blurted out, unable to hide his shock. She couldn't be serious. Sleep in the guest wing?

"Well, I'm assuming I get a room," Scarlett said slowly, watching him carefully.

"You have a room. You've been sleeping in it for days." Fuck propriety. She wasn't sleeping on the other side of the palace. It was out of the question.

Scarlett tilted her head to the side, her long hair swaying over her shoulder. "I am a guest, am I not? Besides, isn't that *your* room?"

"This is your home, Scarlett," he replied. She still had those damn hands on her hips, standing there like the princess she was.

She pursed her lips, contemplating his words. She was standing near one of the room's armchairs, and she ran a finger over the ornate embroidery of the fabric, tracing one of the gold-threaded designs. Finally, she said quietly, "I do not know what it is like to have a home any more. I have not had one since my mother died. Not really."

"This can be your home, Scarlett. If you want it to be." He tried not to shift under her scrutinizing stare as she brought her eyes back to his and her shadows stretched towards him.

"Live here? With you?"

"That is your choice," he said. "If you'd rather a place in the city, I can arrange that, too."

"In the private wing of the palace? Where your chambers are?"

He couldn't decide where she was going with this. He had learned where to look to read her emotions over the past few months. How her fingers curled when she was irritated. How her nose scrunched when she was confused. How her eyes narrowed when she was not impressed. How they shone when she was blissfully happy, although he'd only seen that a handful of times. Her face now, though, was nearly unreadable, like it had been since she'd awoke, as if she were somewhere he could not reach. "I can find you another suite in the private wing, or you may live in my chambers if you wish."

"Then where will you live?"

"I will live wherever I need to live so that you are not alone," he replied, stepping towards her. She looked up at him, the golden flecks bright in her icy blue eyes today.

"Hmm," she said dismissively, stepping back after a moment. "I do rather prefer the sofa in your chambers. Besides, I'd hate for you to be alone in that big wing all by yourself." He saw it for what it was. She was trying. She was trying so damn hard to dredge up who she was, who she had been.

"What makes you think I live here by myself?" he asked, following her out of the guest chamber and taking the lead once more.

"Others live here? Besides the help?" she asked, peering at him as they walked side-by-side. His hand brushed hers, and she didn't yank it back. The closeness of her made his blood hum. While he could have throttled himself for turning her down earlier, he knew she would have regretted it. She'd wanted a distraction from all the trauma she'd repressed for years. That he'd only added to. No, he didn't deserve to touch her at all.

He laughed at her questions now, though. "Yes, Scarlett. I am not some solitary prince living in a huge palace by himself."

"Who else lives here?" she demanded. "I mean, if I have room-mates, shouldn't I meet them?"

"They don't live *in* my chambers," he answered, flicking her nose. "They have their own quarters in the private wing."

"You have family here?"

"Not blood relatives. Gods, no. But they are family, yes," he replied.

"But do you…" Her eyes went wide as she stopped walking, and he knew what she was working out as he paused beside her. "You saw your parents killed by King Deimas and Queen Esmeray."

"I did," Sorin answered softly. "I was in the crowd when they… Well, when they were killed, yes." He didn't need to go into details and tell her exactly how they had been slaughtered in front of their people.

"Oh my gods, Sorin… I don't know what to say."

"You don't need to say anything. It was a long time ago, Scarlett."

"I still… I'm sorry. No child should ever have to see their parent be killed, let alone in such a gruesome way. What that does to a child…" She trailed off again.

"I wasn't exactly a child," he replied, brushing his knuckles down her cheek. "Yes, I was young by Fae standards, but I was several decades old."

"Still… I'm sorry." She bit her lower lip, and the action erased any lingering thoughts of his parents. She cleared her throat after a moment. "So who exactly does live here with you, then?"

"I'm sure you will meet them at dinner. Briar had a heck of time keeping them at bay while you were getting your beauty sleep," Sorin teased as he began leading her to the bridge to cross the river.

"At dinner?"

"Yes, at dinner. If you want to, of course," he answered. "I would like you to meet them. Eliza will be there. And Briar."

"But I already met Briar, and I sort of already know Eliza," she crossed her arms, stopping once more and tapping her foot. "I don't know, Sorin. How many people are going to be at this dinner?"

"Only my Inner Court. You've sort of already met them. They met us at the border." Her lips pursed at the recollection, and he reached for her hand, tugging her towards the bridge that was a few feet ahead of them. "As for Briar, he's not part of my Inner Court."

"Then who is he?" she asked, and he couldn't help but smile as her nose scrunched at the question.

"Briar is the Prince of the Water Court and one of my closest friends."

"Oh my gods," Scarlett moaned. "I attacked a prince today?"

"One, you did not have control over your magic. Briar knows that. Two, you attack *me* on a regular basis," Sorin retorted with amusement.

"Well, yes, but you deserve it because you're an arrogant ass," she snapped, snatching her hand from his. "Doesn't he have his own Court to tend to then?"

"He does. He has his own Court and Inner Court, but I expect there to be some...push back with you being at dinner," Sorin replied cautiously.

"Why?" she asked, stopping in the center of the bridge to look out the floor-to-ceiling windows. They overlooked the Tana River as it flowed down the mountainside, right through the middle of the palace.

Sorin rested his arms on the railing of the bridge, leaning on his elbows beside her. "You are unexpected, Scarlett. I was sent to find a weapon I did not believe existed. Queen Talwyn invoked something called the Blood Vows of the Courts. During a queen's rule, she is allowed to use the vow once with each Court she rules over. The vow requires the prince or princess to obey a command of her choosing without question. I was forced to go. You know our relationship with Talwyn is strained and when they learn that *you* are that weapon, when they learn what you are..." Sorin sighed. "I could need Briar there as a buffer is all. My Inner Court is family, and I rarely have to enforce rank. But two princes may indeed be needed this evening. However, if you do not want to come to dinner, I understand. The choice is always yours."

"A choice." She said it so quietly, he barely heard her, even with his full Fae hearing back intact. Her shadows seemed to flicker, as if they might go out. "I am truly free to go wherever I wish?"

"You are free to wander wherever you feel led. Leave the palace.

Go to the city. Although maybe have an escort the first time, so you do not get lost," he added.

"An escort? You mean you?"

"Me. Briar. Someone from the Inner Court." He shrugged again, but added with a wry smile, "Or go yourself. If I recall correctly, I am not your keeper."

She threw him an unimpressed glare. "I hardly know Briar and have only met your Inner Court when I was being chased by vampyres."

"Oh, I'm sure you will get to know them well enough," he chuckled. "They are obnoxious, cavalier, and intrusive. Come to think of it, you will fit in well."

She gave him a light shove as she muttered, "Prick."

He merely turned, now leaning back against the railing, and pulled her to him. He pressed a kiss to the top of her head as she leaned into him. Again, those shadows flickered. She pulled back to look into his eyes, and he reached up to stroke her cheek, but he was met with a burning, biting swirl of shadows as they darkened around her.

"Scarlett?" Her eyes were wide as she stared back the way they had come.

Where Prince Callan was walking towards the bridge.

He had planned to visit the prince tomorrow, but apparently it was to be now. There was a problem, though.

He leaned over to speak into her ear. "Scarlett, if you do not want to talk to him right now, I understand. I can summon Briar, and he can take you back to our rooms."

She shook her head, her eyes still on the human prince.

"The thing is, the moment he steps foot on this bridge, my entire Inner Court will be summoned. One will be here almost instantaneously. The other two will not be far behind."

She turned to him. Her eyes were dark, as though her shadows had infiltrated them. "Can you tell them not to come?"

He grimaced. "I could, but they will not listen." The look of bewilderment caused him to add, "You will understand when you meet them tonight. But if you do not wish to meet them here, I can request Briar come and escort you back, and I will talk to Callan."

"If he does not step onto the bridge, will they still come?"

"No, not unless he takes that step. It is part of the wards and protection spells to the private wing."

"Can I talk to him first?"

"Of course, Love. You are free to do as you wish. Always."

She looked at him, almost as if seeing him for the first time. Those shadows of hers stroked down his cheek. Then she took a step forward, and they speared from her towards the end of the bridge.

CHAPTER 6
CALLAN

Callan had been watching them for nearly ten minutes. He had seen them rounding a corner in the guest halls. Finn had tried to grab his arm, but he had shrugged him off and trailed them. He had hidden in an alcove as they crossed onto the bridge. She was so relaxed with him. So…carefree. As if nothing could go wrong as long as he was beside her. She had never been that relaxed, that comfortable, around him. She was always prepared to flee. Always prepared to fight her way out of anything. Even when she had been naked in his bed, daggers had always been within reach.

He watched as she lightly shoved the Fire Prince, and he heard her endearingly call him a prick. She was still a wraith, her eyes still haunted, but even the shadows that trailed her had dimmed. And when he had pulled her to him, they flickered. Callan had been sure they were going to go out.

And he couldn't help himself. He had to talk to her. He had to know. She had said she and the general were friends. She had said she couldn't be tied to a throne. If she chose him, wouldn't it be the same? Was she choosing him?

55

He had stepped from the alcove and had begun walking towards the bridge when she had spotted him. Her eyes had widened, and those shadows had swirled. As he came closer, Sorin had bent down and whispered into her ear. Some discussion was had, and when he came to a stop at the edge of the bridge, Sorin's voice floated down to him. "Of course, Love. You are free to do as you wish. Always."

Love. He had called her that the entire trip. A pet name. That's what he had told himself. A name to get under her skin, to tease her like he seemed to like to do. He hadn't meant it as *Love*. Right?

Callan had stilled as Scarlett had begun walking towards him. He made to move toward her, but shadows speared from her and created a wall at the edge of the bridge. He watched as she stopped a few feet from him, cocking her head to study the wall of shadows, like she was unsure of how they had created such an obstruction.

The guard beside the bridge started at the shadowy wall, but Sorin said coolly from down the way, "It is fine, Talis. No need to worry." The guard nodded at his prince and stood back.

Her eyes slid to him. "Hello, Callan." Her voice was as it always had been, yet was far away. Her ears were pointed now, and he couldn't help but notice elongated canines that peeked out when she spoke. She seemed taller. Fae. One of them.

"Scarlett," he breathed. "You are...different."

"Different?" She seemed to mull the term over in her mind. "I suppose. I am not clad in black and armed with weapons. Then again, I've been told I am a weapon."

"That's not what I mean," Callan said, shaking his head. "Come and talk to me."

"I cannot talk to you right now," she whispered.

"Cannot or will not?" he asked, the question coming out sharper than he had intended. She flinched at his tone. He had never seen her flinch in his life. What was Sorin doing to her?

"Are you all right?" he asked, taking a step forward. "Are you safe?"

"Why would I not be safe?" she asked.

Sorin was hanging back, leaning against the bridge railing. His arms were crossed, a bored expression on his face. He had not seen the Fire Prince once since he was led from his chambers nearly a week ago.

"Just please come talk to me," Callan pleaded.

"I am not ready to talk to you, Callan. There is much I need to work through—"

"Then let me help you," he cut in.

"You cannot," she replied sadly.

"And I suppose *he* can?"

"There is much you do not know."

"Then tell me."

"There is much even I do not yet understand," she tried again. Her tone was beseeching.

"And I suppose he holds the answers? How do you know he is not controlling you?"

At the words, Sorin pushed off the railing and came strolling casually along the bridge. "Are you suggesting that I am *forcing* Scarlett to do something?" His voice was dangerous and cold.

"It's happened before," Callan said defiantly. "Or did it? Did Mikale really threaten me?

"Callan, I would not make that up," Scarlett said, hurt flickering on her face.

"Maybe you didn't. Maybe *he* did. Maybe he has orchestrated all of this. To get you here," Callan spat.

"No. That is not true. You know that's not true," Scarlett cried, but a flash of uncertainty crossed her features.

"Then let me go back and confront him," Callan said. "Let me go home where I am free to go where I please and see whom I wish."

"You are not a prisoner here, Callan, but you cannot go back yet," Scarlett pleaded. "It will put you and Cassius in danger."

"Cassius?" Callan blinked, and he let his anger blurt out the next thing he said. "Ah, Cassius. The fourth piece of this equation. Tell me, Scarlett, which of us do you love, by the way? Or do we all serve your purposes in some way or another?"

Scarlett took a step back, and Sorin reached out a hand to steady her. Her shadows receded into her as if she had been punched. Sorin reached up with a finger and drew flames in the air. The symbol shimmered for a moment, then disappeared.

"What do you want me to say, Callan?" she whispered.

"I want you to say to my face that you used me. That you never cared for me," he spat.

"That is not true! I will not say it," she said, shaking her head. "I still care for you."

"I want you to say to my face that you lied to me when you told me he was not the reason you stopped coming to me." He threw an accusing finger in Sorin's direction.

"I did not know him until a few months ago," she retorted, her eyes darkening. She took a step forward, shrugging off Sorin's hand at her back. She came to the edge of the bridge, and Callan met her there, toe-to-toe. Fury lined her features now, but he refused to back down from her. "Ask me what you wish to know, Prince," her voice now lethal.

Callan knew. He knew he was pushing her to a dangerous edge. He knew what she was capable of. He'd watched her cut down vampyres like they were nothing. He'd watched her step on entrails just to inflict more agony and pain.

The sound of rushing water echoed in the space, and the Water Prince stepped from a portal at the other end of the bridge. He stood back, waiting for something, watching.

"Well?" she demanded.

"A few weeks ago, you told me he was a close friend like Cassius. Was that true?" He held his breath, waiting for her answer.

"Yes."

"And now?"

She studied him, her stare penetrating, as she asked quietly, "Are you asking if I have fucked him, Callan?"

The river began to stir below them. The serene waters began churning and waves appeared as if they were rapids. Sorin glanced over his shoulder, and Briar leaned over the bridge, peering down at the water. He stretched a hand out over the side of the bridge, and the waves calmed, but the water still rushed through the palace faster than it had before, like the current had increased in the normally calm, peaceful river.

"Is that what you are asking me, Callan?" she demanded again.

He felt Finn grab his elbow and try to tug him back, but he shook him off. "Yes," he ground out from between his teeth.

A serpentine grin formed on her lips, and her eyes narrowed at him. Shadows slithered and coiled around her arms, her wrists, her torso. She leaned forward, almost as if she were going to kiss him, and tendrils of those shadows reached for him. He flinched back. "You are the first and only person I have ever given myself to by choice," she said with a venomous quiet. "Mikale, however, has also been between my legs, only he took what he wanted. About a year ago. Any other questions for me, Prince?"

Callan recoiled as her words hit him, eyes widening in horror. A year ago. When she'd stopped coming to him. When everything had changed.

"Scarlett," Sorin said softly, placing a hand on her arm, the shadows seeming to embrace his touch. "Go with Briar. He will take you to your rooms. I will be there shortly."

Scarlett looked at Callan, her face hard. "I may have loved you once, Prince, but now I do not know what I feel for you." She turned on her heel and, without looking back, strode across the bridge to where Briar waited for her, his face grim.

"Scarlett," Callan called, and stepped onto the bridge to go after her, but he stilled at the cruel smile that spread across Sorin's face. A second later, Rayner stepped from smoke and swirling ashes behind him. He stepped to Sorin's side and whispered something into his ear.

"Interesting," Sorin said, sliding his hands into the pockets of his charcoal gray pants and leaning a hip against the bridge railing. "Rayner tells me you have been to the other side of this bridge once before?"

"Yes," Callan replied coolly. "I was inquiring after her."

"To call her a whore to her face the moment she woke up?" he asked, raising his brows mockingly. Cyrus appeared from a hallway on the other side of the bridge and stalked across it.

"No," Callan retorted. "I did not mean to make her—"

"You did not mean to hurt her," Sorin corrected. And then Eliza was coming up the stairs and making her way across the bridge. How did they all get here so damn fast? Briar and Scarlett had disappeared. He had not even seen which way they had gone. The river below them had calmed and was now serenely flowing once more. "You know," Sorin continued, taking a step forward now, his Court falling into place behind him. Callan took a step back, off the bridge. "She would have come to you. Had you been patient and courteous and given her a little time, she would have come and explained what she could, but you just couldn't wait."

"You were keeping me from her out of spite," Callan spat.

"I was keeping you from her so that this little scene did not happen the moment she opened her eyes, which by the way, was this morning," Sorin said coldly.

"Mikale. He…" Callan couldn't bring himself to say the words.

"Yes, he raped her, and yes, he would have done so again had we not gotten her out," Sorin said, his lips forming a thin line. "Mikale knows she is Fae and desires her bloodline to merge with his own. That is all we know right now." Callan didn't know what to say as Sorin continued. "Scarlett was correct. You are not a prisoner here. You and your little posse," he said with a smirk at Finn and Sloan, "are free to go wherever you wish. You are free to go to the city. You are free to leave these lands if you think you can make it out and survive amongst what lurks in these mountains without magic. You are free to go wherever you wish in the palace on the *eastern* side of the river. I highly recommend our library. Brush up on some history.

"But allow me to give you your first lesson. The rumors that swirl among the human lands about the Fire Court being the cruelest are true. Step foot on any of these bridges again, Crown Prince of Windonelle, and you shall learn exactly just how true they are." His Court behind him all grinned, callous and wicked. Sorin took a step towards him. Finn and Sloan made to move in front of him, but Sorin raised his hand and flames encircled them. Sorin's voice became venom. "Make her feel like a whore again, and you will learn exactly what it means to be a prisoner in my home. Do I make myself clear?"

"Perfectly," Callan said, his jaw clenched.

Sorin closed his fist, and the flames around Finn and Sloan disappeared. "Eliza, dear, show them to the library, will you?" he said as he turned and began to cross the bridge. He was not even halfway across it when a fire portal opened in front of him, and he stepped through, disappearing from sight.

"He is in a pleasant mood today," Eliza commented, looking up at Cyrus.

"I thought the princeling was going into the river," Cyrus said, disappointment on his face. "Did you see the Mark?"

"Yes," Rayner answered.

Eliza was quiet.

Callan could only stare with his mouth gaping open like a fish at their nonchalant exchange.

"Eliza?" Cyrus hissed, his eyes narrowing at her. "When did you Mark him?"

"Who says I Marked him?" she snapped.

"You are the only one he would trust to give him *that* Mark," Rayner argued quietly.

"For good reason," she returned haughtily.

"When?" Cyrus demanded.

She tsked and crossed her arms. "Before we returned from the mortal lands."

"He hid it from us when he crossed the border?" Cyrus asked, gritting his teeth.

Eliza rolled her eyes. "Careful, Cyrus, you'll give yourself a headache from all that thinking."

Rayner stepped between the two Fae as they glowered at each other. "Enough," he growled.

"Did either of you see her?" Cyrus asked, stepping back to lean against the railing.

"No. The last time I saw her, she was bleeding out in the Prince's arms right after we'd crossed the border," Eliza sighed. "Dinner tonight I suppose then."

"Maybe he can tell you more about her on your little walk," Cyrus said, now eyeing Callan.

"It does not sound like his opinion of her is very high," Rayner supplied thoughtfully, studying Callan as well.

"He is jealous, Rayner," Eliza sighed again. "Jealousy makes people say and do stupid things."

"If that twin flame Mark is Anointed, Sorin will—" Cyrus started.

"Stop speaking," Eliza snapped, stepping from the bridge. She gestured to Callan and his guards to follow. "Come. I will show you to the library."

She led them away towards the back of the palace. When they were out of earshot of the bridge, he said to Eliza, "You were being sarcastic. About Sorin being in a pleasant mood, right?"

"Not at all," Eliza scoffed. "Had he been in a foul mood, you would have indeed ended up in the river. You did not spend much time with him in the mortal lands if you thought that was a pissy mood."

Callan swallowed, slipping into silence. After another minute he asked, "What is the twin flame Mark?"

"Nothing that concerns you," she answered tightly, rounding a corner and stopping before a set of double doors.

"It sounded like it should be concerning to me," Callan argued grimly.

"I tell you what, Princeling," Eliza said, pushing open the doors before them. Inside were rows and rows and shelves and shelves of books, reaching to the ceiling. Not just the ceiling of the second floor they were on, but clear to the top of the palace. All seven levels. The ceiling was the same glass material as the bridges, and the clear blue sky could be seen through it. "You find a book in here about it, and I shall answer any questions you have regarding the twin flame Mark after you have read about it. Good luck."

Eliza turned and left the library, closing the double doors behind her.

"These Fae are real bastards," Sloan grumbled from beside Callan.

"I could not agree more," Callan retorted and set off to look for a book.

CHAPTER 7
SCARLETT

B riar had whisked her away so swiftly she didn't even have a chance to note which turns he took or hallways they went down. She didn't care anyway. She should have had Sorin summon Briar right away. Why she had thought Callan would understand, she didn't know. He had said she seemed different. Of course she did. He only knew bits and pieces of her. If he knew the whole, if he knew her entire being... Well, if he'd known her entire being, things never would have happened the way they did.

Briar was silent as he led her up some stairs. She eyed him in his sea green tunic and gray pants. His shoulder length hair was tied back. As if he could feel her gaze on him, he turned those twinkling, icy blue eyes to her in question. Scarlett looked away quickly and continued to follow him in silence.

After another few flights of stairs, he led her down a hallway and stopped before the second door down. With his finger he drew a symbol on the door in icy snowflakes, and it clicked open. They stepped inside, and she quickly made to go to the bedroom.

"Sometimes it is easier to take off a mask in front of someone who knows nothing of you." His tone was gentle and soft.

She halted and slowly turned to look at him. He had followed her and now stood a few feet away, leaning back against the dining table, his hands braced on the edge. Her shadows reached out to him, and he did not flinch. They swirled around him, searching him, feeling him out. "Do not pity me," she finally said. "I deserve what was said to me today."

"My dear Scarlett, the only pity I feel for you is that you have to deal with Sorin and his whiny Court," Briar said with a grin and a wink, then turned serious once more. "But no one deserves to have another wave slam into them when they are still struggling to recover from a storm."

"And when the storm is unending? When the waves are unrelenting?" Scarlett asked quietly.

"Rage, Scarlett. Rage and scream and cry and fall apart. You are allowed to feel and do all those things, but you do not stop fighting. You do not give up. You become a bigger storm," he answered. He did not reach for her. He did not try to comfort her or tell her what Callan said was wrong. He did not try to make it better.

Scarlett turned and continued to the bedroom. "It's funny. I always thought there needed to be water to feel like you're drowning, but there really doesn't need to be."

"You only drown if you stay in the river. Let him pull you to the shore. It is okay to let yourself be rescued sometimes, Scarlett," Briar replied.

She shut the door behind her.

Sorin entered his sitting room as the bedroom door clicked shut. He glanced to the closed door, then to Briar, who was leaning against the dining table.

"Did she say anything?" Sorin asked. Rage was pulsing through him, and embers filled his vision.

"Very little," Briar answered. There was a swirl of snow, and a sword appeared in his hand. It was pure silver, the hilt gleaming with a large, glimmering sapphire. Ice Razor, the sword of the Water Prince. "She needs a minute, Sorin."

"Are you intending to keep me from my twin flame?" Sorin asked dangerously, flames appearing at his fingertips.

"Of course not," Briar replied dismissively. "But give her a second to breathe, my friend. And give yourself that, too. Come spar and let out that anger before you go to her and help her deal with her own. Five minutes."

"Fine," Sorin ground out, his own black sword appearing in his hand. A water portal appeared, and he followed Briar through.

They came out into a private training room on the top of the palace. The ceiling was fire glass like the bridges, and it let in the autumn sun. Fall was thick in the air, and being high in the Fiera Mountains, snow flurries already graced them some days. Samhain was in just two weeks, and the thought sent him into motion as they entered the sparring ring. Briar parried and deflected, pushing back with his own weapon.

There would be a Samhain feast and ball. Sorin had no doubt preparations were already under way. He would have to go. He'd been absent for three years. His people would be excited and expecting to see him once more. But Prince Callan was here. He would be invited, of course. And Scarlett? A Samhain ball was where Callan and Scarlett had first interacted outside of notes and books. It was the first time they'd danced. It was when their relationship had taken a huge leap forward.

His blade clashed with Briar's once more as he gritted his teeth. Flames danced along his sword as ice shards swirled around Briar's. "You are out of practice," Briar said with a slight smirk.

"I've been training mortals for three years," Sorin replied. "Not much training in that for me. I trained Scarlett I suppose, but unbeknownst to me, she held back her true abilities."

"Is that the reason, or are the effects of taking that Mark without a companion already coming into play?" Briar asked as they clashed again and jumped back from one another.

"Enough," Sorin said. Without missing a beat, Briar sheathed his sword on his back, and Sorin sheathed his own. He crossed to one of the benches around the edges of the room and sat, leaning his head back against the wall. Briar walked over, sitting beside him without a word. "I cannot tell her. Not now. Not yet. She's…"

"She is lost," Briar finished. "But she doesn't realize she has already found her way. She doesn't know she's found you."

"I cannot force her to accept this. Not when I have been the cause of so much of her brokenness. I cannot ask that of her when she is swimming in shadows," Sorin replied.

"Yes, those are interesting," Briar said contemplatively. "Do you know what they are?"

"No. She has rarely spoken of them to me. She calls them the darkness."

"I will see what I can find out from Ashtine when I see her again," Briar answered.

Sorin nodded his head in thanks, although he wasn't sure the Princess of Wind would be much assistance in the matter with her mystical speech and queer personality.

"I should go to her. Make sure she has not drowned," he said grimly. Briar raised his brows in question. "When she is in shock and trying to process something, she goes under the water. But she stays under too long. I thought I was going to have to pull her to the surface this morning while she bathed. Another has had to haul her from the tub in the past," he added, remembering the story Scarlett had shared of that night a little over a year ago.

A knowing smile came across Briar's face. "She may have fire in her veins, Sorin, but her heart is all Anahita. She will not drown. She can breathe underwater."

"What?" Sorin asked, jerking his head to stare at his friend.

"She can breathe. I promise you. She will not drown."

"But when she comes up, she is gasping for breath," Sorin argued.

"If she is gasping for air, it is not due to being submerged. She can create pockets of air under the water. Her body does not know that, so it reacts as it would to survive," he said simply. "She needs to train, not just physically, but with her magic. She needs to learn to control her power."

"I know," Sorin answered with a frown. "I've tried to tell her. She even said she was ready when she knocked me on my ass with a jet stream of water from her palm earlier today." Briar barked a laugh at the words. "But I know her. Callan just shoved her back into a dark place. I'm hoping she is still willing."

"Maybe she needs to see why?" Briar ventured carefully.

"No," Sorin said firmly. "I will not take Scarlett to her. Not now."

Briar nodded reluctantly. "Has she shown any signs of accepting her bloodline?"

"No," Sorin sighed. "In fact, she has adamantly refused wanting anything to do with it."

Briar stood now, a water portal appearing nearby. "She will need to see and meet her sooner than later, Sorin. At least let it be on our terms. See you at dinner." He stepped through before Sorin could reply.

Sorin left the private training pits, walking back to his chambers and taking the various stairs and hallways to give himself a little more time to prepare for what he might find back in his rooms. He opened his door, the wards recognizing his touch. The sitting room was empty, so he crossed to the bedroom. He found her not in the bathing room but curled on the balcony. She was lying on the ground, her cheek pressed to the cool stone floor. Her shadows swirled around her like a cocoon. They were so thick he could hardly see her. He rushed to her side, dropping to his knees. Her eyes were closed, and her breathing was uneven, too fast.

He reached for her and when his hand touched her mass of shadows, her eyes snapped open. The blue of her eyes had turned nearly grey, a muted silver. "Come, Love," he said, reaching for her again. "Let's go inside."

"No," she whispered. "It is too much."

"What is?"

"All of it. I cannot get up right now." She had retreated to wherever she went inside her soul. Her eyes were distant, looking through him.

"Then I will carry you," he replied, preparing to scoop her off the ground. It was warm, but snow had indeed begun falling. Small sporadic flakes stuck to her hair where they slipped through the shadows.

"No," she said.

"Scarlett—"

"I said no." Not angry. Not upset. Just a statement. She closed her eyes and began tracing the stones of the balcony with her finger. Her chest continued to rise and fall rapidly, like she couldn't get a full breath down.

Sorin laid down on that stone balcony, facing her. She did not even open her eyes when she reached for him, her hand resting on his chest. He stilled for a moment. She didn't move, but her breaths began to even out. They began to match his own.

After several minutes, she opened her eyes and looked straight into his own.

"What do you need, Scarlett? How can I help you?"

"Do you still see the light?" she asked quietly, barely audible.

"Yes."

"How?"

"Because I know where to look," he answered gently.

"Then I need you to show me where to find it."

She closed her eyes once more, and they laid on that balcony in the falling flurries. They stayed there for nearly an hour, her breathing now perfectly in sync with his own. Her shadows slowly crept over him until he was part of her darkness. She did not remove her hand from his chest. He did not reach for her. He just sat with her in the dark.

CHAPTER 8
SCARLETT

"How did you fill this closet this fast? And with my exact sizes?" Scarlett called out to the bedroom. The walk-in closet that had been half full when she'd awakened that morning now had every shelf, nook, and cranny full. Sorin's clothing and items were still where they'd been, but now dresses and feminine sweaters and tunics and pants filled the space, as well as shoes and jewelry. She reached for a beautiful, dark purple sweater, the fabric soft as suede between her fingers.

"You've been asleep for days. I had some time on my hands," he answered, his voice drifting in to her.

She walked to the closet and leaned against the doorframe, crossing her arms over her chest. "You had nothing better to do while I slept than build me a wardrobe?" she asked him doubtfully. He was sprawled across the chaise lounge under the window. He wore dark charcoal pants with a dark red tunic and a black jacket.

He propped himself up on his elbows when he spotted her. "You are not dressed yet?"

"With so many options, how can one choose?" she asked sweetly. Truth be told, though, she didn't know what to wear. What kind of dinner was this to be? Formal, like it had been every evening with Lord Tyndell?

"Wear what you're comfortable in, Scarlett," Sorin replied, as though he'd read her mind.

"I'm comfortable in training attire," she retorted under her breath.

"Then wear it," Sorin answered, rising from the chaise and coming to her. Damn him and that Fae hearing.

Scarlett rolled her eyes. "I cannot meet your Inner Court and dine with a prince in training clothes or dressed like Death's Maiden."

"I am a prince," he replied with a smirk. "You have dined with me eating out of a box on my couch."

"That's different," she remarked, waving him off.

He snorted. "How?"

"You and I are different. Besides, I didn't *know* you were a prince when I met you," she replied.

"Would it have made a difference?" he asked, again with that smirk.

"Yes!"

"I doubt it."

"I do have manners," she scowled.

"I would love to see them sometime."

Scarlett gave him a vulgar gesture before turning back to the closet.

"Rude," she heard him call after her.

She surveyed the display of clothing before her again and sighed. He had lain with her on the ground. He had lain with her, letting her sort through everything that had happened. He had not asked to talk about it. He had not told her what had happened after she'd left. He had just crawled into a pit and sat with her in the darkness.

She couldn't decide what to make of it. This male that had contributed to her breaking, lying with her in her shadows. She certainly wasn't going to acknowledge the feelings that were creeping up, not with Callan under the same roof. Not until she could speak with him and try to explain. Explain what, she didn't know.

She finally selected fitted black pants with the dark purple sweater. The fabric was luxurious against her skin. She pinned her hair up off her neck. She was strapping a dagger to her thigh when she came out of the closet and found Sorin waiting for her. He noted the dagger and gave a nod.

"You are fine with me wearing it to dinner?" she inquired, a challenge in her tone.

"I wear multiple weapons everywhere. Why wouldn't you?" he responded simply.

"Well, yes, but you are a man and a trained soldier," she countered.

Sorin winced a little. "Before we go to dinner, some Fae decorum. We are males and females. Men and women are humans."

"Semantics," Scarlett replied with a roll of her eyes.

"Not to Fae. To Fae they are very, very different."

"You are offended?"

"Not me. I am used to you calling me all kinds of endearing names, but yes, others will find it deeply offensive," Sorin answered. He closed the distance between them and took her right hand. "This belongs to you."

Scarlett looked down to find he'd slipped her mother's ring onto her finger. And suddenly she wasn't in the Fiera Palace at all, but she stood in the forest clearing where she had sat with the beautiful man. Shirina appeared at her side, brushing lightly against her leg.

She caught movement out of the corner of her eye and turned to see a giant wolf emerge from the forest to the east. It was the same one she had seen when she'd watched Sorin with Talwyn back in Baylorin. Scarlett stilled, but the panther walked towards it. The two seemed to stare each other down in some sort of stand off, before the wolf gave a bow of its head in Scarlett's direction.

There were other animals here, too. The red bird she had glimpsed in Sorin's rooms that day they'd arrived was soaring in a tight circle above them along with a silver hawk. A large, red stag and a stunning, white horse whose mane and tail looked like flowing water were coming from the trees.

A piercing screech filled the air, and they all whipped their heads to find the giant, black eagle soaring across the sky. It seemed angry. Really, really angry. Scarlett took a step forward, but the horse of water stepped into her path. She reached up to touch its nose. It snorted and shook its mane, spraying her with drops of water.

"Hey!" she protested. The horse's eyes seemed to twinkle playfully. They reminded her of someone else's eyes, but she couldn't quite place them.

"Scarlett."

Sorin's voice was soft, but urgent. She turned, expecting to see him standing beside her, but he was nowhere in sight.

"Scarlett."

None of the animals seemed to hear it. If they did, they didn't seem to care.

The black wolf's ears suddenly perked up, as if it indeed heard something. It was looking past her, and when Scarlett turned to see what had caught its attention, she found herself looking into eyes of the deepest jade green. Mahogany hair flowed around her face on a phantom wind. She had seen her once before, when she had watched Sorin talk to her.

Talwyn.

"Who are you?" her voice was low, dangerous. Those jade green eyes were narrowed as she reached to retrieve a sword that was strapped across her back. She wore leathers, similar to the ones she'd seen Sorin wearing as they'd traveled to the border. Scarlett suddenly found it hard to breathe. Like all the air had been sucked from her lungs. Vines ensnared her wrists, pinning them to her sides.

Talwyn advanced on her, her sword aloft, and pointed it at Scarlett's throat. She had angular cheekbones and a pretty face, and she moved with a queen's grace. Talwyn took a few more steps towards her. Scarlett's throat was burning as she desperately gasped for a breath when white flames surrounded her. The flames seemed to shimmer as they separated her from Talwyn. Talwyn stopped dead in her tracks. The vines around Scarlett's wrists disappeared, and she gulped down a big breath of air.

"Who are you?" Talwyn asked again, the same deadly calm in her voice.

"Scarlett! Open your eyes."

Scarlett snapped her eyes open to find herself back in Sorin's bedroom. He was gripping her shoulders, his golden skin slightly pale.

"Are you back?" he asked, searching her eyes.

She nodded mutely.

"What the hell happened?" he demanded, bringing his hands to her face.

"I think I just met Talwyn."

"You met Talwyn," Sorin repeated, his tone saying just how unlikely he found that.

"I think so," Scarlett answered, biting her lower lip. "I mean, I'm pretty sure it was the same woman, I mean female, from before. We didn't converse. She asked who I was."

"Where were you? Where did you see her?"

"In some forest clearing. I've... I've been there in my dreams."

Dear gods, she sounded absolutely insane.

"You were in Shira Forest?"

"Where?"

"Shira Forest. It's believed Shira Forest is where magic originated and is where the most powerful Fae are bonded with a Spirit Animal. You've been there before?"

"In my dreams, yes, but the Spirit Animals?" Scarlett asked, her brows knitting together.

Before Sorin could answer, they were interrupted by a loud banging and rattling of the main door to the chambers.

"Seriously, you prick? You still have us locked out?" came a male voice from the other side of the door.

Scarlett choked on a laugh, turning to Sorin with wide eyes. "I don't know who that is, but I already like him."

"I told you that you would get along splendidly with my family," Sorin muttered, glaring at the door.

"Aditya," came the voice again. "Get your ass downstairs. Eliza said she's coming up next. She's hungry and cranky, and we all have matters that need to be discussed."

Sorin sighed, looking at Scarlett. "I will explain Shira Forest and the Spirit Animals tonight," he said, brushing his knuckles down her cheek. Then, raising his voice, he added, "Right now, I need to go have a discussion about patience."

"Bastard," the voice called through the door, followed by footsteps heading down the hall.

"Shall we?" Sorin asked, gesturing to the door.

"Talwyn won't... She won't come here, will she?" Scarlett asked. "She doesn't know I'm here, right?" She wasn't ready to face her cousin outside of whatever vision that had been. She had felt Talwyn's power coil around her like a snake, squeezing the life from its prey.

"She likely knows you are in my Court. I will know if she gets close to the grounds and so will the others," he replied soothingly. "And if she shows up and you do not want to see her, you can come up here. The wards around my chambers keep out anyone I do not want in. No one is allowed to portal in or out without my permission."

"Will Callan, Finn, and Sloan be at dinner?" she asked, forcing herself not to wring her fingers together.

"No," he answered gently. "It's just us, my Inner Court, and Briar."

Scarlett nodded once, taking a deep breath. "Eliza is terrifying. We should go eat before she comes up here."

Sorin chuckled, striding to open the door for her. "Yes, Eliza can be quite irritable when she's *not* hungry, let alone when she is."

Scarlett followed Sorin down the hall and staircases leading from the private wing. She had marked most turns and hallways when he'd shown her around earlier that day, so when he led her past the formal dining room, she asked, "We are not eating there?"

Sorin smiled at her as he kept walking. "The formal dining room is for formal meals when we have formal guests. When it is just us," he shrugged his shoulders. "We usually eat in here." He paused outside a door across from the kitchens. Scarlett had assumed it was a pantry or storage room when they had walked by it earlier. "Are you ready?"

She could hear others behind the door, the man who had banged on the door and what sounded like Briar's voice. Scarlett took another deep breath. "I mean, they can't be worse than you, right?"

"That's the spirit, Princess," he said cheerfully, pushing open the door to the room.

"Oh my gods," she muttered under her breath, following him in.

The room fell silent as they entered. It was a den with a large round table in the center. Not the long rectangular tables usually found in the homes of nobility. The table had eight chairs around it. At the back of the room was a long, tall bar against the wall, fully stocked with all the wine and alcohol one could want. To the left of the dining table was a billiards table along with two tall pub tables and chairs. A card table was pushed against the wall as well. To the right of the dining table were two plush sofas and three overstuffed chairs around a fireplace. Blankets and pillows were tossed on them as if people had just been sitting there.

"I changed my mind," Scarlett said, turning to Sorin. A look of confusion passed over his face as he raised his eyebrows at her. "I want *this* to be my chambers. You can have the other to yourself."

She heard a laugh that she knew by now to be Briar's, and she turned to face him. His sun bleached hair was tied back, and the pale blue shirt he had changed into brought out the icy blue color of his eyes and was stark against his dark skin. He rose from the table and came to her. Kissing her cheek, he asked gently, "How are the waters?"

"The waves seemed to have lessened. At least for the time being," Scarlett answered.

"I am glad to hear that," Briar said, squeezing her hand slightly.

From the table a male voice drawled, "She doesn't seem *that* intimidating, Drayce." It was the same male who had pounded on the door minutes before. His head was propped on his fist as he studied Scarlett. She held his gaze, returning the scrutinizing stare. The male's eyes were as golden as Sorin's, and she could see the brilliant recklessness in them.

"Yes, well, dear Eliza doesn't seem that intimidating either at first glance," Briar replied over his shoulder. He turned back to Scarlett. "Would you like a drink?"

"Wine would be wonderful," Scarlett replied with a nod of thanks.

"I'm fine. Thank you," Sorin called after Briar bitterly. Briar only threw him a vulgar gesture over his shoulder. Sorin sighed. "You know Briar Drayce, the Water Prince. He thinks his palace is better and more impressive than mine."

"It is definitely bigger," Briar cut in from across the room with a wink.

Scarlett pressed her lips together to keep her laugh in.

"The jackass that pounded on the door a few minutes ago is Cyrus," Sorin said, gesturing toward the male at the table. "He is my Second in Command."

Cyrus was still studying her and by way of greeting said, "You know how to use that dagger?"

Scarlett smiled sweetly at him, then in less time than it took to draw breath, the dagger was flying across the room, landing directly in front of him. Cyrus didn't even flinch. He only said with a sly smile, "Eliza, I think you have some competition."

Briar jerked the dagger from the table as he passed by, handing both it and a glass of wine to Scarlett.

"Stop speaking, Cyrus. It hurts my ears," chided the female sitting to his right with a roll of her eyes. She had a book open on the table before her that she had been reading quietly during all the bantering. Her red-gold hair cascaded around her in great sweeping curls. Her eyes were the grey of ash and smoke. To say she was stunning was an understatement. Her top was low cut and whorls of tattoos lined her chest and ran down her bare arms.

"You know Eliza," Sorin said. "She is the general of my armies."

"Wait, she's actually a general?" Scarlett blurted, trying and failing to hide her awe. Eliza threw her a knowing smile, saying tightly, "I'm glad to see you are well," before returning to her book.

"As I told you, females fight alongside the males here," Sorin replied simply, as if that explained everything. "If you plan to continue your weaponry and combat training, I suggest taking it up with her." Scarlett's eyes were still on Eliza, who had returned to ignoring them all, when Sorin continued. "And that is Rayner. He is my Third."

Scarlett looked to the remaining male in the room to the right of Eliza. He had a kind face, but there was a darkness to him she couldn't quite place. His eyes were nearly identical to Eliza's except that the grey in his eyes seemed to actually swirl and flow like smoke. His hair was a stark charcoal color similar to Sorin's, but not quite as dark. He gave her a warm smile, saying softly in a cool voice that somehow managed to chill her bones, "It is a pleasure to meet you, Scarlett."

Food suddenly appeared on the table before them, to which Eliza muttered, "Praise, Anala." The book before her disappeared in a burst of flame as she reached for the plate of braised lamb.

Sorin sighed again. "We do have a guest, Eliza."

"From my understanding, she is not a guest at all, but lives here. The *actual* guests are not allowed to cross the bridges," Eliza replied curtly, clearly unconcerned.

Sorin shot Scarlett an apologetic look, but Scarlett just gave him a small smile in return. The whole scene was like a breath of fresh air. They were a family, just as Sorin had said, and it reminded her of simpler times with Cassius and Nuri and Juliette, before orphans had started disappearing from the Syndicate. Tomorrow. Tomorrow she would focus on that and what was being done while she was away. But for now, she felt honored to be allowed into their little world, even if just for the night. Sorin led her to the empty chair next to Briar before he went to get his own drink.

"I have been gone for over three years and no one can even bother to get their prince a drink?" he accused, striding for the bar at the back.

Cyrus snorted, spooning roasted vegetables onto his plate. "While you've been vacationing with the mortals, someone had to deal with Talwyn. You should be getting *me* a drink, asshole."

"He is incredibly needy, isn't he? Poor thing fussing over getting his own alcohol," Scarlett said, taking a piece of bread from the basket that Briar was handing her.

"Says the one who was just waited on by a prince," Sorin quipped while pouring liquor into a glass.

"I can't help it that he's only spent time with me a handful of times and likes me more than you," Scarlett retorted sweetly. "Besides, I'm prettier than you." Sorin turned, drink in hand, and a wary smile was on his face. She batted her lashes at him, taking a sip of her wine.

Across the table, Cyrus gave her an amused smile, and with his eyes on hers, called to Sorin, "I like her."

"I knew you would and dreaded the two of you meeting," Sorin remarked, returning to the table with his drink in hand.

The conversation ebbed and flowed with lighthearted bantering and laughter. They were nearing the end of the meal, having eaten their fill, and Scarlett was beginning to wonder why Sorin had thought he'd need Briar as a buffer when Cyrus asked out of the blue, "Did you find it then?"

The chitchat around the table went silent as all eyes turned to Sorin. His arm was draped casually across the back of Scarlett's chair while he was eating a piece of apple pie. He set his fork down on his plate. "This is not the time for this discussion, Cyrus."

"Bullshit," Cyrus replied. "You've been gone for over three years. We hardly heard from you. Then you finally return, make us babysit a bunch of mortal royalty, and keep us all locked out for days, but let Drayce in." Cyrus gestured at Briar, clearly bitter about being kept out of the know. "He wouldn't fucking tell us anything either, and you return with a—"

"It was not my place to say anything," Briar cut in with exasperation. This discussion had obviously been had multiple times before this evening.

Scarlett could feel the quick glances at her from the others. She thought they had already known who she was. She couldn't have been more wrong, and they clearly did not trust her.

"I should go so you guys can discuss things," Scarlett stated, making to push her chair back from the table.

"Yes," Eliza said, her tone matter-of-fact.

"No." Sorin's voice rang out, pure command. He stared at Eliza, fury lining his features. Scarlett stilled, glancing between the Fire Prince and his general. When he looked at *her* like that, it usually meant she'd be running extra miles in the morning. To her credit though, Eliza stared right back without so much as a flinch.

"It's fine, Sorin," Scarlett said quietly, again trying to push her chair back from the table.

Sorin held firm to her chair so that Scarlett couldn't move it. She threw him a pleading look, but he was looking each of his Inner Court members in the eye. Briar was silent beside her. He reached over and gave her hand a reassuring squeeze, and Scarlett knew then exactly why Sorin had asked him to be here tonight.

"Let her go, Sorin," Eliza said, her eyes still fixed on her prince. "There are matters to be discussed."

"Then they can be discussed while she is present," Sorin answered, his voice low and icy.

"Really?" Eliza asked, her brows rising. "Then let's discuss the mortal prince who has been seeking her out. Let's discuss the little matter of him being in love with her while you bear a new Mark." Her eyes gleamed with challenge.

Sorin did not say a word as he stared back at her.

"Why is the mortal prince here?" Rayner posed quietly.

"Because his life is at risk, and this was the only place to keep him safe until the danger has passed," Scarlett cut in, lifting her chin as she spoke.

"Is he your lover then, Darling?" Cyrus asked casually, taking another bite of his own pie. He reminded Scarlett vaguely of Nuri.

"Are you asking if I am available?" Scarlett asked, her tone sultry as she leaned back in her chair. Sorin's fingers brushed across her shoulder.

"If you're offering, I certainly would not object," he replied with a fiendish glance to Sorin.

"I assure you, *Darling*, you wouldn't know the first thing to do with me and my darkness," she purred. As if in emphasis, her shadows reached for him, caressing down his cheek and neck.

He froze as they trailed along him, then a feral grin crossed his lips. "Intimidating indeed," he crooned.

"Told you," Briar quipped, picking up his drink and knocking the rest of it back.

Scarlett picked up her wine glass, twirling the stem between her fingers. She had originally been willing to leave, to not intrude on their little family squabble, but now that she had been brought into the conversation, she could play. She turned to Briar and smirked. "I now understand what you meant about his whiny Court." Briar laughed, his icy eyes twinkling.

"I'm glad you two find this so amusing," Eliza spat, "but the fact remains that we have no idea what is going on and why your arrival has made our prince, who has never withheld anything from us, suddenly start keeping secrets." Everyone went silent. Scarlett glanced to Sorin, and Eliza continued with soft venom. "Do you need permission to speak?"

"Enough," Sorin growled. He looked murderous as he glared at his general. "She does not need permission to do anything, Eliza. You will not speak to her like this, and you will remember that I am your Prince."

"Do not pull rank on me, Sorin," Eliza hissed, and Scarlett had to admit, she admired the female for her gall.

"Then let's discuss matters, shall we?" Sorin said. He spoke with a calm, lethal rage, and Scarlett froze. She had never heard him speak like that. His tone was uncompromising and threatening. The voice of a ruler. Every one of his Inner Court sat up straighter in their chairs, their eyes slightly widening. It was clear he rarely spoke to them this way. The gold in Sorin's eyes had turned to flame, and it took all of Scarlett not to flinch from him. She looked to Briar out of the corner of her eye. His face was severe, a fellow prince standing in solidarity with his friend. "Let's discuss the fact that she is more powerful than *anyone* in this room. You have all witnessed, in one way or another, just a fraction of what she can do."

All eyes slid to her, and she tried not to shift uncomfortably in her seat. She held their stares and mustered up her bored, uninterested mask, taking a bite of her own dessert like what was being said didn't matter to her.

"She is here because she is Fae, and this is her home," Sorin continued. "The mortal prince is here because she has a heart and a threat was made against his life. She is ridiculously selfless and sought his safety until he can return home. Furthermore, she is Eliné's daughter." All their eyes widened at that revelation, and Cyrus started to say something, but Sorin was not done. "As to whether or not I found the weapon Talwyn so desperately seeks, you are looking at her, and Talwyn cannot have her. Should Scarlett decide to take her throne, our allegiance lies with her. Should she decide not to, our loyalty still lies with her."

Her eyes slid to Sorin at the words. She had told Sorin she didn't want the title. She had told him she didn't want the responsibility of ruling. She had told him she didn't want any sort of Fates deciding her future. As if reading her mind, Sorin continued.

"This information goes nowhere. Briar knows and will tell his Inner Court, but no one else learns this information unless Scarlett decides to share it. The choice is hers, but this is her home, and she belongs at this table." He paused, a long, tense moment of silence, then asked, his words laced with poison, "Anything else you wish to discuss this evening, Eliza?"

Eliza actually seemed like she was going to say more, but Rayner gave her a warning glance. "No, Prince," she conceded, with a bow of her head.

Scarlett met Sorin's gaze then. Her shadows brushed along his fingers, and his eyes softened, the flames lessening.

Too bad Tula isn't here to give you a cookie. You deserve a treat after that little speech, she thought, tilting her head. As though he had heard her thoughts, he smirked at her. She didn't notice the glances that his Inner Court shared. She didn't notice the smile that crossed Briar's face when he reached for her glass to refill her wine. Her eyes were fixed on the golden eyes of the Prince of Fire, where she saw nothing but home.

CHAPTER 9

SORIN

S orin sat in his chambers, sipping at a glass of amber liquor, Cyrus and Rayner doing the same. Eliza had gone to her own chambers when they'd finally retired long into the night, saying she wanted to finish her book and didn't need to sit around listening to 'you three idiots relive memories.' He knew her, though. He knew that despite her hard exterior, she was sorting through everything that had happened the last few weeks. She had been carrying the secret of his Mark since the mortal kingdoms. In the morning, he would find her, and they would sort it all out.

Scarlett had looked exhausted by the end of the night. He hadn't intended on keeping her up that late, but after everything was settled about who she was, games of billiards had ensued. Scarlett had taken every one of them for all they had, other than Eliza, who rarely deigned to play.

"Friends from the Black Syndicate, of course," Scarlett had replied when he'd asked where she had learned to play.

Cyrus had completely missed his shot at the words, cursing as the cue ball flew from the table. "You have friends in the Black Syndicate?" he had asked, his mouth gaping open.

"I am just full of surprises, aren't I, Darling?" Scarlett had chirped with a wild grin, sauntering past him and proceeding to clear the remainder of the table.

"How did you befriend people in the Black Syndicate?" Cyrus asked, as she sank her final shot.

"My winning personality," she said with a smirk, holding out her palm. "Pay up."

Cyrus just stared at her, a new admiration on his face, as he slapped three silver coins into her waiting hand. Sorin had never been worried about Scarlett and Cyrus getting along. No, he had not been entirely lying when he'd told Scarlett he dreaded them meeting.

They had all finally called it a night and walked back up to the private quarters with Briar portaling back to the Water Court. When they entered his chambers, Cyrus and Rayner headed straight to the liquor cart, but he had seen Scarlett wince slightly out of the corner of his eye.

"They do not have to stay," he'd said quietly.

She had merely smiled up at him, a smile she never gave anyone else, not even Cassius, and said, "You've watched me sleep enough, Prince. Go be with your family." She had bid them all good night and slipped into the bedroom.

"So you get sent on a fool's errand and come home with a secret princess?" Cyrus asked, sipping at his drink.

"Cyrus," Rayner said, his grey eyes swirling with the warning in his tone.

"Oh, relax," Cyrus said dismissively. "I'm not trying to start anything. That's just quite a difference, and the story of how it happened must be riveting." He looked expectantly at Sorin.

So Sorin told them everything, or almost everything. He left out the part about her being pissed at him for over a month. Telling the bastards that would result in endless taunting at his own expense, and he didn't reveal any of Scarlett's personal history.

"She has not asked about the Mark?" Rayner asked when he was finished, nodding to Sorin's left hand. Sorin looked down at the Mark that covered the back of his hand, thumb, and index finger.

"She has commented on it, but she does not know what it is or what it means," Sorin answered. "I had to take it. It was the only way I could figure out where she was in the Lairwood House. Through the connection."

"Does she even know what a twin flame is?" Cyrus asked.

"She knows about the idea of the twin flame," Sorin answered, rubbing his temples. "Whether she believes it or not, I do not know. We only discussed it once."

"You haven't told her that she is yours?" Cyrus questioned in disbelief.

Sorin winced. "The timing hasn't been right. She wasn't allowed to make any of her own choices in the human lands. I didn't want to take a choice like this away from her."

"She deserves to know," Rayner said, his voice low. He was always the sensible one of the group, likely because he kept his emotions locked down at all times. "By not telling her, you are taking away that very right to choose."

"I know, but I cannot force it on her. She has had too much of that already," Sorin sighed, draining the last of his liquor.

"Forget that," Cyrus snapped, annoyance heavy in his tone. "Let's talk about the risk of taking that Mark without a companion Mark."

Before Sorin could reply, though, all three of them were on their feet. They had all felt it. She was here. She had crossed their wards. They all crossed the room, stalking to the door, flames licked up and down Sorin's entire body, and when they were gone, he was dressed in dark charcoal clothing, the color of soot and ashes. Fighting leathers lay over the top of the clothes while twin blades appeared at his back. An assortment of knives and daggers were sheathed and secured in various places. Cyrus and Rayner wore nearly identical attire. Cyrus had a bow and quiver full of arrows. Rayner had vambraces at his wrists.

They entered the hall where Eliza met them. Her fighting leathers held more daggers than Sorin's own. "Always in the fucking middle of the night," she muttered, finishing the braid she was quickly working into her hair. Her elegant sword, Flamethrower, was sheathed down her back.

Sorin raised a hand before him and a fire portal opened. As one, they entered and stepped onto the grounds in front of the palace gates. The portal snapped shut behind them.

"She is alone," Rayner said, his eyes entirely swirling with smoke now.

"Luan will not be far behind," Sorin replied grimly, sliding his hands into his pockets.

They all went silent as they waited. Cyrus flanked his left while Eliza was on his right with Rayner beside her. A few moments later, Talwyn stepped from the trees. Her hair was flowing on her winds, moonlight reflecting off it. Three shields of flame and a shield of smoke instantly snapped into place.

Talwyn stopped several feet away from them, a vindictive smile on her lips. She wore her usual brown pants with a white tunic. A moment later, Azrael Luan stepped out of the air to her side. He took them all in and gave a snort of disgust.

"Prince Aditya, you return home," Talwyn said, her voice soft yet severe.

"You gave me permission to do so," Sorin replied nonchalantly, with a shrug.

"I told you to come home weeks ago," Talwyn snapped, displeasure ringing in her tone. "But you begged to stay because you had discovered something." Her eyes narrowed as she continued. "Where is my ring?"

"I do believe your ring adorns your finger."

"Do not be a smart ass," Talwyn growled, taking a step towards them. "Tell me, who bears that ring now?" When Sorin didn't answer, she took another step towards them. "I have seen her, Sorin. She came to the Forest. I have seen it upon her finger. Does she even know what it is?"

"You told me to return with the ring and I have. I have fulfilled my oath to you," Sorin answered with an icy calm.

"Then give it to me," Talwyn replied, matching his tone.

"No."

"Who bears it?" she snarled. "Who is she?"

Sorin could have sworn that, for a split second, her eyes darted to his hands resting in his pockets. "She is none of your concern," Sorin answered. The ground shook, and the winds whipped, but behind their shields and wards they hardly felt a breeze. Sorin merely smirked at the queen. "Still have that temper I see."

"Watch your mouth, Aditya," Azrael snarled, stepping to Talwyn's side once again.

"Let the Queen handle her own affairs, Luan," Eliza crooned from Sorin's right.

"Enough." Talwyn's voice rang clear and commanding through the night. Her eyes came back to Sorin and as she spoke, Sorin could hear the anger being restrained in her tone. So much like Scarlett, this queen that stood before him was. "I am your queen, Prince. Tell me who she is."

"No."

"You will openly defy me?" He could feel her power scraping along their shields, like it was dragging claws down walls of stone. Not one of his Inner Court moved.

"According to the Charters of the Courts, I am permitted to defy you if I believe there is a credible threat to my Court by complying," Sorin replied, stepping right up to the edge of their shields. Talwyn was just on the other side. There were only a few feet separating them. Her jade eyes glowed brightly with rage. "The only work around is the Blood Vow, which you have already invoked. She is a member of my Court, and you, my *Queen*, are the credible threat."

"I may have used my Blood Vow with you," she spat, "but what of the Water Prince?"

"Would you really waste another Blood Vow on this? You have hundreds of years left to reign and only three vows remaining," Sorin replied, calling her bluff.

"This is not over," Talwyn seethed. She closed the distance between them, and he saw her flinch slightly as she brushed the edges of their shields. "You are allowing your bitterness and animosity to cloud your judgment, Prince."

"It must be like looking in a mirror, then," Sorin replied coolly.

"You have no idea what your actions will cost us."

"Enlighten me."

Talwyn's eyes narrowed. He felt a shield of wind surround them, locking out the others. "I know who she is, Sorin."

"I do not believe you," he replied, low and vicious. "But if you do know who she is, then you know where my true allegiance lies."

A smile appeared on Talwyn's lips then, slow and malicious. "And you will discover that in the end, the Fates will plant us on the same side."

Then she was gone. The wind instantly died. The shields came down save for Eliza's as Azrael still stood before them.

"Run along, Luan," Cyrus taunted. "Without the queen here, you have crossed Court borders without permission."

Azrael gave them all a vulgar gesture before vanishing into nothing.

There was silence for only a moment before Eliza sighed. "Can we please go to bed now?"

They walked back up to the palace and through the halls in silence, each departing for their own chambers without so much as a good night. He opened the door to the bedroom as quietly as he could. He didn't know how Scarlett was adjusting to sleeping without a tonic, and he didn't want to disturb her, but when he stepped into the room, he found it wouldn't have mattered. She was standing on the balcony that overlooked the front grounds. Her back was to him, her shadows blending in with the night. She would have had a perfect view of everything that had just happened. She had a blanket wrapped around herself, and she didn't even look over her shoulder when she said, "I felt something. It woke me. I went out to the main room, but you weren't there."

"I'm sorry," he said, quickly crossing the room. "I had to take care of something. I did not intend to leave you alone."

"Talwyn was here. She is looking for me," Scarlett supplied. Her voice was that same monotone voice from when she'd first awoken, as if she were in some sort of trance.

"Yes." He didn't know if he should reach out to her, if he should touch her. So he stood a few feet away, shoving down every desire to pull her to him. She turned to look at him, her icy blue eyes glowing in the night. He hadn't realized how similar she was to her cousin. They were so similar, yet so incredibly different.

"Thank you for tonight," she said. Her face was stoic and unreadable. "It was a sense of normalcy. It felt like a family. It felt like home. Thank you."

Sorin gave her a soft smile. "Thank *you*. For putting up with a little family drama."

Scarlett huffed a laugh, returning to look out over the balcony. "You've seen how my family fights end up. Nuri and I are usually both bleeding by the end." He noticed she no longer gripped the railing at being so high up. If she only knew she could Travel like her cousin, she'd never fear confined spaces again. "Why does she seek me out? What exactly does she want from me?"

"I do not know. I haven't pieced it all together yet."

She turned her head, meeting his gaze again. "But you'd tell me if you knew? You wouldn't keep it from me?"

"No, Love," he replied. He stepped closer to her, unable to help himself. "I would not keep it from you."

"And you've told me everything?" she asked, her eyes searching his own.

"I have told you everything." Before the words had even finished leaving his lips, he felt a searing jolt of pain shoot through his left hand. Gritting his teeth, he pushed it from his mind. "Come, let's have some tea."

Scarlett nodded and led the way back into the bedroom. Tea was already waiting on the low table near the armchairs. She plopped into one, still clutching the blanket around her shoulders. Sorin took up the armchair across from her once more and handed her one of the cups.

"I know you think Fae customs and stories are incredibly profound and all," he started.

"I swear to Saylah, Sorin, if you're about to drop another piece of world shattering information, this tea cup is going down your throat," she muttered.

Sorin blinked at the...at the normalcy of that comment from her mouth. At the peek of who she was breaking through that place she was trapped in. "No, it is nothing like that. This is something I think you already know and just need it explained." Her nose scrunched slightly as she sipped at her tea. "Legend among the Fae is that our magic and power comes from a place called Shira Forest."

Scarlett paused her sipping, her eyes on the fire before them. She had pulled her knees to her chest and draped the blanket over them. Resting her teacup on her knees, she said, "I thought you said the Avonleyans blessed the Fae with magic."

"They did, but it is believed that their magic came from this Forest. It is said Shira Forest is where the gods reside along with the Fates."

Scarlett snorted. "The gods live in a dream world?"

"Shira Forest is a real place. It is just that no one knows where it is."

"Convenient," she grumbled.

Sorin sat back in his chair with a smirk. "I am going to assume you saw an animal there, and I am going to go a step further and venture to guess it was a panther as dark as night." Her head slowly turned towards him. "The Spirit Animals live in the Forest when they are not needed by their bonded ones. The most powerful of the Fae, those chosen by a particular god or goddess, are bonded with their Spirit Animal. In essence, you become bonded to that god or goddess through that bond."

He fell silent and let her process what he'd told her, waiting for the questions he was sure were coming.

"How did you know I saw a panther?"

"Because Shirina made her presence known while you slept. She was often seen at the foot of your bed, watching over you and growling at anyone who dared to approach you. The Goddess Saylah's panther has not been seen in ages, Scarlett."

"But why was I taken there tonight? I saw her in my dreams while I slept. What was the purpose of tonight?"

"I do not know. I have only been there once and that was the night I was bonded with Amaré. How or why you were there again, and how Talwyn was there with you, I do not know."

"Was anyone else there with you? When you became bonded or whatever?" she asked.

"No. It was only me." Scarlett only nodded once and turned back to the fire. "Was someone there with you? When you met Shirina?"

"When I was there tonight with Talwyn, there were other animals there. Not just Shirina," Scarlett said.

It was Sorin's turn to slowly turn to her. "You saw several Spirit Animals there? How many?"

"This time? Many."

"This time? How many times have you been there, Scarlett?"

"That I can remember? Two. The first time I saw two and... The first time there were two animals."

"Which animals did you see?"

"Well, the wolf from the day I saw you and Talwyn speaking in Baylorin was there," she said, fiddling with her teacup.

"Maliq? He is Talwyn's bonded, the wolf of Celeste, goddess of the moon and sky. I suppose it would make sense that he was there if Talwyn was also there with you. Who else?"

There was a quiet cooing, and Scarlett jumped, nearly spilling her tea as Amaré flew in the open balcony door. "That bird. It was there."

Sorin turned to look at the phoenix. "Is that so, my Friend? Care to share?"

Amaré merely clicked his beak and ruffled his feathers slightly.

"You can speak to it?"

"There is a bond that will form and strengthen," Sorin explained, Amaré swooping to his shoulder and nipping his ear affectionately. "You will learn how to communicate with each other. This is Amaré. He is a phoenix and the animal of Anala."

"Goddess of sun and fire," Scarlett whispered softly as she studied the phoenix. Then, a little louder, she said, "There was a horse. It looked like Eirwen, but its mane and tail were like a cascading waterfall."

Sorin smiled. "Abrax. He is Anahita's and is bonded to Briar."

"The silver hawk?'

"She is the wind goddess' and is bonded to Princess Ashtine. Her name is Nasima. They are rarely seen apart. Was Ashtine there as well?"

"No. Only Talwyn," Scarlett answered, setting her teacup on the low table and pulling the blanket up over her arms.

"Were there any others?"

"There was a red stag."

"That was Rinji. Silas's animal and is bonded with Prince Azrael of the Earth Court."

All the Court Spirit Animals had been there? At one time? Along with her and Talwyn? That was indeed interesting. But not as interesting as the next words that came from her mouth.

"And the black eagle?"

"What?" Sorin's head snapped to her.

"The black eagle," she said cautiously. "There... There was a black eagle."

"Altaria... Altaria is Temural's Spirit Animal," Sorin said quietly. "Like Shirina, he has not been seen in ages. Long before the Great War even occurred."

"Why?"

"No one knows. They... Do you remember how Eliza reacted when you spoke of Saylah on our journey here?"

"She was surprised," Scarlett answered. "I know that Saylah is not often spoken of, but my mother gave me my amulet, and I—"

"You owe no one any explanations, Scarlett," he replied softly. "I've told you that."

"But there are... I don't think coincidences are as much of a thing as I once thought they were." She sighed. "I mean, it can't be a coincidence that I've worn Saylah's amulet my entire life and am now apparently bonded with her Spirit Animal."

"No, it likely is not a coincidence," Sorin agreed. He took a deep breath, not entirely sure how she would take the next piece of information he was about to give her. "Shirina and Altaria, along with Ejder, who is Arius's dragon, and Kilo, Serafina's snake, are called the Dark Spirit Animals. To my knowledge, none of them have been seen in centuries."

"Well, that is just…great," Scarlett grumbled, leaning her head back into the armchair and closing her eyes.

"You know that Arius and Serafina and their children are…" Sorin clenched his jaw, not wanting to say the words.

"I know their family are the most feared among the gods, yes," she finished for him. "Again, I don't think there is any sort of coincidence happening here considering I am called Death's Maiden and am feared among most of the continent." After a long moment, she said quietly, "Who was my mother's Spirit Animal? Which goddess was she supposedly bonded to?"

"Supposedly?" Sorin asked with a raise of his brow. "You've seen more Spirit Animals than anyone and you question the bonds?"

Scarlett's eyes met his, and they were blazing gold as she hissed, "As far as I am concerned, the gods and the Fates are just another master coming to stake a claim on my life."

Sorin stilled at the rawness and bitterness in her tone. "You do not have a master, Scarlett. Not any more."

"Keep telling yourself that, Sorin," she bit back. "Just because a prince speaks it, doesn't mean it's the truth. Obviously."

Sorin pursed his lips, but instead of rising to the bait she had so clearly laid before him, he said, "Eliné's Spirit Animal was Paja, the golden owl of Falein, goddess of—"

"Goddess of wisdom and cleverness," Scarlett cut in. "I do know of the gods, even if I don't necessarily believe in them."

"You need to rest. You are cranky," he said, rising and placing his own empty teacup on the low table.

"Could it possibly have anything to do with the fact that you just told me I'm apparently bonded with a panther who serves a goddess everyone fears?" she snapped as she stood as well.

The blanket was loose around her shoulders now, and he could see she wore a black sleeveless nightgown that went to her knees.

"Possibly," he replied with a shrug, "but I'm going to go with exhaustion for this particular mood." The corner of his mouth kicked up despite his effort to keep the half-grin from his face.

"Whatever," she grumbled, crossing her arms. "You still do not sleep in this land?"

He chuckled. "Yes, I need sleep, especially after my encounter with Talwyn."

"And where will you sleep?"

"In the other bedroom," Sorin answered. Scarlett's lips had formed a thin line, and she hugged the blanket tightly around herself again. "What is wrong?" he asked softly.

"Nothing," she replied, her face setting into grim resolve. "Tomorrow you can start teaching me to control my powers?"

"You still desire to do so?"

"Do I have a choice in the matter?"

"You always have a choice, Scarlett."

"You were right," she said after a moment. "I need to learn to control it. It will be one less thing that has control over me."

"I do love those words coming from your lips, you know," Sorin said wryly. She raised her brows in question. "That I was right."

Scarlett rolled her eyes. "I'm glad I could bolster your ego, Prince."

Sorin chuckled again. "I can teach you the control and fire half, but Briar would be better for mastering the water and ice."

"And we can continue our other training?"

"I wasn't joking at dinner, Scarlett. You should ask Eliza."

"Eliza is scary."

"Eliza is just like you," Sorin laughed. "She prefers to be reading or in the training ring, and she takes shit from no one."

"I suppose," Scarlett replied, biting her lip not sounding sure at all. She walked to the bed, pausing as she reached for the blankets to climb in. She opened her mouth to say something, then shut it again. She snuggled in, pulling the blankets up to her chin. "Good night, Sorin."

"Good night, Princess," he said as he strode to the door. He could practically hear her eyes roll as he left the room. His head had barely hit the pillow in the extra bedroom when sleep took him.

"Did you think you could hide from me, my pet?"

Mikale's cool voice raked down her skin while she stood in that cold room in the Lairwood house. She couldn't control her trembling as he took slow, casual steps to her. She backed up until her back hit the wall.

"It is time to come home and fulfill your bargain with me," he said, his eyes turning hard. He was before her now, and he ran his hands down her arms. She couldn't shrink back any farther. "My sister is most upset you have taken Callan from her yet again, by the way."

She opened her mouth to respond, but nothing came out. She couldn't speak. "Oh yes, I have picked up a few tricks of my own," he purred with a cruel smile. "I cannot wait to show them all to you when you return." His touching turned proprietary. "It is strange, isn't it, how I can control you in your own dream?"

His fingers trailed down her chest, down her abdomen, lower. She tried to cry out, but she couldn't. She couldn't even move. She could feel him everywhere, all around her. Tears were slipping down her face.

Finally, he stepped back, surveying her. Then he leaned in close once more and kissed her. He pulled back a fraction of an inch and whispered, "Hurry home, Scarlett. We almost have these wards figured out, then we are coming for them all."

There were hands on her shoulders and a gentle voice saying her name. She lashed out at him, screaming. "Let me go!"

"Scarlett. Scarlett, it's me." She knew that voice. That voice was safe. That voice was home. "Open your eyes, Love. Look at me."

Her eyes flew open, and she found golden ones staring steadily back at her. Her shadows were swarming him, and from the red lines raked down his bare arms and chest, they had not been the caressing shadows. He did not seem to care. Ice and fire swirled around them. He took her hand and brought it to his bare chest. "Breathe, Scarlett. Breathe."

In and out. In and out. She could feel his chest rise and fall beneath her fingers, his heart racing. In and out. In and out. Her eyes stayed fixed on his.

When her breathing had evened out, she wiped the tears from her face. "He was in my dreams, Sorin. He knew how to enter and control my dreams," she rasped.

Sorin's face tightened, and he interlaced his fingers with hers.

"I am sorry I woke you," she said quietly. "And for..." She jerked her chin towards his chest and arms. "That." She went to pull her hand from his, but his fingers tightened. She looked back into his golden eyes and found them searching hers.

"I will always come for you, Scarlett," he said softly.

Fresh tears sprang to her eyes. She took a shaking breath. "I need you to do something for me."

"Of course."

"I need you to stay with me."

"I am not going anywhere."

"No, Sorin, I—" She pursed her lips. "When I would have nightmares, Cassius would stay with me or take me to his room. He's not here, but I need someone to stay with me." Her heart ached. She missed Cassius. It was as if a part of her was missing having him so far away.

"Do you want me to get Callan?" Sorin asked quietly. Her eyes widened as she realized he would. He would let Callan into these very rooms if that is what she asked of him.

"No, Sorin, I do not want Callan," she answered. "I just need... I need someone next to me."

His breathing hitched as her words settled over him. "Scarlett, are you sure?"

"Yes, I am sure, Sorin." Still, he hesitated. She looped her arms around his neck and pulled him to her, pressing her lips to his. She felt him tense under her fingers, and she ran her tongue across his lips, but he wouldn't let her in. "Please, Sorin," she whispered onto his lips.

He groaned as he pulled back to look into her eyes. "Scarlett, this… I will not have the self-control not to touch you if I sleep beside you."

"You don't want to?" she rasped out.

"Gods, Love, that is all I want to do, but not… I would be a bastard to take advantage of this, when you are so vulnerable." She could hear the longing in his voice as he held her stare.

Scarlett pushed herself up into a sitting position. "I *want* you to touch me, Sorin."

"You don't, Scarlett. You hate me. I kept so much from you. Fuck, I can't do this to you. Don't you understand?"

"Don't you understand?" She practically screamed the words at him, and he stilled. "Sorin, he… Mikale touched me in that dream. He touched me, and I could do nothing! And I can feel him. I can feel his hands on me. I can feel his breath on my skin, taking what he wants. I can *feel* him in my very being." Tears were coursing down her cheeks. "I want to feel anything but him. I want to feel *something.* Because I am numb, Sorin. And it is exhausting to not care about anything. It is exhausting to not feel anything. But the only way I can not feel him is to not feel anything at all, and I want to feel *something* that isn't him and isn't threatening to drown me in—"

"Shh," Sorin murmured, pulling her into his arms. "I hear what you are saying, Scarlett. I hear you."

"Please, Sorin," she said through her tears. She didn't care that she was begging. She didn't care how desperate she sounded. She just wanted to feel someone touch her who understood her, all of her.

"This will not fix things, Scarlett." Sorin's voice was low, strained.

"I do not care," she whispered onto his neck. "Tonight, I do not care. Tonight, I just want to not feel *him* touching me."

Sorin's hand came up to cup the back of her head. "Lie back," he whispered, gently nudging her with his body.

She did as he asked, and he climbed under the covers beside her, nestling in close. His fingers brushed her skin as he tucked her hair back over her shoulder. Then she felt his lips barely touch right below her ear. They moved slowly down her neck, feather light. His hand slid over her silk nightgown, slowly exploring her hip, her stomach.

Her eyes closed as every thought zeroed in on his fingers, his mouth. His hand drifted lower over her hip and down her thigh. She felt his fingers grip the hem of her nightgown, and he paused. "Where, Love?"

"Everywhere," she breathed.

Then his hand was moving back up, dragging her nightgown with it, exposing bare skin to him. She lifted her head and arms and let him slide the black silk garment off, and she felt his hardness pressing into her. She didn't care what he did. Not as long as his touch erased any trace of Mikale.

His hand gently cupped her chin and turned her head. She opened her eyes to find Sorin's golden eyes glazed with desire and a glimmer of worry. Holding his stare, she reached up and wrapped her fingers around his hand and guided it down to her breast. She felt him shudder against her as his thumb scraped over her nipple.

His lips were back on her neck, and his teeth nipping and scraping had her closing her eyes once more. He worked his other arm under shoulders and shifted her back pressed against his chest. That hand took over working her breasts as he slid the first hand down her torso, his fingers dancing over her skin as he went. And when those fingers brushed against her the first time, she moaned, pressing her ass into him more.

He swore at the movement, but his fingers kept moving. "I don't know how you can even want this, how you can be this wet for me or anyone after what you have been through, Love," he rasped. "You are simply stunning."

His thumb began to circle that bundle of nerves, and she was lost. She was lost in the sensation of him, of him touching her. She was lost in want and need and desire. She bucked her hips in a silent demand, and he obliged her, finally pressing down on that bundle of nerves at the same time that he pinched her nipple between this thumb and forefinger.

Scarlett cried out, and Sorin's mouth was on hers, as if he wanted to capture the sound. When his tongue slipped inside her mouth, his finger slipped inside her, and she forgot everything else. She forgot about Mikale and his touches. She forgot about Talwyn and her mother. She forgot about Callan and the Inner Court. At this very moment, it was just her and Sorin. She wasn't a secret princess, and he wasn't the Fire Prince.

She moved in time with his thrusts into her, and when he slid a second finger in, a moan escaped from her. She let herself feel the pleasure and the ache that was building and ratcheting up. Those fingers thrust in and out of her slow and hard and almost reverently. "That's it," he murmured into her ear as she rode his fingers. "Take what you need, Love. It's all yours."

Scarlett turned so that she faced him, his hand still between them, between her legs, and plunged her hands into his hair, hauling his lips back to hers. His thrusts became faster, and she broke the kiss to bury her face into his neck, pressing her lips to his skin. The taste of him, the smell of his ashes and cedar and lush smokiness had her whimpering as his hand came up to hold her head there. Then with his fingers still moving, he pressed on that bundle of nerves once more with his thumb and release barreled down her spine. She cried out, the sound muffled as she pressed herself into his neck. His fingers didn't stop moving until she had stopped shuddering and clenching around him. The hand on her head began stroking her hair, and she went utterly lax against him, still trembling from her release. He gently slid his fingers from her as she worked to slow her breathing and fought the darkness that was already reaching for her once more.

"Stay," she whispered against his neck. "Please stay with me, Sorin."

"Sleep, Scarlett," he soothed. His other hand making long strokes down her bare back. Even now, with each brush of his hand, he was erasing the touches of Mikale, and she breathed him in once more as he kept the dark at bay.

CHAPTER 10

CALLAN

A knock came on their suite doors. Sloan went to answer it, and a maid handed him a message. Callan was sitting on the sofa before the fire. After they had left the library three days ago, they had returned here, and he had not left since. He had taken a few books with him, and they lay scattered across the cushions beside him. He had spent the better part of the last few days poring over one in particular. If he was going to be stuck here, he was indeed going to learn as much as he could about the lands that existed alongside his own, starting with this damn Fire Court.

He had learned that Sorin had been the prince of the lands for over two hundred years. Holy gods. How old was he? But more than that, he had learned the four Courts all answered to a single queen who resided in the White Halls in the northernmost part of the continent. The queen, it appeared though, was not just the Queen of the Fae, but had influence over all the continent. If this was true, he wondered if his father had ever had contact with her? Why hadn't he been told of this if he was to rule one day?

"It is from Sorin," Sloan said, reading the note from the maid. "He is requesting we join them for lunch."

"Them?" Callan asked, looking up from the text he was reading.

"He did not specify who will be there, but he wants to update you on matters," Sloan replied gruffly.

"That is a good sign, isn't it?" Finn asked from the armchair opposite him. "They are including us."

"I suppose," Sloan grunted.

Callan didn't say anything. Would it just be Sorin and his Court, or would Scarlett be there, too? Would the Water Prince be there as well? Could he face Scarlett after what had been said between them? He still wanted to talk to her. He still needed answers. But he could have handled things differently. He had just been so relieved to see her safe and up and actually smiling. Not her playful or cunning smile, but a true, genuine smile. A smile he had only seen on her face a handful of times.

"What time is lunch?" Callan asked, rising from the sofa. He was in casual pants and a tunic. The prince had provided them with plenty of clothing options, and he had to admit he found their fashion rather comfortable.

"Someone will be by to escort us in an hour," Sloan answered.

Shortly before noon, there was another knock on the door, and they found Eliza standing on the other side. She smirked at them and said, "Are you lot ready then?"

"Good day to you, too," Callan said, pushing past Finn and Sloan to follow the female who led them from the guest halls.

"Did you find interesting reading material in the library?" Eliza asked smugly as they descended a set of stairs.

"I did. Fascinating history, actually," Callan answered. "Tell me, how does the prince get along with the queen?"

Eliza stiffened slightly. "The queen is not an easy person to get along with—for anybody."

"I think the same could be said of your prince," Callan replied with a raised brow.

A wicked grin spread across her face. "Careful, Mortal Prince, your jealousy is showing."

"I'm not—" but he stopped. He had not realized she had led them to the bridges…and was now crossing one. "We are meeting on the western side of the palace?"

"It would appear so," Eliza said, turning to him and crossing her arms. "Unless you have some objection to that side? Although with the trouble you have been going through to get to the other side, I can't imagine you do."

"Why now?" Finn cut in from his side. "Why are we suddenly allowed on that side now?"

Eliza sighed. "One, because you are being escorted. You are not trying to cross to this side by yourselves. Two, you were sequestered to the other side because his focus was on her. He did not want to have to worry about anything else until she woke. Now come on. I'm hungry."

She turned and began across the bridge again. Callan sighed and followed. If she was leading them to another trap, there was nothing he could do about it. He had never felt so helpless. Then again, he'd never really faced a time when he'd *needed* help, either.

They made it to the other side of the bridge without issue. Eliza led them down two more hallways before stopping in front of a room. She threw the double doors open and stalked in. Rayner held up a stack of papers that she snatched from him as she plopped into a seat and propped her feet up on the long table, despite the fact that it was laden with food.

"These are from Stellan?" she asked, grabbing an apple from the bowl and taking a bite.

"Yes," Rayner replied in his cool voice. "I'd rather not stare at the bottom of your boots while we eat." As he said it, he pushed her feet off the table, and they fell to the floor with a thump. Without missing a beat, she chucked her apple at him. He disappeared into ashes and reappeared on the other side of the table.

"Oh good, we're already throwing food," Cyrus said, prowling into the dining room. "Crown Prince," he added with a slight nod.

He took a seat next to Rayner and began filling his plate. "Please, by all means, help yourself."

"We are not waiting for Prince Sorin?" Callan asked, taking a seat at the other end of the table.

"Gods, no," Cyrus scoffed. "We'd never eat if we waited for him."

"Oh thank Saylah we're not waiting for him," said a feminine voice behind Callan. "I swear he takes longer to get ready than I do."

He turned to see Scarlett floating into the room, her shadows trailing in her wake. She was in all black wearing fitted pants with a black, long sleeve top. Daggers were at her waist, and her swagger was back. If it weren't for the hollowness of her eyes, he would have thought she was completely back to normal.

"I am so glad you are here, Darling," Cyrus said, handing a piece of bread up to her that he had smeared marmalade onto. She breezed by, snagging it and taking a bite.

"So the two of you can torment Sorin together?" Eliza asked. Her boots were back on the table, and she had a new apple in her hand. The previous one lay forgotten on the floor.

"I will gladly accept anyone into our family who can hand Sorin his ass in cards like she did last night," Cyrus replied, putting a sandwich together. "What are you going to do with all that gold anyway?"

"I already spent it on chocolates and shoes," Scarlett answered, finishing off her bread.

"All of it?" Cyrus asked, his mouth falling open.

"And books, of course," Scarlett answered, motioning for another piece of bread.

"But you won…a lot of gold coins," Cyrus sputtered.

"I'm surprised you even remember after the amount of alcohol you drank," Scarlett teased. "I'll have some chocolate sent to your rooms."

"This is the most unorthodox Court I have ever seen," Callan said, his mouth gaping. Sloan and Finn seemed as bewildered as he was. Council meetings with his father's court were formal and quiet and tense. Everyone went silent and eyes slid to them, as though they'd forgotten they were there. Scarlett had perched on the table. *On the table.* She was swinging her legs, eating her bread and jam.

"Good day, Callan. Finn. Sloan, my dear, has your face officially become stuck in that scowl? I knew it would eventually happen," she said with a fiendish grin.

Eliza smirked, and Cyrus barked a laugh. "You seem to be doing well, Scarlett," Callan said slowly, studying her.

"Well, madness can certainly be deceiving, can't it?" she replied, her grin turning feral.

"Where is his Highness anyway?" Cyrus asked, taking a bite of his sandwich.

"He pointed me down the hall and said he had to get something. He'll be along shortly," she supplied with a shrug of her shoulders.

"And what exactly is this meeting about?" Finn asked cautiously.

"It's about Windonelle. What's happening there, and what we can do about it," she answered, her voice softening a little.

"Have you heard news?" Callan asked, looking up in surprise.

"Not exactly," she answered hesitantly. Then she said, "Tell me of your father."

"My father?" Callan asked, his brows rising.

"Yes. Do you know why he wanted a High Force to be trained?" she asked, leaning over Cyrus to take the sandwich that Rayner passed to her.

"Why don't you ask the one who was actually training them?" Callan retorted sharply.

"I have, but he doesn't know *why* your father felt the need to have a High Force."

"Why would any kingdom want a group of elite, highly trained lethal soldiers?" Callan countered.

"To carry out secret missions," Eliza cut in. "Our most skilled warriors are sent out when things need to be handled quickly and discreetly. Things we don't want others to know about."

"And you are wondering what those matters might be for my father?" Callan asked. He shifted his attention back to Scarlett. "If I knew, do you not think I would have already told you? Do you not trust that I have been trying to help you this whole time?"

"I do," Scarlett said, "but maybe you don't know that you know, Callan. Maybe it has absolutely nothing to do with the children disappearing."

"Are you asking him to relay information about his kingdom that was discussed behind closed doors?" Sloan asked now, his voice hard.

"That is exactly what she is asking," Sorin said, striding into the dining hall. He had on an elegant red tunic with gold thread throughout and charcoal gray pants. "You really could not wait an extra five minutes for me to get here before you started eating?"

"When you say we're going to have a meeting at noon, perhaps you should be here *at noon*," Cyrus replied, grabbing another sandwich from the platter.

"Are those pears?" Scarlett asked, leaning over Cyrus's plate and practically crawling on the table to reach for them. Rayner sighed, picked one up, and, on a swirl of smoke, passed it to Scarlett. She sat back on the table, her feet swinging once more. She seemed so comfortable around them, as if she had lived with them her whole life, not merely stayed here for the past several days.

"Are those new boots?" Sorin asked, studying her swinging feet.

Cyrus barked a laugh, and a feline grin spread across Scarlett's face. "I had some money to burn, Prince."

"I have been with you all morning. When did you get to the city?"

"While you were bathing I paid Camilla to go to the city and fetch me a few things."

"Boots?"

"And chocolates and books from the sound of things," Cyrus said, amusement dancing in his golden eyes.

Callan watched as Scarlett tipped her head back in laughter, her shadows ebbing and flowing. Was this how she was when she was alone with her friends in the Black Syndicate? With Cassius and Death's Shadow? She had said to him on so many occasions that he did not know all of her. He hadn't wanted to believe her.

He had wanted to believe that she had felt comfortable enough around him that she could be her entire self, with no pretenses, no masks.

Sorin settled into a chair beside Cyrus. Scarlett stayed perched on the table between them. Her eyes met Sorin's, and she tilted her head to the side like she heard something. Sorin's mouth quirked to the side.

"Well, now that we're all here," Eliza drawled from her seat, "maybe the mortal prince can tell us what he knows."

All eyes shifted back to him now. "As I have already said, Sorin was the one training them. He would know more than I do. My father, it appears, had several secrets I was unaware of. It seems to be a common theme in my life as of late."

Scarlett's brows rose, and she spun to face him, now sitting cross-legged on the table. She met his eyes, her shadows darkening some, swirling a little faster. "I was planning to tell you so many things when we were to meet in the clearing, Callan. I know we are not on the best of terms right now, but we are on the same side."

"Are we?" he countered.

"Why would you think we are not?" Sorin asked. He sat casually in his chair, his hand resting on the table near Scarlett.

"I have been told very little since we arrived here," Callan said.

"And this meeting is to rectify that," Sorin replied, sipping from his glass of water. "What do you wish to know?"

"What have you heard from Baylorin?"

"We got word that they were supposedly close to breaking through the wards Cassius put up to protect the orphans in the Black Syndicate. I am working on some spells to help strengthen them, but have yet to discover why they desire the orphans," Sorin answered.

"You believe Mikale is working with my father?" Callan asked.

"Mikale is currently in charge of the High Force until the Crown Prince returns from his impromptu vacation to Rydeon with his guards and a suitable replacement for me can be found," Sorin replied. "Since he implied numerous times he knew about the orphans, and in light of his ambitions for Scarlett, the fact that he was made the interim general would suggest he is indeed working with the king and whoever is seeking the children."

"A few days ago, on the bridge, you told me of Mikale's desire to merge his bloodline with Scarlett's. Why?" Callan asked, looking to her now.

Sorin's eyes flicked to her as well, then back to Callan. "We do not know for sure."

"But you have an idea." He narrowed his eyes at Sorin as he again glanced at Scarlett.

"We have some ideas, yes," Sorin said.

Callan gritted his teeth at the obviousness of the secrets that were again being kept. "Is it even possible? To merge bloodlines with a...Fae?"

"Of course it's possible," Eliza snapped. "We have the same parts you know."

Callan felt his cheeks heat slightly. "Well, yes, but how...?" Eliza's eyebrows rose in amusement. "What would the offspring of such a union be?" he ground out.

"They would be children," Rayner said, stepping in before Eliza could reply. "But with Scarlett as their mother, they would likely be powerful for demi-Fae. They would rival full-blooded Fae in power."

"They would have magic? Even with human blood in their veins?"

"Any of the races can cross," Rayner explained. "There are many mortals in your lands that can trace their bloodlines back to other beings before the lands were divided."

"There are mortals with magic?" Callan asked, his brows raising.

"There are mortals with magical ancestry. Whether or not they have power, we do not know. If they do, it is likely very weak, if not completely dormant. Since magic is not readily found there, we do not have a way of knowing for sure," Rayner replied.

Callan returned his attention to Sorin. "How could you access magic there?"

Scarlett had gone quiet with the mention and talk of Mikale, and she was staring down at the pear she held in her lap. "Magic is not readily accessible, but there are a few ways around that," Sorin supplied. Another vague answer.

He was about to ask another question when Amaré swooped into the room through an open window. He flew right to Sorin, dropped a rolled piece of parchment into his open palm, and then swooped to Scarlett's shoulder. Sorin read the parchment and stood. Scarlett looked at him, a question in her eyes as she stroked the bird's head, and Sorin smiled at her. Callan knew that smile, knew what it conveyed, because that was the smile he gave to that same woman.

"I'm afraid we need to cancel our magic training today, Princess," he said with a wicked grin.

"Why?" she asked slowly, clearly suspicious.

"I think you will find your afternoon just became completely booked."

As he spoke, a water portal opened in the corner of the room, and Prince Briar stepped through, a silver sword strapped to his back. His icy blue eyes twinkled as they met Sorin's gaze. He nodded once to him, then his eyes went to Scarlett and a grin spread across his face. He stepped to the side to allow someone else to come through the portal.

Cassius Redding.

His eyes swept the room, coming to land on Scarlett, who had gone completely and utterly still.

Sorin's voice went soft and impossibly gentle for the dark prince that Callan knew him to be. "It's real, Love. Not a dream. He is here. I know you need him right now."

Tears appeared on Scarlett's cheeks as she practically fell off the table, Sorin catching her in his arms and setting her on her feet. Amaré flew to the back of a chair. "Thank you," she whispered, and then she was running to Cassius's waiting arms.

Sorin's eyes never left her when Cassius wrapped his arms around her, lifting her off her feet and gripping her tightly to him. Sorin didn't see his Inner Court exchange soft smiles, but Callan did. And again he wondered what secrets were being kept from him.

CHAPTER 11
SCARLETT

Cassius was here. Cassius was sitting beside her at a table in the Fire Court. Scarlett still couldn't believe it. Her hand was wrapped tightly in his as they continued discussing matters happening in Baylorin, and Scarlett kept glancing at him from the corner of her eye. That Sorin had arranged this for her...

She had woken still wrapped in his arms the morning after he'd erased so much of Mikale's touch from her body. Her naked body had still been pressed against him. He'd been right. It hadn't fixed a damn thing. Her darkness still pressed in on her. But he'd also been wrong. The phantom touches she felt on her skin now were his. His hands slowly exploring her skin. His fingers inside her. She didn't regret one bit that she'd begged him to touch her.

When she'd opened her eyes, she'd found Sorin watching her. "Hey, Love," he'd whispered.

"I still hate you," she'd whispered back.

He'd pressed a kiss to her forehead as he huffed a laugh. "Good to know."

Several moments passed, and then she had said quietly, "In my dream, Mikale said that they were close to breaking the wards to gain access to the orphans. Do you think that is possible?"

Sorin pulled back from her to see her face. "A month ago, I would have said no," he had answered, "but now, I do not know. Cassius is powerful. The wards he created were impressive. I do not think they could unravel them in only a week."

"Can we send them a warning?"

"We could send Amaré with a message."

"Okay," she had whispered and fell silent. A moment later, Sorin reached across the space between them and stroked a single finger down her cheek before he had disentangled himself from her. He'd gone out to the sitting room to give her privacy to get up and get dressed without the awkwardness of her having to leave the bed naked in front of him.

He had slept beside her every night since, but nothing else had happened. He was there when she'd wake screaming from nightmares and would stroke her hair or back until she had calmed and fell back to sleep, usually with her hand on his chest to remind herself she wasn't alone.

Her eyes went back to Sorin now as he was telling Cassius what he had found to strengthen the wards around the orphans until they could figure out what the end game was and why. In a swirl of flames, books appeared on the table before them, all with various pages marked. Cassius reached for one with his free hand, as adamant to not let go of her as she was to not let go of him. She helped him flip pages, and he studied them briefly before going to the next.

"These are even more complex than the ones Lord Tyndell had me studying," Cassius remarked, reviewing a page.

"I do not know where Tyndell got books for you to study from," Sorin said, "but these are directly from the Witch Kingdoms."

At the words, Scarlett noticed his entire Inner Court stiffen. "When did you obtain those?" Cyrus asked slowly.

"Not relevant," Sorin said with a dismissive wave of his hand.

"It most certainly is relevant," Cyrus retorted, fire flashing in his eyes. "When did you go there?"

"Later, Cyrus," Sorin said. "The Commander can only be here for a few hours, and I do not want to monopolize his time. You can take the books with you, just keep them hidden. Were you able to obtain any of the information we are hoping for?"

Cassius shook his head. Scarlett had helped Sorin draft the letter to him asking if they had learned anything since she and Sorin had left.

"Not as much as I would have hoped," Cassius admitted grimly. "Mikale is furious. The Council is demanding to know where Scarlett is. The Assassin Lord is even more irate than Mikale. He is working closely with Lord Tyndell. How much he knows of the Lord and Mikale and everything that happened, I do not know. They believe that you enacted the wards with the use of Scarlett's ring, locking Nuri away with the orphans. She does not leave the place where we have the orphans hidden for fear of being tracked down by the Assassin Lord. If he gets ahold of her, he can apparently force her to supply information. How he would do so, Nuri cannot or will not say. I do not go anywhere alone. They seem to think you will come for me because I am important to Scarlett. The number of things I had to do to come here was... It was a lot. Worth it, but I do not know that we could pull it off again. Not one orphan has been taken with the new wards though, so it's working and that's what matters."

"Hiding is not a long-term plan," Scarlett cut in. "You and Nuri being hidden away and constantly watched is no different than being locked away in a tower."

"We are working on it, Seastar," Cassius said gently, squeezing her hand. "We are figuring it out so you and Callan can come home."

Home. She swallowed and snuck a glance at Sorin. He was speaking quietly with Rayner who had come to his side. With a nod, Rayner was gone in a swirl of ashes.

Sorin stood then. "Let's end this for today. We can meet again tomorrow and continue discussing theories. Eliza, if you would escort the Crown Prince and his men back to the eastern side of the bridges."

Eliza stood, and Callan looked none too pleased, but he and his guards followed her out. Sorin gave a slight jerk of his chin to Cyrus who took his own leave, a look of intense curiosity in his eyes as he nodded to her on his way out. Briar had left shortly after he'd brought Cassius, having matters of his own to attend. Sorin closed the distance between them. "He can only stay until late afternoon. I tried to get the others out as quickly as possible. Go find some stars, Scarlett."

He made to leave, but Scarlett caught his arm. "On the eastern side of the bridges?"

"No, Love, you are free to go wherever you wish, as always." Then he was gone.

Cassius turned to her. "The bridges?"

"Come," she said. "Let's walk. Tell me everything."

Cassius filled her in on how Nuri and the orphans were doing. He told her of Drake and Tava. "Nuri must be going crazy being cooped up to avoid Alaric," Scarlett commented as they meandered up a set of stairs.

"Like a caged feral animal," Cassius replied. They had come to the highest bridge on the sixth floor and were stopped in the middle, looking out the window over the Tana River. "Sorin told me. Of what happened with Callan a few days ago."

She turned to him. "When? How?"

"Before your meeting. When he told you he was picking something up. He came to help Briar get me over the border. Briar and I had to work out how I was going to get back, and we sent Amaré to Sorin when we were ready to come to you," Cassius explained.

Scarlett turned back to the full-length windows, folding her arms and resting them along the railing. "I would have stayed with Mikale, you know," she finally said. "To keep you and Nuri and Callan safe."

"I know you would have."

"He is not done. He is biding his time. He is planning something."

"We will be ready for it, Seastar."

"Will we?" she asked, bringing her eyes back to his. "He has already shown I can do nothing against him. He is stronger than me and is nobility."

"From my understanding, you are royalty," Cassius said with a smirk.

"How do you know that?"

"Nuri told me. She knows quite a bit apparently, but is bound by some type of magic that does not allow her to share much. It was quite the feat to get that much from her," Cassius replied.

"It does not matter. I do not want a throne. It is why I walked away from Callan."

"That is not why you walked away from Callan." Cassius was staring down at the river flowing far below them. Scarlett was quiet, waiting for him to go on. "You walked away from Callan because you could not be your entire self with him. You were exhausted from having to keep so much hidden from him. You welcomed the cage when it came because it let you breathe for the first time in a long time."

"How insightful of you," she said sharply.

"I am not saying you did not have feelings for him, Scarlett. I am not saying you used him. Quite the opposite, actually. I think he used you in his own way, but that is neither here nor there. You loved him, maybe a part of you still does, but he will never be able to accept all of you." Cassius shifted, leaning his back against the railing so he could see her face. "Your shadows have lessened since that day on the beach."

"That day on the beach I had no control," Scarlett growled. "I could have frozen you all. I still can't control it. Sorin has been trying to teach me, but it feels futile."

"You have been here less than two weeks, and from what Sorin told me, you spent the first five days either sleeping or vomiting your guts up. You did not learn to fight in two weeks. I'm assuming mastering your power will take time as well."

"Time is something we do not have," Scarlett whispered.

"Seastar, you need this time. We do not know what is coming. We do not know what we will face or when we will face it, but right now, in this moment, you need to breathe. Do not apologize for that. You have sacrificed much. You may have to do so again, but we can sacrifice some, too. Take some time to be happy before you come home," Cassius said.

"How can I be happy when our children are being targeted, Cassius? When you and Nuri are in imminent danger every day because of my actions?"

"You will come for them, Scarlett, but coming back now would be like jumping back into a fight while you are still bleeding from a gaping wound. We are not your responsibility to protect."

"Yes, you are!" she cried. "You carry two titles, Cassius. You are a Commander and a Black Syndicate Imperial. You know that those below you are your responsibility."

"Are we discussing the Black Syndicate or your recent bloodline discovery?" he asked gently.

"I am not a princess nor am I a queen."

"It appears it is in your blood, Seastar."

"Stop."

"Your mother was a queen in every sense of the word. I don't know the story. I do not know how she ruled in this world. I do know how she ruled in the Black Syndicate. I can only imagine how benevolent she was as a true queen, Scarlett. I would have to believe you would be the same."

"Enough. I am not my mother," Scarlett whispered.

There was a long pause of silence then Cassius said gently, "We want you home, Seastar, but we can wait for you. You are worth the wait."

Scarlett sighed, leaning her head against Cassius's shoulder. Home. He'd said it twice now. She felt more at home here in this palace than she ever had in Baylorin, but could a place really be home without Cassius? "Can I be even more selfish and ask you to come here until we figure things out?"

Cassius kissed the top of her head tenderly. "I have thought the same thing so many times, but we both know I need to be there, helping Nuri." They fell silent again, each soaking in the other's presence. "Tell me of Sorin."

"What about him?" Scarlett asked, lifting her head to look into those brown eyes. A soft smile played on his lips, and she knew what he was asking. "It is weird being here with him and Callan. Some days I feel like I can hardly draw enough breath. Thinking of anything else feels like too much right now, even if we do share chambers."

"You share a room?" Cassius asked, raising his brows in surprise.

"Don't act so shocked. We shared a bed all the time," she replied, shoving him lightly.

"You share a bed?" he asked, his brows going higher.

"Only the last few nights. I've had nightmares," she said, her voice falling quiet again. "I wanted you, but…" She trailed off, leaning her head on his shoulder once more.

"I miss you, too," was all he said as they fell into silence once more.

SORIN

Sorin stood in the eaves of the fourth floor watching Scarlett and Cassius on the bridge two levels up. It was nearly time for the Commander to be getting back before Lord Tyndell noticed he was gone. The Lord apparently had no idea Cassius and Nuri had seen them before they had fled, and thus didn't know that they were aware of the Lord's involvement with Mikale. So Cassius had played along, gathering as much information as he could and "trying to work out the wards" they believed Sorin had enacted.

Sorin had let the two have their space and had gone somewhere not even his Inner Court could follow. He wasn't jealous of Cassius. He had stopped being jealous of the man the night Scarlett had told him of the day that Mikale had violated her in so many atrocious ways. He had stopped being jealous of him when he'd figured out exactly who he was to her.

They had started working with her magic three days ago, but

she had not been able to exercise an ounce of control over it. She had not summoned a single ember, drop of water, shard of ice, or lick of flame. She woke every night reaching for him as nightmares filled her dreams. The second night it had happened, she had cried into his shoulder for nearly an hour while he held her close, feeling utterly helpless, and he knew. He knew what she needed. She didn't need him to erase vile touches like she had that first night when he'd felt her come around his fingers and held her bare body all night long.

While some days, what she needed might be him, right now it was Cassius. If that was what she needed, then he would do whatever he could to make it happen.

He also knew it couldn't happen again. Getting Cassius here had been dangerous. They'd had to sneak him out of Baylorin and across the border, which meant getting through Night Child territory. He and Briar had crossed over to cover him for the final few miles, but Briar would have to help him get back. Briar had been right when they had sparred. The consequences of taking the twin flame Mark without a companion were already starting. He could not expend large amounts of his magical reserves right now.

And it killed him that when she said goodbye to Cassius today, he wouldn't be able to tell her when she would see him again.

"Who is he?" Cyrus asked, coming to his side. Sorin had only returned moments ago, but there was ancient magic binding him and his Inner Court. They knew when their Prince left and returned from these halls.

"Cassius Redding. He is a commander in the mortal king's armies. He is also powerful. I suspect Witch blood ties but am not certain," Sorin replied.

"Impressive," Cyrus commented. "But who is he to her?"

"He is not a threat if that is what you are asking."

"I assume you would not leave her alone with him if he were a threat, but is he a threat to you?" He, too, was watching the princess. She and Cassius had sat down, right in the center of the bridge, side-by-side. Her head was on his shoulder, his head resting

117

on hers. Their fingers were intertwined. He kissed the top of her head as he laughed about something she said.

"No, he is not a threat to me either," Sorin said. "I may be her twin flame, but he is her soulmate."

Cyrus was silent for a moment longer before saying, "At lunch, he said 'so you can come home.'"

"He did."

"Will she go back?"

"I do not know."

"Will you let her?"

"I will not cage her."

Silence fell again for a beat before Cyrus said, "I haven't known her long, but I would miss the hell out of her if she is not staying."

"Me too."

CHAPTER 12
SCARLETT

"You need to relax," Sorin said from across a clearing. He was sitting on a large boulder, sharpening one of his many daggers. They were back in the courtyard he had brought her to nearly every day for the last two weeks. The courtyard branched off into five separate training arenas of stone, the walls towering high to contain fire being wielded by Fae who could not yet control it. Each arena had obstacles to work around that grew progressively more difficult.

"It is sacred ground blessed by Anala herself, and it is where we bring the neophytes when they are first coming into their power," Sorin had explained to her when they were preparing to leave his chambers two weeks ago for her first training session. She had come out of the closet strapping daggers to her waist. "And you can't bring those."

Scarlett had brought her hands to her hips. "You are bringing yours and more," she'd protested, gesturing to the bandolier of knives strapped across his chest.

"Yes, but I know how to control and wield my power," he'd replied with a smirk.

"And?" Scarlett had asked, not seeing any sort of connection.

"You need to learn to depend on your magic. That is your greatest advantage. Yes, your weapons are important too, but if you cannot control your magic, it will become a hindrance rather than the great asset that it is," he'd said, crossing the room. He'd plucked the daggers from her hips and portaled them here.

Since that time, she had produced nothing of value. A spark here and there or an ice crystal. Nothing that mattered.

"This is ridiculous. If I'm so powerful, how come I haven't been able to do a damn thing?"

"You have done plenty with your magic," Sorin replied, not looking up from his dagger. How he could just sit there every afternoon and watch her do absolutely nothing was beyond her. He had to have a million other princely things to be doing. "You have frozen branches and thrown fire at poor Briar, to name a few."

"This isn't funny," Scarlett snapped at his teasing tone. Her nightmare last night had been of Juliette's death, and she'd been on edge all day.

Sorin looked up at her terse response, his gaze finding hers. "Everyone starts at the beginning, Scarlett. Everyone starts at this place," he said gently.

Sorin had explained on their first day that most young Fae began to show signs of their power around age seven or eight. Depending on the strength they display, they come here to start training and honing their craft around age ten. Sometimes sooner, sometimes later.

The only task he had given her when they arrived, and the only task he had given her every morning since, was to produce a flame. He didn't care what kind. He didn't care how.

And she had failed at that task. Every. Single. Day.

"Why can't you just tell me how to do it?" she asked. She could hear the whine in her own voice.

"I have told you, it is different for everyone. How I access my magic is different from how you will access it and different from how Eliza and Rayner and Cyrus access theirs. You need to figure out what awakens your magic and then how to control it once it is wide-eyed, or it will control you."

"So I'm just supposed to stand here, all day long, until something happens?" she protested. The whining had turned to ire that ran in an undercurrent in her tone.

"We can do other things to pass the time if you wish," Sorin replied with a coy grin.

Scarlett stuck her tongue out at him, crossing her arms across her chest.

"Love, there are so many better uses for that tongue," Sorin crooned.

"And my teeth, I suppose," she replied, biting the air at him.

Sorin laughed under his breath as he rose from the boulder he'd been sitting on. He sheathed the dagger at his side and crossed the courtyard to her, turning her to face the expanse before them. Standing behind her, she could feel his body lightly pressed against her. He ran his hands down her arms. Once. Twice. Three times.

"What are you doing?" she sighed. "I do not have time for this, Sorin. Every day this takes is a day longer for Mikale to do whatever it is they are going to do."

"If you are not to rule, it is not your responsibility to protect them," Sorin replied pragmatically.

"I do not wish to rule *here*," she corrected.

"You wish to rule in the mortal lands? Then perhaps you should have accepted Prince Callan's offer," he said, continuing to run his hands down her arms.

"Do you wish me to accept his offer?" she asked. "Here I thought you'd grown fond of having me in your bed."

"Shush, you wicked thing," he murmured, and the way he said it made her still. It was lust and desire mixed with awe and wonder. His mouth was so close to her ear, his breath brushed her cheek, causing the few stray hairs that had escaped her braid to tickle her skin.

"Your power," he said, "is an extension of *you.*" His voice was low and soft, caressing her very soul. "It is interwoven into every facet of your being. It is in your strength. It is in your brilliance. It is in your dreams and your fears. It is connected to every thought. Every emotion." His fingers came to her neck, and she leaned into the touch, closing her eyes. Every part of her was focused on those fingers as they made idle circles around her neck, dragging along her shoulder, down her back, stopping just before they dipped too low. She felt her core heat as his fingers began trailing back up her spine. "It courses through every part of you. It is in your blood. It is in your bones. It is in your very essence. It is in the parts of you that you have kept hidden for years, afraid no one would want them. It is in the caverns of your soul, the deepest recesses of your mind. Places even you have not dared to venture. Secrets you keep so hidden even you forgot about them. Be you, Scarlett. Just be you."

She felt like the air had stilled around her. She was in the courtyard with Sorin, and she wasn't. She stood in an empty chamber and before her a panther as dark as night lay sleeping. As if sensing she was there, Shirina opened an eye. She sat up and cocked her head to the side as she studied her. Then she arched her back into a stretch and yawned. She took a step towards her and then another.

"Easy," Scarlett heard Sorin murmur so softly it was barely a whisper.

As the panther neared, Scarlett reached out a hand towards it, and the panther's silver eyes glowed as bright as starlight. She could swear the giant feline was smiling. Shirina stopped before her and bowed her head low. As the panther lifted it once more, Scarlett brought her fingers up, barely brushing its soft fur. Sorin's breath brushed against her ear again.

"Scarlett," he whispered. "Look."

She opened her eyes, and all around her in the cavern, flames glowed. They lined the perimeter, running along the walls. Oranges and golds and reds danced amongst each other in rhythm with her own heartbeat.

She spun around to face Sorin, her eyes wide. Sorin's eyes were bright with fascination. "I did this?" she whispered in disbelief.

"You did this," he answered. She could have sworn that was pride lining his features.

"You didn't help at all?" she asked suspiciously.

"This, Love, was all you," he replied, his eyes staring into hers.

Then she was kissing him, her lips pressing onto his fiercely, and his hands encompassed her face. His tongue ran along the seam of her lips, and she instantly parted them for him. His tongue swept in, and she felt her knees buckle slightly. His hand was instantly around her waist, pulling her closer to him, steadying her. Her own fingers were woven into his hair, and the bandolier of knives pressed into her chest as she pressed into him. She couldn't get close enough. Something was drawing her to him, drawing her home.

He pulled back after a minute, breathing just as hard as she was. She could see the desire lining his face, and his gaze dropped to her mouth. Her flames still burned around them, reflecting in his eyes. He grinned at her as the flames winked out, and he whispered, "Do it again."

"The fire or the kissing?" she breathed.

"Your magic, smart ass, and then maybe I will think about kissing you again," he said, stepping away from her. She scowled at him. She tried to muster that magic, that flame, even an ember again, but all she could think about now was the feel of his lips on hers and the taste of him on her tongue.

Sorin jumped to the top of a boulder. "Come now, Princess, you must not want to kiss me again that badly," he crooned, as he jumped to another one. Flames licked down her arms like he was touching her himself, trailing along her body.

She whirled to him. Frustration overcame her, and she clenched her fists at her sides, darkness swirling around them. She had more control over these damn shadows than she did her magic. She gritted her teeth as she turned to watch him casually leap from boulder to boulder, a teasing grin on his face. Without even realizing what she was doing, she threw those shadows at him. He was in mid-leap when they reached him. They twisted around his arms, and she closed her fists. Those shadows gripped his arms as if they were an extension of her own hands. She threw him to the ground and heard him let out a grunt at the impact. She stalked over to him, pinning him to the dirt with that swirling darkness.

His eyes were wide when she came to stop over him, a feline grin on her face. With a finger, she drew a tendril of a shadow up to his face, stroking down his cheek, his jaw. She traced his lips with that shadow. Then she bent down close. His eyes were dancing with delighted amusement mixed with ravenous hunger. She stopped close enough to share breath with him. "You're right," she whispered. "I don't want to kiss you again that badly."

She stood, pulling her shadows back to her. She leapt onto a relatively flat-topped rock, sitting down and crossing her ankles. Sorin lay on the ground, a slightly shocked look on his face. Scarlett just smirked at him.

"How did you do that?" he asked, slowly getting to his feet.

She shrugged. "No idea, but it was fun."

"It was…"

"Impressive? Remarkable? Superb?" Scarlett offered, bringing a hand to her chest in mock flattery.

"Unexpected and dramatic," he said, flicking her nose with his finger as he climbed up the rock and sat beside her. He leaned back on his palms.

She held her hands up and watched the shadows swirl. She opened her palm in front of her and slowly those shadows began to swirl in the center of it. She concentrated, sending every wisp of dark there, and when it was all contained in one spot, she held it. She could feel sweat forming on her brow as she worked to keep them in one spot until she finally had to let them go. They snaked back along her arms and around her torso. She closed her eyes, panting slightly. How did Sorin do it? That much concentration to control so little and his power was so mighty.

"It gets easier," he said quietly, as if he'd read her thoughts. "With practice, it gets easier to control until it becomes second nature." She only nodded, leaning back on her own palms now. "Tomorrow is Samhain." Scarlett stiffened. How had she not realized that? "We do not have a formal masked ball here, but we do have a traditional masked feast with dancing. Much less formal than things were in Windonelle. It's held in the palace Great Hall. You do not have to attend, but I do. I have been gone for the last three years. My people will expect me to be there knowing I have returned, but you do not need to attend, Scarlett."

"Callan?" she asked, staring across the courtyard. Her shadows darkened, and she twirled them around her fingers absentmindedly.

"He has been invited along with Finn and Sloan," Sorin confirmed. "You do not need to attend, Scarlett," he repeated.

"No, I will," she said, sending those shadows up her arm. "I do not want to sit up in your chambers all night by myself, especially on the night the dead are free to walk among us."

"So you believe in Samhain legends but not the gods and Fates?" Sorin asked, raising his brows.

"I do not wish to tempt either right now should they exist."

"Fair enough."

Silence ticked by for a few minutes, leaving them each to their own thoughts. Scarlett was too occupied by Samhain, both past and future, to concentrate on her magic any more. It would be good to be around people, even if Callan was going to be there. Maybe it would be good to be in a casual setting with him too, rather than a meeting room where Sorin and Cyrus were constantly serving as a buffer.

"Love?"

"Hmm?" she murmured, getting lost in the shadows swirling around her fingertips.

"I am finding there is a necessity arising."

Scarlett stilled at the change of his voice. It was low and intense and rough. She kept her eyes on her shadows as her heart rate jumped. "Really?"

"Yes, but I am afraid you will not view it as such," he answered.

"I'm sorry to hear that."

"The thing is, it is your fault."

"What?" Her head swung to him where her eyes met golden ones burning with, well, *need*. "How is your need my fault?"

"Because you kissed me," he answered, pushing off his hands and sitting up, leaning closer to her. "Then you told me you did not want to kiss me again that badly."

"Because I don't." But her stomach dipped as he brought his hand up. His fingers brushed down her cheek and then her neck, sliding around to cup her nape.

"See, Love, I feel like this is the problem. Either you are lying to me, or I need you so much more than you appear to need me."

Scarlett bit her lip, and Sorin's eyes shot to the movement. That lush, smokey spice mixed with his ash and cedar scent, and a light ache began throbbing between her legs. "Sounds to me like your plan backfired when you tried to use a kiss to get me to access my magic again," she purred with a smirk.

"That it did," Sorin said softly, as his hand fisted gently in her hair and tilted her head back and up to him.

"Sorin?" she whispered.

"Yeah, Love?" His eyes were fixed on her mouth. His other hand was braced on the rock beside her hip.

"I want you to kiss me again."

"Thank fuck," he answered, his voice near guttural. His lips were instantly on hers, and she was kissing him back without any hesitation. Her own hand came up to his chest while his other came to her hip. She let herself get lost in all of him as he kissed her deeply, thoroughly. And when he gently began guiding her onto her back on that rock, she let him. He held her head in his hand, not letting it touch the hard stone as his other hand explored her torso, her hip, her backside.

She let her own hands explore a little of their own, sliding over his broad chest, his shoulders, down his arms. He growled against her mouth when she slid them down his back, and the sound rumbled through her. All she wanted was to feel *him*. She slipped her hands under his tunic, and when she lightly dragged her fingers up his spine, he shuddered against her.

"Gods," he swore, breaking their kiss. "You are…"

"What?" Scarlett whispered. She kissed one corner of his mouth, then the other.

"There are not words, Love. I do not think there are words to adequately describe you," he answered, his hand sliding down her hip to her thigh once more.

She gave him a slight frown. "I'm not sure if that's a good thing."

He huffed a laugh. "Has anyone ever told you that you over-think things?"

"I was trained to kill very prominent people. I was taught to overthink all the things."

Sorin pulled back to look into her eyes. "But you do not have to be that here. You can just…enjoy being."

"Being what?"

"Just being, Scarlett. Just enjoy living," he answered, brushing a light kiss to her lips.

She'd never had such a luxury. She'd never been allowed to just be.

So she brought her lips back to his and kissed him in the court-yard, enjoying every swipe of his tongue against hers and every brush of his fingers and feel of his skin beneath her own. They kissed and kissed until Sorin pulled back, his lips swollen and eyes wild with predatory hunger. His voice was gruff and low. "We should go. We are expected at dinner later."

"You're the prince. No one can really scold you if you're not at dinner," Scarlett pointed out, nipping at his lower lip.

He groaned softly, pressing kisses along her jaw. "No, but Cyrus will come looking for us and not care what he is interrupting."

"Cyrus is a busybody," she murmured, tilting her head back to allow him access to her neck once more.

"That he is, and he enjoys being one. If he knew what we were doing up here right now, he would show up just to tease us," Sorin answered, obliging her silent request and sliding those lips down to her throat.

"I totally would," came an amused male voice.

A string of curse words came from Sorin's mouth as he pushed himself off of Scarlett and took her hand, hauling her into a sitting position. She glared at Cyrus from atop the rock.

"Darling, if I knew that was the kind of magic training you were doing, I'd have offered to train you myself," Cyrus smirked as she adjusted her top and smoothed out her hair.

"Darling, if I thought you had anything to teach me, I'd have asked," Scarlett retorted as Sorin hopped down from the rock and reached a hand up to help her down as well.

Cyrus burst into laughter. She leapt down, landing before him, and Sorin's arm came around to rest casually on her hip. "What exactly are you doing here?" Sorin asked, not even trying to hide the bite of annoyance to his tone.

"Checking on my prince, of course," Cyrus answered, trying and utterly failing to act innocent.

Sorin sighed as he pressed a kiss to her temple and a fire portal appeared before them. He nudged her forward, but Scarlett dug in her heels. "Wait. That's it?"

Sorin raised a brow in question. "What do you mean?"

"He didn't even give you a reason as to why he's up here," Scarlett replied, glaring at Cyrus.

Cyrus's own brows rose in surprise. "But I did. I was checking on my prince."

"Mhmm." Scarlett crossed her arms.

"Come, Scarlett," Sorin urged, again nudging her towards the waiting portal.

"He must have needed *something* to come all the way up here," she protested.

Cyrus exchanged a look with Sorin, and Scarlett glanced back and forth between them. The realization drove any lingering desire from her as she stepped out of Sorin's reach. "He actually *was* checking on you?"

"As we have already established, Cyrus is a busybody," Sorin said, stepping towards her and reclaiming the space she had put between them.

She whirled on the Second. "You don't trust me alone with him? You are aware we share chambers, right? That we sleep in the *same damn bed?*"

Cyrus's face hardened slightly. "I am well aware of your sleeping arrangements, Darling," he drawled. "I am also well aware of your extreme lack of control when it comes to your power and your delightful temper. So, yes, I am not entirely happy with the idea that the *prince* is up here, isolated from everyone, teaching you to try to control your unknown well of magic."

An icy smirk curled up her lips.

"You find this amusing?" Cyrus asked, his brows rising once more in surprise.

"No, Darling. What I find amusing is that your fear is of my magic." A tendril of her shadows curled towards him and slid along his jaw like a finger. She walked towards the fire portal as she said over her shoulder, "My magic should be the least of your concerns."

CHAPTER 13

SCARLETT

S carlett stood in front of the mirror. The teal color of her dress was so dark it was almost black. There was silver along the bottom that faded as it moved up the skirts. The sleeves and bodice were fitted, leaving an open back and deep plunging neckline. Her mask was a beaded beauty of silver and teal. Camilla had curled her hair and pinned it half up, leaving the rest to cascade down over her shoulders. Then she had twisted tiny black orchids into her hair.

Scarlett stared at her pointed ears and longer fingers and limbs. She examined her elongated canines. Her shadows were slight and loose around her. She had been here three weeks, and each day she fell more and more in love with all of it. She actually looked forward to getting out of bed for the first time in a long time. She looked forward to bantering with Cyrus. She loved the food and exploring the palace library. She didn't even mind her magic lessons, despite the frustration they wrought.

She hadn't seen much of Callan except at the lunch meetings they had a few times a week. Sorin was making an effort to include him as much as he could, and Scarlett was content to let Sorin handle things. She'd meant what she said. She had no desire to rule.

She was enjoying not having expectations and demands shoved on her.

She adjusted the mask on her face. She hadn't been lying either when she'd told Sorin she didn't want to sit alone all night in his rooms. She might not believe in the Fates or Samhain legends, but she certainly believed in the thoughts and nightmares that would plague her were she left alone for an entire evening. She studied her image another moment and was about to turn and leave when she found herself staring into dark eyes.

Scarlett whirled around, but there was no one behind her. When she turned back to the mirror, Mikale's image remained, staring back at her, an amused expression on his face.

"My pet," he said with a slight smile, "how lovely you look this evening." Scarlett looked behind her again. Was she hallucinating? Had she finally gone so mad she was seeing things? "Look at these delightful talents I am learning." Scarlett slowly turned back to the mirror. "Tell me, Scarlett, where in his Fire Court has Sorin Aditya hidden you?"

Scarlett watched as her shadows darkened and swirled faster around her, flowing through her hair and around her skirts. "I am not hidden well if you are speaking to me, am I?" she finally managed to say. If she had finally gone mad, it didn't much matter what she said to him, did it?

"If only that were the case," Mikale answered, his smile turning into a sneer. "My source in the Black Syndicate has a few ideas and has heard several rumors, but we are unable to confirm any of them. I am assuming he is responsible for that."

His source in the Black Syndicate?

"I have no idea about what kind of defenses he has," she replied with a shrug of her shoulders.

"I highly doubt that is the case," Mikale retorted, his face taking on a hard edge. "My source is also most upset about the updated wards around the children. However did your beloved prince manage that from so far away?"

"Shall we make a trade, Mikale?" Scarlett asked sweetly. "You tell me who your source is, and I shall reveal how he enhanced his wards."

Mikale glared at her in the mirror. He lifted a hand and stroked her cheek in the reflection, and Scarlett could feel it on her own skin, as if he were indeed standing behind her. "Do not worry, my pet. Soon enough you shall be back where you belong, and we will move forward with our plans."

"Who is we?" she asked, trying to hide her shortness of breath.

He leaned down and whispered into her ear as that hand slid along her throat, down the front of the plunging neckline of her dress. "When you learn who had your mother killed, then you will know the answer to that."

Then he was gone.

CHAPTER 14
CALLAN

Callan stood at one end of the Great Hall listening to the musicians play a lively tune. All around him Fae twirled and danced, laughed and shouted to one another. There were even a small number of humans present. He watched as the Fire Prince made his way through the room, and his people came up to him and shook his hand, welcoming him home. He greeted them all by name. Every single one, as if he personally knew every person in his city. He scooped up babies and children, swinging them through the air to delighted giggles. He ate off trays of food as they came by, like everyone else. There was no high table where he and his household sat and presided over everything. He mingled and laughed and visited with them all.

Callan couldn't deny it was inspiring. It was a vision he had once told Scarlett he had for his own kingdom. He had once told her that he wished to focus on those already in his kingdom's care, and watching Sorin, he realized this was what he desired. He desired people who would see him as one of them, not fear him as a king and ruler.

A flash of vibrant red-gold hair in the corner of his eye caught his attention, and Callan turned to see Eliza striding through the crowd. Gone were her usual leathers, although he had no doubt daggers were still strapped to her thighs beneath the cerulean blue dress she wore. Her mask was a lighter shade of blue with rose gold accents that seemed to reach for her unbound hair cascading all around her. Her sleeveless dress revealed every tattoo down her arms and across her chest. She came to a stop beside Rayner who was in black pants and a black tunic. On anyone else, they would have been considered plain, but on Rayner, they looked regal. His black mask covered his eyes and nose. Eliza grabbed his hand, dragging him to the dance floor. She laughed as Rayner grumbled something to her. Callan watched with no small amount of shock as the two began to twirl around the dance floor.

"It is odd to be on this side of things," Finn commented from beside him.

"We have been guests at various feasts and balls in the past," Callan replied.

"Yes, but here nobody knows who you are. It is unknown that you are a prince for the most part," Finn said simply. "The threats are substantially less. It is just different. That is all."

"It is not all that different," Sloan grumbled. "We are still on the lookout for her."

The words were like a calling as the double doors at the end of the hall were opened, and Cyrus strode in with Scarlett on his arm. She was stunning in her dress of dark teal and silver. Even with the shadows, which seemed to have become a part of her, she looked more like a princess than the wraith she had been two years ago at a different Samhain ball.

Two years that seemed like a different lifetime.

Callan had expected her to come with Sorin and had been more than a little surprised when the prince had arrived without her. Callan had wondered if she would even come when she wasn't with him. Every head turned to look at her as Cyrus led her into the crowd. He leaned over and murmured something in her ear, and she grinned wide, giving him a little shove with her elbow. Cyrus led her to the long table laden with food, and the two began filling plates with the various delicacies that had been prepared for the evening.

"Will you approach her tonight?" Finn asked, his eyes also fixed on her as she moved along the table, chatting casually with Cyrus.

"If I did not know any different, I would think she was from here," Callan said instead.

"She *is* Fae," Finn replied.

"I do not mean like that. I mean, watching her interact with Sorin's Court, one would think she has always lived with them. They are like a…"

"Family," Finn finished. "It is as if you are watching her with her family."

"Do you think this is what she was like with Cassius and Nuri and others in the Black Syndicate?" Callan asked, tracking her as she and Cyrus found a bench along the wall and sat among a few others, digging into their now full plates.

"I do not know. I do not know how you could know that," Finn supplied.

She again broke into laughter at something Cyrus said. "It is almost as if I never knew her at all."

SCARLETT

Scarlett's heart felt relatively light for the first time in days as Cyrus spun her to a song on the dance floor, despite her encounter with Mikale earlier that evening. She had been delightfully surprised by Cyrus's dancing skills. She had seen Sorin milling about with his people. Cyrus had told her he would likely be kept busy by them all evening, especially since he had been gone for the last three years. Cyrus had kept close though, making sure she was never left alone amongst people she didn't know. Eliza and Rayner had joined them for food a while ago, and Scarlett had almost not recognized the female without her fighting leathers.

The song was just coming to an end when a voice from behind her made her freeze in Cyrus's arms. "May I have your next dance?"

Cyrus's eyes were on her with a question, and she closed her own for just a moment, breathing deep. Then she put a smile on her face and turned to face Callan. "Of course, Prince," she replied. Cyrus's hand tightened on her own, and she squeezed it back, conveying she was fine.

"I will get us drinks," he said.

"I will find you in a moment," Scarlett answered.

The next song started up, and Callan held out his hand to her. She tentatively took it and braced herself for the memories that were going to drag her under. All of it was familiar as he began leading her through the steps—her hand in his hand, his hand on her waist, the flow of their steps together, the look in his eyes. After a few beats of silence, he said softly, "I did not know if you would say yes."

"It would be foolish to refuse an invitation from a prince, would it not?" she asked with a tilt of her head.

Callan's eyes narrowed slightly at the words, the same words she'd said to him two years ago. "You look beautiful tonight."

"Thank you."

"That is it? No other remarks?"

"About how I look this evening? What would you like me to say?"

"We used to talk, you know. We used to have real conversations."

"What would you like to discuss?"

She watched as frustration darkened his eyes. "Do you think we will be able to return home soon?"

She stumbled at his words, but he held her up, pulling her a little closer to him. "I do not think it would be safe for you to return to Baylorin until we have figured out Mikale's plans. He could very well use you to get to me."

"You will not return home?"

"Of course I will return," she snapped.

Relief flashed across his face. "If Mikale is the problem, Scarlett," he said slowly, "we can rectify that simply enough. My offer from the garden still holds."

Scarlett blinked at him. Gods, it was hot in here. Her mask was so godsdamned hot. She struggled to keep her breathing even, and her shadows darkened slightly around her. "Callan," she started as evenly as she could, "if you knew all that I am, you would rescind that offer in a heartbeat."

"You have not given me the chance to know all that you are," he retorted. As if realizing his sharp tone, he took a breath and continued more gently. "I thought you had, but watching you here, interacting with Sorin and his Court, it has only made me love you more. It has only made me wish you could be that carefree and relaxed with me."

"That is just it, Callan. I cannot. You live in a world of formality and royalty."

"And this world is not the same? Sorin is as much of a prince as I am. More so even," Callan replied. "You once told me you do not wish to be chained to a throne. Would staying here not be the same?"

"You do not know everything, Callan," she replied softly, searching his eyes. She shoved her temper down. She would not get upset with him. Not tonight, in front of all of Sorin's guests.

"Because you refuse to tell me *anything*."

"I am telling you as much as I can." Smoke curled in her mouth, and her shadows crept down her arms. She glanced around, noting Cyrus on the edge of the crowd, drinks in hand. He was visiting with another male, but his eyes were on her.

"Why does Mikale desire you so badly? Simply because you are Fae?"

"Yes and no," she replied softly. The fire in her veins turned to ice. She saw Callan glance at her hand which must have turned ice cold as well. The temperature had dropped in the hall, and Scarlett struggled to control the stream of emotions that were imploding on her.

"Why can you not just give me a straight answer?"

"Because I am trying to keep you safe, Callan. I am trying to protect you. It is all to keep you safe."

"I did not ask you to keep me safe," he answered, his voice low and gruff. "I would rather be by your side on your adventures than behind you in your protection." When she did not reply, he continued. "You know why I asked you to dance tonight, Scarlett?" She brought her eyes back to his. "I asked you to dance because this is the first time I have been allowed to have a private conversation with you, and even now, it is in front of hundreds and being monitored by his Court." Scarlett swallowed. "You have nothing to say?"

"I am sorry, Callan," she said, her eyes going to the floor.

"No, that is not enough," Callan said, shaking his head. "Look at me, Scarlett Monhroe. Look at me and tell me why you allow him to help you and see all of you and not me. What has he done that has allowed him such an honor?"

She slowly brought her eyes back to his. Her shadows slithered around her wrists and hands, hovering just within a breath of Callan's own. He went slightly rigid, his eyes widening. She could see Finn and Sloan out of the corner of her eye, making their way through the crowd to them. Cyrus had shoved the drinks into the hands of the male and was doing the same. Without missing a beat in the dance that was coming to an end, she stepped closer to Callan. "My answer has not changed since the day you asked me on the journey here. He understands my darkness, Callan, and he does not fear it," she said, her voice low. "He has never once looked at me with the unease I see in your eyes. He does not have guards coming to protect him from me."

"Cyrus is making his way here, too," Callan countered.

"Cyrus is making his way here to guard *you*, Prince." Her shadows crept forward once more, but then ashes and cloves and cedar wrapped around her.

"May I steal her for the next dance, Crown Prince?"

Her shadows paused as the song ended. Callan's eyes were fixed on her own behind his mask of forest green, his hands still holding her to him. She stepped in closer to him so she could whisper in his ear. "This is only a glimpse of who I am, Callan, and you can hardly stand to face it. The light is easy to love, isn't it? But what of the darkness? What would you do with all of me?" Finn and Sloan were behind him, and she sent her shadows creeping towards them.

She felt a hand on her elbow. "Dance with me, Scarlett."

"Yes, please quit hogging the Crown Prince all to yourself." There was Eliza, taking Callan's hand and pulling him away and across the hall to dance. Callan's eyes were still on her though.

"Scarlett."

She finally broke Callan's stare and turned to Sorin. He was in what she had come to realize was his usual attire—charcoal gray pants, red tunic, and black jacket. His mask was red with gold and only covered his eyes.

She sighed, noting where Cyrus had stopped in the crowd when Sorin had reached her. He stood, waiting for a signal from his prince.

"You have duties to attend to Sorin. I will have Cyrus escort me back."

"You will go be alone on a night the dead are free to roam?" A small smile graced his lips.

She did not return it.

"I feel as if I am one of them anyway. Maybe I would enjoy their company."

Sorin's face turned hard, and he clenched his jaw. "One dance."

"You have people to greet and speak with, Sorin."

"I can take a break." He extended a hand to her as another song began, a slow paced ballad.

She sighed again and took his hand. "I do not need a keeper."

"Wouldn't dream of it, Princess," he said, pulling her to him.

They danced in silence for the first minute. She felt herself gradually relax as he led her around the floor, her hand grasped gently in his and held to his chest. "Do you want to talk about it?"

"No." She felt ice rise in her again, and a moment later heat warmed her hand.

Another beat of silence. "Numerous people have asked who you are this evening."

"Oh? And what did you tell them?" she asked, arching a brow behind her mask.

"That you are darkness incarnate and blessed by Saylah herself," he said with a shrug.

"You did not," she scoffed, pinching his shoulder where her other hand rested, her mouth quirking to the side.

He grinned at her, relief seeming to pass over his eyes as he tugged her closer. She could feel every inch of him pressed up against every inch of her. "I thought of telling them you are the most stunning female in this room."

"They can clearly see that, although Eliza might take that title this evening," she said with a small smile, her eyes snagging on the female dancing with Callan on the other side of the hall.

"No, she doesn't," Sorin said, his voice low and husky.

Her eyes went back to his, where she found him looking at her like she was the only person in the room. She felt her cheeks flush and was suddenly glad for the mask, but she held his gaze. They said nothing for the rest of the dance, and their eyes did not leave each other. The world melted away, as though it were just them. The only two stars in the sky.

When the song ended, she went onto her tiptoes to whisper in his ear. "When you are done with your princely duties this evening, come find me." She let her shadows curl around his ear as she stepped from him, turning to make her way to the doors.

She was nearly to them when Cyrus fell into step beside her. "Leaving so early?"

"Stay, Cyrus. Enjoy yourself. As I've repeatedly told your prince, I do not need a keeper," she replied, the guards opening a door for her.

"Perhaps not, but I'd love to keep you company," he said coyly, his tone becoming sensuous and flirty, attempting to lighten her mood as he followed her through the doors.

She paused in the hallway, looking over her shoulder at him. She smiled, a cruel thing, as her shadows darkened around her. She sent them swirling to him, and the guards at the doors shrank back, looking to Cyrus for orders. "Show me your darkness, and I'll show you mine, Darling."

She saw Sorin emerge from the doors, Eliza and Rayner coming up behind him a moment later, but Cyrus held up a hand to halt him. Sorin signaled the guards to close the doors, which they promptly did. Cyrus stepped farther into her shadows, flames wreathing his own wrists and winding through his hair, swirling with her shadows. "Darling, my darkness was left in a clearing, exacting revenge for my love, who was slaughtered in front of me. I can certainly dredge it back up if that's what you desire, but I find it much more fitting to unleash it on my actual enemies." Scarlett saw the others stiffen. Her own shadows seemed to freeze in place. He took another step towards her. "We all have shadows, Scarlett. We all have nightmares. We all have regrets. We all have darkness. You get to decide how much control that darkness gets over you."

Scarlett held his eyes. "What was her name?" she asked softly.

"Thia." The pain that flashed across his face was heart-wrenching.

"How?"

She could tell he understood the question. Not how did she die, but how did he continue to laugh? How did he continue to put one foot in front of the other? How did he not let the darkness win?

"Time. It's hard to see a way out," he said softly. "Most do not understand that the darkness can be beautiful, but you don't learn that until you've come to understand that the darkness is not something to defeat but something to befriend. All stars are born in the dark, Scarlett. The darkness allows us to see them. You decide if they are worth fighting for."

Her shadows swirled, and Cyrus let his flames mingle with them. She held his gaze as she said quietly, tears glimmering in her eyes, "My mother was slaughtered in front of me when I was nine. Slowly. I hear her screams of pain in my sleep, but they get over-shadowed by the constant replaying of when I was forced to kill my sister by plunging a dagger into her heart to save a little girl after I was raped in exchange for the freedom of my family."

"Holy fuck," she heard Eliza mutter in horror.

"Mikale visited me tonight, before the feast, touching me. His hands roaming where they willed. He told me that if I figured out who had my mother killed, I would figure out who is behind the attacks on my people in Baylorin. I either feel nothing at all or I feel everything all at once, and I can't decide if it's truly worth it any more, Cyrus. I sometimes don't believe I will find my way back. "

Sorin began striding to her in an instant, but Cyrus gripped her hands first and replied, "I'll let you in on a secret, Darling. The stars are always worth fighting for."

A fire portal burst to life behind her. Sorin scooped her into his arms and stepped through.

CHAPTER 15

CALLAN

Callan watched the Prince of Fire finally coax a small smile from Scarlett and tug her closer to him. He watched her hold his gaze, as if there were no one else in the entire godsdamned world.

"You need to let her find her way, Princeling," Eliza said, clearly noting where his attention still lay.

"What?" he asked, pulling his gaze from Sorin and Scarlett to the female he was dancing with.

"She is sorting through a lot of new information right now. You need to let her do so."

"You mean I need to let *him* help her sort through it all."

"Sorin. Cyrus. Prince Briar. The cook. The shop clerk in the city." Eliza shrugged. "Whomever she turns to, not whomever shoves themselves into her path every chance they get." She gave him a pointed look. "You could have just danced with her, but instead you pushed her. She will come to you. When she is ready. She cares too much about you to just walk away." The song ended, and Eliza stepped from him. She opened her mouth to say something else, but her attention snagged on the entrance doors. Callan followed her gaze to see Cyrus and Scarlett walk through the doors. A moment later, a flash of shadows.

A flame had Eliza reaching up and snagging a note from it. Her lips formed a thin line, and she muttered a curse under her breath. She had pulled a lethal-looking hairpin from her hair as she incinerated the note and strode quickly for the doors. Rayner was already there as Sorin casually walked through, following Cyrus and Scarlett. Whatever had happened would apparently take all five of them to deal with it.

Callan turned and walked in the opposite direction, out through the mezzanine doors. Stone steps led from the balcony and wound down to a path that led to the main gates of the Fiera Palace. He found himself striding quickly down the path. He had been to the city with Finn and Sloan a few times and could find his way, even if it was dark. He would find a tavern and drink himself into oblivion for the night.

"Maybe we shouldn't leave the palace at night," Finn suggested, falling into step beside him, Sloan on his right.

"We've been told we're not prisoners. We can do as we wish," Callan snapped, ripping his mask from his face.

"They have alluded to dangers in these mountains numerous times, Callan," Finn tried again.

"Do you not have swords?"

"Yes, but we do not have *magic*," Sloan drawled.

"Then stay here," Callan bit back as he prowled past the entrance gates. The guards didn't even acknowledge him.

"What is the plan here then, Callan? We're to stay here until you convince her that you are meant to be together or until she convinces you that you're not?" Sloan sneered after him.

"Shut your fucking mouth," Callan snarled. The moonlight illuminated the road, but the shade of the trees still made his eyes strain as he followed it.

"This is her world, not yours," Sloan growled.

But another growl made them all go still.

Two enormous black wolves emerged from either side of the road, snarling softly. Finn and Sloan immediately shoved him behind them, swords angled. Callan glanced over his shoulder. He hadn't realized how quickly he'd been walking. He must have been near running for how far behind them the palace was now. There was no way they'd outrun wolves that big.

A beautiful female seemed to step from the very night right in between the wolves. She had flowing mahogany hair with white flowers woven into it that seemed to float on a gentle phantom breeze. She wore a cobalt blue dress that grazed the ground and had a bracelet around her wrist along with twin swords strapped to her back.

"Well, this is interesting," she said, cocking her head to the side. The movement was as lupine as the wolves beside her. "What is a mortal Crown Prince doing in the Fire Court?"

"I am here as a guest of Prince Sorin," Callan said, grateful he sounded more confident than he felt.

"Is that so? Interesting indeed," she mused. She reached a hand out, scratching the ears of the wolf on her right. "I hope my pets did not alarm you?" When none of them spoke, she said, "You look like your father did when he was your age." Callan started. His father? So he had indeed had dealings with the Fae in the past. "Did you come with her then?" the female continued when still no one spoke.

"With who?" Callan countered.

"The female who bears my sister ring," she replied, holding up her right hand. The ring that glittered in the moonlight looked exactly like the ring he had often seen on Scarlett's finger. The ring she had said her mother had given her.

"I do not know whom you speak of," Callan lied.

The female clicked her tongue. "From royalty to royalty, Crown Prince, let's not begin this relationship by lying to one another." She took a step towards them but came no further.

Royalty?

"Are you the Princess of the Wind Court?" Callan asked, racing through all the history he had read the last few days.

A smile spread across her lips. "No, although the winds do obey me." A gentle breeze blew past them, ruffling his hair in emphasis.

"Along with the earth." She held open a hand and a small white flower bloomed in the very center of it, which she then crushed in her fist, letting the pieces float away on her breeze.

"Then…" He started at the realization and bowed his head. "That would make you the Fae Queen."

"Indeed it would," she confirmed. She took a few steps to the right, almost like she was beginning to pace. "You have figured out your riddle. Now for me to figure out mine, hmm? A mortal prince is a guest of the Fire Prince." She seemed to spit out the words 'Fire Prince' as if they tasted sour. "You have returned with him at the same time he brings a female and my ring home, which would suggest you are important to her." She paused her pacing, her jade green eyes snapping to him and narrowing. "Are you her husband?"

"No." The word came out more bitterly than he had intended.

Her smile became a knowing one. "No, but you wish to be. Interesting. She is your lover?"

"Yes," he ground out from between his teeth.

"Still?" Her brows arched in surprise.

"That remains to be seen."

"Interesting."

"Stop saying that," Callan hissed. Finn elbowed him in a clear warning to watch his tone.

"Do you have an objection to the word?"

"I have an objection to the repetition of it when you fail to explain what exactly you find so interesting."

"Where are you off to in the night by yourselves?" the Fae Queen asked with a smile, resuming her pacing.

"If you must know, to the city to find a tavern and drink," Callan drawled.

"There were not drinks at the festivities this evening?" she asked, noting the masks they now held in their hands.

"Why does it matter to you?"

"Callan," Finn hissed.

"It matters to me when a mortal prince is in my lands, and I am not informed of it. Do you know the mess it would create if something should happen to you, Crown Prince of Windonelle? I'm sure the Prince of Fire did not think of such things when he brought you here with her," she said with a sneer. "Who is she?" She leveled those jade eyes at him, and they seemed to glow.

Callan just stared back at the Fae Queen with a frankness he couldn't hide. He wasn't going to tell her anything.

"You care for her so much you would defy me? How charming. You are either very brave or very stupid," she purred.

"What?" Callan asked, looking at her sharply.

"Who attempts to steal her affections from you?" the Fae Queen asked, her eyes narrowing slightly.

"Who doesn't?" Callan muttered under his breath.

Her brows rose again. "Is she that beloved by so many?"

Damn that Fae hearing.

"Yes," Callan sighed. "She keeps many secrets and apparently bears many titles, but she is kind to those who cannot defend themselves, and her loyalty knows no bounds if you manage to secure it."

"Tell me, mortal prince, should you succeed in winning her over, how shall you feel in ten years when you are aging and she is not? How shall you feel in twenty years? Fifty? When you are old and wasting away on your deathbed, and she does not look much older than she is now?"

"What do you mean?"

"Surely you know the Fae are immortal, do you not? Prince Sorin himself is centuries old. She will have a Staying in a few years, and her body will age no more," the Queen said with a wave of her hand. "And your children? Will they inherit their mother's immortality, or shall they too waste away while she remains young, seeing her grandchildren and their children and their children's children die as well?"

"Stop," Callan ordered quietly.

"Things you should consider, Crown Prince, should you not, if you are to pursue her?" the Fae Queen asked with a half smile. "Unless you believe she would bind her immortal life to your own? To die when you die?"

"I would never ask that of her," Callan spat.

147

"Good," she replied coolly, her face going cold. "Come, Prince, let me buy your drinks this evening."

"I think we will just head back to the palace," Callan said. "It was a pleasure to meet you, Your Majesty." He turned to head back to the palace, but soft growls emanated from the wolves at her sides.

"Oh no, your Highness," the Queen purred. "I insist."

The earth below his feet shook. The road itself was moving, drawing them to her. She stood, not coming any closer. Almost like she couldn't. The wolves snapped their jaws, and Finn and Sloan angled their swords once more.

"Those are not necessary," she said sweetly, and vines appeared from the very ground they stood on, wrapping around their swords and swallowing them down into the earth.

"And what would my father say of the Fae Queen taking me against my will?" Callan demanded, pushing down the fear in his gut.

"I shall not harm you, Prince," she said with a smirk. "I only wish to visit more. I am sure there is much we can learn from each other, and I would like to discuss a matter I require your assistance with."

"What could I possibly assist you with that you cannot do yourself?" Callan asked, as they were shoved next to the wolves.

"I need to learn if my suspicions as to who she is are correct," the Fae Queen answered, "and now that you are outside his wards, we can talk more freely."

His wards. That's why she had been pacing and not coming any closer. "You are not free to go anywhere you wish in the lands you rule?" Callan asked casually, following her down the road.

"I suppose I am, but I do not want him to know I have been here. If I cross his wards, he will immediately be notified of my presence," she replied tightly.

"Because you do not get along," Callan said, recalling Eliza's words.

"My dealings with the Fire Prince are not your concern."

"As my relationship with the *female* is not yours." The Queen glared at him. "Perhaps, your Majesty, if you would like my cooperation, we could start with names."

"But I already know your name, Crown Prince Callan Solgard," she answered. At his quizzical look, she added, "I do know the ruling families of each land, Prince. As a queen, it is my duty to know the reigning powers."

"Has my father ever been here?" Callan asked. "I mean to any of the Fae Courts?"

"No. I have not had direct dealings with the mortal kings. We have eyes in the lands, but do not usually have direct contact, which makes it all the more interesting that you are here," she answered. They could see the city entrance ahead, and she paused. "Rather than go to the city and have my presence immediately reported, may I suggest we go to my home? I assure you the drinks are just as woe-forgetting."

Callan glanced at Finn and Sloan, who had remained quiet, letting him deal with the nobility as they always did. "I suppose that would be acceptable," he said cautiously.

"Delightful." And before he could say anything further, she took him by the arm, barely giving Finn and Sloan enough time to lunge for him before they were all pulled through the very air.

CHAPTER 16

SCARLETT

They were in the training courtyard on a bench along the entrance. Sorin was sitting with his legs stretched out before him, his ankles crossed. She was on her back, stretched along the bench, her head resting against his thigh, staring up at the sky. When he had stepped through the portal last night and set her down, she had silently walked to the dressing room, changed into a nightgown, and crawled into bed. After a moment, she heard him shuffle to the bathing room, and a while later, the bed shifted. Neither of them spoke. She tossed and turned, unable to sleep. After nearly an hour, Sorin silently got up and walked to his bookshelf, came back to the bed, ignited a soft flame, and read to her. She had no idea how long he had read, likely an hour or two, before she'd finally fallen asleep.

He let her sleep in this morning. She did not even feel him get out of bed. When she did finally wake, she did not go down to breakfast with the others. Camilla had come to clean their room, and she had sent her away, nestling down in the blankets. Her shadows seemed to overtake her.

Then Sorin had returned to the room.

"Up," he demanded, throwing open the curtains.

"You don't give me orders," she had growled, pulling the covers over her head.

He had proceeded to pull the blankets off the bed. All of them. "Up."

She threw him a vulgar gesture.

He had sauntered to the side of the bed, his hands in his pockets. He'd leaned over her and smiled. She knew that smile. That smile meant hell awaited her in training. That smile meant he was going to kick her ass by either making her run until she puked or make her actually try in weapons training. "Up, Princess. We leave for the courtyard in ten minutes. You can either get into training clothes, or you can go in that." He gave a pointed look at her nightgown.

True to his word, ten minutes later he brought them here. He'd walked straight to this bench and sat. She had narrowed her eyes at him, followed him to the bench, and here they were.

"If we are just going to sit here all damn day, I could have stayed in bed," she grumbled to him, toying with her shadows at her fingertips.

"I cannot decide," he said through his teeth, "whether to discuss my Second, who got drunk off his ass after bringing up Thia last night, or to ask when you were going to tell me godsdamned Mikale made contact with you again." His golden eyes were flame, and Scarlett sat up, swiveling to face him.

"You are upset with me?"

"Why did you not tell me of Mikale?"

"You were busy, Sorin," she sighed. "I wanted you to enjoy the feast, your people. You've sacrificed so much for them."

"I am never too busy for you," he said, the flames banking in his golden eyes as they searched hers.

"You are a prince with responsibilities. I get that. I've lived with that for the last two years."

"I am not him. It is not fair of you to compare us. Our lives are very different. Our responsibilities are very different."

"Yes, they are. You have even *more* responsibilities." Sorin opened his mouth to say something, but she cut him off. "How is Cyrus?"

"Cyrus is hungover," he replied, his lips thinning. "So naturally he is in the training ring with Eliza working off a temper." Scarlett grimaced. "He rarely speaks of her."

"Did you know her? Thia?" Scarlett asked, her eyes falling to her lap.

"Yes. She was a very powerful female. She was arrogant and a smart ass, and I've never seen anyone else so thoroughly have someone wrapped around their finger." He paused for a moment before saying, "The mission to save your mother. Do you remember in that story that Cyrus and I had a fight? He had wanted a very powerful female to stay on our side of the border, but I had pulled rank and she..."

Scarlett's eyes snapped back to his as her heart stuttered. "The female was Thia? Your bad call..." She trailed off, unable to say it.

Sorin nodded, pain and sorrow filling his eyes. "I told you that one bad call had so many rippling effects... Thia was his twin flame."

He seemed to be watching her carefully. "Those are real?"

"Of course they are real. Rare to find your own, even rarer to risk the Trials, but they are real."

"How long were they together?"

"Nearly two hundred years."

Scarlett started. "He still laughs and jokes and..."

"He did not. For many years. That he does so now is indeed remarkable. To lose your twin flame is to lose a piece of your soul. But I think his purpose in telling you of her, Scarlett, is that despite whatever hell you are forced to endure, there are still things worth living for."

The stars are always worth fighting for.

Cyrus's words from the night before echoed in her mind.

"He will always be alone?"

"He is not alone. They are not just my Inner Court. They are my family. He is my brother. As for a partner, he has taken other lovers, but none have come close to Thia. No one likely ever will.

He may find someone else at some point, but he is perfectly content with how things are for the time being." When Scarlett did not reply, he said, "Tell me of Mikale." He was leaning forward, his elbows resting on his knees now with his fingers interlaced, looking at the ground. She could hear him working to control his tone.

She swallowed. "He came to me in a mirror. When I was getting ready, he was there. He touched my reflection, and it was like he was touching me. I could feel him." She shuttered remembering the feel of his fingers on her neck. "He does not know where I am. I mean, he knows I'm in the Fire Court, but not exactly where I guess. He tried to get me to tell him how you were hiding me and told me his source in the Black Syndicate was upset about the newly enhanced wards around the orphans. When I asked who his source was, he told me if I figured out who had my mother killed, I would figure out who was behind everything."

"The Assassin Lord? You think he knows who I am?" Sorin said quietly.

"He wouldn't have had my mother killed though," Scarlett answered, toeing the dirt of the courtyard with her boot.

There was silence for several minutes. "I did not know you were there. When Eliné was killed."

"I was nine. I do not remember much of that day. It had been an ordinary day, but I remember my mother tucking me in that night. She had lingered, hugging me extra long, telling me how very much she loved me. There were tears in her eyes. I remember thinking it was strange, and I couldn't fall asleep after she left my room.

"I went to find her, to ask her for some warm milk, and saw her leaving down the front walk in her cloak. Normally, this wouldn't have been odd. She was often called out for healing services at all hours, but she did not have her bag of supplies with her. I grabbed my own cloak and followed. She turned down an alley and when I followed, she heard me. She went pale and rushed to me. She asked me over and over what I was doing there. Tears were running down her face. Then she stilled, as if she heard another noise. She slid her ring onto my finger, hid me inside a trash bin in the alley, told me to close my eyes and not to make a sound.

"But I heard everything. There were two men. One asked where her ring was, how she would fight without it. I didn't know what it meant. Then he asked where she had hidden me. He had gone to the healer's compound for me first, but I was gone. I could see out of a little hole in the side of the can. I couldn't see the man who was speaking, but the one I could see was all in black, even had a mask over his face. He drew a dagger from his side, and my mother backed against the wall. The dagger was completely black, blacker than your own blades.

"I will spare you the details of how he took her apart. How she screamed. How I clamped my hands over my mouth to keep him from hearing me. I couldn't look away. I watched everything. He left the alley when he was done. Left her in pieces there. I vomited over and over in that trash can and sat in there for I don't know how long. Cassius eventually found me, somehow. He took me to the Fellowship where I was hidden away by the Assassin Lord, until everything began happening with the orphans. But now I wonder, if she had had her ring, if she could have fought." Her voice cracked in her throat as Scarlett tried to hold back the tears. "If I had not followed her, maybe she would have been able to save herself."

"No, Scarlett," Sorin breathed. "You cannot blame yourself. He said he came for you first. Had you not followed, you would have both been slaughtered."

"But she would have had a chance with her ring." Scarlett spun it around her finger. "She could have come home, to you and Talwyn, and fixed whatever the hell had gone wrong."

Sorin tilted her chin up with a finger. "No one gets to see what could have been, Scarlett, but you cannot focus on what is behind you if you want to move forward."

"Perhaps," was all she said, laying back down on the bench, resting her head on his thigh once more. The sky was clear blue, not a cloud to be seen. "Few know the details of that night. You officially know all of my secrets, Sorin Aditya."

Sorin began playing with her braid. "You have endured much in your short life, Scarlett Monrhoe."

"I am tired, Sorin," she said softly. "So, so tired."

"I know, Love, but you're not alone. You can rest here."

"Can I? Even here am I not still drowning? Is Mikale not finding me? Are the orphans not still sitting ducks? Do you not wish me to take a throne and take on the problems of two entire Courts?"

"Scarlett, you are alone in none of those things. Mikale cannot have you. We will figure out the orphans, and as for the Courts, that choice is yours. If you do not take the throne, nothing will change about how I look at you. If you want to move to a house in the mountains and live out your life there, I will make sure you are safe and fulfilled."

Scarlett fell silent as she looked up at Sorin, who was still fiddling with her braid. This day was absolutely perfect. Sitting with him, talking and being real. It was just perfect and wonderful, and she could breathe.

"Sorin?"

"Yeah, Love?"

"I don't blame you. For my mother's death. You are not responsible for that."

Sorin stilled, clearly not knowing what to say, but then he stiffened at the same moment she felt it. It was like an icy breeze with no wind. The hair on her arms stood on end, and gooseflesh appeared. They were both instantly on their feet. The boulders in the courtyard seemed to vibrate until one of the smaller ones exploded. A shield of flame from Sorin instantly surrounded them and bits of rock bounced off of it.

"Shit." His voice was pure dread. Scarlett watched as, with a finger, he drew some sort of symbol with flame that disappeared as quickly as he drew it. His eyes came back to hers, and he said, "I am so sorry."

"For what?" Scarlett asked, her eyes widening.

But Sorin turned to face the entrance to the courtyard, shoving Scarlett behind him.

"Hello, Prince of Fire."

Talwyn stepped into view, and Scarlett paled. Her radiance was even more profound in person. Talwyn's hair was braided to the side and over her shoulder. Bits of ivy and purple flowers were interwoven into it. She wore brown pants and a white tunic with fighting leathers over the top. Daggers and weapons adorned her, including twin blades strapped to her back. On her finger, she saw her ring, the twin to the one on Scarlett's own finger. Scarlett balled her hands into fists, trying to hide her ring from view.

"What are you doing here, Talwyn?" Sorin's tone was vicious.

"I told you our conversation was not over," Talwyn replied, her own tone as malicious as his.

"Then we will discuss this elsewhere. I will come to the White Halls. You have my word," Sorin replied.

"Your word means nothing to me," Talwyn drawled with a sneer.

A high-pitched whining sound reached Scarlett's ears. It sounded like claws were scraping down the stones of the courtyard walls. Scarlett pressed her hands to her ears, crying out as she dropped to her knees, the sound excruciating.

"I do believe it is time we met outside of the Forest, don't you?" Talwyn lilted.

"Stop this, Talwyn," Sorin snarled. "This is between you and me."

Scarlett could hear the panic in his voice. She had only heard that in his voice one other time— when he'd thought she was dying from the shirastone dagger wound in her side.

"It was between you and me until you brought others into it," Talwyn sneered, her eyes flashing with ire. As if blown in by unseen winds, Callan, Finn, and Sloan appeared, bound with vines around their wrists and gagged.

"Callan!" Scarlett cried. She shot to her feet and made to run to them, but Sorin gripped her wrist, keeping her inside his shield. Finn's eyes were wide as he beheld them all. Sloan's face was twisted with rage, but Callan's gaze was fixed on her. She couldn't read his face, his eyes.

No. No! This wasn't happening again. She flashed back to a

cold dungeon cell when Cassius, Nuri, and Juliette had been led into the room to get to her.

The earth buckled beneath her feet, and Scarlett found herself stumbling outside of Sorin's shield and towards Talwyn. She was ripped from Sorin's grip, and she felt his flames reach for her, but the air was sucked from them.

"Don't worry, Prince of Fire," Talwyn crooned. "I am not going to do anything to her. We just need to talk." Talwyn snapped her fingers, and Scarlett was trapped in a swirling vortex of wind with no way out.

"Sorin!" she cried, but her voice was carried away on the whirling winds.

Ashes and smoke appeared behind Sorin, and Rayner stepped from them, his blades drawn.

"Welcome, Ash Rider," Talwyn drawled. "I assumed you would arrive shortly after I did."

Rayner's eyes went from Sorin to Scarlett and back.

"She is your concern, Rayner, not me," Sorin yelled. He drew his own swords from his back, and Scarlett's breath caught as flames ignited down the blades. He stepped towards Talwyn, but a gust of wind slammed into him.

Scarlett cried out as he was thrown backwards, but again her voice was carried away by the whirlwind she was trapped in. Rayner vanished into smoke and reappeared just outside the vortex.

"Rayner!" she cried. "Help him!"

"He can handle himself, Scarlett," Rayner replied, his voice calm and steady, even though he was yelling to be heard over the raging winds. He was walking around the whirlwind, his hands up with smoke and ashes pouring from them, as if searching for any weakness in the vortex.

"She just threw him against a wall!" Scarlett cried.

Still focused on the tempest before him, Rayner shot a quick glance to Sorin. "He is not using the full extent of his power, Scarlett. He is barely tapping into it."

"Where are Cyrus and Eliza?"

"They are coming as fast as they can," Rayner answered. Then he swore under his breath as he realized there was no way to get to her.

"Go to Callan and the others. Help them!" she screamed at Rayner, but he made no move to do so.

"She has them in invisible wind prisons, Scarlett. They cannot hear anything that is being said. They can only watch it happen. We cannot get to them."

"Tell her to give me that ring, and we can end all of this now," Talwyn was saying to Sorin. Scarlett watched in horror as what she had thought was a bracelet began uncoiling from around Talwyn's wrist like a snake. It sparked and crackled like lightning, turning into a whip that Talwyn now held in her hand.

"It is hers, and no one tells her to do anything," Sorin growled. He stepped forward again, and this time when the winds blasted towards him, he held his footing.

A wicked smile spread across Talwyn's lips. "Don't waste your strength, Sorin," she taunted. "We both know you are feeling a little...less than these days."

Talwyn brought her whip back, but before she could bring it forward, it was wrapped around a flaming blade from behind. Talwyn whirled in surprise. Eliza stood behind her, holding that sword. It was the most gorgeous blade Scarlett had ever seen.

"I underestimated your speed," Talwyn snarled.

"You underestimate me a lot, your Majesty," Eliza tossed back.

If looks could kill, Eliza would have been dead from the glare that Talwyn threw at her.

Cyrus appeared at Rayner's side, swearing viciously when he beheld what she was encased in.

"Cyrus, go help Callan!" Scarlett cried again, but he, too, made no move to do so.

Talwyn jerked her arm, and the whip came back to her. She turned back to Sorin. "None of this is necessary, you fool," she growled.

"You are the one who accosted us, my *Queen*," he answered. The venom that dripped from the word queen was palpable.

"Enough of this," Talwyn cried. With a sickening thud, Sorin and every member of his Inner Court were hurled to the edges of the courtyard on winds that would have ripped trees from the ground. Restraints of what appeared to be tree roots grew from the cracks of the stone walls pinning the others to them. Sorin was on his feet in an instant, but Talwyn was already on top of him, her whip coiled around his throat.

"I know who she is, Sorin." Her voice was low and cruel. "I know why she has that ring. How dare you keep her from me. She is my own blood."

Scarlett stilled inside the whirlwind. She knew. She knew they were cousins. How had she figured it out? How long had she known?

"I know you care nothing for me," she continued to Sorin, "but do you truly hate everything and everyone in the White Halls that much? Did your love die with Eliné?"

Sorin was struggling against that whip around his throat. Flames surrounded his hands as he tried to wrench it free. His Inner Court was thrashing and cursing against their own restraints.

"Do it, Sorin!" Eliza cried from where she struggled.

"No! Don't!" Cyrus bellowed.

Talwyn clicked her tongue. "What ever will you do, Sorin? Shall you waste that slowly draining well?"

Scarlett couldn't focus on what they were saying. She couldn't even try to decipher what they were referring to. Her breathing was ragged. Her shadows were whipping around her, slamming against the walls of the wind vortex. She could hardly draw a deep enough breath into her lungs, and she wondered if Talwyn was doing that, too.

Trapped. She was trapped. She was locked up. In a cage. Again. She was helpless as she watched them. She looked at Callan, eyes wide in disbelief. Sloan looked murderous as he struggled against his bonds. Finn was taking everything in, calculating. She looked at Eliza and Rayner. She looked to Cyrus, fighting with all he had not to get to Sorin but to get to *her*. His eyes were fierce as he locked them onto her own. "Fight!" he bellowed at her. "The stars are worth it!"

She turned and saw Sorin struggling. Sorin, who had not left her, who had come for her every single time. Sorin, who had come down into the pits of hell for her, coming back every time she slipped and slid back in. Sorin, her light in the darkness. She flashed back to laying on a cold stone floor. She flashed back to another wicked grin of victory, of eyes delighting in her misery and suffering. Not again.

Not again.

Not again.

The stars are always worth fighting for.

Flames, white as starlight, erupted all around her. The whirlwind blew apart. Talwyn screamed as she was blasted across the courtyard, the thick tree roots holding the Inner Court slackened. Scarlett landed on her feet, floating to the ground on her shadows. She needed a damn blade. She ran across the rocky ground of the courtyard, desperate to get to Sorin. She wasn't even halfway to him, and Talwyn was already getting to her feet, shock and fury mixing on her features.

"Eliza! She needs a sword!" Sorin shouted.

Eliza cried out words in the Old Language. She was scrambling to her own feet, all of the Inner Court were, but none of them were moving fast enough to get to Scarlett before Talwyn.

Flames appeared before Scarlett, and when they were gone, a sword lay before her. The blade was the black metal that Sorin's weapons were made of, but the hilt shone as white as the flames that had erupted from her moments earlier.

"No!" Talwyn screamed.

Scarlett had the sword in her hand before Talwyn could take another step. As soon as her fingers touched the hilt, the same white flames encompassed the blade. As she held that blade before her, she felt all the rage and fury and hurt and pain and loss that she'd experienced these last years come crashing into her. She had finally found a place she belonged. She had found someone who came for her. She had found people who did not fear her darkness but understood it. People who wouldn't leave her alone. She had found home.

To hell with whoever tried to take that from her again.

She felt Sorin and the others racing up behind her, and she felt Talwyn rally her power to blast them back. She knew what to do in her bones. Her power was yanking at the leash, straining to take over.

So she let it.

She placed the tip of the blade to the ground, and a wall of that same white flame erupted between them and Talwyn, shooting towards the sky. Talwyn's power could not cross it.

"How did you come across that sword?" Talwyn seethed, not at her or Sorin, but at Eliza.

"There's that underestimating again, your Majesty," she answered with a derisive grin. Scarlett could feel the hatred emanate off of Talwyn. She brought that whip of lightning up again, and this time when she brought it down, Scarlett met it with her own blade, stepping through her fire.

"Stay behind the flames," she heard Sorin command his Inner Court.

"I know who she is, Sorin," Talwyn crooned. Her voice had become lilting and calm again.

"Enough," Scarlett said. Her voice rang out, pure and commanding. Talwyn's eyes snapped to her own.

"You do not give orders here," Talwyn replied, a thin smile forming on her lips.

"I think you will find everyone here would disagree with you," Scarlett replied, matching Talwyn's icy tone.

"Have you finally come to claim your throne at last?" Talwyn asked, as a ball of the same lightning energy of her whip appeared in her hand.

"Scarlett!" Sorin cried, his voice full of warning. She felt him step beyond her wall of flame, and, as if in slow motion, she saw Talwyn send that ball of energy hurtling towards him. She had no idea what she was doing or how she did it, but a ball of her white flames met Talwyn's orb of energy in the air, and the impact of those two powers meeting sent a blast through the courtyard that sent every one of them flying into the high walls surrounding them.

Scarlett stifled a scream at the cracking of bones in her forearm as she slammed into the stone wall. Sorin was at her side in an instant, a shield of flame surrounding them both. Rayner appeared out of smoke and ashes beside them, holding the sword that Eliza had summoned for her. He added his own shield to Sorin's and a few moments later, Cyrus and Eliza had joined them, reinforcing with their own shields. Sorin helped Scarlett to her feet, and she choked down a scream at the stabbing pain in her abdomen. She knew that pain. Her ribs were bruised at best, broken at worst. As Talwyn approached them, Scarlett pushed past that agony, adding a layer of white flames to their shields.

"This is a family matter," Talwyn hissed, her face white with rage.

"*This* is my family," Scarlett replied. The pain in her arm was sharp, and her vision was blurring as she tried to breathe around the pain in her ribs, but her voice did not waiver. Her knees did not buckle.

"There is so much you do not know," Talwyn answered, and Scarlett could have sworn there was a hint of panic in her voice.

"I know enough," Scarlett replied, and frost began creeping up the walls of the courtyard.

Talwyn's attention turned to Sorin, hatred filling her eyes. "You have failed yet again, Prince."

"Do not speak to him like that," Scarlett snapped, and a dagger of ice appeared at Talwyn's throat.

Talwyn merely brushed it aside. The dagger clattered to the floor, shattering. "Best to stick to fire tricks in the Fire Court," Talwyn replied sweetly. "And what of your mortal lover?" She turned, advancing on Callan, Finn, and Sloan.

"Leave them alone," she seethed at Talwyn. She made to step from the shields, but Sorin gripped her arm.

"I will get them," he panted.

"No," Scarlett said coolly. She speared her shadows out from herself. They slithered along the ground straight to Talwyn. Scarlett wrapped them around her ankles and yanked, sending Talwyn sprawling to the ground.

This time, when she made to step from the shields, Sorin let her go. She strode quickly to Callan and the others. With a thought, the vines encompassing them were burned to ash, along with whatever invisible shields were around them. Talwyn was back on her feet, winds whipping around her and lightning flickering at her fingertips. Flames surrounded Callan and his men, shielding them from Talwyn.

"How did you do that?" she demanded.

A smile, as serpentine as Talwyn's had been, formed on her own lips. She took a step towards the Fae Queen. Her shadows curled around Talwyn, sliding up her body, wending around her throat. "I know more tricks than fire and ice," Scarlett purred. She watched Talwyn wince as the shadows bit into her skin. "If you ever come near Prince Callan or his guards again, I will kill you."

"You could try," Talwyn replied, her voice low with challenge.

Scarlett only gave her a bone-chilling smile, and let those shadows bite a little farther into her skin before reeling them back into herself.

Talwyn's eyes slid to Sorin where he still stood behind Scarlett's flames. "Prepare her well, Prince. In the little time you have remaining. She needs to control it to wield it, not just throw a magical tantrum when her life is in danger...or the lives of those she loves."

Then, just like the night Scarlett had watched from Sorin's balcony, Talwyn disappeared, as if she'd never been there at all.

CHAPTER 17

CALLAN

Callan lurched for Scarlett as Talwyn disappeared. Sorin and his Court were across the courtyard racing towards them. He caught her before she slumped onto her clearly broken arm. Things had gone wrong. So horribly wrong.

"Are you all right?" she rasped, pain contorting her features as she cradled her arm to her body. And her eyes. They were silver and shimmering with unshed tears.

"I am fine, Scarlett," he whispered, brushing sweat-laden hair from her face. There was a cut along her cheekbone, and blood was trickling from it. "I am so sorry."

"For what?" Confusion flitted across her face, but before he could explain, the Fire Court stood before him.

"Go, Rayner," Sorin ordered. "Find Beatrix quickly."

Rayner stepped into smoke and ashes, and Sorin opened a fire portal before the rest of them. Callan stood, scooping Scarlett into his arms as he did so. She stifled a scream. Sorin stared at him, his eyes narrowing slightly, and his hands curling into fists at his sides. He couldn't possibly know he'd been with Talwyn last night, could he? Callan glared back, hugging Scarlett to his chest a little tighter. Her face was pale as she breathed through her teeth around the pain. "Go through," Sorin said with a jerk of his chin to the portal.

Callan stepped into a bedroom, Finn and Sloan right behind him. When Sorin stepped through last, the portal snapped shut. "On the bed," he said. Callan moved across the room and laid her down as gently as he could onto the huge fluffy comforter. She hissed at the movement.

"What do you need?" Callan asked, sitting on the edge of the mattress beside her, gripping her other hand tight.

"I'm fine, Callan," she said around a grimace. "You are truly all right? She didn't hurt you?"

"Not a scratch on me, my Wraith," he murmured soothingly, rubbing his thumb along the back of her hand. She closed her eyes, tears leaking from the corners to mix with the blood on her cheek. He looked at Sorin to find hard eyes gazing back at him. Eliza and Cyrus were dispersed throughout the room, looking rather uneasy, their eyes warily darting between him and Sorin. "I thought Fae could heal themselves?" Callan ground out to the Fire Prince.

"She can, but her bones are broken in more than one place, and she just used more magic at one time than she ever has before. She hasn't built up enough stamina and power reserves to dive that deeply so quickly and still have magic to heal herself," he snapped. "Our Healer will be here momentarily."

Her breathing was becoming uneven, and she tried to sit up, biting down on a scream at the pain. "Scarlett, a Healer is coming," Callan soothed, trying to push her back down. Her eyes were darting frantically around the room.

"She is going to be sick from the pain and from being shoved so deeply into her magic," Sorin said tightly, sending a trash basket to him on a flame. Scarlett immediately vomited into it. She sat up, trying to catch her breath, clutching her abdomen. Her whole body was trembling now. Callan ran a hand down her back. Her body was like ice, though flames danced at her fingertips, swirling amongst the shadows. Smoke furled from her mouth as she vomited not the contents of her stomach but ice and water. She cried out in pain with every convulsion.

"Breathe, Scarlett. Breathe. The Healer is coming," he murmured.

Helpless. He was utterly helpless to help her. Her shadows were thickening with each ragged breath. The magic she had displayed moments ago? Holy gods. It had been a hundred times more powerful than what she'd done on the day they'd arrived here.

"You need to let me near her."

"What?" Callan turned to Sorin, who seemed to be trembling himself. With restraint, Callan realized. "No. She is here because of you! Why did you not protect her?" he snapped

"Let him take your place, Prince. Her magic is raging, and she will not be able to control it much longer. Her magic will run wild, not caring what it costs her," Eliza said, her tone a warning.

"No."

"Either move your ass willingly, or I will do so for you," Cyrus growled from near the balcony doors.

"What can he do? He said himself we are waiting on a Healer."

"This is not a pissing contest, Prince. Move your ass," Cyrus snapped, beginning to prowl towards him.

"Callan," Finn hissed.

With a glare at all of them, he reluctantly moved from the bed. Sorin was beside her faster than Callan could blink. He watched as he took her uninjured arm, placing her hand flat against his chest. "Breathe," he soothed, stroking her hair with his other hand. "Focus. Make us match. Like we have done every other time."

Every other time. They had done this before. Sorin had helped her through whatever this was before.

"Where is the Healer?" Scarlett gasped out between breaths.

"She is coming. You can do this. You've been through worse. I've put you through worse. Do you remember that time I made you run so long you vomited and then I made you run some more just because I could?"

"Do you remember the time I punched you in the face?" she muttered.

"There you are, Love," he whispered, pressing a kiss to her forehead. Callan's heart constricted as she leaned into him, her forehead going to his chest, just above her hand. "Breathe, Love." Sorin's voice was so tender, so gentle. He loved her. Sorin loved her as much as he did. Callan suddenly felt like *he* was going to be sick.

Her trembling lessened while she sat, focusing on her breathing, Sorin's hand soothingly rubbing her back. No one said a word as they watched the Prince steady the Wraith, her shadows brushing down his cheek, his arms. "None of today was your fault. Do you understand me?" Sorin said gently but firmly when her breathing had evened out, tilting her face up to look into her eyes. Callan could see the doubt flickering in them. "Scarlett, they are safe. They are unharmed. It was not your fault."

There were running footsteps, and an older woman rushed into the room, Rayner a step behind her. She was the same Healer who had been there that first day here. She crossed the room to Sorin, took one look at Scarlett's arm, and pressed a hand to her cheek. White light flared from her hand, and Scarlett was instantly asleep. Sorin gently laid her back on the pillows and stood back to let the Healer work. They were murmuring quietly to each other as she focused on Scarlett's broken arm. Then she shifted her attention to somehow magically binding her ribs that had Callan gaping slightly.

While their focus remained on Scarlett, Callan took the moment to look around the room. The suite was huge. A desk and bookshelves lined the walls. Two overstuffed chairs sat in the front of the fireplace, a male's cloak draped over one. His eyes drifted to the balcony doors where Cyrus still stood, leaning against the wall, his arms crossed. There was a chaise beneath the window, and weapons lay strewn across it. Weapons he recognized. *Her* weapons.

He looked around the rest of the room. Were these her chambers or his? He glanced to Eliza, who stood by the bedroom door, whispering with Rayner, but she met his eyes. Her lips formed a grim line. To her right was an open door to a dressing room, and he could glimpse female clothing hanging. Her room then.

"She will sleep for a couple hours and be pain free, but she will need to take it easy the next few days. She will be sore, and those rib breaks will take some time. She is weakened from draining her magical reserves improperly," the Healer said, her voice crackled with age.

"Thank you, Beatrix," Sorin replied, bending to brush a kiss to the woman's cheek.

"And you, Prince?" the aged Healer asked, a half smile on her lips. She raised her hand to his forehead where a gash was still healing, presumably from when Talwyn had thrown him against the wall. A flare of white light and it was gone. Not even a mark. "Anyone else?" The Healer surveyed the room. When no one replied, she took her leave.

Sorin's gaze settled on him and his guards. The gleam in his eyes was half feral as he surveyed them. Cyrus and Rayner casually stepped between the two princes. "Another place, perhaps, Sorin?" Rayner said coolly.

"Take it to your sitting room," Eliza drawled from the doorway. "I'll stay with her."

Sorin stalked past her, leaving Callan with little choice but to follow when Cyrus and Rayner looked at him expectantly. He entered the sitting room and immediately recognized it as the room they had come to when they'd first arrived in the Fire Court. This had to be Sorin's private chambers. Not hers.

"How the fuck did she get past our wards?" Sorin seethed at Cyrus and Rayner, flames appearing in his eyes.

"I don't know," Cyrus answered bitterly, violence and rage dancing across his features.

"I already have spies looking into it," Rayner added in his quiet, lethal voice.

"Not a single one of us felt her? That is not fucking possible." Sorin's gaze was murderous as he leveled it at Callan. "Where were you when she took you?"

"We were not at the palace," Sloan cut in with a snarl.

"What do you mean you were not at the palace?" Sorin asked with a deadly, calm rage.

"As I recall, we are not prisoners and are free to leave when we wish," Callan retorted.

"When? When did she come for you?" Cyrus cut in. Rayner had

positioned himself between the princes once more. They were both tense as they glanced from one another and back to Sorin.

"Last night. We were going to the city to drink after you lot all left with Scarlett. She met us on the path. In fact, she knows exactly where your wards stop and would not cross it herself or allow her wolves to cross," Callan answered.

"Her fucking wolves are in the mountains?" Sorin snarled.

Rayner was gone in smoke before the words had finished leaving his lips.

"If she would not cross the wards, then how did she obtain you?"

Callan swore. "I went with her willingly, all right?"

"You did what?" Sorin roared.

"Shit," Cyrus muttered, putting a hand on Sorin's shoulder.

"On it," Eliza called from the other room, clearly having heard every bit of the conversation.

"You willingly went with the queen for what purpose?" Sorin ground out from between his teeth.

"She wanted information on Scarlett. She asked for my help. I did not know that it would turn into this. I would never have agreed to such a thing," Callan bit back, working to keep his voice even.

"What kind of information did she want?" The venom in his voice made Callan flinch, and Finn and Sloan tensed, hands on their swords.

"Something to do with her ring. She said she had been trying to talk to her, and you had been preventing it. Having been in a similar situation, I could relate," Callan replied tightly.

"For what purposes did she want the information?" Sorin was visibly trembling again. With restraint or rage, Callan didn't know. Probably both.

There was a sound of swirling water and the Water Prince appeared. Why he was here, Callan didn't know. Briar took in the scene, locking eyes with Cyrus for a moment. "She was hurt?"

"A broken arm and some broken ribs," Cyrus confirmed grimly. Flames encompassed the room. "Beatrix was already here. She is sleeping and will be fine."

"How?" Briar demanded

"Our beloved queen learned of one of her weaknesses and took full advantage," Sorin replied. "She used *them* to bait her and shove her deep into her magic. When it collided with Talwyn's, we were all blasted into the damn walls. Then I come to learn that he went with her willingly and that he gave her information."

The Water Prince's eyes snapped to Callan. "What did you tell her?"

"I know little, so there is little for me to tell her. I would never have knowingly put Scarlett in danger. You cannot seriously believe I would."

"Your actions—" Sorin started, taking a step towards him.

"Sorin, let's go to the sparring ring. We will figure it out," Briar interrupted, a wicked-looking sword appearing in his hand amid a swirl of snow.

"Not until he tells us exactly what was said," Sorin snarled. Flames now appearing at his fingertips.

"Sorin, I more than anyone know what is coursing through you right now, but you are in no condition to be expending this much power," Cyrus said cautiously, a sword appearing in his own hand. "We will have them escorted back and discuss things later."

"We will discuss them now," Sorin seethed, and a blade wreathed in flames was in his hand.

"Eliza, we might need you," Cyrus called.

"You moronic males," the female chided, stalking from the bedroom. "This is why Drayce was summoned. So that I would not be needed." She was still in the leathers she had been in at the courtyard, her magnificent sword strapped to her back.

"He is riding a very dangerous edge. Briar and I will not be enough," Cyrus snapped.

"Cyrus, escort them back to the other side of the bridges. If I were you, Crown Prince, I would stay in your rooms the rest of the day," Eliza said in a bored tone.

"You are locking us in our chambers?" Finn asked in disbelief.

"No. I am suggesting that should you want to avoid a fiery Fae temper tantrum, you may want to make yourselves scarce, but the choice is yours," Eliza ground out.

"They are not dismissed, General," Sorin snarled.

Eliza erupted. She was a living pillar of flames the color of her hair, and Callan was shoved to the ground by Sloan. "They are, Prince," she snarled back, "or you and I shall have it out right here, and *she* sleeps in the other room, directly in the path of the destruction you and I would wreak. Or have you forgotten sixty years ago in Threlarion?"

Sorin bared his teeth as he stood perfectly still, glaring at her. Callan had seen Scarlett move through the world as a Wraith of Shadows. He had seen Death's Shadow herself. And the female ablaze before him rivaled them both. He could not decide of the three, who was the most terrifying.

"Let them go to their chambers, Sorin," she said calmly. "I will personally go to them and find out exactly what was said and report back."

"No," Sorin snarled.

Eliza's face went positively vicious. "Briar, please stay with Scarlett," she growled as she drew her blade from her back. "And get me a portal to the grounds."

Instantly a water portal appeared behind Sorin, and Callan could only watch in horror and amazement as that female flung herself at the Prince of Fire, tackling him through that portal.

"They are in the front so we can monitor," the Water Prince said gravely, crossing to the bedroom.

"You lot can get another escort or wait for me," Cyrus said without looking at them and following Briar.

Callan pushed himself to his feet and trailed them. Scarlett was sleeping soundly, the Healer's magic apparently putting her into a deep enough sleep that she had slept through all the commotion. Color had returned to her cheeks some, and her arm lay across her chest. She still wore the loose pants and tight shirt she had been wearing. The shirt was bunched up some, baring her midsection, and he could see where her abdomen was bound for her broken ribs.

He pulled his gaze from her to where the Fae males now stood out on the balcony. Finn and Sloan had followed them out and stood frozen, their faces pale. Callan quickly joined them and stilled as he watched the General and Fire Prince fighting on the front grounds. Each hit was precise. Their swords were blades of flames, sending sparks flying. He moved so fast, Callan could hardly keep track of him. Rage and temper fueled his every move. This was who had been training his father's High Force?

And Eliza? She flipped and twirled and moved in ways Callan didn't know were possible. Maybe the movements weren't even possible unless one was Fae. She held her sword in one hand and a dagger in the other, and for every thrust and attack and parry Sorin came at her with, she countered it with her own.

A ring of flames radiated from them as their blades met again with a force that shook the palace grounds. Callan could feel the faint vibrations from where he stood. "What exactly happened sixty years ago?" he asked, not entirely sure he wanted the answer.

The Fae males didn't take their eyes from below as Cyrus answered, "Sorin and Eliza had a disagreement. They leveled an entire neighborhood in Threlarion."

"You mean figuratively, right?" Finn said slowly.

"No, Sentry, I do not. It was an abandoned neighborhood, and they had enough sense to ensure it was empty before they got into it. But when they were done, they were both so bloody you could hardly recognize them, and there was nothing but rubble around them."

"They won't get that far today, will they?" Callan asked, unable to pull his gaze from the lethal beings below.

"I do not think so. It is why Eliza removed him from the palace itself, but should they seem close, Briar will intervene. Briar and Eliza together will be able to restrain him if necessary," Cyrus explained. "However, the fact that Scarlett lies sleeping in this building will prevent him from touching his deepest wells of power for that kind of destruction."

"This is all because of Queen Talwyn?" Finn asked.

"No," Prince Briar answered. He sounded distant, and his icy blue eyes were glowing. "This is because someone he cares deeply for was put in danger and hurt."

"Fae may be civilized and powerful, but in many ways, we are just as primitive as the wild animals of the forests and mountains," Cyrus cut in. "We can become just as feral when those in our charge, when our family, are in danger, and when it is one's— Well, when it is someone we care so deeply for, the urge to protect and defend can overtake us, despite our discipline and control."

There was a deafening boom as the blades below met again. Palace guards were standing around, watching the two. Callan couldn't smell fear like the Fae could, but it was tangible in the air around them. "Sorin needs to cease this," Cyrus murmured to Briar. "Until she accepts it, he can not expel this much power."

"I am tunneling into my power as quickly as I can," Briar replied. "I have been doing so since Eliza's message."

"Then do so faster," Cyrus bit back. "Unless we have Beatrix wake her..." Those glowing blue eyes turned to Cyrus.

Callan couldn't have heard right. Or maybe he misunderstood? They weren't seriously talking about waking Scarlett, were they? There was no way she could fight right now. The Healer had said she would sleep for a few hours and then needed to rest for a few days. They couldn't wake her up and expect her to pick up a sword. They wouldn't do that to her.

When another blast of power shook the palace, Briar turned to Cyrus. "Summon Beatrix. I could stop him, but it will get messier. She will stop it immediately."

Cyrus drew the flame message, and a few minutes later, the Healer rushed in. "We need you to wake her," Cyrus said, not bothering with formalities or explanations.

"She will be in intense pain," the Healer warned.

"Then it shall pull him from this madness faster," Cyrus ground out.

"You will use her for this purpose?" Callan demanded. "You will make her suffer even more?"

Briar turned those icy blue eyes upon him, and Callan forced himself not to squirm under the intensity. "We would, and perhaps you should see why."

Beatrix and Briar strode through the doors and back into the bedroom. Callan made to follow, but Cyrus stopped him. "Stay. Watch, Prince."

So he did. He watched as a few moments later, a water portal appeared on the grounds below. He watched Briar emerge, cradling Scarlett in his arms, the Healer with them. He watched as Briar gently set Scarlett onto her feet in the grass, supporting her as she cradled her middle. Eliza saw them, too, but too late to stop her next blow. Flames radiated from them, and Briar sent out a blast of water, dousing the flames and shielding Scarlett, the Healer, and himself. He watched as Sorin whirled and stopped short, his flames vanishing into nothing but wisps of smoke.

CHAPTER 18

SORIN

He couldn't see past the blinding rage. All he could feel was fury and terror. Scarlett had been hurt. She had a broken arm, broken ribs, and multiple bruises. She had been fucking bleeding. He hadn't been able to protect her. She had been shoved into her magical well so deeply, she couldn't even begin to heal herself.

And it was all because of that fucking mortal prince.

"Sorin!" Eliza cried. "Calm the fuck down!"

She caught his feint and met his blade. He had not sparred with Eliza in years. They had not fought in sixty. Her own flames clashed into his, and the reverberations could be felt in the ground beneath him. Eliza flipped back as he thrust again, and she barely avoided the hit.

"Sorin, you will level this whole damn place!" she ground out between her teeth as he struck again. "She is in there! She is safe! She is healing!"

He knew this. In the back of his mind, he knew what she said was true. He knew he was being irrational, but the savage rage coursing through his veins could not be quelled. He could not quiet it, could not douse it.

"He put her in danger!" he seethed, attacking again.

She caught his blade between her own sword and dagger, shoving him back. "He did not know! Talwyn is cunning and conniving. He was tricked. He is a mortal who knows nothing of the rest of the world, Sorin."

"He is a mortal who is in love with her and thought Talwyn would help him take her from me," he snarled.

"She is no one's damn property," Eliza growled, and Sorin had to shield against her own attack. He was panting as he dodged her blow, forced to retreat a few steps. "The two of you need to back off and give her space to figure out her own shit."

"Why do you think I have not told her of the twin flame bond?" Sorin seethed again.

"Because you are a fucking coward," she sneered.

Sorin felt his power surge up, and with it pain that he blocked out, lunging for her once again. He saw her dredge up her own power, and just before their blades met, her eyes widened in horror. Power emanated from their strike, and he felt a spray of water. Great. Now fucking Drayce was here to try to quell him, too.

He whirled, ready to take them both on with the blinding rage that burned through him at the thought of his twin flame being in such danger, and he froze. The flames along his blades guttered, and his eyes widened.

Briar was not alone. Beatrix stood near him, reproach and disappointment all over her face. Briar's arm was looped under Scarlett's shoulders, supporting her as she stood barefoot in the grass. She hugged her arm to her chest. He could see her grimace as she took a breath. The pain against her ribs had to be agony. Her eyes locked onto his, worry filling them.

"Sorin?" Her voice was barely a whisper, but he felt it in his soul. He felt her in his mind, using that bond she didn't even know existed.

What is going on? They said you were in danger. That I was needed.

"What is she doing here?" he demanded. The rage was there, boiling just beneath his skin, but he couldn't do anything. Not with her before him. "Get her back to our chambers. She is in pain."

"You need to stop, Sorin. You are not in a place to be expending this much power. She was the fastest way to reach you," Briar said. His voice rang with authority.

"That is not your call to make," Sorin snapped.

"Sorin." Scarlett said softly again, as though she were awake but still as sedated as possible. She took a step towards him and stifled a cry. She slowly lowered to her knees, Briar easing her down.

Sorin's chest cracked. He dropped his sword to the ground, rushing to her. "Love," he whispered, dropping to his own knees before her and taking her face in his hands. Her eyes had returned to their usual icy blue color, but they were dull and filled with pain as she sucked in a shallow breath.

"Make her sleep, Beatrix," he growled.

"Wait," Scarlett gasped, thrusting out a hand to stay Beatrix. She studied his eyes. "You are not all right."

"I am," he said softly, brushing her hair back. "I am fine, Love."

She pulled back slightly, glancing around at the others and up at Briar before her eyes came back to his. "Come back with me. I need you."

"Of course," he replied. He stood in a fluid motion, gathering her carefully into his arms. She cradled her arm, and tears leaked from the corners of her eyes. "Put her back to sleep."

"No," she gasped again. "Not until you are back."

"I am right here, Scarlett." He stepped through a fire portal, not caring if the others followed.

"You are not all right. Something is wrong," she said softly. Despite the exhaustion in her eyes, there was a clarity. He set her gingerly on the bed, flinching at her slight grimace. He stood and saw Cyrus...and the mortal prince.

His lip pulled back from his teeth and a low growl rose in his throat. Cyrus stepped between them, but before he could say a word, she spoke again.

"Sorin, I need you," she whispered, her hand reaching up and brushing his.

That was all it took. He understood now. He understood on the deepest of levels how Thia had so thoroughly wrapped Cyrus around her finger. He understood why seeing Scarlett in mortal danger had driven him to a brawl with his General. He understood the utter insanity that encompassed Cyrus for years when Thia had died. He understood that it did not matter that the person who put Scarlett in such danger stood in this room. She needed him, and his entire world revolved around that need.

Without a word, without another glance at Callan or his guards, Sorin toed off his boots. Water licked down his body, erasing the blood and sweat courtesy of Briar. He walked to the other side of the bed, laying down beside her. She reached out her hand once more. He took it gently, pressing a soft kiss to her fingertips, and placed it against his chest.

"Your heart is racing," she said around another grimace.

"Please let Beatrix help you sleep again."

She turned her head, looking into his eyes. He could hear the question in them.

Are you back?

"You brought me back, Love. Now rest," he murmured, pressing a kiss to her temple.

"You will stay?" she asked cautiously, suspicion etching along her features.

"Always," he whispered, running his nose down the length of hers.

Beatrix pressed her hand to her cheek, and Scarlett seemed to sigh in relief as she slipped back to sleep.

"Get out. All of you," he growled to the room. He didn't look away from the princess sleeping next to him to see if they obeyed or not. It did not matter.

CHAPTER 19

CALLAN

Callan felt a tug at his elbow at the Prince's growled order. He looked down to find a female hand there. Eliza had a grim look on her face, jerking her head to the door. His feet felt like lead as he followed her from the room. His mind was reeling from the events of the last hour.

The Fae Queen had asked for his help in obtaining an audience with Scarlett. She had said she had been trying to speak with her since her arrival, but Sorin had been interfering. She had explained that the ring was a family heirloom and incredibly valuable to her family. She only wished to know how Scarlett had come across it. Then she had asked if Scarlett had any tattoos. When Callan had told her no and that he indeed had knowledge to know if there were any hidden ones, the queen had become somewhat more with-drawn. She had also asked about Sorin's tattoos, but he had so many visible now that he couldn't tell her if any were new or not.

Callan had not known her plan until minutes before. They had eaten breakfast at her home. The White Halls, she had called it. When she returned to bring them back to the Fire Court without warning, she had trapped them in some sort of soundless prison and portaled them. He could hear nothing of what was going on outside the inaudible bubble. He could see the screaming and yelling. He watched as Scarlett was shoved into a swirling vortex, her eyes wide in terror.

But when Scarlett had exploded with her magic, his own terror shifted from terror for her to fear of her. She had wielded those flames as if they were extensions of her. She had threatened a gods-damned queen for him. Her concern had been for him and his safety. Even when she was writhing in pain, she questioned if *he* was hurt.

They all walked into the sitting room in silence, Briar gently closing the door behind them.

"Bold move, bringing her down into that," Eliza said softly.

"It was the only move we could make," Cyrus replied gravely.

The Water Prince was standing off to the side and looking nearly as livid as Sorin had before Eliza had tackled him through a portal. His eyes were as hard as chips of ice as he stared at Callan.

"Drayce," Eliza warned. "Perhaps it would be wise to go speak with Sawyer and make sure Talwyn doesn't make a similar visit to your own Court."

"I assume you two have things under control from this point?" Briar asked, his eyes dragging to her.

"We do. I doubt he will leave her side until she wakes," Cyrus answered.

Briar only nodded before exiting through a water portal.

Callan immediately felt himself relax a touch being out of his presence. "Whose rooms are these?" he asked, looking around the sitting room. Finn and Sloan were waiting by the main door. Even Sloan still looked a little shaken by the whole ordeal.

"They are the prince's private chambers," Eliza replied. "Come, I will escort you back to your own."

Callan obeyed, falling into step beside her. As they walked down the corridor, he steeled himself enough to ask, "Will you tell me if I ask which are *her* rooms? I assume they are not far from his."

"You assume correctly," Eliza said as they rounded a corner. "You were just standing in hers."

Callan stopped short, Finn nearly running into him. "They share rooms?"

"There is more than one bedroom in those chambers, Prince, but yes, they share the space," Eliza replied, not stopping for them.

"He does not even give Scarlett her own space?" Callan demanded, quickening his pace to catch up to her.

"He gave her the option," Eliza said with a shrug. "Despite what you seem to think of him, he is not forcing her into anything. In fact, he is doing quite the opposite." Her last words held enough of a bite to them that Callan knew not to press the matter, despite wanting to know what she meant.

Against his better judgment, he said, "It seems like he is deciding plenty for her."

"Like what?"

They went down a set of stairs before taking another corner. "He keeps people from her for starters."

"Like you?"

"Queen Talwyn said she has been trying to speak with her for weeks as well."

"Ah," Eliza said as the bridges came into view. "Tell me, Prince, what did the queen promise you in exchange for selling Scarlett out?"

"I did not sell her out," Callan retorted, leashing his temper.

"No? What did she ask of you?"

"Why would she ask anything of me?"

"Because the queen does nothing without motive. The queen does not grant favors out of the goodness of her heart," Eliza sneered.

"Maybe not to those who oppose her so openly," Callan countered.

"Do not guess at things you know nothing of, Princeling. What did she offer you in exchange for your services?" When Callan was silent, she went on. "You accused my prince of not protecting her moments ago, of willingly allowing his— Someone he cares deeply for to be injured. The fact of the matter is, had you not been involved in this, things would have gone very, very differently. Had

181

Scarlett not been distracted by you and your companions, her focus would have been on defending herself and not rescuing you."

"I was not told of the queen's plans."

"Of course you weren't. She doesn't tell anyone her plans, except maybe her lover, but before you so brazenly trust her over our own Court, perhaps you ought to consider your own motives for doing so. What did she promise you in return?"

They had crossed the bridges and were nearing their own suite.

"She asked me if she had any tattoos. When I told her no, she seemed upset by that. Then she asked about Sorin's tattoos, but I could not tell her anything about those. She was also very interested in Scarlett's ring. She has a matching one and said it was a valuable Fae family heirloom."

"Did she say why she was so interested in whether or not Scarlett had any Marks?" Eliza asked, following them into their rooms. She shut the door behind her, leaning against it. Finn and Sloan immediately departed for their own rooms, clearly not seeing a threat any more.

"Marks?"

"The tattoos," Eliza said impatiently, gesturing to the swirls and ink that adorned her own skin.

"No."

"And what was your reward for being her source of information?" Eliza asked. Callan just stared at her, holding her gaze. "Ah, a guessing game it shall be then." She tapped her chin as if thinking long and hard. "Considering everything you've done since your arrival here has revolved around Scarlett, I'm going to guess it has something to do with her. Did she offer to help give you a private moment with her?"

"No," Callan said through gritted teeth.

"Did she offer to send you back to your mortal lands and deliver her there?"

"No."

"I don't have time to guess all day, Princeling," Eliza said, her tone going cold. "You can either tell me what happened, or Sorin will come to extract it himself."

"I am not afraid of him," Callan snapped. That was a gods-damn lie. He was terrified of the prince.

"You should be," Eliza said, a cruel smile spreading across her face. "Our methods of obtaining information are most unpleasant, and because this has to do with *her*, he will use whatever means necessary."

"He loves her?" Callan asked.

"I think you know the answer to that."

Callan bristled inwardly at the answer. "Does she return the sentiment?"

Eliza paused, studying him carefully. "We all have our suspicions and opinions on that, but the truth remains to be seen," she finally answered.

"Tell me your best guess," Callan challenged.

"It is not my place. Tell me what she told you."

"She did not tell me anything. She gave me access to a book for a few hours, which I spent all night reading."

"What sort of book?" Eliza asked, her brows rising in surprise.

"A book of Fae customs and history," Callan answered. The shock and adrenaline of the day's events were wearing off, and exhaustion was sinking in. He crossed to the liquor cart in their sitting room, pouring himself a knuckle's length of whiskey.

"Was that your asking price?" Eliza asked, watching him carefully.

"No. I asked her if Fae royalty were required to marry royalty and nobility as is custom in the mortal lands. From the little bit I've been able to observe since being here, the lands seem similar in that at least."

Eliza noticeably stiffened at his words. "They can be," she replied slowly.

"Instead of giving me a straight answer, which seems to be a common Fae trait, she pulled a book from the air and told me it was mine to peruse until she returned me here." He took a sip of the alcohol.

"And what did you learn?"

"I learned that marriages are often arranged between powerful bloodlines to breed power into the royalty."

"Did that ease your worry of their relationship?"

Callan clenched his jaw, a muscle feathering in it. "Not particularly, since it has been hinted that her own bloodline is powerful. Is that not why Mikale wants her? Is that why Sorin wants her?"

Eliza bared her teeth at him and a growl left her throat. "Careful, Princeling," she warned. "What else did you learn?"

"I learned that Fae believe there are bonds between souls and that two in particular surpass any other type of relationship."

"And...?"

"And that while Sorin has the twin flame Mark on his left hand, Scarlett does not." When he had read those particular pages, he had sunk to the couch in his small room in relief. The twin flame bond took precedence over anything and everything. It was a bond deeper than marriage, deeper than love. It was an inexplicable union of the souls that persisted beyond death. The Marks were taken together, though. "Who is his twin flame then?"

Eliza's eyes hardened. "That is not for me to say, especially since you seem so willing to divulge information to Queen Talwyn. If she knew that sort of information, she could use it against him."

"You said if I found a book about the twin flame bond, you would answer my questions."

"I did," Eliza said with a nod.

"So they take this Mark and that's it?"

"No," Eliza said slowly. "The Mark is an offering of their souls to each other. A Claiming Rite is spoken when the Mark is given and initiates the Trials. They must face four Trials that strengthen their bond. If they complete them all, the bond is Anointed, sealing them as each other's for eternity. It is rare to find one's twin flame."

"And what of one's soulmate?" He had read about those, too. Twin flames were equals in every way. They were companions and lovers and linked in magic and soul. But a soulmate was one's closest friend. There was no physical component with soulmates, just a kindred soul connection.

"What of it?" Eliza asked.

"Are they soulmates? Sorin and Scarlett?"

"What do you think?"

"I think it would make sense if they are. The connection they seem to have. How he can talk to her, help her. How protective he is of her."

"If they are, would you hold it against them?"

"No. I would not like it, but I cannot control such a thing."

"And you could control other facets of their relationship?"

He paused at her question. "Are soulmates ever lovers?"

"No. There is no romantic intimacy between soulmates. Only a deep love and connection of the soul," Eliza answered.

"He wishes for more from her."

"Does he?" Eliza asked, cocking her head to the side.

"It is evident in the way he looks at her. I am not stupid or blind to such a desire, as I am sure it is a mirror of my own," Callan replied coldly. Eliza did not respond. "What does his twin flame have to say about his lusting after another female? Does she not live in this palace?"

"The twin flame bond is not always accepted by both parties," Eliza answered with a shrug of her shoulders. "It does not happen often, but sometimes one or both do not want the bond, despite the pull of it. Sometimes the Fates get it wrong. Just because it exists does not mean one must submit to it."

"She rejects the twin flame bond, or he does?"

"I did not say either of them rejects it. I do not know where she considers her home to be."

"Could you be any more vague?" Callan asked in frustration, running a hand through his brown hair and pushing it back from his face.

"I'm sure I could," Eliza replied with a smirk.

"Can you give me one straight answer? A yes or a no?" Callan asked, gripping his glass tighter.

"That depends on the question."

"Are Sorin and Scarlett soulmates or not?"

"No, I do not think that they are," Eliza answered.

"Will he reject his twin flame bond for her?"

"You said one straight answer. I have fulfilled my end of that bargain," Eliza said, pushing off from the door. She pulled it open, looking over her shoulder. "I suggest lying low for a few days, Princeling."

As the door clicked shut behind her, Callan hurled his glass at it. It shattered everywhere, alcohol sliding down the door. Finn came rushing from his room, a dagger in his hand.

"What the hell, Callan?" he barked, lowering his dagger at the empty room.

If Eliza wouldn't tell him anything, he'd figure it out himself. "I am going to the library," he growled to Finn, wrenching the door open, his boots crunching on the shattered glass.

CHAPTER 20

SCARLETT

S carlett woke with a groan. Her arm was stiff and sore, but the shooting pain was gone. She sucked in a breath and gasped. Her ribs were healing, but her entire body ached. She was exhausted. Her very soul felt drained.

"Take it easy, Princess. Sorin will kill me if you wake up and hurt yourself more," came a female voice.

Scarlett's eyes fluttered open, and she found Eliza sprawled in the chaise beneath the window, a book in her hands. The army general wore pants and a tunic the color of ash. Her fighting leathers and weapons were discarded on the floor beside the chaise, although a dagger was still sheathed at her side.

"Where is he?" Scarlett asked, looking around the room.

"He had to tend to some Court matters with Cyrus, and Rayner had his own tasks."

"So you got stuck with babysitting duty?" Scarlett inquired, using her good arm to push herself into a sitting position. She breathed through her teeth at the sharp pain in her ribs. She moved her arm back and forth, wincing slightly with the movement.

"I volunteered," Eliza replied with a shrug of her shoulders.

"How many days have I been asleep?"

"Only one."

Scarlett's eyes widened. "How have my arm and ribs healed this much in only a day?"

"Didn't Sorin tell you Fae heal quickly? Add Beatrix to the mix, and you should be good as new in a few days' time. Although your depleted magical reserves may delay things a bit. There is a tonic by the bed to speed your healing," Eliza answered with a nod to the nightstand. Her red-gold hair was free and flowing down her back. Scarlett could see her tattoos peeking out from beneath the collar of her tunic. Eliza followed her gaze and said, "They're Marks."

"What do they mean?" Scarlett asked.

The two females hadn't spent much time together the past few weeks, so she wasn't sure if Eliza would find the question prying. She had eaten dinner with Sorin's Inner Court every evening, becoming more comfortable with them each day. She had quickly become close with Cyrus and delighted in giving Sorin as much shit as possible with him. She could tell beneath the wit and endless bantering was a brilliant mind that was constantly calculating and assessing everything at once. After spending just a few hours with him, she knew why he was Sorin's Second, and he had even given her tips on her archery skills a few times.

Rayner was still a mystery to her. He was kind whenever she saw him and always had a soft smile for her, but he was quiet and reclusive. She rarely saw him outside dinner and even there he only spoke to quiet tension. When he spoke, though, you listened. He was like a wise old man who you knew held untold wisdom if you just listened at the right times.

Eliza, however? She could still hear her voice telling her to leave them at that initial dinner and see the challenge in her eyes to Sorin. Eliza had been civil to her, but hadn't spent any more time with her than necessary. To hear she had volunteered to watch over her was a surprise. Even on the short journey here, Eliza hadn't said much to her. Her sole focus had seemed to be keeping Sorin under control for some reason. She'd always managed to appear when tensions were rising between Sorin and Callan. She clearly had no problem with challenging him when she thought what he was doing was ill-advised.

Eliza closed her book and laid it beside her on the chaise, those gray eyes fixing on Scarlett. "Some Marks are symbols. Some Marks are tests. Some Marks are used in spells and enchantments. Some Marks amplify certain aspects of one's power."

"And yours?"

Eliza studied her a moment, then asked instead, "What do you know of the Courts?"

Scarlett blinked in surprise. "Not a lot," she admitted. "I know there are four. I know the names. I know the sitting royalty. I know little more."

Eliza nodded. "I'm told that the mortal kingdoms place a lot of stock in bloodlines."

"They do," Scarlett answered shortly, reaching over to the tonic sitting on the bedside table. She swallowed it down and nearly choked on the bitter taste.

"The Fae Courts are no different, except that our families are built up for magical power, not just royalty bloodlines. Those with powerful magic are betrothed to those of similar power to strengthen the bloodlines," Eliza explained. She was looking down at the floor as she spoke, tracing idle circles onto the rug with the toe of her boot. "Marrying outside of your Court is not permitted. The only exception is if your twin flame is from another Court, and even then the bond has to be Trialed and Anointed before it is accepted. Queen Eliné had been working hard to break that stigma, and we were beginning to see more marriages amongst the Courts, but it's still frowned upon by many."

"But why?" Scarlett asked. "In the mortal lands, sometimes marriages are arranged between the kingdoms to strengthen their relations."

Eliza snorted. "I don't pretend to understand the workings of the Courts and their arranged marriages. The Courts hold petty grudges against each other, especially amongst the Western and Eastern Courts.

"My mother, though, was of the Earth Court. She was incredibly powerful and was given to a male of equal power. I was conceived, and it was impossible for me to not be more powerful with their combined bloodlines. From the day I was born, it had already been determined that I would be given to the Earth Prince for marriage. His parents had been slaughtered by Deimas and Esmeray like the other royals had been, but he was older than Sorin was when it had happened. He was in a much better position to take over ruling his Court and did so without thought or question. Queen Henna, and later Queen Eliné, had to do little advising to him.

"However, when my power began manifesting at age eleven, it was fire, pure and strong, and my mother's husband realized that he was obviously not my father. She had had an affair with a male from the Fire Court, whom she believed was her twin flame, but they were too afraid to undergo the Trials. I still don't know who he is to this day, but instead of my powers being unparalleled earth magic, they are fire. My fire magic is second only to Sorin's."

Scarlett's mouth fell open a little at the revelation. She had seen Eliza use her flames here and there, but had no idea she was that powerful. "When my mother's husband learned the truth, he slit her throat in front of me. Then he gave me this Mark," she said, pointing to the whorl of ink directly over her heart. "It prevents me from bearing children. He told me he'd rather die than have any more of his relations with a drop of Fire Court blood in their veins. He dropped me over the border of the Fire Court and left me to fend for myself or die. There has long been tension between the Fire and Earth Courts. This only added to the hostility between them."

Eliza fell silent as Scarlett rose from the bed, pushing down a cry at the pain, and came to her side. "You cannot bear children? Sorin told me it is very difficult for Fae to conceive. Are you sure?" But she trailed off when she saw the look on Eliza's face.

"I cannot bear living children," Eliza corrected. "I have conceived children three separate times. After enduring that pain three different times, I will not attempt it again. I never told my partner. It was my burden to bear alone."

Scarlett wrapped her arms around the female and pulled her into an embrace. "No one should have to bear that alone."

Eliza stiffened at first and then returned the hug gently, careful of her ribs. When Scarlett pulled back, tears glistened in Eliza's eyes. "I share it because…" Eliza trailed off, looking out the window. Scarlett let her gather her thoughts, waiting for her to continue. "I share it because you watched your mother be killed in front of you. I share it because you've experienced hell, a different sort of hell than me, but a hell nonetheless. I share it because you were to be given to another simply because of the power that courses through your veins. I share it because you went up against Talwyn, for all of us, not knowing what power you would face. I share it because I want you to know you are not alone." Then she added quietly, "No one else knows. Of the losses."

Scarlett understood the request in her words. "It is not my tale to tell, and it will not leave this room," Scarlett replied simply. After another beat of silence, she asked, "Your lover was not your twin flame?"

"No. I don't believe so. The connection could have maybe settled into place eventually, but he was killed by Night Children many years ago," Eliza said, bringing her eyes back to Scarlett's. There was something on her face that Scarlett couldn't read as she said tentatively, "Finding your twin flame is extremely rare and taking the Mark is a test few dare to do."

"Sorin said it is an offering of the soul," Scarlett recalled vaguely from that night on the beach.

"It is indeed." Eliza paused, seeming to want to say more, but then deciding against it.

"How did you meet Sorin then? How did you become the general of his armies?"

"A soldier on patrol found me the day I was dumped over the border and brought me to the palace. I worked as a kitchen assistant for years, but I would sneak out whenever I could and watch the soldiers train. I studied everything they did. Not just weaponry but war strategies and battle formations. As my power grew, I was taken up to train with the other neophytes. Sorin caught me in the training ring one night with a sword I had swiped from discarded weapons that had been deemed no longer usable. He told me if I wanted to swing a sword, I needed an opponent who would swing back. He sparred with me that night. The next morning, I was summoned to the training pits beneath the palace. I clawed my way through every training ring to the top, and Sorin had been watching, keeping tabs on me apparently. He eventually asked me to be the General of his armies.

"This Mark is my Mark of Loyalty to him and the Fire Court," she said, pulling back the collar of her tunic and pointing to the Mark on the left side of her chest near her shoulder. It was a flame with a sword through it. It was in nearly the same spot as the one on Sorin's chest and looked identical. "Cyrus and Rayner bear one as well."

"Most of the other Marks enhance my abilities, and allow me to do things like summon weapons from my flames, among other things."

Scarlett tried not to stare at the female before her. She had faced her own battles. Alone. She had clawed her way through piles of shit to get to her position. Alone. She had even watched her mother murdered in front of her. Sorin had been right. They were kindred spirits.

"Eliza," she ventured slowly. Eliza merely cocked her head to the side slightly, and Scarlett tried not to squirm as those ash grey eyes seemed to see right through her. "Sorin told me that if I wanted to continue my own physical training, I should ask you to train me. Would you be willing?"

"Training with me is grueling and hard," Eliza replied, warning in her tone. "My strongest warriors curse me on a daily basis."

"I imagine it's similar to training with Sorin when he's being a cranky prick," Scarlett scowled. Memories of running for miles and getting knocked on her ass flashed through her mind.

Eliza laughed. "At least you'll know what to expect."

"Thank you," Scarlett said. "For sharing with me."

"Thank you for coming," Eliza replied. "The others will not say it to you, but I hope you decide to stay."

Scarlett felt her cheeks heat at the compliment. "I don't remember much after Callan carried me here from the Courtyard," she said, "but I remember being woken and told Sorin was in danger. Did that happen, or was it a dream?"

"It happened," Eliza said gravely.

"He is all right?" Scarlett asked, her heart skipping a beat.

"He is fine, Scarlett. He told me to summon him when you woke, which I can do when you are ready."

"No," Scarlett replied hastily. "He has responsibilities here. I do not need to monopolize all of his time."

"I think he'd prefer if you did."

"When you are a prince you do not always get that choice," Scarlett answered. "He has been gone for three years. He needs to tend to his people."

"Then let's have some tea," Eliza replied with a small smile.

The two were still sitting together on the chaise, sipping tea, their shoes off, feet tucked underneath them, when Sorin entered the room a couple of hours later. He stopped short, looked them up and down, and brought his fingers to his brow with a groan. "How long has she been awake, Eliza?"

"She's sitting right here. Ask her yourself," Eliza replied casually, as though she were speaking to a sibling and not a powerful prince.

Scarlett merely smiled sweetly up at him over her teacup as his eyes went to her with an unamused glare. "How is your arm?"

With a smirk, she twisted it to give him a vulgar gesture and replied, "I've been awake for a few hours, thank you."

His unamused glare went back to Eliza. "I told you to let me know when she woke up."

"Did you?" she asked with mock surprise, raising her eyebrows. "Oops."

"It took nearly five years to get you to say more than three words at a time to Cyrus and Rayner, but you and Scarlett are thicker than thieves in a few hours?" Sorin asked, his tone conveying just how unlikely he found this to be.

Eliza shrugged. "She doesn't have a cock. That makes a big difference. I've been telling you for years we needed another female in the family."

Sorin closed his eyes in a slow blink at the reply, then drawled sarcastically, "We could hardly handle one of you, dear Eliza. Two ought to be most enjoyable."

CHAPTER 21
SCARLETT

Scarlett lay awake, staring at the ceiling. Sorin was sleeping beside her, as he had been every night since she had asked him to stay. Nothing else had happened since that night either, which both relieved and slightly disappointed Scarlett. He had let her and Eliza have time to themselves nearly the entire afternoon, and Eliza had helped her bathe since she had still been in the clothes from the courtyard.

When Sorin had returned, he had hovered like a mother hen. And had continued to do so for the last two days. He brought her meals and wouldn't let her out of the bed unless she had to see to her needs, at which point she had to shut the door in his face.

He had tried to explain it to her, that Fae males felt an instinctive drive to serve and protect. Guilt, she had realized. He had felt guilt at what had happened to her in the courtyard.

"Sorin, in this very room, you looked at me and told me none of what happened was my fault," she had said quietly.

"It wasn't," he had replied quickly, worry flickering across his face.

"Nor was any of it yours," she had answered gently.

"Not being able to protect you——"

"I do not need protecting, Sorin," she had cut in.

"That is not what I mean, Scarlett. You do not need protecting or rescuing."

"Read to me?" she had asked then.

He had, for nearly two hours, until she could tell he was exhausted. He had fallen asleep almost immediately, and here she was, going more than a little stir crazy. She needed to get up, to move around. She needed to get out of these rooms. She was trained in the damned Black Syndicate. She could be stealthy, even with an injured arm and ribs. They were healing quickly anyway. She was mostly just sore at this point.

She sucked in a breath, bracing herself as she gently eased herself to a sitting position. She slid from the bed with expert quiet. She was in loose fitting training clothes, which were fine for walking around the palace. She slid her feet into slippers. Sorin hardly stirred. She supposed he was used to her waking screaming or thrashing from nightmares, not from her silently slipping from bed. Now to get out the door.

She pulled the door, grimacing at the abdominal muscles she had to use to do so. The door mercifully was silent as it slid open, and she slipped out. She braided her long hair back while she crossed the sitting room and strapped a dagger she found near the door to her thigh. She was in the hallway a moment later, and she let out a long breath. It had been a long while since she had had to sneak anywhere.

She silently padded down the hallway. The palace was silent at this hour, everyone asleep, save for the night watch guards stationed here and there. They nodded to her as she passed. She moved slowly across the bridges, not really wanting to tackle stairs tonight. Another left and a right, and she found herself before the level's library entrance.

As she walked along the balconies of the massive library, she could see various levels below, lit by torches and candles. She heard a noise ahead among the stacks and froze. She did not really want to interact much with anyone, but it was too late as a figure emerged from between the shelves. She instinctively protected her healing ribs as they nearly collided.

"My apologies," a man yelped, dropping the books he was carrying. "I did not know anyone else was in here." He had stooped to grab his books, but Scarlett knew who it was before he stood upright.

Callan's eyes widened at who stood before him. "Scarlett." He scanned her, noting her wrapped middle and arm. "What are you doing here?"

"It's a library," she said with an eye roll. "I'm here to get a book." She realized a moment later that with that sarcastic comment, she had not put on the mask she usually wore with the prince. Then again, he'd been seeing plenty of things that went far beyond that mask these days.

"Of course." He shifted on his feet. "How are you?"

"I've been better," she admitted with a weak smile. "Are you okay? Did Talwyn hurt you?"

"No. Nothing like that," he said in a rush of words and a peculiar look.

They stood awkwardly together in the silence, neither knowing what to say. "Well, this is stupid, hmm?" she finally murmured.

He huffed a laugh. "We can finally converse in the open, and we do not know what to do with ourselves."

"What are you reading?" Scarlett asked, glancing at his stack of books. "Hopefully something to keep your interest? Unless you are looking for something to help you fall asleep?"

"No, I—"

She reached out with her good arm and plucked a book from the top of the stack. *The Heart of the Beginning*. She looked up at him with a quizzical look.

"I figured since I am to be king one day, I should know as much as I can about our land and relations, so I have been studying the history of the Fae," he explained with a small shrug.

"Smart. Have you learned anything interesting?" she asked as she thumbed through the book.

"Some, yes. Listen, can we walk somewhere so I can set these down?" he asked, lifting the stack of books in emphasis.

"Of course. Sorry." She followed him to a little alcove with a table. More books and papers littered the surface. "How much research have you done exactly?" she asked with a raised brow as he plopped the books onto the table.

"I have some time on my hands here," he said, rubbing the back of his neck. He turned to face her fully. "I am sorry. About what happened in the courtyard."

"What could you possibly have to be sorry for?" she asked.

"Sorin did not tell you?" Again he had that peculiar look.

"Tell me what?" she asked slowly.

He took a deep breath. "The Fae Queen did not kidnap me. I went with her willingly."

Scarlett stilled. She could hardly draw a breath as she said as evenly as she could, "Why would you do that?"

"It had seemed like a good idea at the time, to get to know another leader of the lands. To build relations."

"Oh, Callan." She didn't know what else to say. When she'd asked how Talwyn had crossed the wards to get to Callan and the others, Sorin had only said they were working on it and that it wouldn't happen again.

He swallowed. "She had questions. About you."

"I'm sure she did," Scarlett muttered.

"Why?"

Scarlett waved the question off. "What kind of questions?"

"She commented on your ring, about how it is a Fae family heirloom. She wondered how you obtained it. Then she asked if you had any of the tattoos the others have."

"She asked if I had any Marks?" Callan nodded. "How curious," was all she could say as he looked expectantly at her.

"Which part? The Marks or the ring?" he asked, running a hand down the stubble along his jaw.

The action caught her off guard. How many times had she watched him do that when they were strategizing in the same hours of the night in his own private rooms?

"All of it, I suppose," she said with a sigh. She eased herself into a seat at the table. "Tell me what you've learned."

Callan took a tentative seat opposite her. "You are not at all curious about her questions?"

"Not tonight I am not. Tell me the most interesting thing you have discovered."

Callan studied her. "There used to be two Fae Queens who ruled the Courts. They were sisters, but some say there was a third sister. That Esmeray was that third."

"So I've heard. What did you learn of them?"

Callan shrugged. "Most accounts say that Deimas and Esmeray tried to overtake the Courts to get to the mortals. I am not surprised that their history books are so different from our own, I suppose."

"Most accounts? Are they not all the same?"

"No," Callan said, leaning back in his chair. "One book I read said the Fae Courts were just caught in between a bigger conflict between Esmeray's territory and Avonleya. It claimed that Deimas and Esmeray were seeking something across the sea, and Avonleya refused to let them even come to visit. That such a slight would ignite the Great War seems a little far-fetched though."

"Yes, but did it ever say what they were looking for? Or what Deimas was?"

"What do you mean what Deimas was? He was mortal, wasn't he?" Callan asked with a raise of his brow.

"But he had magic. How else did he and Esmeray lock away the Avonleyans? If Esmeray was as powerful as the Fae Queens, that explains that. But what of Deimas?" Scarlett pressed. She chewed on her bottom lip as she pondered this. Callan was quiet, and after a few moments, she realized he was staring at her. She cleared her throat and straightened in her chair.

"What else have you discovered?" Scarlett asked, leaning forward to look at his various notes and books.

"Myths and legends mostly. It's all so different from the history we were taught. It paints the Fae as mortal protectors, not as a race seeking to enslave us."

Scarlett pulled one of his pages of notes towards her, skimming his neat and precise handwriting. Handwriting that was so familiar to her. "And what are you inclined to believe?"

Callan shrugged again. "Honestly, I do not know what to believe any more. Some things seem so far fetched. There was one book that spoke of something called a World Walker who was apparently a being that could walk between the worlds somehow."

"Interesting," Scarlett murmured, flipping through his pages of notes. She stilled as she read the page title. *Twin Flames and Soulmates*. "What is this?" she asked, tapping the paper with her fingernail.

"More research," Callan said, reaching to take the papers, but she grabbed them, twisting out of his reach. She stifled a cry at the pain in her abdomen from the movement as she read his notes.

"Why are you researching this?" she asked.

"I heard of the twin flame bond mentioned in passing and wanted to know more about it," he said cautiously.

"This is old blood magic, Callan," she said, her eyes moving rapidly over the pages. She saw her name jotted in the margins with a question mark beside it. "Why is my name written here?" She brought her eyes to his in time to see him wince.

"I am trying to figure out how you fit into their world, Scarlett," he finally conceded with a sigh. "No one will give me straight answers about anything, so I decided to take it upon myself."

"You think I am one of these? To whom?" she demanded, waving the page of notes at him.

"I do not know, but it would explain why you fit in so well among them."

"I fit in among them because I am *Fae*, Callan," she said shortly.

"I know, but you interact with them as if you have known them for years. You are more comfortable around them than you were around me when we were sharing a bed for a year, and you have only shared quarters with him for a few weeks." His eyes widened as the words left his lips.

Scarlett stared at him, blinking slowly. Without a word, she extended her hand with the notes back to him. "Why are you really researching all of this Callan?"

"Everything I said was true, but also to help you. Why can he help you and I cannot?" he demanded, his eyes hardening as he took the papers from her hand.

She studied him a long moment. All of him so familiar to her still to this day. "All right then," she said, pulling a book towards her.

"What are you doing?"

"It's my history. Maybe I should learn some of it too, don't you think?" she asked, flipping the book open.

"You are going to sit here and read with me?" There was wariness in his tone.

"Unless you have some objection to it?"

It was his turn to study her.

"I do not have an objection. I can think of another who might?"

"He is not my keeper," she said simply, and she began to read.

It was hours later when she crossed the bridges again, slipping silently into Sorin's rooms. She silently closed the door behind her, padding across the sitting room. She was sore. She knew she had overdone it sitting at that table for so long with Callan, each of them offering interesting bits of history or research they came across. The space between them was still tense, but it was something she supposed.

She carefully pushed open the bedroom door and stepped inside. Sorin still lay in bed where she'd left him. She unbuckled the dagger from her thigh and slid her feet from her slippers. Then she stood, debating whether a hot bath would ease her aching middle.

"Take the tonic on the nightstand for the pain," came a voice from the darkened room. She scowled at him in the darkness, and he chuckled, rising from the bed. He grabbed the vial from the bedside table as he came to her, uncorking it and extending it to her.

"When did you learn I was gone?" she asked, tipping back the vial, its honey taste trying to mask the bitterness of it.

"Love, I felt you get out of this bed," he replied with a smirk she could just make out in the glow from the hearth.

"You did not," she scoffed, handing him the empty vial.

"I did. Granted, I thought you were going to the bathing room and did not want the door slammed in my face again. When you did not return after an hour, I sent word for a pain relieving tonic to have ready for you. She added a sedative to help you sleep."

Scarlett rolled her eyes, making to move towards the bed. Dammit. She was so damn sore.

"I'm surprised you didn't try to stop me when you heard me leave the room then," she ground out, trying and failing to hide her grimace of pain. She didn't fight him as he gently lifted her into his arms and carried her to the bed.

"Scarlett, I understand it is hard for you to let yourself be taken care of. I understand that Fae protectiveness is new to you and takes such a thing to a whole new overbearing level. It took every shred of self-control to let you leave this room tonight and fight that urge to make you stay in bed, despite knowing you would come back in this state," he said pointedly, pulling the comforter up and around her. "I am trying though."

"The mother hen look is not good on you," she said softly, feeling the tonic begin to take effect.

"I'll try to remember that," he said with a soft chuckle, as he climbed back into the other side of the bed.

"I just couldn't sleep. I was getting restless," she murmured into the dark.

"I know, Love, but maybe one hour in the library would have been wiser than three?"

"You know where I was?"

"I am the prince of the palace, Scarlett, and you are, for all intents and purposes, a princess. I was sent a message by every night watch you passed."

"Why did you not tell me Callan went with Talwyn willingly?" she asked. She wanted to roll onto her side and face him, but knew that would be impossible, so she turned her head.

He seemed to know though, and propped himself onto an

elbow, looking down at her. It was somehow more intimate than kissing, laying in the dark, staring into his golden eyes. "He told you?"

"He did. Why didn't you?"

"Because I know he is important to you. I did not want this to fracture your relationship with him further."

"I think he is still hoping things will return to how they were," she said quietly, feeling the tug of sleep.

"I think you are right," he agreed, gently stroking soothing lines down her cheek, along her jaw.

"I do not know how to tell him that…that I do not know if I will remain in Baylorin when we take him home," she said, her eyes growing heavy.

Sorin's finger paused its movement for a split second before continuing. "Oh?"

"He is researching things. In the library," she murmured. She hardly knew what she was saying any more.

"What kinds of things?"

"Mainly history."

She heard the smile in Sorin's words as he said, "Is he now?"

"Yes. He is also researching twin flames and soulmates."

Sorin's fingers stilled completely this time. Her eyes fluttered open at the interruption, and she found him watching her closely. "What has he learned?"

"We didn't discuss it much." She couldn't read his expression, although her mind was so muddled from the tonic, there was prob-ably nothing to read there, anyway. She was just babbling at this point. "He said he thought someone here might think I am their twin flame or soulmate, and that's why you all are so protective. I couldn't tell him the truth."

"Which is what?" Sorin asked slowly.

"That you all think I'm a princess and that's why you're so fussy," she answered with a half smile.

"You *are* a princess," he said, resuming his soothing stroking on her face.

"I think you might be mine though," she said, as sleep finally overtook her.

"Your what?" she heard him press, but sleep pulled her under before she could reply.

CHAPTER 22
SCARLETT

S carlett wandered along the banks of the Tana River in the gardens behind the palace. The thin dusting of snow they'd gotten that morning had melted in the afternoon sun, and the evening chill settled over her bones. She drew her cloak tighter around herself. It was thin, but the only thing she could find so it would have to do, she supposed. She had left a note for the others that she would not be at dinner this evening. She just needed some time to…

She didn't know what she needed time for. She had awoken that morning feeling tired and empty. It had been nearly two weeks since the courtyard dramatics. It had taken five days before Sorin had finally relented and allowed Eliza to begin training her in the mornings. Scarlett flexed and rolled her wrist on the arm that had been broken under her cloak. While it had healed well enough under Beatrix's care, it was still sore after a day of wielding weapons and practicing combat moves.

Eliza had seemed to sense something amiss this morning during their training session. Scarlett had known she was being sloppy and making careless mistakes, but Eliza hadn't said a word about it. In fact, she had backed off on her own maneuvers.

And had apparently reported such to Sorin because when he came to take her to the Courtyard for their afternoon magic training, he had looked her over carefully before asking too casually how she was doing. She hadn't been able to focus there either. He had ended their time together earlier than normal and asked to walk back to the palace with her rather than portal, but she had declined. When they'd gotten back to their rooms, she had gone straight to the bathing room, shutting the door behind her. She hadn't bathed, though. She had waited until she'd heard him leave to have his usual afternoon briefing with his Inner Court. Then she'd left her note, grabbed a cloak and somehow found herself walking in the cold evening air.

Her thoughts were everywhere today. Cassius. Nuri. The orphans. And memories she worked so hard to keep shoved down seemed to be clawing their way to the surface. Not just Juliette and Mikale, but memories of punishments from the Assassin Lord and images of pain she'd inflicted upon her assignments.

All of it pressed in on her today. Cyrus had said it had taken time to find his way out of the dark. That the stars were always worth fighting for. And she had been trying. Every day she had been fighting through the unending and relentless grief and panic and guilt that crashed upon her. And today she awoke not feeling like she had any fight left in her.

Today she awoke and felt utterly and completely empty.

Scarlett hadn't realized she'd stopped beside the river. Her hands rubbed at her arms as she stared across it to the mountains towering in the distance.

She didn't know how long she'd been standing there when she felt the pulse of heat behind her. How he had found her, she didn't know, but she sighed at the sound of his boots on the earth. She didn't even bother to look over her shoulder at him when she said, "I do not want company, nor do I wish to speak right now, Sorin."

"I did not come to do either of those two things, only to bring you these." She couldn't decipher the emotions in his voice when she turned to face him. A heavy cloak was wrapped around his own shoulders, and his breath was visible as he watched her, his face solemn. He held a bundle of fabric in his arms, and Scarlett arched a brow at him in question.

"It's freezing out, Scarlett," he said quietly, taking a small step towards her. "I know it gets far colder here than it does in Baylorin, and it's not even technically winter yet." He picked up something off the top of the bundle and held them up. A pair of gloves. She didn't say anything, just glanced at the remaining item in his arms. "A fur-lined cloak," he said by way of explanation.

She said nothing as she turned back to face the river once more, and she felt him come up beside her. He handed the gloves over, and she silently slid them on. The insides were fur-lined too, and her frozen fingers burned at the sudden warmth.

"Hold this," he instructed, holding out the other cloak to her. She obeyed, and he quickly unclasped the thin cloak she currently wore and slung it over his shoulder. He reached wordlessly for the thicker one, unfolding it and wrapping it around her shoulders. His eyes came to hers as he quickly did up the buttons, and she couldn't help but think of the short journey here when he'd often done the same.

She'd felt like this at that time, too. Lost. Unrelenting grief. Unyielding pain.

A flood of heat wrapped around her, and she knew it was his magic as he reached over her shoulder and pulled up the hood for her.

"Do you need anything else?" he finally asked softly.

Yes? No? She wanted to feel something, anything, but the emptiness beckoned. She knew she could find a short reprieve at his hands physically, but she'd still be left with...this. These broken pieces of herself.

Pieces he'd contributed to shattering.

The thought had her turning from him and continuing to walk along the river without a word.

She rounded a small bend, and the path was so covered by trees, the sun had not reached these parts. The snow that had been falling the last few days had not melted, but had accumulated. She stopped at the edge, stooping and scooping up a handful of the cold flakes.

She wanted to cry, but tears would not come. She didn't have it in her to rage or scream or do anything really. She scooped up another handful of snow, letting it drift back to the ground.

"It's okay, you know." His soft voice floated down to her, but she didn't look up at him. There were several moments of silence. She had stilled, not knowing where he was going with this. The soft crunch of footsteps sounded, and then he was stooping down beside her. "It is okay to have hard days, Scarlett." His tone was impossibly tender. "It is okay if some days the only thing you manage to do is survive. That is okay."

At those words, she finally turned to him. Eyes of gold, full of concern and understanding and an emotion she wasn't ready to acknowledge, met her own. "I feel like all I've been doing is surviving, Sorin," she whispered. "I don't want to just survive any more. I want to *live*. I want to feel something other than...this."

Scarlett tipped her hand, dumping the snow and watching it fall back to the mound. Sorin was quiet beside her for another long moment. "The things you have experienced in your short life," he paused, as if trying to find the words. "Those are things that will get easier to live with over time, but they are memories that you will still carry with you forever. They are memories that will still sneak up on you at the oddest times, when you are not expecting it."

"I don't know what is wrong with me today," she whispered.

"There is nothing wrong with you, Scarlett. You just had a hard day. That is okay."

The silence stretched on between them once more. She finally stood, and he rose beside her, a steady presence. She looked out over the river once more, saying quietly, "Briar told me you only drown if you stay in the river." She swallowed as the last of the sun dipped behind the mountains, and the night enveloped them. How long had they been out here?

She turned to face him, pulling her cloak tighter around herself. "I don't want to be in the river any more, Sorin." Her voice cracked on the last words.

His arms were around her in the next breath, pulling her to him, like he'd been waiting for this moment. As if he'd known it was coming. "I am not going to let you drown, Scarlett."

She let him hold her in the dark, breathing him in and soaking in his warmth. As he sent another flood of heat through her, she grumbled, "I hate the cold."

Sorin huffed a laugh, pulling back to look into her eyes. "Are you ready to go back to where it is warm?"

She only nodded, and a fire portal appeared before them. He took her hand in his and led her through into the warmth of his sitting room. Reaching up, she pushed back the hood of her cloak and took off her gloves. Sorin was taking them from her a heartbeat later, and he sent a fire message of some sort as she reached up and unbuttoned her cloak. He took that from her, too, striding to the hooks near the main door and hanging them upon it.

"I asked Camilla to send up some food," he told her as he came to her once more. "I am assuming you did not eat."

"I didn't. Thank you," she answered, walking over to the fire and holding her hands out to it, watching the flames flicker and dance among each other. After several minutes, she turned to ask Sorin a question and found him sitting on the brick red sofa, his head propped on a hand on the arm of it, watching her, a soft smile playing on his lips.

That look she wasn't willing to acknowledge was again glimmering in his eyes, and the question she had been about to ask flew from her mind as she met his eyes. "What?"

The smile turned into a slight frown. "You look tired."

"My soul is tired," she sighed.

"Yes, but you look physically tired as well. You need to rest more. The more magic you do, the more energy your body will use up. It is what feeds your magic. You need to make sure you are eating enough and getting enough sleep," he replied.

Scarlett rolled her eyes. "I really thought we were past this whole mother hen thing." His small smile made another appearance. "How was dinner?" she asked, turning back to the fire once more.

"It was fine, I suppose. As fine as it can be without you there."

"Don't say things like that."

"Say things like what?"

"Like it makes any difference if I am here or not. I am not a part of this Court. It wouldn't matter if I returned to Baylorin tomorrow."

Sorin was silent for so long that she finally turned back again to see if he had left the room. He was still seated in the same spot, his head propped, but his eyes were narrowed slightly. "Come here."

Scarlett wrinkled her nose. "No."

"Why not?"

"I don't want to."

He huffed a laugh. "Please come here," he patted the spot on the sofa beside him.

She sighed and crossed the small space. She sat down, tucking her feet up underneath her, propped her elbow on the back and angled to face him. He stretched an arm towards her, resting it just behind her elbow, and turned to face her as well.

"While I do not particularly enjoy you going off to be by yourself, I understand the need to do so from time to time. I understand hard days, Scarlett, I do, but do not for one second think that your missing presence is unnoticed or unfelt. Do not for one second think you do not make a difference. Do not—" Sorin broke off as she broke eye contact with him, her eyes dropping to her lap. His fingers brushed against her arm on the back of the sofa. His voice was even lower when he spoke again. "Do not for one second think that you do not matter."

There was a knock on the door, and Camilla called out, "Prince Aditya? I have the food you requested."

"Thank you, Camilla," he answered, not moving an inch. "Please leave it by the door. I will grab it in a moment." There was the soft thunking of a tray and light footsteps leaving down the hall. Still, he did not move to retrieve it.

His fingers were making light strokes on her arm. "Scarlett—"

"Don't, Sorin. Please just…don't," she whispered.

Sorin stood then and crossed to the door, bringing the food in and bringing it back to the sofa. He set it on the end table, and the smell of braised meat and fresh bread floated over to her. He fixed her a small plate and sat down once more, extending it to her. She reached for it, but when she went to pull it towards herself, he held firm, until she brought her eyes back to his. "I will never stop, Scarlett. I will never stop telling you that you matter and that you make a difference. I will never stop telling you that you are a necessity in my life, and I sure as shit will be sure and say it extra on the hard days."

He released the plate to her, and she didn't say anything as she brought it to her lap and ate the small dinner in silence. He had conjured a book from somewhere and read beside her while she ate, lost in her thoughts once more. The words he had just said settled deep within her. All of them. And not just this evening. Words from time in Baylorin floated back to her. The little things from tending to her wound after Alaric had hit her to ensuring she ate along the trip here to bringing her gloves tonight. He always seemed to know. He knew when to push her and when to let her be. He knew how to coax her out of foul moods and when she just needed someone to sit with her in the quiet.

"Did you get enough to eat?" he asked, noting her now empty plate.

She nodded mutely, and he took it from her, setting it back onto the tray on the end table. He picked up his book and began reading once more.

"What are you reading?" she asked quietly.

"A story about an arrogant creature of shadows who turns out to be an unknown princess," he answered, not looking at her.

Scarlett groaned.

"Wait, I'm not done," he continued. "She meets a devilishly handsome and splendid prince and—"

"I regret asking," she murmured, leaning back into the sofa.

The book closed, and an arm came around her shoulder. There was a soft brush of lips against her temple that had her leaning into him. He pulled a pillow from beside him and placed it in his lap. "You need to rest, Scarlett."

"You don't need to sit in here with me, Sorin." They usually spent their evenings lounging with the others in the den, playing cards or billiards or simply visiting.

"I am exactly where I need to be, Love," he answered, gently pulling her down to the pillow.

She turned onto her back so she could look up at him. His fingers grazed along her cheek, her jaw, her forehead. "Why do you think she took me from here?" she asked thoughtfully.

Sorin's brow furrowed at her question. "Who?"

"My mother. Why do you think she found it better to raise me in the mortal lands? What was she hiding me from? And why?"

"I don't know," he said softly. "It is something I have often pondered though."

"Today, tonight, while I trailed along the river, I thought of how my life might have been different. If she had made different choices. If I had been raised as a princess instead of a healer's daughter taught to kill and torture…" she trailed off.

"You cannot think that way. There are too many what ifs. Too many variables. You likely would not have met your sisters if that were the case. Or Cassius."

Her heart clenched at the sound of his name. "That's true, I suppose, but I also wouldn't have experienced the losses I have either," she sighed. Sorin was playing with a piece of her long hair now, twirling it around a finger while his head rested against a hand propped on the back of the sofa. "I should really change or bathe or something." She was still wearing her training clothes and had her boots propped on the end of the sofa.

He smiled and flames licked up and down her body. A moment later, she was in soft lounge pants and a top with two small straps. "Now you don't have to get up."

"That is rather convenient," she murmured, although she could still really use a bath. She could feel the day clinging to her. He was still watching her as he wound a lock of hair around his finger, the soft smile back on his lips. That look back in his eyes. "You've been looking at me like that all night," she whispered.

"How have I been looking at you?"

She couldn't bring herself to say it. She couldn't form the words. She didn't want to form the words because what if she was wrong?

No. Today, on this hard day, she couldn't face it if she was wrong. So instead she said, "Thank you, Sorin."

His finger halted its twirling. "For what?"

"For pulling me from the river tonight."

"Thank you for trusting me enough to give me the privilege of doing so despite everything," he answered, fingers grazing her cheek once more.

She reached up and allowed her own fingers to brush along his cheek, his jaw. "I told you that day in the Courtyard, Sorin. I do not blame you for my mother's death. You are not responsible for that."

He leaned into her touch, closing his eyes briefly. "Thank you for that, Scarlett."

She brought her hand back down, resting it on her stomach as she turned her head to watch the flickering flames once more. After a few minutes, she heard Sorin pick up his book and begin reading.

Minutes or hours later, she didn't know, she felt familiar strong arms scooping her up as she groggily nestled into his chest. At some point she had fallen asleep in the comfortable silence, Sorin just *there* if she needed him. The bed dipped as he got in on his side, and she rolled to him. His arm came around her, tucking her into his side, her cheek on his chest and leg draped over his.

She was still in the same position when she woke the next morning, Sorin's arm wrapped tightly around her. She soaked him in. All of him. Her soul feeling lighter, so much lighter than it had yesterday. She lifted her head to find him watching her, that same look on his face from the night before.

"Good morning," he said softly, brushing stray hair back from her face.

"Morning."

His fingers lingered in her hair, and he said, "Today will be a better day."

She felt her cheeks flush slightly, but she held his stare, whispering, "Today I'm going to do more than just survive." The arm wrapped around her squeezed gently. "But on the hard days, promise me that you'll pull me from the river."

"Always, Love," he answered. "I promise I will always pull you from the river and help you find the stars."

She pushed herself up to him and pressed a soft kiss to his cheek, but he turned as she pulled away. His hand coming to her nape and holding her in place, his eyes locked on hers. "You, Scarlett Monrhoe, will never stop being a necessity in my life." His lips met hers in a gentle kiss. Short and sweet. He pulled back just far enough to look into her eyes. "Are you up for training today, or would you like me to tell Eliza you won't be there?"

"No, I want to train today," she said, shaking her head. "I feel... better today."

He brushed one more kiss to her cheek. "Go get ready then. She will be an ass if you are late."

CHAPTER 23

SORIN

"When are you going to tell her?" Rayner asked, his voice as smoky as the ashes that obeyed him.

They were on the upper decks of the library, and from where they stood, Sorin could see Scarlett sitting with the mortal prince a few levels below. Hidden by shelves and alcoves, the two had no idea they were there. He'd had to check on her, though. He'd just spent two hours of magic training with her, but he had still found himself needing to lay eyes on her. After the words she'd said a few days ago, after it had taken him all damn day to reach her wherever she'd retreated to inside her soul, he found himself needing to check on her and reassure himself she was all right.

Scarlett was bent over a book, a finger absent-mindedly twirling her hair that was unbound since bathing after their training session. She chewed on her bottom lip as she read. What she found so fascinating, what she was researching, he didn't know. Across from her, Callan was bent over a book as well, but Sorin saw the glances he'd make at her every now and then.

"I don't know," Sorin finally answered his Third. "She is trying to figure out who she is. She is facing traumas she has repressed. She is working through truths hidden from her. I would be a prick to lay this in front of her now as well. To add one more thing to what she is already processing."

"Is this not another truth being hidden from her? Isn't the fact that you kept so many truths from her to begin with the reason there are trust issues now?" Rayner asked from where he stood at his side.

"There are not trust issues now," Sorin snarled.

Rayner arched a brow at him.

Sorin turned back to watching the princess and the human prince. He wasn't lying to himself. She did trust him. Had she been furious when she'd woken? Yes. Had she put walls back up? Yes. But she'd also taken them back down. Each day she was here, she let more and more of herself out. Let him see more and more of her. He woke up next to her each morning and found himself counting down the hours until their magic training when it was just the two of them up in the Courtyards. He loved having her beside him at dinners amongst his family and delighted in how she'd fit right now, just like he'd known she would.

"She will not reject it, Sorin. You have to know that," Rayner supplied after another bout of silence.

He knew that, too. Deep down in his gut, he knew how she felt about him. Despite her threat to break him. No, he knew she wouldn't reject it. But would she view it as another cage? She was so adamant about not being chained to a throne. Would coming to his side not be just that, even if she chose to renounce her own birthright?

Callan said something he couldn't hear, but it had her looking up over her book and giving him a cautious smile. She didn't say anything in response, just slid her eyes back to her book.

"If you know she will not reject the twin flame bond, if you know she will choose you, then why not tell her?" Rayner pressed quietly.

Sorin sighed. "Do I deserve her, Rayner? Do I deserve to call her such a thing? After how I failed Eliné? After how I failed *her*?"

Rayner leaned on his arms on the railing overlooking the balcony of their level. "Eliné was not your fault, Sorin."

"She says the same."

"Accepting forgiveness offered when it is not requested is often harder than asking for it. Or do you not want to accept it as a way to continue punishing yourself?"

Rayner, his quiet, observant, peace-keeping Third, could be more of a busybody than Cyrus.

"We should go. I want to bathe before dinner," Sorin said, pushing off the railing.

Rayner didn't move to follow, his eyes still fixed on Scarlett below. "You need to tell her, Sorin."

"You need to stop meddling," Sorin muttered. He heard Rayner's dark chuckle as he left the library.

He walked back to his chambers, stripping off his tunic while he crossed the sitting room. He bathed quickly, and when he came out of the bathing room, he scented her and followed it until he found her laying on the sofa, a book propped above her.

Leaning over the back of the couch to peer down at her, she didn't look at him but a small smile graced her lips. She wore fitted, black pants and a red sweater that made her hair shine like starlight.

"Did you not read enough in the library today?" he asked.

She frowned slightly as she met his gaze. "Is there really such a thing as reading too much?"

"For you? No, I do not think there is."

She closed the book, reaching over her head to place it on the end table. "Are you ready to go then?"

"We still have a little time. Can I take you somewhere first? I have something for you," he said as she rose from the couch as graceful as a dancer.

"What is it?" She crossed to the door and slid on silver, silk slippers. The portrait of casual ease. A picture of what he'd one day envisioned sharing his life with someone to look like. Simple conversations. Comfortable give and take.

He closed the distance between them, opening the door for her. "Come now, can you not just wait and see?"

"No," she chirped. "I'm not big on surprises, as you are well aware." She turned and smirked at him.

He gave a long-suffering sigh. "Cruel thing, there's that wicked tongue again." She said nothing, but the smile he had only ever seen her give to him had returned. "How was your day?" he asked as he led her up several flights of stairs to the seventh and top level of the palace.

"It was good," she answered. "Eliza taught me a new move with twin short swords."

"A move I have no doubt you have already mastered?" he asked with a raised brow.

"I'm good, but not quite that good," she laughed, reaching the top landing. He turned left down a hall. "The blades on many of your weapons are so dark. What are they made of?"

"There is a steel mined from the Fiera Mountains. It is the strongest steel on the continent and is said to only be rivaled by steel found in Avonleya," he answered.

"But they cannot kill a Night Child?"

"No. You still need shirastone for that. Shirastone nullifies magic. That is why it is effective against the Fae." He stopped in front of a glass door, and she looked at him expectantly. "Have you been here before?"

She shook her head, curiosity all over her face.

He pulled open the door and let her go in first, following behind her. The inside was warm, and plants and flowers grew and bloomed all around them. The walls and ceiling were entirely of glass to allow in maximum sunlight. Scarlett had stilled, her mouth slightly opened in awe. She turned to him. "It's a glass greenhouse," she breathed.

"That it is," he said with a smile. He took her hand and led her along a path that wound through the various trees and vegetation. She stepped closer to him, her eyes wide in wonder as she took everything in.

"It's like stepping into another world."

"My mother had it built," Sorin said, and she turned to face him at that, to give him her full attention. "She loved her people and loved ruling by my father's side, but she was from a small village near the Xylon Forest in the southern part of our territory and missed the forest terribly. So my father gave her this space to build her own little forest. He called it the Princess's Garden. It spans half the roof of the palace. The other half of the roof is the private training pits we use."

Scarlett stopped and stooped down, brushing her fingers over the petals of a vibrant red and orange flower. He crouched beside her and snapped one off, handing it to her. "The fire rose," he said. "It only blooms in the Fire Court."

She took it gingerly and tucked it up into her hair near her ear. "What was her name? Your mother?"

Sorin stood, pulling her back up with him. "My mother's name was Elliya, and my father's name was Branton."

He led her farther along the path in silence, letting her take in all the beauty his mother had cultivated here. They came to a small pond in the center that had a bench beside it. He saw her sniff the air then ask, "Is that salt water?"

He smiled. "It is. It didn't used to be, but I had to make modifications to it."

"Why?" Her nose was scrunched as she looked at him, confusion in her tone.

"Because I wanted that to be able to survive and thrive here." He pointed down into the pond at a vibrant multi-colored sea star in the center of the sandy bottom. It had taken him nearly an entire week to figure out the spells to keep this section of the garden in tropical warmth. Briar had come and told him exactly what he'd need to do to keep that sea star alive and had searched the Water Court for this particular one.

Scarlett dropped to her knees beside the pond. Her hands were clutched to her chest as she watched it move along the sandy bottom, fish darting to and fro around it. He slowly lowered himself down beside her, and when she met his gaze, silver pooled in her eyes. "I don't know what to say, Sorin," she whispered. "It's beautiful." She looked back at the sea star, reaching out and skimming her fingers over the top of the water. Rings rippled out under her touch and seemed to shimmer. "Thank you for bringing me here. And for…" she trailed off as she stared at the sea star.

She faced him once more. "For everything, Sorin. Thank you for all of it."

He cupped her cheek, his thumb wiping away the stray tear that had slipped free. "It is my pleasure, Scarlett."

She leaned against his shoulder, and he tucked her in tighter. Quiet fell around them while they watched the small pond life. After several moments she said quietly, "I wish I could have met your parents."

The statement startled him a little, and his chest tightened at the thought of his lovely mother who had walked these very gardens with him so often when he was a child. At the thought of his father who had made time to personally train him a few hours every week, not just in weaponry, but in running a Court. He swallowed thickly. "Me too, Love. Me too," he said, pressing a featherlight kiss to her cheek, but he stilled when she brought her fingers to his own cheek.

Holding his gaze the entire time, she brought her lips to his, and he couldn't suppress the slight shiver it sent through his body. It was a short grazing of lips on lips. She pulled back just far enough that he could feel her breath on his lips as she spoke. "They would be so proud of you, Sorin."

He didn't know what he'd been expecting her to say, but it wasn't that. The emotion that flooded through him at the words had tears burning at the back of his eyes. His hand slipped into her hair, and he pulled her lips back to his. She immediately opened for him, and his tongue swept in, tangling with hers. Her hand was still on his cheek, and the other came up and gripped his side, fingers digging in slightly.

"Dinner," he murmured when they both came up for air. "We need to go to dinner."

"Dinner is highly overrated," she hummed back onto his lips.

He smiled against the kisses she was gently gracing one corner of his mouth with and then the other. "Overrated, but essential," he replied, disentangling himself from her. "Especially with the magic you have been practicing every day." He stood and extended a hand down to her, wiggling his fingers. "Besides, I can hear your stomach, Princess."

"You cannot," she snipped, slipping her hand into his. He interlaced their fingers as he led her from the garden and back to the stairs. He could have portaled them down to the den, he supposed, rather than taking the seven flights of stairs, but he didn't think she'd keep her hand in his once they were with the others.

And he was right. When he pushed open the den door and the others all turned to them, she dropped his hand and strode for her seat, throwing a flirty grin at Cyrus. Rayner, however, gave Sorin a pointed look over his glass while he sipped at some liquor.

"Drink, Love?" he called to her, ignoring his Third.

"Wine, please."

He set her glass down before her and slipped into his usual seat to her right. The food appeared before them, and they all scooped noodles and sauce and salad onto their plates.

They'd only taken a few bites when Cyrus sighed slightly. "Talwyn sent a message right before dinner, Sorin."

"Did she now?" He glanced at Scarlett out of the corner of his eye. She was spinning noodles on her fork, acting uninterested, but he knew better.

"She summoned the Royals for a meeting in two weeks," Cyrus continued.

"For?" Eliza demanded.

"She's not really known for sharing things in advance, is she?" Cyrus replied bitterly.

"She is not, but it usually has to do with something Ashtine has picked up on her walkings," Rayner cut in.

Sorin sighed. "No use in worrying about it tonight."

Scarlett had set down her fork and picked up a piece of bread. As she took a bite, her right hand came up and brushed down his forearm, giving it a quick squeeze before she reached for her wine glass.

Conversation ebbed and flowed some more until Eliza said, "Did you hear that Lord Winston's son is trying to regain their lost seat?"

"Lord Winston? Isn't he the Lord that was killed a few years ago in Rydeon?" Cyrus asked, dessert appearing before them. From the variety of fruit tarts, Sorin searched for two pear ones and scooped them onto Scarlett's plate. She gave him a little smile, picking up her fork.

Rayner huffed softly. "For good reason. He was selling women and children out of his estate for horrific purposes. The Rydeon king stripped the family of their council seat after it was all revealed."

"That man actually deserved to have the Wraiths of Death sent after him," Cyrus commented.

"Do we know it was the Wraiths?" Eliza mused. "Was that ever confirmed?"

"From the rumors of how he was carved up and clearly alive for all of it, there is no way it couldn't have been them," Cyrus answered, leaning back and sipping at his liquor. "You said you have friends in the Black Syndicate," he said, eyes sliding to Scarlett. "Did you ever hear of the missions the Wraiths of Death were sent to carry out?"

Scarlett had been silently eating her pear tarts. She brought another bite to her mouth as she said, "I'd hear of them here and there."

"Did you ever travel to the other kingdoms? Do you know where the Black Syndicate is?" Cyrus asked.

"Do you?" she countered.

"No, but I am not the one who supposedly has friends there." He took another sip of liquor. Sorin wasn't sure if he should intervene here or not, so he let Scarlett handle his Court unless she looked to him for help.

Scarlett leaned back against her chair, swirling the last of her wine. Sorin's arm was draped along the back as it usually was during the dessert portion of the evening.

"Supposedly? You doubt my words, Darling?" Scarlett said with a soft, wicked smile curling up the side of her lips.

"It is incredibly improbable," Cyrus returned. "Weren't you living in a noble household? How would you have met people from the Black Syndicate?"

That smile on her lips grew wider, and Sorin watched as a mask slipped over her features. "How did *you* become the Second to the Prince of Fire? You weren't born noble."

The entire table stilled.

Cyrus's face was hard as he held Scarlett's stare. She merely sipped her wine once more, waiting. "What would you, a Fae princess hidden away in the human lands, know of my history?" he asked too quietly. Sorin tensed at the tone. The violence dancing on the edge of it.

"Down, kitty," Scarlett purred. "No need to get your claws out." She took another sip of her wine, clearly unconcerned. "I can smell an orphan from a mile away, Darling. I can tell someone who wasn't raised by nobility but has found themselves living in such a world of propriety and politics. So tell me, Second of the Fire Court, did you not befriend anyone that could benefit you? That would ensure your survival to see the next sunrise or next meal in your belly?"

Cyrus was utterly still as he surveyed Scarlett with a new under-standing. When he did not answer, Scarlett's tone was hard as she continued, "It seems we have more in common than you thought, hmm?"

"It would appear we do, Darling," Cyrus finally answered. He raised his glass to her from across the table, and Scarlett inclined her head.

"Do you know the Wraiths then?" Rayner asked quietly.

Scarlett's eyes slid to him. "Everyone knows of the Wraiths."

"Yes, but did you ever meet them?" Eliza pressed.

"If I had, would you like me to arrange a meeting?" Scarlett mused, draining her glass.

"Badass women who are feared amongst the entire continent? Yes, I would love to meet them," Eliza said, a thread of wistfulness in her tone.

"Should I ever see my friends again, I'll see what I can do," Scarlett replied, setting her empty glass down. She turned to Sorin. "I'm tired. I'm going to head back early tonight."

"I will walk you back," he replied, getting to his feet.

They said good night to the others, and he followed her from the den. They had walked the steps up to their floor in silence and had entered their rooms when he gripped her arm to stop her as she made to move to the bedroom. She turned a questioning glance to him, and he pulled her to him. "Hey, Love."

The mask was gone, and the corner of her mouth twitched. "Thank you. For not saying anything about…all of that tonight."

"Your story is not mine to tell," he answered, his hands sliding down to her waist.

"Sorin, I…" She closed her eyes and huffed out a breath, a stray piece of hair fluttering. He waited, brushing that hair back from her face. She opened her eyes again and met his. "I don't deserve you. I don't deserve all that you've done for me."

"Who says? Who decides what we deserve? Do I deserve to be touching you right now after all I kept from you?" he countered, voicing the same thoughts he'd said to Rayner earlier that evening.

"I told you that my mother's death was not your fault," she argued, her tone hardening a touch.

"Do I deserve such forgiveness?"

"Of course you do. You deserve happiness, Sorin."

"My Love, so do you. You deserve every happiness."

He didn't know how long they stood there, eyes locked on each other, before she rose up onto her tiptoes and pressed a kiss to his cheek. "Whether I deserve you or not, Sorin, I'm grateful you came into my life."

She freed herself from his hold and crossed to the bedroom, presumably to get ready for bed. She did look tired. She wasn't resting enough as she dove deeper into her magic. He crossed to the hearth, giving her a few minutes of privacy to change and wash up. He stood, watching the flames flicker. He would never cage her. He would never ask her to assume a throne, either as queen or at his side, that she did not want. But he also knew that if she returned to Baylorin to stay, he would follow her there. He would follow her to the farthest star.

CHAPTER 24
CALLAN

"Do you spend your entire day in here?" Scarlett asked, plopping a small stack of books onto the table.

Callan looked up, a little surprised. They had met in the library nearly every day in the weeks that had followed the Courtyard incident. The surprise was not that she was here, but that she was here so early in the day. Normally, she met him in training clothes later in the afternoon. She had explained she trained with Eliza in the mornings and had magic lessons with Sorin after lunch, so they had begun spending a couple hours before dinner together researching in the library. She wasn't in training clothes today, though, either. She wore gray fitted pants with a soft blue sweater and a black cloak around her shoulders. Her hair was out of its usual braid and flowed down and around her shoulders.

She sank into the chair across from him, pulling a pear from her cloak pocket and taking a bite. "Are you sure they allow food in here?" he asked her with a raised brow.

"It's a pear, Callan, not a four course meal," she answered, pulling another from her pocket and tossing it to him.

He caught it with ease as he said, "You are early today."

"Sorin has a meeting this afternoon with Talwyn so our magic lesson was canceled today," she answered tightly.

"Talwyn is coming here?" Callan asked, stiffening.

"I do not know where they are meeting." She pulled the book from the top of her stack and flipped the cover open.

"That would probably explain the three extra guards trailing me today," he grumbled, returning to his own book before him.

"More than likely," she said with a smile.

"I am surprised he does not have a dozen guards with you," Callan muttered under his breath.

Scarlett looked up from her book and gave him an impish grin. "Oh, he does. They're getting me more books."

"Your guards are looking for books?"

"Levels below us," she answered with a wink. "They were getting on my nerves."

"Some guards," Callan said with a huff.

"Maybe they learned from Finn and Sloan," she crooned.

He looked up from his book and gave her an unimpressed smirk. She was staring at her own book, her hair falling like a silky sheet over her shoulder. He'd always loved her hair down, out of the braid that meant she was all business. She'd always seemed more relaxed when her hair was down.

He was about to comment on it when he noticed the book she was reading. "You can read that?"

She brought her eyes to his. They were pure icy blue today, made even bluer by the pale blue of her sweater. "I can. It is the Old Language of the Fae."

"You learned it that quickly? I have been studying it here and there and find it incredibly complicated."

"Apparently I was born knowing it," she said with a shrug.

"Are all Fae born knowing the Old Language, then?"

"No. Only some," she said, returning her eyes to the book.

"The most powerful ones," he supplied.

"I suppose so," she replied shortly.

He chose to take the strong hint in her tone and drop the subject. They sat together in silence for the next half hour, each left to their own books, when she sat back, tapping her fingers on the table. "Have you learned any more about what Deimas and Esmeray supposedly wanted across the sea? What supposedly set off the Great War?"

"That is incredibly random," Callan said, sitting back in his own chair.

"Just something I've been thinking about. I mean, it'd have to be pretty big if they went to *war* over it." She began twirling a piece of her silver hair around her finger absent-mindedly while her shadows curled around her arms.

"I have not, although I did read something that suggested Deimas and Esmeray were not the ones who isolated Avonleya, but that Avonleya set up a powerful enchantment to keep them out," Callan remarked. She tapped her fingers on the table again.

"That would be a twist," she murmured, seemingly more to herself than to him. "Deimas and Esmeray would have searched for the work around...and sought out help from the Fae. From her sisters."

Interrupting her musing, Callan asked, "What do you mean a work around?"

Scarlett's eyes came back to his, pulling her from her thoughts. "Sorin said there is always a work around to magic. Even enchantments and spells. Avonleya was apparently very powerful. More powerful than the Fae. Deimas and Esmeray would have sought the work around if whatever they were seeking was that important and valuable. Nothing else you can think of?"

"Not that I can recall, but I will look through my notes," he offered.

"No, that's okay," she said with a wave of her hand. "If it's only been mentioned once in all your research, it's likely not truth anyway. Just speculation." She leaned back over her own book, her hair falling around her once again.

Before he could stop himself, he blurted out, "Have dinner with me tonight." She stilled. She seemed to stop breathing entirely as her eyes stayed fixed on the book before her. "It is just a meal, Scarlett, not a marriage proposal," he added slyly. Her eyes dragged up to his at the words, and he forced a half smile at the scrutiny in them. Her damn hair swayed around her as she sat back in her chair once more. Still, she said nothing. "We can expand where we interact, can we not? I mean, for an entire year we met solely in my chambers. Now we seem to only speak in a library. We are allowed more than one location at a time, are we not?"

For an entire minute, she said nothing. Callan forced himself not to squirm under her intense gaze. She made no movement. It was a preternatural stillness he'd realized only Fae could achieve. He was about to tell her to just forget he'd said anything when she said slowly, "All right."

"Really?"

The corner of her mouth twitched up. "It's just a meal, right?"

"Right. Yes," Callan fumbled.

"All right then. Send word as to when and where," she said, returning to the book before her.

"I will."

And despite himself, despite everything he knew deep down, he allowed a little part of himself to hope.

Scarlett strode into Sorin's chambers, two books tucked under her arm. She didn't know why she hadn't thought of it sooner. Books written in the Old Language likely had more history than those in the common tongue. She knew Talwyn had been meeting with Sorin and the other Royals today. About what she didn't know. Her mind kept going back to what Callan had said about Deimas and Esmeray seeking something across the sea. She wondered if Sorin knew anything about that particular theory or what they might have been looking for. Maybe he'd be back by now and she could ask him about it.

She paused by the table to set the books down and said as she did, "Darling, what a pleasant surprise." She'd sensed another presence as soon as she'd opened the door. She'd scented him a moment later.

Cyrus chuckled from the sofa in the room. "Hello, Scarlett. You didn't read enough in the library today?"

She turned to face him, leaning against the table and crossing her arms. "As I've repeatedly told Sorin, there is no such thing as reading enough. Besides, it's research." She tapped the books in emphasis.

"Sorin said you were doing research with the mortal prince. You are spending a lot of time with him," he commented too casually.

"Jealous, Darling? You're simply taking too long to make your move," she crooned with a smirk. Cyrus didn't fall into their usual flirty banter, though, and the look on his face made her stomach flip-flop. "Where is Sorin?" she asked as nonchalantly as she could. "I thought you two were meeting with Talwyn this afternoon."

"We did." His tone was grim.

"How did it go?"

"Not well."

She straightened, the dread in her stomach growing. "Where is he, Cyrus?"

"Not here."

"Where is he?" she demanded again.

"He has gone where he goes to drink and brood. When he wants to do so alone."

"I'm afraid he doesn't get that option today. Where is he?"

Cyrus sighed. "I didn't wait here to take you to him. I just wanted to let you know he likely will not be home until tomorrow sometime. So you wouldn't worry. If you want someone else to stay in these chambers with you tonight, I will do so."

"No. He does not get that option either. Where is he, Cyrus?"

"He will not let you in."

"Cyrus!" she snapped, smoke curling in her mouth and her shadows darkening.

"Fine. He has a mountain home up in the highest peaks. He has wards all around it, and he doesn't let any of us in. He goes there when he wants to be alone."

"You mean when he wants to throw a fit," Scarlett said. "Take me to him."

"He will not let you in," Cyrus repeated.

"The fuck he won't. Take me to him."

Cyrus, finally accepting she would not back down, sighed. "I cannot portal, Scarlett. I have no way to get you there."

"Then summon Briar. He can make me a portal."

Without a word, Cyrus reached up and sent a fire message to the Water Prince. A few minutes later, Briar stepped into the room. He bowed slightly to Scarlett. "I saw what happened today," he said grimly.

"He is at the chalet, and she insists on going to see him," Cyrus replied.

Briar's eyes settled on her. "He will likely not let you in," he said slowly.

"As I have already told Cyrus, he does not get that option. Take me to him," Scarlett snapped, striding towards them. Cyrus and Briar exchanged a look and a water portal appeared.

All three of them stepped through, and Scarlett blinked at the brightness of the snow-covered mountainside. She had forgotten they were entering the cold winter months, that Winter Solstice was quickly approaching, and wished she'd had the foresight to grab that fur-lined cloak Sorin had gotten for her. Before them, nearly a quarter of a mile away, was indeed a mountain home. It was smaller than she had been expecting, but there was smoke coming from the chimney.

"We cannot portal any closer. His wards prevent it," Briar said from beside her.

"He will not let you in, Scarlett," Cyrus said again. "He has never let anyone else into that house."

"No one?" she asked, turning to him incredulously.

"Only once," Cyrus said gravely, his eyes studying the chalet.

Scarlett began walking, trudging through the snow. Sorin had come for her. Sorin, who did not leave her alone. Sorin, who had sat in the darkness with her so many times, who had pulled her from the river. She would climb down into his pits with him just as he had done for her.

She could feel Briar and Cyrus watching her as she made her way among the drifts. This was taking too long. She was also not wearing proper footwear for this, she thought as she looked down at her now soaking wet silk shoes. Not trusting her own power yet, she glanced over her shoulder at Cyrus, who sent a small flame ahead of her, melting a path to the front door. For Sorin, she could do this. She felt the zing of the wards push against her magic, but she punched through, picking up her pace on the now clear ground.

She finally reached the front door and knocked tentatively. There was no reply, but she could feel him somehow, on the other side of the door. She could feel his temper and his bleakness and his misery.

She knocked again, more firmly. This time she got a growled response telling whomever was at the door precisely what they could go do to themselves.

Brooding indeed.

She banged on the door with her fist. "If you're going to throw a temper tantrum, Prince, at least let me drink with you," she yelled through the door.

She felt him pause. "Tell your escorts nice try, but I will be home tomorrow."

"I am not your damn messenger, and I demanded they bring me to you. They tried to deter me from coming. Let me in, Sorin," she replied, wiggling the locked door handle.

"I will be home tomorrow, Scarlett," he snarled back.

Scarlett.

Not Princess. Not Love.

She looked over her shoulder, biting her lip. Briar and Cyrus still stood, watching her. Cyrus's arms were folded across his chest. With her Fae sight, she could see his 'I-told-you-so' expression on his face.

Fine. He wanted to be a prick? She would play that game.

"Sorin Aditya, you stubborn ass, let me in!" she cried, banging her palm on the door.

Silence.

"I will sit out here. All fucking night, Sorin. I will sit here in the snow and the cold."

"Tell Cyrus that if he does not take you home, I will kick his ass from here to Threlarion."

"My home is wherever you are. If you demand I go home, I am already there. Let me in."

Still, the door remained closed. He was really not going to let her in? After all they had been through? After all she had shared with him?

No. That wasn't an option.

"You promised, you lying bastard!" she screamed now. She could feel the tears pooling in her eyes as she banged on that door with clenched hands. Her shadows wreathed her fists, the wood of the door groaning under each hit. "You promised you would not leave me alone in the darkness. You came for me, and I have come for you. I am yours, and you are mine. Let me in!"

She heard both Briar and Cyrus gasp at her words, but she didn't care. Let them think what they wanted.

Then she heard Cyrus swear as that door slowly cracked open.

Sorin looked like every emotion she could feel emanating off of him. His eyes were hollow. His dark hair looked like he'd been running his hands through it repeatedly. He wore a short-sleeve tunic with his pants, his jacket presumably shucked off in the space behind him and his feet were bare.

"What do you want, Scarlett?" he asked after a long moment of silence, staring at each other. She could smell the liquor on his breath.

"Let me in, Sorin," she whispered. She saw him glance behind her, and she peered over her shoulder. Cyrus and Briar stood, shock on their features.

"We can talk tomorrow," he said, his eyes coming back to hers.

"Fine. Then I shall sit with you in the darkness. Let me in," she said, trying to push past him. He was immoveable, though, not budging an inch. She reached up to touch his cheek, anything to bring him back to her, but he jerked out of her reach.

232

Oh, she recognized this kind of temper, and it did not scare her. She smirked at him. A smirk she knew would make him see red. His nostrils flared. "Go home, Monrhoe. I will be back tomorrow."

"No, *Aditya*," she said with quiet calm. "Let me in."

"I do not want company right now," he growled.

"I do not care. You've shoved your face into my business when I didn't want company numerous times," she retorted, crossing her arms. "Let me in." He did not move.

"Quit being a stubborn brat," he ground out.

"Quit being an obstinate jackass," she retorted. The two stared each other down, glaring at each other.

"So what? We will just sit here and get drunk together?" he asked with a sneer.

"If that is what you desire, yes."

"And what if I desire something else?" His eyes raked over her, and she fought the urge to flinch. "Or is that reserved for your mortal prince?"

"Do not be a prick," she growled. "You do not get to call me a whore because you're having a hard day, but if that kind of release is what you need, I'll go find someone for you to be with."

He blinked at her, and she saw the flicker of surprise pass across his eyes before they became unreadable again.

"Tell me what happened." She rubbed her hands over her arms, trying to warm herself. His eyes flickered as he noted the movement, her wet shoes, but he still did not move to let her pass.

"No."

"Why?"

"Because they are not your burdens to bear," he snarled.

"So you will punish yourself by bearing them alone?" she snapped back. "That's not how this thing works between you and me."

"There is no you and me," he hissed. Scarlett stilled at the venom in his words. "There is you, and there is me."

"I don't believe that for one second. We've been through too much together."

"Then maybe that is my punishment, hmm? Going through all this trouble to get you here for nothing."

The words slammed into her, and she stumbled backwards from him. "I understand that you had a shitty day, but that does not entitle you to be cruel to me, Prince of Fire."

"I told you to leave. You did not listen," he snarled, his face colder than she had ever seen it.

"So it gives you permission to speak to me like I am garbage?" she demanded. She could feel her shadows hovering at her fingertips, and she trembled with the effort to control them.

"You have called yourself that on more than one occasion," he said with a shrug.

Tears burned in her eyes, but she refused to cry in front of him. Not this time. Not when he was the cause of it. Again.

He stared at her with cold indifference. She heard footsteps behind them, and Sorin's eyes flickered to the movement. "Your escorts are coming to claim you," he sneered, stepping back to shut the door.

"We are not done here!" she cried, spearing her shadows out from her to block the door from closing.

"Oh, I think we are. I have nothing else to say to you."

"Then I have something to say to you," she retorted, stepping right up to the threshold of the door, going onto her tiptoes so she was inches from his face. "You are a fucking coward. You crawled into the pits of hell for me, and when I come to claim you, to return the godsdamn favor, you shut me out. You push everyone who loves you away. You push *me* away. You say it is to protect us, to keep us safe, but it's really to keep yourself safe. You know how I know that? Because we're the same, you and me. We're the same in every fucking way."

And she couldn't stop them. She couldn't stop the tears from running down her face, hot and angry and full of hurt.

"You sit up here in this fucking house, throwing a fit, sulking and feeling sorry for yourself because you think you what? You deserve this? You deserve to suffer? To be alone? No one deserves that, Sorin. And I certainly do not deserve to be told I am a whoring piece of shit, least of all by you. The only person I have shared my darkest secrets with. You don't get to call me trash when I am the one who risked baring my entire soul to you. Stupid? Naïve? Maybe, but I am not your godsdamned punishment. I am not some piece of property that you have been inconvenienced with.

"If you do not want this thing we have, that is fine. I can find my own way. I do not need to stay here." Her shadows swirled around her, a vortex of darkness. "I can find the stars somewhere else with someone who won't toss me back into the river and shove my head under water when they have a bad day. Someone who won't treat me like a fucking burden."

Sorin's face had paled. She felt a hand at her elbow and whirled to see Cyrus at her side, ire on his face. Briar stood next to him, just as furious. A water portal opened behind them.

Sorin stepped from the chalet, reaching for her, his fingers brushing her other hand. "Scarlett—"

"Do not touch me," she spat, jerking her hand from him and stepping back into Cyrus. His arm curled protectively around her waist, and a shield of water sprang up between her and Sorin. "It is certainly not a necessity right now."

"Scarlett, wait," he tried again, his hand dropping to his side. He flung the door of the chalet open wide and stepped aside. "Come in. I will let you in. Come in. Please."

"I have dinner plans with my *mortal prince* tonight," she sneered. "I'll see you when I see you."

She turned to step through the portal, but she didn't miss Cyrus's words to his Prince as she did so.

"You are a fucking idiot."

CHAPTER 25

SORIN

Sorin made to follow Scarlett and Cyrus through the portal, but Briar stepped into his path, the portal snapping closed behind him. He threw fire at the shield of water Briar still had up, and the flames hissed as they sputtered out.

"Get out of my way," he snarled at Briar.

"No," he retorted with quiet rage. "You can give her a gods-damned minute."

"I need to talk to her," he growled, hurling more fire at that shield.

"You have said plenty to her," Briar snapped back, the water of his shield beginning to turn to steam at the onslaught of Sorin's flames.

"Get out of my way," he snarled again.

And then he felt the blow to his face. Briar had punched him square in the jaw.

Sorin growled, spitting blood onto the ground, but he did not retaliate. He had deserved that hit. More than deserved it.

"Did you hear any of what she said to you?" Briar snarled, circling him, his icy blue eyes glowing. Every feral Fae predator trait and instinct was evident on his face. He was defending Scarlett. Their Princess. Their Queen.

Their princess, yes, but *his* twin flame. He had shredded her. He had said far worse things to her than Mikale or Callan. He had known exactly where to hit because she had bared her soul to him. He was the piece of shit. Not her. Never her.

Ice flooded through his veins as Briar bared his teeth at him. The Prince of Water and Ice come to defend their Princess against the Prince of Fire. He let the ice slow his blood. "You let Talwyn so far under your damn skin, you did not even hear what Scarlett said to you. She practically screamed the Claiming Rite at you without even knowing what she was saying. You insufferable fool," Briar spat.

You came for me, and I have come for you. I am yours, and you are mine.

"If she walks away from you, from us, from all of this now, it is entirely your fault," he snarled again, ripping his ice from Sorin's veins. His own magic took over instinctively, flooding him with heat.

I can find the stars somewhere else with someone who won't toss me back into the river and who won't treat me like a fucking burden.

Her words rattled around his head and wrapped around his chest, squeezing tight.

"Let me go to her," he choked out.

"She does not want to see you," Briar growled back. "It's interesting, isn't it? We told her the same thing of you. That you did not want to see anyone, speak to anyone. She did not care. She demanded we take her to you. She would not let us be. Over and over we told her you would not let her in, but I saw it on her face. She was convinced you would. She was certain you would let her in. If we had refused, I am certain she would have attempted to kill us both, then she would have clawed her way through every hell to get to you.

"And I thought maybe you would. I thought maybe you would not refuse your godsdamned *twin flame*. I thought maybe this would be what it took to get her to feel that bond. So I brought her to you, knowing what kind of foul mood you would be in. Thinking there was no way you would take it out on the female who owns your heart. And then you pissed all over it." Each word felt like a dagger to his chest.

"Let me go to her," Sorin said again, a slight snarl this time.

"Are you finally getting over yourself?" Briar sneered.

"How intriguing this scene is," came a cool voice from the trees beyond.

Both males whirled to see a mortal man leaning against a tree, his hands in his pockets. A man Sorin recognized. Mikale.

How the fuck was he here?

The Fae males had been so busy arguing and fighting, he had missed the warnings of the wards. His mind had been so overtaken by Scarlett, he'd missed this crucial imposition.

"Who are you?" Briar demanded, his sword appearing in his hand in a swirl of ice and snow.

Mikale chuckled. "That will be of no use." He waved his hand through the tree. A mirage. He was an illusion.

"What do you want, Lairwood?" Sorin ground out.

"You took something that belongs to me," Mikale growled. His eyes were nearly black as he stared down the Fae princes.

"She belongs to no one," Sorin snarled, flames flickering in his eyes.

"She is clearly dividing your own alliances," he said with a bored sigh. "Send her back to me, and we can all go about our business. Our efforts can be focused elsewhere, away from your Court."

"Go to hell," Sorin spat.

"You have been so careful to keep her hidden from me, Prince of Fire. Until today. Until a little bit ago, when all our tricks and spells picked up her essence. Right here in this very space. It took me a while to work out this illusion spell, unfortunately, and it seems I have missed her. She has disappeared from my tracking spells once more." He took a step towards them, and shields of fire and water sprang to life. Rage filled Mikale's face as he ground out from between his clenched teeth, "Where is she?"

"Somewhere you will not find her," Sorin growled.

"Very well, Prince of Fire. There is more than one path to what

I desire. This would have simply been the easiest." With a cruel, bone-chilling smile, he was gone.

"Was that...?" Briar asked, turning to Sorin.

"Yes," Sorin answered. "Yes, it was."

"How did he get here?"

"Apparently, he is accessing magic somehow. I have been using my own to hide her from him, but today, with all the words exchanged between us... The enchantments slipped. Because I am weakening," he said quietly.

Briar swore. "Why didn't you fucking say something? I would have helped."

"I did this. Let me go to her," Sorin said, not meeting his friend's eye.

A water portal appeared, and the princes stepped through into Sorin's private chambers. Cyrus leaned against the liquor cart. He smiled cruelly at the bruise that hadn't yet healed on Sorin's jaw. "You deserve that, you stupid bastard," he snarled, sipping his drink.

"I know," Sorin replied. "Where is she?"

"She left a message for you. She said you'd understand it when you heard the words," Cyrus said casually, swirling the ice in his glass.

"What is it?" Sorin ground out.

"Her exact words were: Tell that Fae bastard when he's ready to tell me what's going on, I'll be waiting. Until then, he can go fuck himself, and my wellbeing is none of his concern."

Sorin closed his eyes at the memory of Cassius delivering those same words months ago. "Where is she?"

"She gathered a few things and went to Eliza's rooms when we returned. Good luck," Cyrus said with a smirk.

Good luck indeed.

Sorin trudged down the hall a few doors and stopped before Eliza's room. He knocked once, and the door flew open. Another raging female stood before him, fire in her eyes. "What the fuck did you do?"

"Where is she?" was all Sorin said.

"She's gone to have dinner with the mortal prince. Do not interrupt them," Eliza snapped, and she slammed the door in his face.

He slid to the floor outside Eliza's rooms in the hallway. For hours he sat there, waiting for her. It was nearly midnight when she came silently down the hall. She was in an amethyst colored dress with silver thread in the skirts. The bodice and sleeves were fitted. It was simple and elegant and perfect on her. Perfect for a dinner with a prince.

He stood as he scented her, grateful there wasn't another scent so thoroughly entwined with her own, and she froze at the movement. Her shadows instantly thickened around her. She was nearly ten feet away from him and stood with a stillness only Fae could achieve.

He didn't say a word as she silently moved towards him. She didn't bother to look at him when she strode right past him and into Eliza's rooms, shutting the door behind her.

He inhaled deeply and knocked gently. "Scarlett. Please come talk to me." He could feel her, just on the other side of the door. If he didn't know any better, her scent was so close she was leaning against the door itself. But that door may as well have been an ocean for the distance she'd put between them. He leaned his forehead against the door. "Love, please."

There was movement on the other side, and he nearly fell to his knees as the door opened, but it was Eliza who stood there. Her face was a mixture of wrath and sympathy as she said quietly, "She went to bed, Sorin."

"Did she say anything?"

"She said she would come to you in the morning."

"Will she?" he asked, desperately searching her eyes for any hint of hope.

"I believe she is a female of her word, and when she says she is going to come for you, she will." Eliza stared back at him, her gaze hard. She was not going to let him in tonight.

He turned and silently went back to his chambers. The emptiness of them weighed on him. He could still smell her. In the air. In the bedroom. In the sheets. He couldn't even lay in the bed without her, so he sat in a chair before the fire.

I can find the stars somewhere else with someone who won't treat me like a fucking burden.

He would never be able to sleep tonight. Not until he talked to her. He stood again, pacing back and forth before the hearth, waiting for her to return. Her words from weeks ago floated back to him.

I think you might be mine, though.

CHAPTER 26
SCARLETT

Scarlett lay awake in Eliza's extra bedroom. Her dinner with Callan had been just that. A casual dinner. She had almost canceled on him, too broken by what Sorin had said to her earlier that day, but she'd be damned if she'd let his words wreck her. He had been the one to pull her from the river. Screw him for trying to hurl her back in.

They had dined in Callan's guest suite, Finn and Sloan joining them. Sloan was even almost smiling by the end of the evening as they shared tales of adventures in Baylorin. She was impressed to hear that Sloan had actually fought in battles before becoming one of Callan's personal guards. Finn had grown up with Callan and had been trained to be his personal guard since birth. The three were the best of friends, and she had felt a slight twinge. They reminded her so much of her and Nuri and Juliette.

Sorin had been brought up only once, and she had simply said she wished not to discuss this land or its occupants for the evening. The others had seemed inclined to agree and that had been that.

It was much later than she'd intended when she had walked back to the private wing of the palace, feeling lighter than she had when she'd gone to the guest wing.

Until she had seen him outside of Eliza's rooms, waiting for her.

She didn't have it in her to fight with him anymore. She could feel that darkness pulling her down, down, down. She could feel her shadows stretching around her as that darkness yawned open. She didn't want to go there. She didn't want to let that out of its cage. Not against him.

So she had walked past him without a glance and slumped against the door once inside Eliza's suite. Eliza was sitting on her sofa, reading a book and sipping tea, when she met her eyes with a questioning look.

Scarlett had heard him beg her to talk, but she couldn't. The wound he had dealt her was still too raw. She had shaken her head at Eliza, and her friend had gotten up from the couch, coming to her.

"Tell him I will come to him in the morning," she had whispered, barely audible.

Mercifully, Eliza had waited until she was in the bedroom with the door closed before talking to Sorin.

And here she was, unable to sleep without that male body next to her. The bed felt huge and cold. She knew she could warm it up, but she didn't trust herself enough to tap into her magic without someone else in the room.

She walked back out to the sitting room and found Eliza waiting for her, a second cup of tea steaming beside her own. "Cyrus filled me in on everything that was said, the parts you left out," she said quietly as Scarlett picked up the teacup and took a sip, settling in beside Eliza on the couch. "He was wrong and out of line."

"He was." It was all Scarlett could think of to say.

"He has it in his head that he needs to protect us all, and he takes failure harder than anyone I've ever met. Talwyn knows exactly how to push his buttons. Did you know he trained her in her magic?" she asked.

"No," Scarlett said softly. "How? Her magic is earth and wind."

"Yes, but magic basics are the same. Control, discipline, and knowing your limits are all similar. He was her private tutor growing up. He was your mother's Second and Hand to the Queen," Eliza explained. "I do not know the particulars of what she said to him today. Cyrus would not tell me, but she knows what wounds to reopen, Scarlett. It does not excuse his behavior. Nothing of what he said to you was remotely permissible. Just..." Eliza pursed her lips as if trying to decide the words to say. "You said yourself you are the same. I trust you know what it is like to be in a pit you are trying to crawl out of and that you can slip, even on your best of days. I trust you know you lash out at those you love the most."

"I know your Fae customs. I have been researching them and learning," Scarlett said after several moments of silence, both lost in their own thoughts. "I know he has a twin flame out there somewhere, but I wish he didn't. Does that make me an awful person?"

Eliza seemed to weigh her words before she replied. "No. It doesn't, but finding one's twin flame is so, so rare, Scarlett. The majority of us do not find them in our long immortal lifetime."

"What would you do though? If you bound yourself to another, and they later found their twin flame?" Scarlett asked.

"I think if I cared enough about another to bind myself to them and they found their twin flame, I could not ask them to give that up for me if they desire to be with them instead," Eliza said slowly.

"If you knew there was a chance that they would one day find their twin flame, would you risk giving that much of yourself to another?"

"I think that if you found someone to trust enough to give your entire self to, it would be well worth the risk of losing them and worth the time you did have with them," Eliza answered softly. Scarlett was quiet as she stared into the hearth, sipping on her tea. "Let me ask you a question now. Which prince does this pertain to?"

Scarlett jerked her head to Eliza at the words. "There is nothing between me and Callan anymore."

"There is definitely something there," Eliza said with an unbelieving laugh. "He wishes for so much more though."

"Callan and I have a complicated history. I almost didn't go to dinner tonight, but it felt good. To eat with friends and reminisce about Baylorin. To know the stories being told, without feeling like I was on the outside looking in."

"Is that how you feel with us?" Eliza asked, tilting her head to the side, her red-gold locks falling over her shoulder.

"Sometimes," Scarlett admitted. "It feels like I have known you all for ages, but I have only been here a few months. You all are a family, and I am...still an outsider most days. It is not anything that has been done or said. It just takes time. I did have people, before Sorin. Before..."

"I know."

"Callan was one of those people in an odd way, and I miss the others. Especially today."

"The male that Sorin brought weeks ago?"

"Cassius. Yes. I miss him most of all," Scarlett whispered. She leaned her head on Eliza's shoulder. "Sorin eases that heartache most days. Most days, just being around him gives me the strength to push through. He... I don't know how to explain what he is for me. Most days, though, he is a rock that steadies me in a storm that does not cease. Today was not one of those days."

"Some days are hard. Sometimes simply making it through the hard days is enough," Eliza said, leaning her own head against Scarlett's. That little bit of contact from a friend who understood just how hard some days could be eased the ache in her chest slightly. The knowledge that sometimes just surviving was enough for one day almost made her sigh in relief.

"Tomorrow will be hard, too," Scarlett murmured.

"No matter how tomorrow goes, you are not alone," Eliza replied, "and I do not mean Sorin."

"Thank you," Scarlett whispered, squeezing Eliza's hand.

Sorin

The main door creaked as it opened, and Sorin was instantly on his feet in the sitting room, but it was Cyrus.

"She's training with Eliza in the private pits," he said by way of greeting, leaning against the door with his arms crossed. "You look like shit."

Sorin had hardly slept. He'd been up since before the sun, watching the clock tick by the minutes, then the hours. The bruise on his cheek had healed completely overnight. He'd gone over so many things he wanted to say to her and played out every scenario of how she would respond. Then, of course, there had been the dinner with Callan. What had transpired there? Not that it was his business. They were not bonded. She was free to find release else-where. She had basically told him she would find him his own release if he needed it.

When he all but called her a whore.

"I hope you plan to do more than stand there in stone-cold silence when she finally comes back," Cyrus drawled.

Sorin snorted. "If she does not kick me out on my ass first."

"You'd deserve it, you know," Cyrus retorted.

"I am well aware."

Cyrus stared at him for a moment before saying, "Briar said the mortal who tried to keep her managed to appear to you two."

"He did," Sorin admitted, sitting back down on the sofa. "Although I am starting to believe he is not a mortal at all, which would make his desire for Scarlett and her bloodline a lot more logi-cal. Mixing her bloodline with human blood would not do much, but combining it with another magic wielder would be tempting to say the least."

"Why not approach Talwyn, though? If his desire is more power?"

"I do not know. Perhaps he has heard of our benevolent queen," Sorin sneered.

"You let her get to you yesterday," Cyrus said quietly. "Why?"

"She is upset with me. I am keeping Scarlett from her. She is worried about something, so she is lashing out at me, and she knows exactly where to strike," Sorin answered tightly.

"You let her come between you and Scarlett. She was right there, Sorin. She all but said the Claiming Rite."

"You think I don't know that?" Sorin snapped. "I do not need you to remind me of my failures. Talwyn did that enough yesterday."

Cyrus's lips formed a thin line, a muscle feathering in his jaw. "What do you need from me?"

"Tell Rayner to check in with our spies in the mortal lands, especially the Windonelle capital. See if he can learn anything about Mikale. We are going to need to inform Talwyn soon if we cannot figure it out. Ashtine will need to be sent in," Sorin said. "Keep it quiet. I do not want her to know unless we have to."

"Anything else?"

"Try to keep the mortal prince occupied today," he ground out.

"I'll see what I can do," Cyrus answered. "Send word if you need something."

Sorin nodded, staring into the darkened hearth before him as Cyrus left the rooms. The minutes began to tick by again. He stood, pacing in front of the fireplace. He was about to just go up to the training room and beg on his knees for her to speak to him when the door opened again, and she slipped in.

She wore her training clothes, and she was drenched in sweat. She had trained hard this morning, likely trying to work through all her emotions. He could see it in her eyes as she stilled at the sight of him. She reached up and pulled the string from her braid, shaking out the plaits as she crossed the room to their bedroom without a word.

He waited a few minutes to see if she would come back out, and when she didn't, he took a deep breath and followed her path. The door to the bathing room was closed. So he waited.

And she took her time. He knew she was drawing this out as long as possible. He knew her well enough to know she was dreading this conversation. She was dreading the possibility of what else would come from his mouth. She had given him pieces of herself that she'd given no one else, and with that had come a tentative trust that he had shattered in the span of a few minutes.

When she finally emerged, she wore fitted black pants with a black tunic. Her hair hung loose around her shoulders, still wet. He stood near the balcony doors, and with half a thought, her hair was dry. She didn't acknowledge the gesture. She just crossed her arms and leaned against the doorframe of the bathing room, waiting. Her shadows slithered along her like vines of ivy, and he flashed back to a rooftop in Baylorin when he had first laid eyes on her and Nuri together. Death's Maiden stood before him now, not the female that he had spent months convincing to take down her walls...and then watched them all spring back up in a matter of seconds. She had put on her full armor for this conversation, retreating to that predatory place inside of herself.

He'd spent hours perfecting exactly what he was going to say to her, and now that she stood before him, he didn't know what to say to make her stop looking at him like he had ripped her heart from her chest and stomped on it.

Her eyes pinned him with a stare, gold and fiery today. "I've no treats for you this morning, Prince. Speak." Her voice was as cold and dark as the shadows that adored her.

But he couldn't. Words escaped him. He literally could not form them as she stared at him. He had expected to see hate and anger in her eyes, and while fury certainly stared back at him, he was not prepared for the hurt she allowed to shine through. This female who had always worn so many masks. Who had finally stopped wearing them around him.

Hurt. That is one mask he had never seen. Pain, yes. But this type of hurt? This was caused by betrayal. He had caused this. He had done this. There were no words to say that would make this right.

After another minute, she huffed a laugh of disbelief. "I am not going to stand here all day, Sorin. Either say something, or I will take my leave."

He made to take a step towards her, but when she stiffened at the movement, he froze. "I am sorry, Scarlett. I am so sorry."

"Keep going," she said coolly.

"There is so much. I do not even know where to begin."

"Start with one."

"You came for me," he said quietly.

248

"Of course I came for you," she snapped. "I thought that's what we did for each other. I thought... Of course I came for you."

"I am sorry that I hurt you."

"I am sorry that you knew where to strike," she replied with a cold bite.

Sorin swallowed. "You were right, Scarlett. We are the same. You are my equal in every possible way, and I had no right to speak to you like I did."

"No, you did not. You were in the dark, and instead of letting me in to keep you from blotting out the stars, you tried to shove me back into that river, back under the water. How ironic it is that *you* are the one who helped me realize that only I can decide who and what gets that kind of power over me. What's even more paradoxical is that I thought *you* were one of two people who would never try to shove me into a damn cage." He could see the silver pooling in her eyes. He could see her resolve to not let them fall. "I am not your godsdamned punishment," she whispered with venom, her eyes going to the floor.

He didn't hold back his own tears as two slipped down his face. It took every bit of self-control to keep himself from going to her. "No, Scarlett Monrhoe," he choked out. "You are anything but a punishment. You are a bright star I do not deserve."

"I trusted you!" Her voice cracked, and his knees nearly gave out at the sound of it. Then she was striding across the room to him, her shadows mixing with flames of bluest wildfire. "I trusted you with all of me, and you used it against me. You shut me out. You fucking took what you wanted from me and shut me out." She shoved him at the last words with such force he stumbled backwards. His chest burned where she had touched him, from the shadows or the flames he didn't know.

"I am sorry, Scarlett. Tell me what I need to do. Tell me how to fix this," he pleaded.

"There is no fixing this, Sorin! You may as well have been Mikale yesterday. You all but told me you only keep me around to get what you want from me. That I was a necessary burden."

"No! No, Love—" He reached for her, but she stepped back, interrupting him before he could say more.

"Don't you get it, Sorin? There is no Love. There is no you and me. There is you, and there is me." The words were stones being hurled at him. Words he had so carelessly snarled at her. Tears were flowing uncontrollably down her cheeks as she screamed at him. "You broke this! You broke us!"

And he felt it then, in his soul. He felt it splinter. His left hand burned in agony as that unfinished Mark faded slightly. It wasn't gone, but it was definitely lighter, a faint gray color rather than the stark black of his other Marks. He was going to be sick.

Then he was sick, violently sick, as she disappeared into the air.

CHAPTER 27

SORIN

In between bouts of hurling his guts up, Sorin managed to send fire messages to his Inner Court and Briar. They appeared almost instantly in his rooms.

"Where the hell is she?" Eliza demanded, looking around the room with wide eyes.

"She Traveled," Sorin answered hoarsely.

"You said she hadn't learned how to do that yet," Cyrus said slowly.

"She has done it one other time. It is how we got out of the Lairwood House."

Rayner was gripping his arm, helping him to his feet as he wiped his mouth with the back of his hand. Vomit coated his tongue, his mouth. Briar handed him a glass of water.

"Then how did she do so now?" Cyrus pressed.

"We… Emotions were high," Sorin ground out. "As you can imagine."

"Where the hell is she?" Eliza demanded again.

"I don't know."

"Then find her," Eliza spat.

"I can't."

"What do you mean you can't? You're her twin flame. Find her," Eliza ordered, her words cool and clipped.

"I. Can't." Sorin said again.

Cyrus's eyes went wide as he reached out and snatched Sorin's left hand. He swore at the sight of the faded Mark. "What did you do?" he whispered in horror.

"Where is she?" Eliza demanded once more.

"He can't feel her, Eliza," Cyrus said, disbelief in his voice. "He can't find her."

Eliza stalked from the room, the door slamming behind her.

"I can't feel her. I do not know where she is," Sorin's eyes went to Briar's. "Which means my enchantments are down."

This time Briar swore viciously. "I cannot help, Sorin. Not without knowing where she is."

"Rayner," Sorin started, turning to him.

"I am already on it. All of our resources are combing every territory," he said softly.

Sorin swallowed. He tried. He braced himself and looked inward, down that bond between their souls, but the threads connecting them had all but snapped. There was only one left, and it was stretched tight. He didn't know how long it would last.

Thick silence fell in the room, no one knowing what to say. And in that silence all he could hear was Scarlett screaming at him, pain and hurt entrenched in every word.

You broke this! You broke us!

"She said there was no fixing this," he said quietly to Cyrus. "You are the only one who has had a twin flame. Is she right?"

"I don't know, Sorin." His voice was somber, still in shock. "Thia and I had fights. There is no denying that, but we had been Anointed. Our bond was firmly in place and was always stronger. We weren't in the Trials. You aren't even in the Trials. You are the only one with a Mark."

Silence fell again.

I trusted you with all of me, and you used it against me. You shut me out.

He had shut her out. Talwyn had berated him all afternoon about his failures. About Eliné not trusting him with information about where she was going. About his failure in the mission to recover her. About those that were lost in that mission. Then she had started in on how he was continually failing her, starting with keeping Scarlett from her. He had pushed Scarlett away, not wanting Talwyn to be able to use her against him. He had shut her out, knowing she was a weapon that could and would be wielded against him. He had done it to protect her...and if he were being honest with himself, to protect himself as well.

Eliza burst back into the rooms, Prince Callan and his guards in tow.

"What is he doing here?" Sorin growled. Briar had used his magic to clean up the vomit from the floor, but at the sight of Callan, Sorin thought he would hurl all over again.

"Tell your fucking pride to take a seat," Eliza snarled. "You two are the two people in this Court who know her best. Where the hell is she?"

"He cannot find her," Cyrus said. "We've already discussed this."

"Yes, he can. He knows her. Where would she go?" She turned to Callan. "Where would she go, Prince?"

"To Cassius," Callan said firmly. Sorin didn't know how much Eliza had told him, but apparently it was enough that he grasped the gravity of the situation. "She would go to Cassius."

Sorin shook his head. "That's where she would want to go, but she knows it's not safe. There are wards around the Tyndell Manor. He might not even be there right now."

"Nuri?" Finn supplied.

"No. She would not go to Nuri," Sorin said darkly.

"You males are so dense," Eliza seethed. "Where would she go to feel safe? Before coming here, where did she last feel safe?"

"That woman hasn't felt safe in years," Sloan grunted from the far wall. "Why else would she be constantly in the shadows? I had never seen her unarmed until dinner last night."

Everyone turned to him. This guard, who had always showen such animosity toward Scarlett, seemed to know her better than they thought.

"Except once," Callan said slowly. "The day we surprised you two at your apartment. She was completely relaxed and comfortable and completely unarmed...and came to you for protection." He could see the dread on his face as he looked at Sorin.

"Baylorin?" Cyrus said in shock. "Could she even Travel that far without proper training?"

"I do not know the depths of her power," Sorin said, shaking his head. "She was...upset enough to unknowingly dive deep into her magic."

The mortal kingdoms. He could portal to the border, but it was over a day's ride nonstop to get to Baylorin. He would never get to her before Mikale tracked her down. He needed to Travel, and he only knew two other Fae who could do so.

"We need Talwyn and Azrael," Rayner said quietly from where he stood near the balcony doors, always separate from the others.

"Ashtine could go," Briar cut in.

"And report everything back to Talwyn? Take Scarlett back to Talwyn instead of here? I don't think so," Cyrus growled.

"She would not take her to Talwyn—"

"But she would tell Talwyn everything she learns," Sorin cut in.

"The only other options are Talwyn or Azrael," Briar drawled. "I would rather take my chances with Ashtine."

"But Ashtine won't be able to get her out. She'll only be able to find her swiftly. We still have to get to her," Eliza cut in. "We should leave right now. Sorin and I can go. We've done this before."

Callan and his guards stood by silently, not being able to contribute anything, but the mortal prince looked sick with worry.

Were Talwyn and the Earth Prince really his only options? Sorin ran his hands through his hair.

"There is another way," he said slowly. A very risky other way.

"What other way?" Eliza demanded.

Sorin's eyes slid to Briar. "It lies beneath the Black Halls."

Briar's eyes went wide in shock and fear. "Absolutely not."

"She could do it. She could get us there and back," Sorin argued. "Talwyn would never need to know."

"You are not seriously suggesting we let her out to ferry us across the border to the *mortal* lands, are you?" Briar demanded. "I know you are in a panic right now, but for fuck's sake, get your head out of your ass."

"She wouldn't need to be let out. We would just need her to create an enchantment to get there and back," Sorin argued.

"Please, for the love of Anala, tell me we are not talking about the Sorceress," Eliza said, her face going slightly pale.

"More like for the love of Arius if we're talking about her," came the muttered response of Cyrus.

"Who is the Sorceress?"

Everyone turned to Callan. Sorin had forgotten the mortals were even in the room, but before he could explain, Briar spoke. "The Sorceress is not from this world. No one knows where she came from or how she got here. She was incredibly powerful until she was caught hundreds of years ago and imprisoned beneath the Black Halls in the Underwater Prison." He turned back to Sorin as he finished. "A prison that only *I* can access and allow others to enter, and I will not do so now."

"Instead, you will bring Talwyn into this? You will hand her over to Talwyn who will not care what she does to her as long as her revenge is completed?" Fire ignited in Sorin's veins, and he knew his eyes had turned to embers. Briar's were glittering like ice as the princes squared off.

"Blood magic is forbidden for a reason, Sorin. The costs are too great." Briar's tone was as icy as his eyes.

"No cost is too great for her!" Sorin bellowed.

"She will use that exact attitude to her advantage," Briar argued.

The entire room fell silent. Rage and panic were emanating off of Sorin, and the others were hardly daring to breathe, let alone move.

"We cannot release her without Talwyn, Sorin. You know this. I may control who enters the Underwater Prison, but the queen's blood is keyed to the cells," Briar said slowly.

"I have already told you that I do not want to let her out. I just need her to create an enchantment."

"Then go to the Witches. Go to Hazel," Rayner cut in quietly, still leaning against the wall near the balcony.

"The Witches do not practice blood magic. Their spells will not be powerful enough, or I would ask Beatrix. It must be her. You know this. Briar, please." The longer they debated this, the closer Mikale would be to discovering her if she were indeed in the mortal lands.

Briar looked as if he couldn't believe what he was hearing, and he shook his head in disbelief when he said, "You promise her nothing. You *give* her nothing. We talk to her, and see what she has to say. That is it, Sorin."

"Fine. Agreed. Yes," Sorin said in relief as a water portal appeared behind Briar.

The two princes stepped through directly into the Underwater Prison. Sorin could see the merfolk who guarded the compound swimming in the waters beyond the windows. Briar led the way quickly down various halls and down into the depths. Neither prince said a word as they walked. Magic could not be used beyond the point they had just entered as an added security measure against the inmates.

Sorin had only been in the Underwater Prison a handful of times accompanying Eliné when she'd needed to speak with prisoners. He honestly didn't even know how many were imprisoned here, let alone why. He only knew the foulest and deadliest of the world's creatures were sent here if they were ever captured, and once you entered a cell, you never came back out.

Briar paused before a staircase. "Her cell is down these stairs. She is the only one on this level. Are you absolutely sure about this, Sorin?" Briar had placed a hand on Sorin's shoulder. A friend concerned for his friend.

"I am," he answered. "She is worth it, Briar."

"Give her nothing," was all Briar said as he turned and descended the stairs.

The set of stairs was short, only twenty or thirty steps, and they found themselves standing before a cell. The bars of the cell were made of shirastone from the Shira Cliffs in the Wind Court.

Immune to magic and deadly to magic wielders. Sitting in the corner of the stone cell was a thin woman. Her knees were bent up, her arms encircled them. Her forehead rested on her knees. The woman's jet black hair fell around her like a drape of midnight sky. She wore a plain beige shift, but her skin was so pale, even that was stark against it.

The Sorceress slowly lifted her head at the sound of their approaching footsteps, and her electric violet eyes settled on them. Her mouth twitched up at the side, and her head tilted in curiosity.

"Visitors? How unexpected." Her voice was smooth and even, elegant yet tinged with a hint of madness. The Sorceress studied the princes, those violet eyes moving slowly over them. "A Prince of Fire and a Prince of Water and Ice." She pushed herself to her feet, uncoiling from the ground like a giant serpent. "Those were not your titles the last time I had visitors. The thrones you now sit upon were occupied by others."

She came to the bars of the cell and raised her hands like she would wrap her long fingers around them and then stopped herself, seeming to remember just what those bars were made of. She inhaled deeply, as if she were breathing in fresh air, and her eyes fluttered closed. "Such power you wield. Yet you, Prince of Fire, there is something extra in your blood. Faint, but it is there." Those eyes of hers fixed on him, and her half smile grew slightly.

"I am not here to discuss my power nor the Water Prince's," Sorin replied, finally finding his voice and stepping forward.

"Then what would you like to discuss, your Highness?" she purred.

"I am in need of your...expertise," he answered carefully.

"My power was stripped from me when I was imprisoned in this wretched cage. Surely you know this?"

It was true. The Avonleyans had used ancient blood magic to strip her of her magical abilities and had given them to others, creating entirely new bloodlines— Shifters and Witches.

"Yes, but they did not take your knowledge," Sorin answered, taking another step closer.

Her half grin became a full one. "No, they did not. What do you require of me, Prince?"

"I need an enchantment to carry me and two others to and from the mortal lands."

"Are there no longer horses outside these walls? Your legs seem to be working just fine. Surely you can walk there?" she answered coyly.

"I need the speed of Traveling," Sorin answered.

"And your queen will not aid you? Her mother's abilities run in her veins, do they not?"

"The queen is not to be part of this," Sorin replied through gritted teeth.

"Interesting," the Sorceress mused. "What is it you seek in the mortal lands, Prince of Fire? For if you are seeking my help, it is something great indeed."

"My business there is none of yours," he snapped.

"An object of power?" she asked, as if he hadn't spoken at all. "If it is power you desire, Prince, I can help with that. Bring me to your side, and the world will be yours."

Her words made the hair on his arms stand on end. "I do not desire power."

"No? Then only one other thing would drive you to seek *my* help," she mused once more. Her eyes met his as she said, "Love." When Sorin didn't answer, she continued. "After all, love is what drove Eliné and Henna to seek my help."

"What?" Sorin asked, the word escaping him before he even knew what he was saying. "Eliné and Henna never came to see you."

The Sorceress laughed, a cold and chilling sound. "Love drove them to me, Prince of Fire. A fierce love of their people, their kingdoms. They beseeched my help to defeat Deimas and Esmeray."

"And you denied them?" Briar asked, speaking for the first time.

"They were unwilling to pay the price for my aide," she said simply. Then that eerie smile formed on her lips once more. "Unfortunately, your parents became the cost for refusing my offer, although maybe not so unfortunate for the two of you, given the thrones you now sit upon."

Sorin shoved down the images of his mother and father being butchered in front of him in the city center. "Enough of this," he ground out. "We do not have the time."

"I have all the time in the world, young prince," the Sorceress scoffed, looking at her nails and scowling. "In fact, I am rather enjoying the company."

"Will you help me or not?" Sorin ground out, stepping closer still to her cell bars.

"The Fae Queens were unwilling to pay my price. What are you willing to pay?"

The Sorceress stooped and began drawing in the dirt of her cell.

"What is your asking price?"

"Sorin, we give her nothing," Briar hissed from behind him.

The Sorceress looked up at them under lowered lashes. "What is it worth to you?" She stood then, studying him once more. "You say it is not power you seek, but what you seek does have power. What you seek is power and love and...death." She smiled fully then, and it was terrifying. "A twin flame. How unexpectedly intriguing."

"Sorin, let's go. She will not aid us," Briar said, gripping his arm to pull him back.

"I did not say I would not aid you," the Sorceress cut in. "I asked what you are willing to pay."

"And I asked your cost," Sorin bit back.

The Sorceress stooped and began drawing in the dirt once more. "I am intrigued, young prince, so I shall make you a deal. I shall require no payment right now. Your debt to me can be fulfilled at a later time."

"And what will that debt entail? Your freedom? Because if that is the case, the answer is no, and we are done here." He may be desperate, but he wasn't that desperate.

"Do you know what nourishes me, Prince of Fire?" the Sorceress asked, continuing to scrawl in the dirt.

"I imagine whatever food you are provided," Sorin drawled.

"That food feeds my body, yes, but it does not nourish me. No, my nourishment is far more refined." This time when she smiled, her teeth appeared, and Sorin saw sharp elongated canines like his own and like a Night Child's.

"Blood? You want me to get you blood?" Sorin asked. That could be accomplished easily enough. Hell, he'd bet Callan would give a cup of his own mortal blood if it meant getting to Scarlett quickly.

"Not just any blood, young prince," she crooned. "In exchange for my services, you shall provide me with the blood of a god."

"A god? Even if I found one, they are formless. They have no bodies to supply blood from," Sorin argued.

"Then you have nothing to fear, do you?" she asked, her drawings becoming more intricate and precise.

"Sorin, no," Briar warned. "We promise her *nothing*."

Finally, she stood and came to the edge of the cell. "Here is my offer to you, Prince of Fire. I shall supply you with an enchantment that will allow you to Travel to and from one location, carrying two companions. In exchange, you shall provide me with the blood of a god to be brought to me."

"So you can kill a god?"

"Who said anything about killing a god? I just want a drink of something divine after centuries of starving," she said coldly, her eyes darkening.

"And what if I never find a god to fulfill such a request? What if I should die before my end of the bargain is fulfilled?" Sorin asked.

"Then I suppose the joke is on me, Prince of Fire," she replied, that half-smile returning. "But, should you indeed find the blood of a god, I get to decide when I call in the debt."

Sorin stood still. The blood of a god? That was impossible. What she was asking was impossible. Even still, if he somehow managed to find one, how would she even know? The deal seemed like a godsdamn trap and yet—

"Time is of the essence, is it not, young prince?" The Sorceress was at the bars again, and this time she did wrap her fingers around those shirastone bars. They hissed and steamed under her hands, but she hardly flinched at the magic burning her palms. "What is she worth to you? Would you damn the entire world to save her?" she purred softly.

"Sorin, do not do this. It is a trap," Briar called, pulling him back from the bars, but Sorin dug in his heels. "We will find another way."

Sorin wrenched free from his grip and came to the edge of the bars. "What do you know that you are not sharing?" he growled.

"I know that those who seek her are not mortal, young prince," she whispered softly. "I know that should they secure her before you do, your world is damned anyway. I know that she will be used in ways you cannot even comprehend. I know that she will suffer in ways you cannot even fathom."

"She is playing you, Sorin, exactly as I said she would," Briar cried, but he could do nothing here. His magic could not be accessed this deep in the Prison.

"How? How can you know these things?" Sorin asked, ignoring his friend. He felt like he'd so often seen Scarlett look, as if he couldn't get enough air into his lungs.

"I may be locked in a cell, but as you said, my knowledge was not stolen from me like my gifts were. Make your choice, Princeling. My offer will not last forever," the Sorceress snapped, stepping back from the bars.

"It is a bargain," Sorin said. "Give me what I need."

"Sorin!" Briar roared from behind him, but it was done. As the words left his lips, there was a faint burning on his left forearm, and he looked down to find a new Mark there. A flame with three diamonds surrounding it. A Bargain Mark, to remain until the debt was fulfilled. But rather than being black like his other Marks, this one was a deep red.

"Give me your blood, young prince," the Sorceress said, extending her hand to his.

"My blood?"

"It is *blood magic*, is it not? The name would imply that blood is needed. The enchantments of my cage do not allow me to access my own blood, for obvious reasons, thus I need yours. A slice along

261

the palm will do just fine," she said simply. Her eyes glimmered with anticipation.

Sorin pulled a dagger from his side and sliced a gash along his palm, blood instantly welling. The Sorceress inhaled deeply again, as if the smell of his blood were as fragrant as flowers. "Such interesting tales your blood tells," she mused as Sorin extended his bleeding hand to her through the bars.

She gripped his wrist, her fingers freezing against his skin, and twisted his arm sideways. The blood ran down his arm, dripping onto the symbols she had drawn there. She moved his arm so his blood imbued each one, then she released him. He snatched his hand back out of the cell.

"Until next time, Prince of Fire," she said, her chilling grin returning.

He felt Briar grip his arm right before he was pulled through a rip in the world.

CHAPTER 28

SORIN

S orin was no longer standing before the Sorceress's cell but in his old bedroom in the Baylorin apartment. Callan had been right. This was the only place she had ever felt safe in the mortal kingdoms. His apartment. With him.

Sorin turned to Briar and was about to speak when he realized all was not quiet here. He froze as sound drifted into the room. Not sound. *Music.* Piano music. On Fae silent feet, he went to the doorway leading out to the main room and braced himself against the door frame, trying to steady his breathing. Briar came up behind him and stilled.

Scarlett sat at the piano playing with all the passion and abandon Sorin had seen those months ago in this same place. She had been a wraith then. A hollow shell, lost in her own dark hell. Her music then had been sadness and sorrow, and today it seemed no different.

But it was.

There was a fragile hope as she moved along those keys, her eyes closed, and her entire body feeling every single note. Her silver hair flowed around her as she moved her fingers over the keys of ebony and ivory.

When she came to the end of one of her songs, he nodded to Briar and pushed off the doorway.

"Be swift, Sorin," he whispered. "We do not have magic here, and we do not know how or when the Sorceress's enchantment will bring us back."

Sorin nodded and began walking towards Scarlett, Briar closing the door behind him until it was only open a crack. Sorin added extra force to his steps to make sure she heard him as he approached, unsure if she knew he had been standing there listening. He had expected her to immediately stop playing, but she opened her eyes, hardly glancing at him. She gave him a sad smile and continued to play, not missing a single note. In fact, she scooted down the bench a little ways, making room for him to sit.

Tentatively, he sat beside her, and her eyes closed once more. He could see her eyes were puffy, and her face was splotchy from crying, but tears no longer wet her cheeks. She inhaled deeply and then began a new song. She began a piece so moving Sorin could hardly breathe. It sounded ancient and young all at once. A movement of notes so intricate and precise with no room for error. The piece seemed as if it held every emotion possible— joy and grief, sorrow and hope, fear and courage, dark and light. He watched as those small delicate fingers flew over the keys, then he looked at Scarlett. Silent sobs were shaking her shoulders, and yet she somehow managed not to miss a beat, and he knew in that moment exactly which song she was playing.

The song crescendoed as it reached the end, as if in triumph over whatever the composer had been battling. The final notes rang in the empty room, and Scarlett was breathing hard, her fingers still pressing down on the final chords. He looked down to see her hands trembling slightly.

After nearly a minute, she whispered, her breath shaky, "That was the piece that…" Her voice caught.

"I know what piece that was, Scarlett," he replied gently, resisting the urge to reach out and touch her.

"You remember?" she asked in surprise.

"It is the piece that made you want to learn to play. The piece you heard the first time your mother took you to the Theater District." Some of the tension in her body seemed to relax a bit at his words.

"You came for me," she whispered, her eyes fixed down on the keys. "I… I don't know how I got here. I didn't know how I would get back to you, but… I was hoping you would. Come for me, I mean."

"I will always come for you," he said carefully.

"I told myself…" She swallowed, brushing her fingers along the smooth ivory, not playing any notes, but as if relishing the feel of them under her fingertips. "I told myself that if you came for me, I would play that song. That even though you have the power to utterly destroy me, I would still give you this piece of my soul. I told myself that—" Her voice cracked again before she swallowed thickly and went on. "I told myself that even if you did not want it, there is still no one else I want to share it with. I do not care if that makes me stupid or naïve, but even after everything you said to me, I still want you to be that person for me. I still choose you."

He felt wetness on his own face. "I am honored, Love. I am honored and humbled that you still offer me something I do not deserve."

Her eyes finally met his. They were the palest blue as she looked at him. "You deserve happiness, Sorin. You deserve love and joy and hope and happiness. You deserve it as much as I do."

Slowly, to allow her time to refuse, he brought his hand to cup her cheek. "I am so, so sorry, Scarlett. You are my equal in every way. You are my mirror." He felt her lean ever so slightly into his touch. "You are not a punishment. You are not a burden. You are the brightest star in my darkest of skies. You are my necessity."

She held his stare as she said, "You know every part of my soul, Sorin. You've seen every dark corner and every cracked crevice, and you have not once balked. You have not once looked away. You have sat in the pits of hell beside me, telling me the light still existed even though I could not see it. You have rescued me from the river in every way that counts. The least I can do is show you that I am not all darkness."

"I have always known you were more light than dark, Scarlett," he said softly.

"You have. Even when I have not," she replied. "But you do not get all of me, if I do not get all of you. You do not get to shut me out. You do not get to tell me to leave. There does not get to be a you and a me. There must be a you and me."

"I am yours, and you are mine," he whispered, not breaking her gaze.

She leaned forward then, stretching up to press a light kiss to his cheek. Her soft lips on his skin sent heat rushing through his veins despite his lack of magic here. She pulled back, stopping inches from his face, their breath mingling. He was going to kiss her. He wasn't going to be able to stop himself. His last bit of self-control was dissolving as she said softly, "I meant what I said on the beach last summer, Sorin. I hope you find your twin flame some day, but until then, I claim you."

"What?" he started, jerking back from her.

She smiled softly, turning back to the piano, her fingers beginning to play another piece. "Whomever takes you from me shall have to prove she's worthy of you, Sorin Aditya. Until then, I claim you. As my mirror. As my kindred soul. If you will have me as yours."

Her mirror. Her kindred soul. The words clanked against his heart, grating down his bones. She seemed to be holding her breath, waiting for his answer as she played a slow ballad along the keys.

"Scarlett," he said, swallowing. Her fingers stumbled at his tone, and she sucked in a breath. He gently gripped her chin between his thumb and forefinger, turning her head to look at him. Dread shone in her eyes, as if she were anticipating him saying no. As if he could ever say no to her. "It would be my greatest joy to have you as such a thing. But there is more that needs to be said on this subject, and here is not the—"

"Really, *Renwell?*" came a drawling voice from the doorway. "Hiding her in plain sight was not the best move, unless that was not your plan at all? Unless you decided to accept my offer and deliver her to me on your own?"

Scarlett and Sorin both shot off the piano bench, Sorin shoving her behind him. Mikale stood there with two guards and a snake's smile on his face.

"What offer?" Scarlett asked from behind Sorin.

"He did not tell you?" Mikale replied with a raise of his brows. Then he clicked his tongue. "Has he continued to keep such secrets from you? Even after he managed to steal you from my house? I am beginning to wonder if the *general* did indeed come to accept my offer, considering his alliance with the Water Court seems to have been mended. Tell me, did you bring your counterpart along to help control her?"

"What is he talking about, Sorin? Briar is here?"

At her words, Briar emerged from the bedroom, his sword drawn. His normally dark skin had slightly paled as he tried to adjust to being without his magic.

"Mikale somehow appeared near the chalet yesterday," Sorin started.

"Yes, that was most entertaining," Mikale cut in smoothly. "You seem to have caused quite the rift among two long-time allies, my pet. I particularly enjoyed seeing the Water Prince land a nice blow to the face of the Fire Prince."

Scarlett whirled back to Sorin, her eyes darting to Briar. "We took care of it, Scarlett. I was going to tell you. Once we had... Once things were better—"

"Were you though?" Mikale asked, stepping farther into the room, the guards flanking him and more filing in behind them.

"What was the offer?" Scarlett demanded, stepping from behind him to Sorin's side. He reached for her hand, but she jerked it out of reach.

"He said if I brought you back to him, he would focus his efforts elsewhere, away from the Fire Court."

"What efforts?"

"He did not specify, and I did not ask. I told him the same thing I will tell him now: He can go to hell," Sorin snarled at the man.

"What have you done?" she hissed quietly to Mikale.

"I have done nothing...yet." The smile that filled his face was wicked and horrifying.

"What will you do?"

"To get you back where you belong, my pet? I have been authorized to do whatever it takes."

"By who?"

"I gave you a hint. Have you not figured it out yet?"

"I took care of the bastard who killed my mother. Years ago. I would love to give you a demonstration as to how," Scarlett said quietly, violence glittering in her eyes.

"But not the one who ordered her killing," Mikale purred in reply.

"Why? Why am I so important to you?"

He clicked his tongue again, taking a step towards her. Her shadows coiled around her, preparing to strike like snakes. "Come with me, and I will tell you everything. I will keep nothing from you." He held out a hand to her.

Sorin watched, with no small amount of horror, as her shadows slowly slithered from her, reaching tentatively towards him as if curious.

"Scarlett." Sorin said, his tone full of warning.

"Interesting, isn't it, *General?*" Although Mikale addressed him, his eyes were fixed on Scarlett's. She stared back, her head tilting slightly to the side at his words.

Sorin glanced at Briar, but two of the guards blocked his access to them. Briar's eyes were wide with terror as he watched Mikale and Scarlett. "What is interesting?" he snapped at Mikale.

"That shadows always return to the darkness," Mikale crooned.

Scarlett took another step towards him. Her shadows swirled around her. "What does that mean?" she asked quietly.

Sorin reached for her, but her shadows pushed him back, and then they shoved down his throat, choking him.

Scarlett!

But whatever was between them was not fully repaired. He couldn't reach her.

268

"You have heard that before, haven't you, my pet? Perhaps in an alley with your sisters by your side?"

"How could you possibly know that?"

Mikale's dark eyes glittered with wicked fury. "The Witch's death served more than one purpose."

Scarlett's face tightened at the mention of her sister. Sorin didn't know what this exchange meant. He didn't know what they were discussing, and her next words only increased his bewilderment.

"Who is your king?" she whispered with venomous quiet.

"Who is yours?" he purred back.

"How? How do you know this?"

Mikale's face twisted from fury to delight. "Tell me, have they figured out these delights that adore you?" He swept his fingers through one of the shadows that was closest to him, as if he were running them through water. The shadows shuddered around his touch.

"What do you know of them?" She was less than five feet from him now, and her only protection from him was those shadows that she sent slithering towards him, wrapping around his throat.

Mikale didn't even flinch. His smile only widened. "You have only scratched the surface of your sweet Darkness. Come with me, and I will show you all of its secrets." His tone was soft and gentle, coaxing, as he took another step towards Scarlett, his hand still outstretched. She took another hesitant step towards him, and Sorin could do nothing. He was utterly helpless as she lifted a hand to reach for his.

Scarlett!

"That's it, my pet," Mikale purred. He stretched his hand closer to her.

He felt it at the same time Briar shouted, "He is entrancing her, Sorin! He is using the powers of the Night Children!"

But before he could try and lunge for her again, there was a flash of light.

Four flashes, actually.

And a giant panther stood before Scarlett, snarling and growling and roaring with ferocity. Her enormous fangs were bared at

Mikale, and his guards all shrank back. There was a bird's cry as Amaré swooped around the room, coming to rest on Sorin's outstretched arm, and a whinny as Abrax stood before Briar, stamping his hooves.

"No!" Mikale bellowed, and Scarlett blinked, her eyes widening. Her shadows released him, and Sorin lunged for her as she stepped back. He wrapped his arm around her waist, tugging her back against him.

"This is not over, Princess," Mikale seethed. "You will come with me, and it will be of your own choosing. I know what he thinks you are, but Darkness always returns home."

Shirina snarled again, and another bird let loose a battle cry. A silver hawk rose into the air and with a flap of her fair wings, a mighty gust of wind swept through the apartment. Windows shattered, and Sorin threw himself over Scarlett as she dropped to the ground, covering her head. He could feel her trembling beneath him.

I am yours, and you are mine. We will leave here together.

He threw those words down that fragile bond over and over again.

The panther growled low, taking a step towards Mikale, and he let out an audible hiss as he stepped back. "You will all fail," he seethed at the panther.

Shirina snarled again, and Mikale and his guards scattered, rushing from the apartment.

When they were gone, the three Fae stood in stunned silence. Shirina was pacing by the now shut entrance door, her hackles still raised as she stood guard.

Sorin slowly rose, helping Scarlett to her feet. Briar walked to them, Abrax tossing his head in agitation. The silver hawk came to settle on Briar's shoulder, and he reached up to stroke her head.

"My landlord is going to wonder what the hell we did in here," Sorin grumbled, glass crunching under his boots.

"You're obnoxiously rich. Just buy the damn building," Scarlett muttered, her eyes on Abrax and Nasima.

"I am glad to see your delightful tongue is back," he retorted, to which she stuck that tongue out at him in return.

They both turned as Briar began speaking. "Go, Nasima," he said, stroking the bird's feathers again. "Tell her everything you saw."

Nasima let loose another cry as she flapped into the air and disappeared in a flash of light.

"She will go to the Wind Princess?" Scarlett asked.

"Yes. She and her Court have libraries full of ancient books and history long forgotten by the rest of the world," Briar said, his face grim. "And she is... You will understand when you meet her someday."

Sorin turned back to Scarlett to find her frowning down at her still bare feet amid the broken shards of glass. "Are you ready?"

"For what?" she asked, looking up at him.

He held his hand out to her. "To go home."

She studied him for a long moment, then her eyes darted to Briar. "You really hit him in the face?"

Briar grinned at her. "Yes, Sunshine. Hard enough he spat blood."

"Good," she said. Then she turned a questioning look upon Sorin. "How exactly are we getting home? I can't bring us all back. I don't know how I—"

"It's okay, Love. I found a work-around to get to you."

There were small flashes of light as Abrax and Shirina disappeared. Amaré remained on Sorin's shoulder. He still held his hand out to her, and warmth flooded through his left hand as that Mark imperceptibly darkened when she slowly slid her fingers into his waiting palm. "Then let's go home."

CHAPTER 29
CALLAN

C allan shot to his feet as Sorin, Briar, and Scarlett appeared from thin air. They had all been sitting in Sorin's great room waiting. Eliza had nearly worn a path in the carpet from her pacing. He'd never seen the general so out of sorts. Judging by Cyrus and Rayner, who stood solemnly near the fireplace whispering amongst themselves, they hadn't either. The princes had been gone well over an hour now, and all of Callan's questions about this Sorceress had gone unanswered. The Fire Court was apparently too preoccupied with their own worries and thoughts to bother answering him.

Callan looked Scarlett over as she pulled her hand from Sorin's. She appeared fine. No obvious injuries, but her eyes looked haunted and hollow. Her eyes looked like they had the night of the engagement dinner at Mikale's. What had shoved her back to that place?

Her gaze swept over them all. "A welcome home party just for me? How unexpected. Although you could have put in a bit more of an effort into the decorations," she quipped, bringing a hand dramatically to her chest with a feline grin that didn't quite meet her eyes.

Eliza pushed past Callan as she strode for Scarlett. "Next time please just lock yourself in my rooms, and allow me to kick his ass for you," she snapped as she pulled Scarlett into a fierce hug.

Scarlett gripped her back just as tightly. "Deal, my friend," she whispered.

All the Fae males looked slightly shocked at the exchange happening before them, and Callan was inclined to agree. He had never seen Eliza convey any type of sentimental emotion.

After a few more moments, the females pulled back from each other, and Eliza's gaze went to Sorin. The violence that entered her eyes told Callan exactly why she was the general of his armies. "If you ever—"

Sorin held up his hands placatingly, cutting his general off. "I do believe you will be the first in a long line of those who will come to her defense, Eliza dear," he sighed, glancing around at everyone in the room.

Cyrus and Rayner came up behind Eliza, their faces just as hard and full of promised bloodshed as the general's. It still took him by surprise, the irreverence they had for the fact that he was their prince and ruler.

"Damn, Prince," Scarlett scoffed with a smirk, a hand going to her hip. "They really do prefer me over you." Sorin threw her an unimpressed glance, which she completely ignored to Callan's own satisfaction. Her attention went to Cyrus as she purred, "Hello, Darling."

Cyrus closed the space between them, and he held Sorin's stare as he bent down and gently kissed her cheek. He whispered something in her ear that Callan couldn't hear, but the Fae in the room clearly could. Sorin's face went from unimpressed to displeased. The others all snickered, and Scarlett's cheeks turned slightly pink at whatever it was he said.

Finally, her gaze settled on Callan. Surprise flitted across her features at his presence, but it was quickly replaced by a grim resolve. She strode to him and said, "I have need of you."

He didn't fail to notice how Sorin straightened at her address to him. She had come to him, not Sorin, for whatever it was she was needing.

"Of course," Callan answered, eyeing her curiously.

"Are you free? Right now?"

"I do not exactly have a lot of pressing commitments at the moment," he replied with a half smile and raise of his brow.

"Then come with me." She turned and headed for the main door, snatching up a dagger and buckling it to her waist as she went. Everyone was staring at her as she pulled the door open and turned to him. He stole a quick glance at Sorin, who was watching her closely, as if trying to read her.

Callan went to her side, and she gestured with a hand. "After you."

"We will need an escort," Callan said tentatively.

"*I* am your escort," she replied coolly, and her tone dared anyone to say otherwise. As she made to follow him out, he heard Sorin call after her, and Callan stopped, turning to watch.

Scarlett paused in the doorway, her back still to the Fire Prince. She closed her eyes and seemed to be breathing deep. She opened her eyes again and slowly turned to face him. Sorin took a few steps towards her, pausing as her shadows thickened.

The two stared at each other, and Callan could swear no one was daring to breathe as they observed them. She tilted her head to the side as if she heard something. Honestly, sometimes he thought they could read each other's thoughts, but then she said, "You shall get no treats from me, Prince. Not for a long while. So speak if you have something to say."

"Tonight. You will speak with me?" he asked tentatively. "We need to finish a conversation we were having."

"That sounds like it would be a necessity," she said slowly. Deliberately.

A flash of relief passed over Sorin's features. He swallowed and only nodded mutely, understanding whatever meaning those words held.

Without another word to any of them, Scarlett turned and shut the door behind her. She grabbed Callan's hand and began pulling him down the hall. When they had gone down a set of stairs, she let out a sigh. "There was a book," she said.

Callan nearly stumbled a step. "A book?" he asked.

"Yes," she replied, pulling her hand from his and pushing back her hair from her face. He could still see the hollowness in her eyes.

He grabbed her wrist, bringing her to a stop in the stairwell. "What is wrong, Scarlett?"

She only shook her head. "It has been a long couple of days, Callan. I do not wish to speak about it right now."

"You do not wish to but maybe you need to," he pushed gently.

She shook her head again. "No, Callan. I— Mikale found us there, and he said some things…"

Callan's eyes widened in surprise. "Are you all right?" he asked, looking her over again. He didn't know why. Any injuries Mikale would impose would not be external. They would be internal… causing those haunted eyes that looked at him now. Without letting himself consider it, he pulled her to him. She stiffened for a moment, then relaxed against his chest. Her arms came up around his neck. Her head rested on his shoulder. He said nothing as the Wraith let him hold her for the first time in months.

CHAPTER 30
SCARLETT

S carlett knew it was late. Callan had gone back to his rooms hours ago when she caught him sleeping on the books. He had tried to convince Scarlett she needed to go back to her own quarters and eat something. She had waved him off, saying she would head back shortly. That was at least two hours ago.

He had held her in that stairwell. He had let her soak up his strength. Had given her a tether to hold herself together. She had needed it. She had needed a friend, and he had been there. It had been unexpected and welcomed.

She sat in a secluded alcove on the first level of the library, nestled in an oversized chair. It had taken Callan a little while to track down the book she had wanted to see, *The Heart of Beginning.* While he had searched for it, she had asked him questions of his own family, and how long they had been the ruling family of Windonelle. He had told her they could trace their ancestry back to the beginning. That the Solgards were the only family to have ruled the western human kingdom since Deimas and Esmeray had sacrificed themselves to keep out the magic wielders.

To see my king's throne restored.

It was a night that sometimes visited her dreams, but one she

276

rarely thought of otherwise. Not until Mikale had uttered those words.

The shadows always return to the Darkness.

They had crashed into her like a cresting wave. She had thought it impossible that he could know of that night in that deserted alley. No one had ever come looking for the man they had killed that night. There had never been a whisper of him again. So she had tested him. She had asked who his king was, and he had replied exactly as that man had.

Who is yours?

She was learning there was no such thing as coincidences. Not in the utter mess of horse shit her life had become.

He knew. Mikale knew they had killed that man. That man had said he was there to visit kin that resided on this continent. Mikale had said Juliette's death had served more than one purpose.

Revenge. He had made her kill Juliette out of revenge as much as to prove his control over her.

Where had they come from? The Lairwoods had long been Hands to the human king in Windonelle. Just how distantly related were they from the man who had come across the sea then?

She thumbed slowly through the book. She had seen mention, somewhere in here, of the other continents of their world. Distant lands and kingdoms long forgotten by those of this continent.

She skimmed each page as quickly as she dared. She was exhausted. She'd hardly slept the night before, and the emotional turmoil she'd been in since that mountain house had drained her. But this... She knew it was important.

Her fingers stilled as she came to a paragraph that listed several other kingdoms. Orlandria. Maraa. Asterolia. Avonleya. Solember. Where these kingdoms were located, she had no idea, but it was a start.

She rose from her seat and ventured toward the shelves. This was old knowledge. Knowledge, perhaps, from before the time of the Great War. She went deeper into the tombs and stacks of books. As the passages grew darker and darker, she grabbed a torch down from the wall so she could see the books' titles better. Many of them were in the Old Language, which she was starting to recognize and differentiate from the common tongue. But others were in languages she had never seen.

Farther and farther she crept, running her fingers along book spines. The passageway got mustier and damper until she came upon a bookcase set into the wall. The books on these shelves were centuries old. Older. There was an iron bracket near it, and she set the torch in it, illuminating all the books. The first shelf was books in the common tongue. The second shelf was books in the Old Language. She pulled a book from the third shelf, waving her hand at the cloud of dust that sprang forth. Gingerly, she opened the book and sank to the floor, crossing her legs beneath her.

Spells. This was a book of spells. Sorin had said Fae could do spellwork, but not well. He had said spellwork was honed and crafted by the Witches. There were spells in this book for everything. Healing. Wards. Strength. Curses.

Blood Oaths.

Dividing territories.

Creating keys.

She turned back to the bookshelf. The entire third shelf was spell books. She placed the one in her hands gently on the floor beside her. Gods, she was filthy. Her black pants and tunic were covered with dust and dirt as she sat on the floor. The dust was so thick on the stones it was clear it hadn't been disturbed in years.

Her attention turned to the bottom fourth shelf. All the books on this shelf were written in a language she did not know, but they seemed to all be of the same language. The letters and symbols appeared the same, at least. She reached to pull one off the shelf, and as she did, there was a creaking and groaning. She shot to her feet, pulling the dagger from her side and angling it as the bookshelf slid into the wall.

Of course this was here. Of course there was a magical book-shelf in the recesses of this library. Because she needed more surprises in her damn life right now.

She sighed in frustration when the bookcase stopped moving, leaving only a sliver of the books accessible. Cautiously, she stepped forward to look at the opening and found a staircase wending down into the dark. She yanked the torch from the wall and plunged it into the opening before her, but it did little. Just illuminated more steps leading somewhere she could not see.

She stood at the top of that stairway, biting her lip. Did Sorin even know about this place? She couldn't venture down there tonight. Not with only a dagger. She'd need a few more weapons and candles and a plan.

She stepped back out of the passageway, studying the opening. She couldn't just leave it open. Based on every book she'd ever read that contained a secret passageway, she supposed the book that had opened the doorway would also close it. The book was one of the few still accessible on the bookshelf, and sure enough, when she pulled it again, the bookshelf slid back into place.

Holding her breath, she gently tugged on the book next to the secret switch, and breathed a sigh of relief as nothing surprising happened when it came free. It was in that odd language she didn't recognize. She flipped through it. How could she learn to read this? Maybe Sorin knew what it was.

She set it down beside her and picked the spell book back up. She should really go up to bed, but that meant seeing Sorin. She knew he'd be up, waiting for her. And while they had talked in his old apartment, those wounds were still fresh. She forgave him. She really did. But that didn't mean things wouldn't be tense and awkward for a while. She was just too emotionally drained to handle it right now.

Fine, she was avoiding him.

So she opened the spell book and began to read.

"Scarlett."

The voice was soft as familiar hands gently shook her shoulders. There was a cold stone floor beneath her cheek, and her breathing hitched as she shot straight up, reaching for the dagger at her waist.

"It's me, Scarlett," Sorin said in a low voice. "I did not mean to startle you."

She whipped her head around, taking in her surroundings. The library. She was in the dark stone passages of the library.

Not that room in the Lairwood House.

Home. She was home, and she must have fallen asleep reading…

She looked down beside her at the spell book and the other book. Then she looked over her shoulder at the sealed secret passage behind her.

"Scarlett," Sorin said again, drawing her eyes to his. He was crouched before her, his face carefully neutral, but she could see the wariness in his eyes.

"What time is it?" she asked blearily. It had been late when she'd come down this passageway. Who knows when she'd fallen asleep.

"It is well into the night," he said. He studied her, as if trying to decide if he should say or do anything.

"How did you find me?"

"Did you not wish to be found?"

"No. I didn't mean it like that…" She trailed off.

Yes. Tense and awkward. Exactly as she had feared.

He watched her a little longer, and she tried not to flinch under his stare. Finally he said, "I will sleep in the other bedroom, Scarlett. Come to bed. Rest and sleep."

He made no move to reach for her. Just remained crouched before her.

"I wasn't hiding from you," she said quietly. Only partially a lie.

"All right," he replied doubtfully.

"I was reading."

"Hmm," he said, glancing at the books beside her. "With your eyes closed in dark passages of the library I did not even know existed?"

So he didn't know. Which meant he had no idea about the secret passageway, either.

She smacked his knee as she scowled at him. "I fell asleep while reading, smart ass."

A flash of relief flickered in his golden eyes, and it softened something in her. Hesitantly, she reached for his hand, interlacing her fingers with his. His fingers tightened around hers, and he sank forward from his crouch onto his knees. She swallowed. She supposed they could have this conversation here, in a dark forgotten passageway of a library.

She gently pushed the ancient books aside as she rose to her own knees before him and took his other hand in her own. She swallowed again before she said softly, "It will take me a little time..."

"I know." His voice was low and tender. "I hurt you in unacceptable ways, Scarlett. I would not expect you to just be okay after everything. I do not expect it all to be fixed overnight."

"I can't..." Scarlett paused, trying to find the words. "I still choose you, Sorin. I can't picture a world without you in it. I do not want to be in a place where I shut you out. I know—" Her voice caught a little, and she swallowed again to compose herself. Sorin just patiently waited for her, his eyes full of an understanding sorrow. "I know I said I could find the stars with someone else if you did not want this, if you did not want me. That I could find my way in the darkness on my own. But I do not want anyone else. Maybe it is a weakness, but I do not wish to be alone in my darkness. And I still choose you, Sorin. I still want you because... Because I do not hate you. I do not know what exactly that means, but I want no one else to come for me. I want it to always be you."

There were tears on her cheeks and his as she looked into his golden eyes. He let go of her hands and slowly, giving her time to dismiss him, he brought his hands to her face. "Scarlett Monrhoe." Her name on his lips caressed something deep in her soul, and it took all of her self-control not to lean forward and kiss him. "My home is wherever you are. There will never be a world where there is not a you and me because should you be ripped from me in this world, I will cross them all to find you. I will always find you. I will always come for you. I will always choose you. I will always want you." A sob escaped her as he asked, "Can I hold you?"

She almost choked on the laugh that came out of her. "That would seem like a necessity, Prince."

Then he was pulling her into his arms, and she was wrapping herself around him, breathing in that ash and cedar scent. Everything had been so broken. It had only been two days, but it had felt like an eternity with this chasm that had come between them.

Callan had held her, had helped her keep it together, until she could get to this moment. Not just today, but the last few years. Callan and Cassius had helped her keep the pieces from falling apart so she could get to this place. So she could find the one where her soul could rest, and she could take a breath.

It wasn't fixed completely. It wasn't perfect. But it was all she needed.

CHAPTER 31

SORIN

Sorin held her in that dark passageway for long minutes. He had been disappointed when she had not come to dinner. He had become anxious when no one had seen her since she'd disappeared with the mortal prince. He had become downright worried when the clock chimed midnight. And when she still had not come to their rooms two hours later, after he had checked with Eliza to make sure she had not gone there, he knew she was avoiding him.

He had checked with his palace guards, who had said they had seen her enter the library with Callan, but Callan had left alone. That wasn't to say she couldn't have snuck out unseen, but she was likely still in the library. He had found a stack of books in an alcove on the first floor and had picked up her scent among the book-shelves. He had followed it down and down and down. Of course she had found long forgotten passages in the library.

He had illuminated a small flame beside him as he navigated the dark passageways until he had found her. Sleeping on the stone floor in front of a bookcase of ancient-looking books, two beside her on the floor. She was covered with dust everywhere. Her clothes. Her face. Her hair.

Sighing, he had woken her, completely expecting an argument about her coming up to bed, which is why he had told her he'd sleep in the other room. Hell, he'd go sleep in the guest wing if that's what she wanted.

He had not expected the words she had said. He had not expected her to reach for his hand. He had not expected to be holding her close to him as the torchlight nearly burned out. He would have gladly held her there all night, but she eventually pulled back.

"I'm exhausted," she admitted.

He stood, extending a hand to help her up. She carefully picked up the two ancient books that were lying on the floor and reached for his hand.

"Can I take these out of the library?" she asked.

"Princess, I don't know that anybody even knows these books are down here. No one will know if they are taken from the library," he said with a laugh.

"They might be older than you, Prince. I just wanted to make sure I wasn't stealing priceless antiques of some sort."

"Some day, Love, we will find another use for that wicked tongue of yours," he sighed as they emerged into the first level of the library. He shoved his hands into his pockets, mainly to keep himself from reaching for her. They exited and began the trek to the bridges and up to their quarters. He created a portal for them, but she shook her head.

"Can we just walk and...be together?"

"Of course." They crossed the bridges and headed for the stairs. She carried the books protectively in her arms, and he could not see the titles. "Can I ask what you felt the need to be reading well into the night?"

"Research."

"Regarding?"

"Some things Mikale said," she answered darkly. He waited for her to explain more, but instead she said, "How did you get to the apartment today? In Baylorin."

"I found a work around to be able to get to you," he answered.

"What was the work around?"

"Old ancient magic."

"Mikale is not mortal."

"No, he is not," Sorin confirmed, thinking back on the Sorceress's words.

"Can you portal to other continents?"

"That is random."

"I suppose it would seem so," she mused quietly, lost in her own thoughts.

"You have to know where you are going to portal," Sorin explained. "You have to have been there before, or be able to see where you are going somehow."

She fell quiet again as they climbed the stairs. They were halfway up when she said, "What of blood magic?"

"What?" he asked, jerking around to look at her.

"Blood magic. Could one use blood magic to cross the seas? To cross the worlds?"

"Blood magic is ancient and powerful, Scarlett."

"Yes, yes. I know. Twin flames and soulmates," she said, waving her hand dismissively. "But is it powerful enough to do such a thing? To transport beings from other continents? Other worlds?"

"I suppose it might be, but the cost would be… Magic is always a give and take. The cost of doing something like that would be abominable."

"Hmm," was all she hummed in response.

"What did he say that made you start looking into this?" Again he tried to see the books she held, but she had them clutched to her chest.

"Nothing," she said, waving her hand again as they started down the corridor to their suite. "It's just research. To learn more about our history."

He wanted to ask more. He wanted to push her. He could tell she knew more than that. He could tell she had figured something out. Two days ago he wouldn't have hesitated to do so. But now? After everything they'd just gone through, he didn't dare.

They entered their chambers, and she began to cross the room.

"I'm going to bathe real quick," she said, pushing open the door to their room. Sorin paused, halfway there, waiting.

She looked over her shoulder as she said, almost inaudibly, "I sleep better when you are beside me."

"You are sure?"

A small smile graced her perfect lips. "It is a necessity, Prince."

"As you wish, Princess."

She disappeared into the bedroom, and he exhaled a breath he hadn't realized he'd been holding. She was back. With him. She was here.

He glanced at the clock on the mantle. It would be nearing dawn soon. If anyone knocked on their door before noon, the ensuing fight would make his match with Eliza a few weeks ago look like swordplay. And after Scarlett finished with them, they'd have to deal with him.

He created fire messages to be waiting for his family once they woke, then he trudged into the bedroom. She was in the bathing room with the door closed. He walked to the dressing room and stripped off his shirt and put on looser pants.

He was walking back out to the bed when he saw the books she had carried up from the library sitting on the chaise. He picked up the top one, finding it written in a language he didn't recognize. Where *did* these books come from?

The second book was written in the Old Language and was a spell book, but not like any spell book he had ever seen before. These spells were incredibly complex; something he would expect a Witch to have.

Before he could get any farther in the book, the bathing room door cracked open, and she came out not in one of her nightgowns, but a shirt of his. It was huge on her, and there was no small amount of primal satisfaction at seeing it on her, wrapping her in his scent.

She crossed the space between them and took the ancient book from his hands with a smirk. "Busybody."

"Can you read the other book?" She could read the Old

Language without instruction. Could she read other languages as well?

"Not yet," she answered, setting the spell book atop the other one and making her way to the bed. He dried her dripping hair with a breath of heat, and she nodded her thanks to him. Then she blew out the candle on her side of the bed before she slipped between the sheets.

"Do you know what language it is?"

"Do you?" she countered.

"No," he answered, sliding into the bed.

She rolled over to face him, her hand tucked under her cheek. "It seems old. Older than the Old Language," she mused.

"You plan to learn it? How?"

She clicked her tongue. "So interested in my reading habits suddenly, Prince."

"What was Mikale talking about today? He mentioned an old alley and your sisters," he asked softly.

In the dark, he could barely make out her face as it hardened, and she pursed her lips. "That is a tale for another time."

His stomach dropped at the words. A wall. She had put a wall back up between them. He had expected it but to hear it confirmed...

"Scarlett," he started.

"No more tonight, Sorin. I cannot do any more tonight," she said softly. He could hear the wariness in her tone. "I am *not* training tomorrow."

"I already sent messages to Cyrus, Rayner, and Eliza that if anyone comes to our rooms before noon, your shadows will throw them off the balcony."

"Mmm," she hummed. "I knew you were my new favorite for a reason."

He reached across the bed and stroked a finger down her cheek. She sighed deeply as she whispered, "I missed you."

Before he could reply, her breathing shifted, and she was asleep.

CHAPTER 32
SCARLETT

"Good night," Scarlett chirped, placing her hand upon the door handle.

"Next week then?" Finn called from the table where they had been playing cards.

"Is this a standing weekly dinner invitation?"

"Would you accept such a thing?" Callan countered from where he stood beside her.

"Next week then," she agreed with a smile.

She slipped from their rooms and headed for the bridges, but before she entered the main atrium, she turned down a side hall. She had been exploring this side of the palace the entire last week and had found a little used closet. She slipped into it now and unstacked boxes. She opened the bottom one and pulled out the pants, tunic, and jacket she had stashed there a few days ago.

Silent as a wraith, she took off the pale green dress she had worn to dinner. She breathed deep as she slid on the clothes. It wasn't her usual suit of stealth, but it was nearly identical to Eliza's uniform she so often wore around the grounds.

She went to the corner and pulled an old sheet off the brooms and mops. She had stashed weapons behind them, and she strapped

288

them to her body by muscle memory alone. In one of the dagger sheaths, she shoved three candles and matches. Then she braided back her hair and slung a lightweight cloak around her shoulders.

She had been watching the guards all week, too. She had learned their schedules, the places they left unguarded. They all reported unusual movements to Sorin. If she were seen going to the library this late, he would be told.

So she would not be seen.

She wasn't ready to tell him her theories yet. Not until she had proof. Not until she had all the pieces.

Coincidences were not a thing in her world. She was learning it was all connected.

And she was in the damn center of it all.

She closed her eyes and took a deep breath. She pulled her hood up and drifted down into that place she'd been ignoring for months. She took a step from the cage where she kept Death's Maiden locked up tight. She let that darkness rise and writhe and twist, her shadows darkened as they embraced that darkness.

In less than three minutes, she was inside the library and striding amongst the shelves of books, deeper and deeper into the passage-ways. She sent her shadows ahead of her, feeling out the way so she did not need to light any torches.

Not until she had opened the passageway did she light a candle as she peered down into the darkened staircase. She looked behind her to see a small lever on the wall. A way to close the door from the inside.

And reopen it, she hoped as she pulled it.

When the door had slid completely shut, she pulled a long knife from her belt and began her descent.

PART TWO
THE STARS

CHAPTER 33

CALLAN

C allan looked up from the book he was reading and stole a glance at Scarlett seated across from him in the library. They had continued to meet in the library nearly every afternoon. When she had returned from the mortal lands, she had started researching something in the Old Language books and had become even more interested in what King Deimas and Queen Esmeray had sought in Avonleya.

A weekly dinner had also become a thing ever since that first one a few weeks ago. He looked forward to the relaxed and casual dinners when it was just them and Finn and Sloan. She seemed to enjoy them, too, although that might be because she tended to hand Sloan his ass in billiards nearly every week.

She was leaning back in her chair, biting her lower lip in that way she always did when she was reading something particularly interesting. It was her hand, though, that caught his attention. As she read, crystals of ice crackled and danced at her fingertips. Fire. Water. Ice. Whatever magic training she was doing with Sorin seemed to be paying off. Maybe that meant they'd be able to return home soon.

He'd seen her displaying those powers more and more since she had returned from the mortal lands on the day Eliza had literally dragged him to the Fire Prince's private chambers, demanding to know where she had gone. The two Fae princes had left through a water portal to go speak with this Sorceress person. He, Finn, and Sloan had taken seats while they'd watched Sorin's Inner Court pace and bicker and snap at one another.

She had never spoken of that day or told him what had happened between her and the Prince of this Court, and no one else had bothered to either, but he could not get her from his mind. How she had leaned into him in that stairwell. How she had let him hold her for those minutes while she had collected herself.

"You are staring, Callan," she said, drawing him from his thoughts. Her eyes were still on the book before her.

"How would you know?" he teased, reaching over and flipping her pages.

"You idiot!" she exclaimed, her eyes snapping to his in dismay.

He gave her a teasing grin. "Let's get out of this library today," he said.

"And go where? It is freezing outside."

"A walk in the gardens?" Callan suggested.

"Again, it is freezing outside," Scarlett argued, flipping the pages back to where she was in the book.

"You have fire magic. You can keep yourself warm," he pointed out, glancing at her fingers.

"I have fire magic that I am still learning to control and would never use around you right now," she said flatly.

"I am getting restless here day after day," he grumbled, leaning back in his own chair and stretching his legs.

She studied him for a moment before sighing and saying, "All right. Let me get my cloak, and I'll meet you at the bridges in a few minutes." She grabbed two of the books off the table for 'light reading' as she called it and disappeared out the library doors.

Ten minutes later, they were out in the gardens of the palace. She was bundled in a fur-lined cloak, the hood pulled up over her silver head and her hands shoved into the folds. "I don't know how I let you talk me into this," she muttered. "I hate the cold."

Callan chuckled as they meandered down a worn path between hedges and flower bushes. "Or you have been spoiled by a fire palace. It gets just as cold in Baylorin."

"I hated the cold there, too," she grumbled, pulling her cloak tighter around herself.

"You are in a mood today," he observed. He might be missing Baylorin, but he was savoring every moment with her, out in the open, no secrecy involved. And with each day in the library, with each informal dinner, she let a little more of herself out of whatever cage she maintained. She lowered the mask a little more.

She scowled at him from under the hood and continued walking in silence. Snow was falling gently around them. Big, fluffy flakes that were getting caught in her hair that flowed down over her shoulders and out from under her hood. She suddenly said softly, "You are ready to return to Baylorin." A statement, not a question.

"Why do you say that?" he asked, reaching over and plucking a snowflake from her hair. It melted instantly against his fingertips.

"I can tell," she said with a shrug. "Extended vacations sound nice in theory, but in reality…" She shrugged again and gave him a knowing smile.

She wasn't wrong. While a month or two of not being noticed had been refreshing, playing house guest was growing tiresome. He was ready to go home. He sent correspondence to his father weekly, trying to justify his prolonged absence, but his father's patience was growing thin as well.

"And you? Are you not ready to return home?"

She stiffened slightly at his question, her shadows seeming to shudder. "While I will return to Baylorin, I do not know that I will stay there," she finally replied.

"What do you mean you will not stay there?" Callan demanded, stopping dead in his tracks.

She paused and turned to face him. "I mean I do not know that I can entirely be myself there."

"But you can here?"

"Callan, look around you. There is magic everywhere. No one

bats an eye at my shadows or fire or water. I mean, for the love of Saylah, I'm *Fae*. My entire being is changed when I am there."

"And what of Cassius? And Nuri? The orphans?"

"I said I will return, Callan," she snapped. "But when things are taken care of, I do not think I will stay."

"You mean you will come back here."

"And if I choose to do so?" She crossed her arms, tapping her foot in frustration. The pose and movement were so familiar to him. An action he'd seen her make a hundred times when they'd been theorizing about what was happening in the Black Syndicate.

"And what of me?"

"You are the Crown Prince. You shall one day rule as king. Nothing has changed for you."

"Everything has changed," he countered. "Everything has changed if you are not going to be there."

"What does my absence change? You are the Crown Prince, whether I am there or not. You will be king whether I am there or not," Scarlett argued.

"But you will not be my queen!" He regretted the words as soon as they left his mouth, closing his eyes in a grimace.

She stilled in that way only Fae could do. "Nothing has changed between us, Callan."

"Of course not. Not with him here," Callan returned bitterly.

"Callan. Nothing has changed. I still do not desire to be a queen, no matter how many different ways it is offered to me. I still do not desire to be chained to a throne."

"How is my throne any different from his?"

Scarlett's face hardened. "Do you see me parading around on his arm, Callan? Have you seen us steal kisses or sneak away to be alone together? Have any of our interactions appeared to be courting or betrothing?"

"You share chambers, Scarlett," he said pointedly.

She huffed a laugh. "You and your noble propriety," she scoffed with a roll of her eyes. "Do you know how many nights I slept beside Cassius in the Tyndell Manor? Did you know Drake is the one who carried me into the bath the night Mikale took what he desired? I share chambers with Sorin because I wake nearly every night screaming from nightmares, and he knows how to reach me when the shadows and the fire and the ice overcome me. I will not apologize for that. I will not apologize for ridiculous decorum having no place in my world, in the things I have experienced."

She brushed past him, heading back to the palace. "Scarlett, wait! I am sorry," Callan called, rushing to catch up with her.

She paused, letting him come to her side. "You need to stop waiting for me, Callan. We are too different. Our worlds are too different."

"I tried, you know," he snapped. "After six months of you not coming to my rooms. After six months of no explanation. After that dinner at the Tyndell Manor that evening when you hardly looked at me. I tried. I tried to find a Court Lady. I tried to find someone who *wanted* to be my queen. But none of them... None of them spoke to me like I was anyone other than a Prince. None of them called me Callan. None of them wanted to discuss books. None of them knew anything outside of the wealth they grew up in. None of them challenged me the way you do. None of them made me want to be a better person, a better ruler, the way you do."

She stood, gaping at him slightly in surprise. "I was— I *am* Death's Maiden, Callan. I am part of the Black Syndicate's Wraiths of Death. It would never be possible. You have to know that."

"No matter how many times you say it to me, Scarlett, I will not believe it. We would figure it out. We *could* figure it out."

"No, Callan, we couldn't. There are parts of my world you would not be able to get past," she said, shaking her head as if trying to wake up from a dream.

"Like what? Your magic?"

"Like the fact that I've *killed* people, Callan. Like the fact that Nuri and Cassius are part of me, come with me."

"They are not an issue. They live in Baylorin," Callan countered.

"And Sorin?"

"What of him?"

"He is my... He is part of me, too. This Court is part of my family," she exclaimed, gesturing widely with her arm.

"Sorin is your what?" Callan demanded.

"I don't know what he is!" she cried. "All right? I do not know. He understands me on the deepest of levels. He is my mirror."

"He is your soulmate?"

"I don't know."

"I can live with that, Scarlett," he said, reaching for her hand. "I can live with him being your soulmate."

She looked down at her hand clasped in his own and stared at it. Then she gently pulled her fingers from his and whispered, "I don't know if I can live with that."

She turned and walked back to the palace, silent as the wraith she was, leaving him out in the cold and snow.

CHAPTER 34
SORIN

orin sat in his bathing pool, the steam wafting up from the water. The entire afternoon had been spent trying to sort out the never-ending issues with some Earth Court merchants, and he was exhausted. Cyrus had done well in his absence, but the Earth Court wanted to renegotiate their Marking fees for the third time in three years. He'd listened to concerns and calmed his panicked shopkeepers and business owners. He and Cyrus had gone back and forth on what they should do. Then he had received the summons from Talwyn, addressed to all the Court Royals, for an urgent meeting to be held at dawn. They were only allowed to bring their Seconds to such gatherings.

His thoughts drifted to Scarlett as they always seemed to when he had a quiet moment. She had forgiven him for the debacle at the chalet, but she hadn't forgotten. She was more subdued around him and didn't share things as readily. It was almost like being back in Baylorin when he had been trying to coax secrets from her. He didn't blame her. It was his own fucking fault. He knew she was trying, but she had been partially right that day she had screamed at him. He had broken them. The repairing was excruciating.

She had come out of that day with a renewed will of shoving

down things she didn't want to face, throwing herself into her training. All of it. Physical, weaponry, and magic. She could summon flames of various colors at will. She had recently begun simultaneously crackling ice at the tips of her fingers. Her shadows still hung around her shoulders, but they seemed muted these days and sometimes flickered. She was still cautious, despite him and the others telling her how well she was doing. She refused to use it outside the courtyards unless she was alone or solely with him. The others stopped by the courtyard every once in a while to see how things were progressing, but other than that, they had no idea what the true extent of her power was. Neither did he.

He wasn't surprised that she was progressing so quickly. He had trained her in combat and weaponry. He knew she would do whatever was required of her to obtain something she desired. To her, mastering her magic was protection and safety. He knew she was a quick study and would likely learn her craft faster than others, but Talwyn had been right that morning months ago. Summoning it and wielding it were two very different things.

He winced as he shifted on the bench of the tub. While Scarlett was getting stronger, he was getting weaker. The bond was thicker than the thread that had threatened to snap that day, but it was not the bridge it had once been. Even with concentrated efforts to reserve his magic, he could feel it, slowly draining away day by day. He grew tired more quickly, and the others were noticing. He had argued again with Cyrus yesterday about telling Scarlett about the Mark. He couldn't do it, though, because he knew her. He knew she would accept the Mark to save his life, and he wouldn't force something upon her, not when she had been forced into so much in her short life. And he damn well wouldn't make it appear as if he only came for her because she was his twin flame.

He scented her then. Out in their room. She was back early from her usual sessions in the library with the mortal prince, and something was wrong.

Sorin quickly exited the bathing pool and toweled off. He pulled on his charcoal pants and slid on a white shirt. He was just finishing the final button as he entered the bedroom to find her out on the balcony in the gently falling snow, large fluffy flakes getting caught in her flowing hair. Flames were in her hands. Practicing. She was always practicing her magic when they were alone. The flames were various colors, but he could swear he glimpsed black amongst them.

She turned quickly at the sound of the door, extinguishing the flames instantly. "You are doing well with your magic," he said, crossing the threshold to the balcony.

"The fire seems far easier to control than the water," she replied. As she said it, she held her palm open and a small orb of water formed…and then splashed into her hand. She sighed in frustration.

Sorin leaned against the railing, bracing his hands behind him. "Talwyn was right on that," he said. "Your fire magic will be dominant when in the Fire Court."

"I can control ice just fine, though," she argued. In emphasis, ice crystals danced at her fingertips amongst her shadows.

Those shadows of hers. Those she could control with a half a thought these days.

"Is the ice not easier to control than flames? Water is a liquid. I imagine it is harder to control than ice," Sorin offered.

"So I just don't do anything with the water magic then?" she asked.

"Gods, no," Sorin exclaimed. "When you go to the Water Court, I suspect you will find it easier to access that power. With practice and training, you will be able to access them equally, no matter where you are."

"When I go to the Water Court?" Her brows rose at the idea. "I can go there?"

"You are no one's subject, Scarlett. You can go wherever you please," he replied softly.

"Your meetings went well today?" she asked, summoning a bracelet of flames around her wrist. Each bead of the bracelet was a flame of a different color.

"As well as can be expected with the Earth Court," Sorin answered, watching her work as she called each flame forward, one by one.

"Eliza said your Courts do not get along," she replied, not looking up at him.

"No, we do not."

"Why?"

"Various reasons. Old blood feuds," he shrugged. "Things to discuss at another time."

"Hmm," she hummed, her brow scrunching in concentration. Those flames around her wrist froze, became a bracelet of brilliantly frozen flames of ice. "How did I do it? How does she do it? Disappear into nothing?" Scarlett mused after a beat of silence. The ice bracelet vanished, and she absent-mindedly began rolling a string of flames between her fingers, snaking it along her knuckles.

Sorin straightened at her questions. She hadn't spoken much of that day.

"It's called Traveling. Few Fae can do it," Sorin answered.

"Can you?"

Sorin shook his head. "No. I can create fire portals because I am the Fire Prince, but I cannot Travel. You have Traveled before that day, you know," he answered with a wry smile.

"When?" she demanded. Her flames blazed, and she flinched slightly.

Sorin chuckled under his breath as he extinguished her flames for her. "In the mortal lands. You traveled us from the Lairwood House to the beach."

"But how did you know I would have the ability?" she pressed.

"Because your mother could Travel."

She considered this for a moment. "Do you know who my father is?"

Sorin shook his head. "I do not have any idea. She was not with child the last time I saw her. Not that I was aware of anyway."

"My mother told me he had been a sailor and that he was dead. She kept so much from me, I wonder if that is even true." She had ceased with her magic and had braced her arms on the railing, looking out over the mountains before them. He wished he could capture the moment as snow gently drifted down around her.

Sorin shoved down the desire to go to her. While he still slept beside her every night and they still flirted incessantly, they had not kissed since that day in the Princess's Gardens when he had shown her the sea star. Gods, he had wanted to. He had wanted to touch her again since the day she had begged him to after her first nightmare. Feeling her come around his fingers had him imagining her doing so around other parts of him. Had him thinking about how he'd make her come in other ways, too. But after the chalet, after the way he had so thoroughly shredded her, he would wait. He would let her come to him if she ever chose to do so again.

Then there was the mortal prince. Where things stood with him, he had no idea. She continued to meet with him nearly every day in the library, and once a week, she had dinner with the mortals in their guest suite. He was always a moody bastard at his own dinner with his Inner Court those evenings. She always came back to their rooms in the wee hours of the morning, the mortals' scents wrapped around her, along with another scent he couldn't figure out. It smelled of musty dirt and earth.

"How do I learn to Travel?"

Sorin considered the question. "I do not know," he admitted. "It is different from portaling. Portaling opens a doorway between two points. Traveling is bending the air between time and space, like folding a map to make two points closer to each other and stepping through a rip in the world."

"Do you know any other Travelers?"

"The Prince of the Earth Court is a Traveler," Sorin replied darkly. Then after a moment, he added, "We should talk to Rayner, though. He may be able to help."

"What exactly is Rayner?" Scarlett asked, curiosity taking over her features.

"After all these months, you finally ask of him?" He had been waiting for her curiosity to get the better of her. He was surprised she had held out this long.

She shrugged indifferently. "It seemed rude to pry."

"You love to pry," Sorin said with a pointed stare.

"Fuck off," she replied with a roll of her eyes.

Sorin gave her a teasing grin. "Rayner is an Ash Rider. He can move among smoke and ashes, including across the territories," Sorin answered. "It is like his own personal portal except that he can move mostly unnoticed and unseen if he desires."

"So when he's gone all the time, he's..." she trailed off.

"Rayner is my Third, but he is also a spy. He is constantly in other Courts and lands gathering information and reporting back. Ash Riders are rarer than Travelers. Wind Walkers are the same," Sorin explained. At the look of confusion on Scarlett's face, he added, "Wind Walkers are able to move among the winds, just as Ash Riders move among smoke and ash. In fact, because the winds are constant, they do not need to rely on smoke or ashes and can be even more discreet."

"Do the Earth and Water Courts have rare gifts as well?"

"Yes and no. Not in the way Fire and Wind do, but do not discount them. The Earth Court has the Artists. They are the only Court that can bestow Marks."

Scarlett's brows rose at that. "The tattoos?" Her eyes raked over him, pausing where she knew many of his Marks adorned his skin.

"Yes. Highly skilled Artists can charge astronomical fees for their services."

"Interesting," Scarlett mused. "And Water?"

"As for Water, they can imbue water to make weapons suscep- tible to magic. It is how my blades can become wreathed in fire. They were dipped in such water. Additionally, water is all around you and can be used as a looking glass if the right Fae is on the other side," he answered with a knowing smile.

"Briar?" she guessed.

"He is a Water Gazer, among others, yes," Sorin answered.

"How far can someone with the Traveling gift actually go?"

"What do you mean?"

"I can clearly Travel across the territories, but how far can I go? Can I Travel across the seas? Or is it like portaling where I have to know where I am going?"

"I do not know," he said slowly. "Why the sudden interest in such things?"

"Inquisitiveness, I suppose," she replied, waving her hand

dismissively. She sounded as if she were half-listening at this point, clearly pondering something.

Secrets. She was keeping secrets from him. He had startled her a few times in their rooms when she had been poring over those ancient texts she kept hauling up from the library. She kept them hidden somewhere. He had gone back down to that passageway himself, to see if he could glean what books she was reading, but the shelf was always full, not one book missing.

She was staring out over the balcony again, playing with her shadows that swirled around her, lost in her thoughts.

"You have been preoccupied these last few weeks," he said cautiously, leaning against the balcony rail once more.

"Have I?"

He clenched his jaw, not knowing how far was safe to push her yet. "What have you been researching in all those books you have been reading lately?"

"Various things," she answered vaguely as she shaped her shadows into flowers.

"Such as?"

"The territories. The Avonleyans. Deimas and Esmeray."

"Deimas and Esmeray?" he asked, unable to hide his shock at the admission.

"You said Talwyn has been upset with you because you didn't find the weapon for her to seek her revenge. That is what caused your...mood that day," she said, glancing at him sidelong.

He had told her about that meeting, about some of the things that Talwyn had said to him that had put him in such a state of mind. He didn't know she had started researching things because of it.

She shrugged. "I thought if we could find something to give her to seek that revenge, maybe she would stop being such a raging pain in your ass." She shrugged again, as if it were nothing.

He swallowed. "Have you learned anything?"

"About Deimas and Esmeray? Not much," she admitted.

"But you have learned other things?"

Scarlett took a step back from the railing as she said, "I suppose we should go find Rayner. See if he can help me learn how to Travel."

Too much. He had pushed her as far as she was willing to go today.

"I was thinking we could take a night off," Sorin said, a half smile curling on his lips.

"I don't need a night off," she replied without looking at him.

"You may not *need* a night off, but I would like to show you the city."

Scarlett turned to face him. "You'll take me into the city?"

"I did tell you that you could go into the city whenever you wanted to," Sorin reminded her.

"I know, and I have been a few times on quick errands with Eliza, but never out for fun. There's just been so much going on, and we were going up to the courtyards every day. And now there's the— I just forgot there were other things to see," Scarlett said, looking out over the balcony once more. From up here, you could just see the start of the city beyond the sprawling grounds.

"There will always be something to tend to or something to train for. There will always be people vying for your attention and places to run to, but it is just as important to take the time to look at the stars and feel the sun on your face and enjoy good food with excellent company," he said.

"Excellent company? Are Eliza, Cyrus, and Rayner to join us as well then?" she teased with a smirk.

"My dear Scarlett," he purred, coming up behind her, "when shall we find a better use for that wicked tongue of yours?"

Her citrus and embers and jasmine scent filled him. The Mark on his left hand burned as desire coursed through him, and he hid his grimace. She turned to face him, her composure more alluring than ever. Her voice was low and sultry as she said, "Oh Prince, you shall find out just how wicked I can be when you see what I'm wearing out tonight."

Sorin had no doubt it was true as she sauntered past him, swinging those damn hips of hers just right, and went to dress for a night in the city.

CHAPTER 35
SCARLETT

S carlett sat across from Sorin at a small table in a little restaurant along the Tana River. Since most of the residents of the Fire Court possessed fire magic, the city was kept as warm and toasty as the palace by the various business owners and patrons. The hostess had greeted Sorin by name, addressed as Prince Sorin of course, and immediately taken them to this table. Scarlett hadn't asked if he sent notice ahead or if he just always had a table on stand by.

Eliza, of all people, had helped her get ready for the night. For a female who was more comfortable on battlefields and with books in her hands, she certainly knew fashion well enough. Scarlett wore a tight forest green dress that made her hair shine in the setting sun. It boasted sheer panels that ran along her midriff, and the sleeves were sheer as well. The back was open and exposed. Tiny beads of silver adorned the whole thing. Eliza had used two ornate floral hairpins to sweep half of her hair up. The rest she had curled down her back. Then she'd sent her on her way to meet Sorin at the palace entrance, promising to join them for dancing later in the evening.

"I've heard him talk about this city so many times I could recite everything he's going to say," she'd said with a wave of her hand.

"Let him show you Solembra. We will show you the nightlife." The feral gleam in her eyes had Scarlett laughing as she'd sauntered down the hall.

The guards had given her appreciative glances when she'd passed, and the look on Sorin's face when he'd seen her would forever be etched in her memory. How he had stilled. How his eyes had swept her up and down. Twice. How, when he finally began moving again and reached her side, her toes had curled when he had whispered directly into her ear, "You shall start rumors tonight in that dress, Princess."

They had walked the half mile or so to the City. With Sorin beside her, the biting cold of winter was stifled. She didn't even need her cloak, and Sorin had sent it to whatever pocket between the realms where he stored everything else it seemed. He had pointed out various places on their way to the restaurant. Next time, he promised, he was taking her to the artist's district.

The sun was setting as they sat beside the Tana River. Despite it being winter, the magic of the Fire Court kept the river from freezing, and she could hear the rushing sounds of the water. Not quite the waves of the sea, but they quieted her soul nonetheless. They had already ordered, and she sipped at her wine. He studied her, taking a drink of his own, before he said, "You were back earlier than usual from the library today."

She paused, slowly setting her goblet back onto the table. She leaned back in her chair, her eyes gazing out at the Tana. "We weren't in the library long today. Callan was restless and wanted to walk the gardens. It was freezing, so it did not last long."

"Let's try again," he said gently. "You were upset when you came back to our rooms earlier than usual today."

She brought her eyes back to his where he was patiently waiting for her. "He grows restless and is ready to return to Baylorin." Sorin was silent, waiting for more. She sighed. "I told him that while I will return to Baylorin, I likely will not stay in Baylorin when everything is taken care of. He did not take it well."

"I am sure he did not," Sorin said, taking another drink of his own wine. She couldn't read the expression on his features.

"We argued."

"I am gathering that."

Her gaze slid back to the river, and she strained to hear the waters over the din of the restaurant. "About more than me not staying in Baylorin."

"Oh?"

"He still holds out hope that I will be his queen, that we will be together. No matter how many times I tell him or reasons I give him that it cannot be so."

"Do you want it to be a possibility?" Sorin asked evenly.

"No," she answered softly. "I still do not desire to be chained to a throne." Sorin was quiet, letting her ponder, letting her volunteer whatever was on her mind. "He questions what you are to me," she ventured carefully.

"Does he now?"

"He thinks you are my soulmate."

A faint, almost sad smile crossed his lips. "I am not your soulmate, Scarlett."

"Because you were my mother's?"

"No. You can actually have more than one soulmate, but I am not yours." He paused a moment before he added, "Cassius, however, is your soulmate."

Her brows rose in surprise. "How do you know?"

"I am ancient as hell, remember?" he said with a wink.

Cassius was her soulmate. She let that truth plunk into her soul and sink to the bottom. Now that it was said, the obviousness of it stared back at her.

"Do you wish you were my soulmate?" she asked, picking up her wine glass just to have something to do with her hands.

He was quiet, contemplating. "No, Scarlett, I do not wish I was your soulmate."

She was both crushed and relieved at his answer. Soulmates were intimate friends, but nothing beyond friendship. She had stared at her hand clasped in Callan's when he told her he would be fine with Sorin being her soulmate, and she had realized the truth.

She wouldn't. She wouldn't be fine with that at all.

She did not want him to be her soulmate. She wanted more than just soulmate intimacy. The thought of him with another female made her want to rage and vomit and cry all at the same time.

But he had a twin flame. Somewhere out there. And despite her conversation with Eliza, if she ventured down that road, should his twin flame come along, the urge to kill her on sight would be strong.

"I am closer to you than I am with Cassius," she said quietly. "You know things I have never told him."

"What are you to me?" he asked, his eyes studying hers intently.

"A pain in your ass?" She batted her lashes at him as she took a sip of her wine.

He barked a laugh. "That you most certainly are."

The sun dropped the last beat behind the mountains, and there was a sizzling sound. Scarlett's eyes widened as she looked frantically around the restaurant.

"The river, Love," Sorin said calmly. "Look at the river."

She turned back to the water as flames rushed along the banks on either side, starting at the palace and flowing down the river and out of sight. She had seen the fires in the palace but had thought it was part of the palace magic. She did not realize it spanned the entire length of the river. The flames lit up the banks and the little businesses that dotted its shoreline. She could feel the heat from the blazes and couldn't help but gape in wonder as small seals jumped as they swam downstream.

Finally she tore her gaze from the water and turned to Sorin, who was staring not at the river, but at her. His eyes were practically glowing. "They are the Twilight Wildfires. They start at the river's source and go along the entire length to the border until dawn."

"They are beautiful," she breathed, turning back to the river.

"That they are," he replied.

The food arrived, and Scarlett ate some of the most divine seafood she had ever encountered. After finishing off a piece of raspberry glazed cake, they had meandered around the city a little more. The Twilight Wildfires cast a twinkling glow along the streets, illuminating their path, until they came upon the dance club and found Eliza, Rayner, and Cyrus waiting for them outside.

They were handed drinks as they entered. Well, the others were. Apparently everyone here knew exactly what they drank. "Wine," Eliza said to the hostess over the music, with a nod of her head to Scarlett. A few moments later, she had a glass in her hand and was following them through the crowd to a reserved table. This one, she was fairly certain, was always on reserve for them.

For hours they danced, and she silently cursed them all for taking so long to show her this side of the Fire Court. Cyrus whirled her around the dance floor, expertly guiding her through some popular Fae dances. She drank, Eliza pressing a full glass of wine into her hand whenever hers was empty. Even Rayner took her around the dance floor a few times. She laughed, carefree and joyful, with a family she didn't know she had been missing.

Cyrus had just finished twirling her around to a particularly fast-paced number. She was breathing hard, laughing as Eliza sauntered over and began dancing between Cyrus and Rayner. Then she spotted Sorin across the room. He was sitting at their table, and his attention was fixed solely on her.

What are you to me?

His words from earlier that evening came floating back. She had deflected and had been grateful for the Twilight Wildfires interrupting that particular conversation because she didn't know the answer.

But that was a lie.

Cassius had told her once that there was a connection between her and Sorin. Mikale had sneered that everyone could see it. Callan was beyond paranoid about it. She hadn't believed them.

That wasn't true either.

If she were honest with herself, she hadn't allowed herself to believe them. She kept boundaries in place, kept feelings pushed so far down, to keep herself safe. Just as she had screamed at Sorin that day in the mountains. She'd known what he was doing because it was what she did herself. She was used to doing the protecting, constantly guarding those she loved. She had loved Callan once, but even then, she was constantly watching for threats and lived in the shadows.

But the way Sorin was looking at her, as if she were the only person in the room, despite the chaos and revelry going on around him, she allowed herself to peel back the outer most layers of whatever it was they were. She allowed herself to entertain the idea of letting herself love him, the one who always came for her. The one who let her work through things. The one who knew every secret her heart held. The one who did not fear her darkness.

She had meant it when she'd said she hoped he found his twin flame someday, but the deepest parts of her did not want to share him with anyone. A horrible part of her prayed to whatever gods would listen that his twin flame was already long gone from this world, and they wouldn't find each other until the After. Even then, she didn't want to share him.

She pushed aside the shame that washed over her at the thought of that for her friend, about what kind of person that made her. She shouted to Cyrus over the crowd and music that she was going to take a break. Cyrus smirked at her, as if he knew something she didn't. Sorin's eyes locked onto hers as she made her way towards him, and she held them the whole way there. She slid onto the bench beside him at their table.

"Hello, Prince." Her voice was low, sensuous.

"Hello, Princess." Sorin's voice was thick, and a predatory hunger filled his eyes.

"You are not dancing?"

"Cyrus informed me that I had you all evening and that I could share you for a while," he answered, sipping from his drink.

"I think we've finally proven they do actually prefer my company over yours," Scarlett replied with a wink.

He huffed a laugh. "It only seems natural, I suppose." He paused, drumming his fingers on the table before him, seeming to debate saying something.

"Do I need to find a treat for you tonight, Prince, or are you going to say what you're wanting to?" she asked, running her finger along the rim of an empty glass on the table.

"Love, that dress is all the treat I need tonight," he purred.

She placed a hand on his upper thigh, and he stilled, watching her closely, studying her as he had all night. "Are you sure? I think I've finally thought of a better use for my tongue," she replied, her fingers inching up his thigh.

Without taking his eyes from hers, he drew a fire message in the air. Then he knocked back his glass of liquor as if trying to clear his head. He brought his hand up, the one with the unfinished tattoo, to her cheek and dragged his fingers slowly along her cheek, her jaw, along her neck to her shoulder. As he lazily pulled them across her collarbone, he leaned forward so she could hear him over the noise of the club. "My dear Scarlett, I have done nothing but think about all the uses I could find for that tongue since the day I watched you spar with Cassius in that training barracks. It has really been quite distracting."

And it was her turn to still.

"Then," he continued, his breath hot in her ear, "I thought of all the things I could do with *my* tongue."

His fingers had slowly trailed down from her collarbone, stopping right at the top slope of her breast. Her breathing hitched, and her core heated.

She swallowed as she breathed, "Who's starting rumors now?"

His laugh was deep and carnal. "What kind of rumors would you like to start, Love?"

Sorin's eyes followed his own fingers as he dragged them down between her breasts. Down slowly to her navel, then curved and slid down to her thigh. He started making idle circles on that thigh, slowly, so slowly, working his way back up.

She was done. She was done flirting. She was done keeping him at arm's length. She was done. "Sorin," she ground out, "let's go."

A slow smile spread across his face as he leaned in even closer, so that his mouth was right next to her ear. She could feel his lips brush the shell of it as he whispered, "As ravenous as this dress makes me for you, Princess, not tonight."

She actually groaned. Out loud. "Why?"

He didn't move, still whispering into her ear, "Because, Scarlett

313

Monrhoe, you are drunk on wine." She started to protest, but he continued over her. "And the first time I take you, I want you completely aware of every single way I worship you."

Scarlett felt a pulse of heat behind her, and she turned to find he had opened a portal. Eliza was standing beside it, a look of pure amusement on her face. She scowled at her friend as Sorin said, "Take her home, Eliza dear."

She turned back to him. "You are not coming?"

"Love, if I came home with you now, I would go back on everything I just said."

"Then come home," she purred.

But then Eliza was taking her hand, tugging her to her feet. Scarlett was still staring at Sorin, a look of pure desire on his face, when Eliza pulled her through the portal, holding in her laughter.

CHAPTER 36
SCARLETT

S carlett felt the bed shift. She opened her eyes a fraction to find the room still dark, with no sign of the sun any time soon. She lifted her head slightly and swore. Gods, her head hurt. Damn wine.

She reached with her hand to find the spot next to her warm but missing the male that was supposed to be lying there.

"Sorin?" she sat up in bed, panic setting in. She was still in their room. She was still in the Fire Court. She was still safe.

"I did not mean to wake you," he said softly, coming out of the closet. He was fully dressed in elegant charcoal clothing, fine gold and copper threads running throughout it. A crown of flame cast a soft glow above his head as he buttoned the cuff of his shirt. He looked not like a prince, but like a king.

Scarlett slid out of bed and crossed the room to him, shivering slightly. Her nightgown was sleeveless, low cut, and only went to her knees. The fire that had been smoldering embers in the hearth leapt to life with a glance from Sorin.

"You know, Love," he said in that low voice that skittered along her bones and made her toes curl, "the things you wear to bed are about as wicked as your dress was last night."

She hadn't heard Sorin come home. In fact, when she'd felt the bed shifting a few moments ago, she'd thought it was him getting into bed, not getting up.

"Where are you going?" she said to him now as he buckled on his sword belt. She rubbed her hands down her bare arms, watching him.

"I have a meeting," he answered.

"That you must be at before the sun rises?"

"That I must be at *when* the sun rises," he corrected, sliding on his red jacket.

A burst of flame appeared in the air right next to his head. Sorin reached up a hand and pulled a piece of paper from the flame, reading it. "I must go," he said, leaning down and brushing a soft kiss to her temple. "Cyrus is waiting in the sitting room, but when I return we need to talk." She couldn't read the expression in his eyes as he turned to leave.

"I want to come," Scarlett said. "I'll just be a minute." She started toward the closet, but Sorin caught her arm.

"You cannot come, Scarlett."

"What? Why not?" she demanded. He had never, not once, told her she couldn't go somewhere.

"This meeting," he paused, weighing his words. "It is at the White Halls."

"It is with Talwyn?"

Sorin nodded.

"About what?"

He hesitated. "Princess Ashtine has news about Mikale and movements in the mortal lands."

Movements in the mortal lands? He'd never mentioned any of this to her.

"Then I am definitely coming." She tried to pull her arm free, but Sorin held tight. Some primal part of her bared her teeth at him as she pushed down the memory of someone else holding her tightly and leaving bruises.

"You cannot come, Scarlett. It was a summoning of the Princes and Princess of the Courts. That is it."

"But Cyrus is going," Scarlett argued.

"We are allowed to bring one member of our Court with us to these summonings."

"Then bring me instead of Cyrus," she cried.

"I can't do that," he said, releasing her arm.

"What do you mean you can't do that? Of course you can. You're a prince!"

"Meetings like these do not involve just the Courts, Scarlett. They involve dealings with the entirety of the continent. Relationships with the other territory leaders. It is strategizing and planning. They are things you would not understand. They are things you do not *want* to be a part of. Cyrus needs to be there as my Second."

He started to make his way to the bedroom door to leave. She had been secretly working on combining her shadows with her magic, utilizing those incessant shadows that she had come to love. She took those shadows and slammed them into her fire, producing a wall of impassable shadowfire in front of the bedroom door.

"Scarlett." He turned back to her. She could just make out the shock lining his features in the dark of the room. "How did you do that?"

"That is not your concern right now," she seethed. "Take me with you."

"Scarlett, I must go. I cannot be late."

"I can help with this. I have information that—"

"Scarlett, I do not know how to make this any clearer. My Queen has summoned me. I must go. If I am late, she will collect me herself, and it will not be pleasant for anyone," he pleaded sharply, frustration coloring his tone. She could tell he was choking down on his temper.

"So because Talwyn says jump, you have to ask how high?" Scarlett spat.

"Yes! That is how this works! She is my Queen, Scarlett." Sorin's voice was rising. Angry. He was angry with her. She had never heard him angry like this with her. Worried? Concerned? Irritated? Yes, but never anger directed at her. It only escalated her own fury.

"Yes, she is your Queen, but what am I?"

Sorin froze, and when his eyes fixed upon her this time, they were flames. He stalked back to her and a trail of fire was left in his wake. As he reached her, a column of flames erupted around them, and Scarlett forced herself to quiet the surprised cry that rose up inside of her. She had known he was powerful. She had known he was the Prince of Fire for months now, but he had never displayed it at this level, not even in the face of Talwyn. Flames of red and gold and wildfire blue snaked through his hair and rose from his fingertips. He seemed to almost be floating on flames.

His voice was lethal, the ire as sharp as the blade at his side, as he said, "That is an excellent question. You tell me, Scarlett. What are you?" Scarlett didn't know what to say, and when she didn't speak, he continued. "You told me, over and over again, you do not want this. You do not want your bloodline to dictate your path. You do not want the Fates to decide your future. You do not want to rule. You do not want to be chained to a throne. You do not want to be my Queen. You do not know how you feel about Callan. You have said you do not belong here. You do not feel like you belong there. You wanted the choices. You wanted to decide. So I have left those decisions up to you. So tell me, Princess, what are you? What are you to the Courts? To the world? What are you to me?"

Scarlett felt like he had punched her in her gut. She would rather he had actually punched her. Her shadow flames blocking the door guttered into nothing, and Sorin's own power dampened. There was a light knocking on the door before it opened. Cyrus stood there, clearing his throat awkwardly, obviously having heard their fight.

"Sorin, we must go. Briar just sent a warning."

The Prince before her merely nodded at Cyrus, then turned back to Scarlett. She couldn't even look him in the face. He gripped her chin roughly, forcing her eyes up. When she finally met his gaze, he spoke again. His voice was just as lethal, but the edge had softened a touch. "You are mine, and I am yours, but what are you to me? What am I to you?"

"I don't know," she snapped. "We must suddenly define something so undefinable?"

"When you decide what you are, I will accept your choices. But until then, when my Queen summons me, I must go. I do not have a choice."

"Then go," she spat. "I do not care."

He dropped her chin, his mouth forming a thin line, and strode to Cyrus. The doorway before them transformed into a portal of fire, the crown of flames above his head glowing brighter than it had before.

"He doesn't have a choice, Scarlett. Not until—" Cyrus began softly, but Sorin threw him a look that clearly told him to keep his mouth shut.

"I. Do. Not. Care," she repeated, enunciating each word. "You all can go to hell."

She saw Sorin's back stiffen, and he stepped through the portal without a glance back to her, Cyrus a step behind.

The portal snapped shut, and Scarlett screamed in frustration. Flames appeared in her palms, and she hurled them into the fireplace. She found herself wishing she could talk to Cassius, and she cursed aloud for not knowing how to control her Traveling yet.

She had information that could help them. Each week, after her dinners with Callan, Finn, and Sloan, she snuck down to that passageway. At the base of the stairs was a huge cavern with books in that strange language. She had found two other books down there in the Old Language. Translations. They were translations of the other language, and she had indeed been teaching herself how to read it, and along the way she had found information about the Avonleyans and their continent. She wanted to go down there now but couldn't risk being seen going there during the day.

As she turned to throw more flames, not caring if she burned his entire fucking palace to the ground, she froze in place at the panther that sat across the room from her. Its eyes were glowing as it watched her, its tail switching back and forth across the floor.

"Shirina?" she whispered cautiously.

The panther didn't move as she inched closer. When she was a foot away, Shirina stood. Scarlett reached out her hand, and the instant her hand touched the animal's soft fur, she felt the pull at her navel. As if in slow motion, she watched the bedroom disappear, and she found herself standing in the middle of a grove of trees. The trees were in full bloom with flowers of purple and turquoise and rose gold despite the frost and snow on the ground around them. She turned to find a large castle looming behind her. The sky was cloudy and gray, the wind chilly. She stood barefoot in the snow. Shirina stood at her side and nuzzled her hand.

"Where did you take me?" Scarlett asked her quietly, scratching behind her ears.

"Where indeed?" came a voice from behind her. It was icy, cold, and cruel.

Scarlett turned slowly to face the female it came from. She was tall and young. She looked like a mortal in her early twenties. Her features were sharp and angular. She had long brown hair that was braided down her back, and she wore a black suit of some sort with leathers over the top. Scarlett could see the sword strapped to her back, peeking over the woman's shoulder underneath the cloak she wore. Her skin was golden brown, but her eyes were a deep shade of violet as she pierced Scarlett with her stare.

"It has been an age since a Spirit Animal has visited our realm," said the woman. Shirina elicited a low snarl beside Scarlett, and the woman tilted her head to the side, as if contemplating something. She looked back at Scarlett. "The panther brought you here? You did not come on your own?"

Scarlett didn't know if she should answer. She didn't know if she should do anything.

Shirina decided for her with a nod of her head.

"I see," the woman answered. Looking Scarlett up and down, she added, "You best come change, your Majesty. You cannot see the Oracle looking like that, even if you are a Queen."

Scarlett looked down to find she was still wearing her night-gown. Her eyes darted to Shirina, who nudged her forward with her nose. She started to follow the woman, Shirina in step beside her. "I'm sorry, but *where* am I?"

The woman looked over her shoulder, a wicked smirk lining her lips. "You are in the Witch Kingdoms."

Scarlett felt the blood drain from her face. Sorin had told her some about the Witch lands. They were a realm of cruelty and bloodshed. The Witches themselves were harsh and brutal, showing no mercy. She didn't let the terror color her tone. She dug deep, pulling up every shred of arrogance and swagger she could. After all, as Death's Maiden was she not just as cruel and brutal? "And you are?"

Those violet eyes glared back at her, just as wicked as this whole damn realm felt. "I am Hazel Hecate, the High Witch."

CHAPTER 37

SORIN

S orin and Cyrus were rushing along the hallway to the Council Rooms in the White Halls. They were late, and Talwyn was going to be pissed. They were nearly to the doors when he felt it. He felt her terror as it hit him like a blow to the face. It hit him so hard, he stumbled and nearly went sprawling to the floor.

"What the fuck?" Cyrus cried, catching Sorin by the arm and keeping him upright.

"She's gone," Sorin rasped. He could hardly breathe.

"Who's gone?"

Cyrus yanked his arm, pulling him into a nearby alcove. Sorin leaned over, bracing his hands on his knees. He could feel her, yet he couldn't, almost as if she were too far away.

"Get it together, Sorin," Cyrus hissed. "Talwyn cannot see you like this."

"She is gone," Sorin hissed again. "Scarlett is gone. I should not have left her like that. Not after we are already on uneven footing. We need to go back."

He made to turn to go, but Cyrus gripped his shoulders. "We

cannot go back right now. Talwyn would hunt you down and drag you back here herself."

"Something is wrong. She is terrified. I can feel her terror," Sorin said, trying to wrench free of Cyrus's grip.

"You had a fight. It was nothing compared to the one a month ago. After this meeting, you can go to her and work it all out," Cyrus started.

"You do not understand," Sorin snarled. "She is not in the Fire Court."

Cyrus slammed him into the wall. "You need to pull it together, Sorin. There is no way Talwyn will let you go to her right now. Without her taking the Mark and acknowledging the bond, she is not considered your highest priority," he barked. "We'll send Rayner to her. Can you find her? Or is it like before?" He glanced at Sorin's left hand as he said it.

Sorin sent his mind down the bond as fast as he could, and the farther down it went, the more he could feel his power fracturing, his soul splintering. He'd been conserving his power as much as possible for weeks, but there wasn't much left. This morning had taken a toll on him. It was as if his magic couldn't replenish, and when he came to the end of it...

Finally, he found her and when he pulled back, he traced a flame symbol in the air, sending a fire message to Rayner.

"She is in the Witch Kingdoms," he said to Cyrus as the flame disappeared.

"Fuck," Cyrus murmured. "Are you sure?"

"Yes. It explains the terror."

"How the hell did she get to the Witch Kingdoms?"

"I don't know," Sorin said, adjusting his tunic as he straightened.

"Rayner will find her. He will get her out," Cyrus said, his voice tight, like he was trying to convince himself as well as Sorin. "If we haven't heard from them by the time we leave, we'll go there ourselves."

"It should be me going," Sorin muttered. "She will not forgive me for walking out on her. Not again."

"Sorin, she is our family, too. She is our prince's twin flame.

323

Rayner will not fail you," Cryus replied. Then he added softly, "And she will forgive you. The bond is stronger than the fights. At least it was for me and Thia."

Sorin only nodded, stepping from the alcove. He shoved his hands into his pockets as he sauntered into the Council Room, pushing his own fear down deep, and awaited word from his Ash Rider.

CHAPTER 38
SCARLETT

S carlett looked in the mirror in the room the High Witch had led her to. She was wearing a black bodysuit of some sort. It was tight and hugged her in all the right places but somehow incredibly flexible, allowing her to move with ease. Atop that, she strapped leathers on. They were different from the fighting leathers that she wore in the Fae lands. These were a thicker leather, but somehow lighter. The boots were warm on her feet and went over her knees. Shirina sat beside the entrance, her silver eyes ever watchful. Her ears perked up, and she cocked her head to the side, just as a swirl of smoke appeared in the reflection of the mirror behind her near the hearth and Rayner stepped from ashes. His eyes settled on her, relief flooding them as they scanned her for injuries.

"Are you hurt?" he asked, his low voice thick with worry.

"No," Scarlett answered, tilting her head to the side as she watched him in the mirror. "How did you find me?"

"Sorin sent me," Rayner answered, coming to stand beside her. He reached over and tightened a buckle at her shoulder.

"How did he know where to find me?"

Ignoring her question, Rayner asked, "Does anyone know you are here? Have you been spotted?"

But before Scarlett could answer and press about how Sorin knew how to find her, the door to the room flung open. The High Witch stalked into the room, her violet eyes glowing with ire. Her voice was cold and unforgiving as she hissed, "Do you know what we do to males who come to my lands, who enter my home, without permission, Ash Rider?" She drew the sword that was strapped to her back as she finished speaking, leveling the blade with his throat.

"Forgive me, High Witch," Rayner replied, bowing low at the waist. Scarlett was somewhat shocked at the deep level of respect from someone just as terrifying as the High Witch. "I come on an errand of my Prince."

"Your Prince should know better than to send males here without warning. You shall be his reminder," she snarled as she made to step towards Rayner.

Without giving herself a chance to think about what she was doing, Scarlett stepped in front of Rayner. Her voice was authoritative, commanding, and her eyes glowed blue with flames, her shadows poised to strike. "He came at my request. He is one of mine."

The High Witch studied her with those violet eyes for a moment, seeming to consider something. "You claim him?"

"I do. He is my family," Scarlett answered.

"Intriguing," the High Witch said, studying her a moment longer. "Follow me. The Oracle is expecting you."

Shirina stood at the words and padded after the High Witch. She paused at the door, looking back over her shoulder as if beckoning Scarlett to follow. Scarlett had only taken a step when she felt Rayner grab her elbow. She slowly looked down at his fingers on her arm and dragged her eyes up to his, biting back on the snarl at that grip.

"You are going to the Oracle?" he asked darkly.

"It would appear so," Scarlett answered. She tugged her arm, and Rayner let go at once. She again began to follow Hazel and Shirina, and Rayner fell into step beside her.

"Who does the High Witch think you are?" he whispered as they walked along a corridor. They were several feet behind the High

Witch, and Scarlett wondered if a Witch's hearing was as keen as the Fae and Night Children. Based on Juliette, if she had indeed been a Witch, she could only assume it was.

"She called me a queen. I didn't think it wise to correct the High Witch," Scarlett whispered back.

"The Oracle is not someone to be trifled with," Rayner warned as they rounded a corner.

"Then it's a good thing I'm not planning on fighting her," Scarlett drawled. "Is it a her?"

"No one knows. We assume so since it is a Witch," Rayner replied, "but it appears differently to everyone."

"What do you mean?" They were outside now, walking down a snow-covered dirt path to the forest that sprawled behind the High Witch's castle.

"I mean how she appears to me, she will not appear to you. You might see an old blind woman, hunched over and walking with a cane, while I might see a great bird."

Rayner caught her by the waist as she tripped over a fallen branch, and she threw him an appreciative glance. Once he had steadied her, a plume of smoke appeared before them and from it he drew the same sword that Eliza had summoned for her in the courtyard the day Talwyn had appeared there. "Here," he said, handing it to Scarlett. "Eliza sent this for you."

Scarlett gave him an appreciative nod and slid it into the sheath along the back of her leathers. They walked for at least another five miles, traversing through the trees and across babbling brooks not yet frozen over by the winter weather. The High Witch never once looked back to see if they were still behind her, but Scarlett had the feeling she could indeed hear every word they were saying.

"What is she when you see her?" she asked Rayner.

"I have never seen her."

"Never?" Scarlett turned to him in surprise.

He shook his head. "Very few have ever seen the Oracle. So few, in fact, that some believe it is only a legend."

Scarlett only nodded as they continued on. They had begun to climb a steep cliff-side, and Scarlett found herself even more grateful for the clothing Hazel had provided for her. The boots were excellent for gripping the rocks. Shirina was bounding ahead of them, back and forth, up the rocky slope, a shadow of night against the snow. Hazel had clearly climbed this cliff-side many times, knowing exactly where to step and grip to make quick work of the climb. Rayner had gone before Scarlett and helped her up onto a cliff edge where Hazel stood waiting beside a cave opening.

"The Oracle lives here?" Scarlett asked, peering around Rayner into the dark of the cave before her.

"You are not permitted to take weapons in with you," Hazel replied in answer.

Scarlett glanced at Rayner, uncertain of what to say to that. He had placed himself between her and the High Witch, and he straightened to his full, towering height as he said, "You expect my Queen to enter a cave unarmed?"

"If she wishes to see the Oracle, I do," Hazel retorted harshly.

Scarlett looked to Shirina, who was now sitting beside the cave mouth, her tail switching behind her. The panther gave a slight nod of its head, and Scarlett reached behind her, grabbing her sword. She handed it wordlessly to Rayner, then stepped around him. There was worry swirling in his gray eyes as she met his gaze, and she tried her best to give him a reassuring smile.

She stepped towards the cave mouth, but Hazel held up a hand, halting her. "You cannot bring any weapons in with you."

"I do not have any other weapons," Scarlett argued. "I have nothing hidden. I swear it. I came here in a nightgown, remember?"

"You have fire and ice running in your veins and shadows at your beck and call, do you not?" Hazel replied, a cunning smile on her lips.

"I can't give you my magic," Scarlett balked.

"Of course not," Hazel said. She made a motion with her hand and a table appeared beside her. On the table sat a small vial, just like the vials of tonic Scarlett had taken nearly every night of her life. "This will temporarily nullify your powers. When the Oracle is finished with you, they will be released back to you."

"Scarlett," Rayner warned from behind her. "We should wait for Sorin."

"You question your Queen?" Hazel asked sharply. Then she turned those violet eyes upon Scarlett. "You would wait for permission from a male?"

"No. I mean—" Scarlett started, stumbling over her words.

"Is he your keeper?" the High Witch snarled.

"I do not have a keeper," Scarlett bit back.

"Are you someone's subject? Someone's property? Someone's pet?"

"No," Scarlett growled from between her teeth.

"Your Spirit Animal brought you here. The Oracle does not often take visitors. I cannot guarantee you another visit if you do not go now." When Scarlett still hesitated, the High Witch stepped closer to her. Looking directly into her eyes, Hazel said in a dangerously quiet voice, "You are a Queen. You do not need permission to do anything and certainly not from a male. You make the choices that will affect you and your people, and you make them without regret. You choose, and you handle the consequences, whatever they may be. You do not look back, only forward. Now make your choice."

Scarlett shot one last wary look to Rayner, then stepped forward and swallowed the contents of the vial in a single gulp. It tasted exactly as her daily tonic had, and she felt her magic instantly vanish. The shadows she had grown to love faded into nothing. Hazel smiled widely, gesturing to the cave. "See what awaits."

Scarlett walked slowly forward into the cave, letting her eyes adjust to the darkness. It was pitch black and without her shadows to scout the way before her, she moved cautiously, relying on her enhanced Fae senses. She had walked for nearly five minutes in total silence when finally a glow appeared ahead. Swallowing hard, she took a deep breath and stepped forward once more.

She didn't know what she had expected to see or what the Oracle would be, but she did not expect what stood before her as the passageway opened up forming a wide circular cavern. In the center of the room stood a woman.

Stood Juliette.

She was barefoot, her feet dirty from the dirt floor of the cave, and she wore her black tunic and pants. The same clothing she wore on the nights they were dispatched to take care of the worst of the worst. Her hands were clasped lightly before her.

Not real, Scarlett told herself. She was not really standing before her. That was impossible.

But Scarlett could not take another step into the room. Her breathing grew ragged, her chest tight.

"Hello, sister," the Oracle said, her voice soft.

"I am not your sister," Scarlett said quietly. "Juliette is dead."

"Am I?" she asked, with a tilt of her head.

"Yes. I stabbed you in the heart myself. I watched the life leave your eyes. It's haunted me, whether I am sleeping or awake."

"You merely released me from my mortal body. My essence lives on," the Oracle said, taking a step towards her. "I came here. To wait for you. To see you."

"How? How is that possible?" Scarlett whispered, her voice cracking.

"Blood magic," Juliette said grimly. "Powerful, ancient blood magic."

"You knew I would come here? How?" Scarlett asked, unable to hide the shock and surprise in her voice.

"I am a Witch, Scarlett," Juliette answered. "I am a powerful Seer. I saw what you are to become. I had originally thought it meant you were to be a queen beside Callan. It is why I tried to push you towards such a path. But then I had more and more visions. And now…"

"And now?" Scarlett asked, swallowing thickly.

"You were made for such a time as this, sister," Juliette said, reaching out and grasping Scarlett's hands with her own, repeating words she'd said with her dying breaths.

"No," Scarlett whispered, shaking her head in denial. "No. I am not a queen. I was not made for a throne."

"Then what are you?"

"What?"

"Then what are you?" Juliette repeated, her amber eyes fixed on Scarlett's orbs of icy blue.

"What kind of question is that?" Scarlett demanded.

"If you are not a queen, if you are not to care for those who cannot care for themselves, what are you to the realms?"

"I don't know," Scarlett snapped, jerking her hands from the Oracle's. "I stopped knowing who I was the minute I drove that dagger into your heart."

"You did not cease to exist when my heart stopped beating," Juliette chided gently.

"But I did," Scarlett whispered. She sank to her knees, and Juliette dropped with her, reaching for her hands once more. "I shattered the moment I drove that dagger into your heart. He destroyed me."

There it was. She had said it. The thing she had never allowed herself to admit to anyone. Not Sorin. Not even herself. Mikale had wanted a broken pet, and he had accomplished that task the second he'd made her kill Juliette. She had been shoved into a pit. She had been forced to walk through a hell, and she didn't recognize the person that was emerging on this side of that journey.

"Yes, but he has come for you," Juliette answered with a soft smile.

"Mikale has come for me. Over and over. Last time, I nearly went with him. Sorin and Briar think he was entrancing me, but he wasn't, Juliette. I was not under some Night Child spell. A part of me thought it would be easier—" Scarlet swallowed against the lump in her throat. "That maybe it would be easier just to go with him, let him finish breaking me. If it would keep those I love safe. If it would keep the orphans safe."

Juliette reached up and brushed tears from her face. "Mikale is not of whom I speak, my friend. I speak of the one who comes for you. I speak of the one who came for you before he even knew who you were. I speak of the one who has searched for you since the dawn of time."

"You speak as if I have a twin flame," Scarlett scoffed.

Juliette barked a laugh. "We grew up and trained together, Scarlett. I *know* you are not this dense."

"No," Scarlett whispered. "He is not mine."

"You know that isn't true," Juliette retorted. "You have screamed it at him in your most desperate moments."

"How could you possibly know that?" Scarlett asked with a sidelong look at Juliette. She still could not believe she was sitting here, speaking with her. Maybe that potion she'd drank did more than nullify her magic...

"All powerful Seer. Remember?" Juliette said with her wicked grin as she gestured to herself.

Scarlett snorted. "Careful, sister. Your vanity is showing."

"I'm still me," Juliette scoffed. "Just different, I suppose. Just as you are still you, only...different."

Scarlett didn't say anything to that as she looked around the dark cave cavern. "You will reside here now? Forever? What of the previous Oracle?"

"Those are secrets I am not allowed to reveal, even to a queen of the realm," Juliette replied quietly.

"I am not a queen," Scarlett repeated, but Juliette said nothing in response. Just waited for her, as she always had. As Sorin did. Waited for her to collect her thoughts.

"I have been terrified. To let myself love him," she whispered into the darkness of the cave. "I have been terrified that someday his twin flame would come for him, and I would lose him forever. As I have lost you."

"He has proven himself to you. Over and over again. He will always come for you. He will always catch you."

Scarlett swallowed, looking down at the dirt covered floor. "Does he know?"

"He has told you. In so many ways," Juliette confirmed, her voice solemn.

Scarlett jerked her head up to meet Juliette's eyes. "He knows? How long has he known?"

"He bears the Mark, yes?" Juliette asked, holding up her left hand, showing Scarlett the back side.

The Mark. The unfinished tattoo on his hand.

"He is— I did not know…" Scarlett trailed off.

"Of course you knew, Scarlett. There is a difference between knowing and acknowledging. Just as there is a difference in your knowing and acknowledging your purpose in this world."

"I am not a queen," she snarled at Juliette again, growing tired of the cage she kept trying to shove her into.

"Why? Why does the title scare you?"

"I am not the one for this, Juliette," Scarlett cried. "I do not know the first thing about leading, about ruling."

"You would not be alone. Others would be with you. Sorin would be with you. If you ask him," Juliette argued.

Scarlett huffed a harsh laugh. "Being alone does not scare me."

"No, it does not. But what of being required to depend on others? As you did when you and I and Nuri worked in tandem? What of being required to rely on others so deeply once again? Letting them in on the scheming and the planning? What of allowing someone to rescue you instead of doing the protecting? You fear letting others close. You fear loving others that deeply once more far more than you fear being alone," Juliette said softly.

"Do you have any idea what I went through after that night? Nuri withdrew from me. You were gone. I wished he had just killed me alongside you!" Scarlett cried.

"I know, Scarlett. I *know*," Juliette said, squeezing her hands. "But it had to happen this way. For me to get here. For *you* to get here." Scarlett was silent as she stared into the eyes of her friend, her sister, who stared back unblinking, her eyes glowing with challenge. "You do not back down from anything, Scarlett. I have never seen you back down from a fight or admit defeat. You think he broke you, and maybe he did. But look at what rose from those ashes. Look at the strength, at the power, at the beauty of those shadows and that darkness on your soul."

"Give me a different task," Scarlett begged. "Anything else. Please!"

"I am not the one who gives such assignments," she answered with a shake of her head.

"Oh, yes. The fucking Fates," Scarlett drawled, rolling her eyes. Juliette smiled, amused. "You reject the Fates, sister?"

"I reject the idea that my life is to be decided for me."

"Just because you have a destination, is it not your own choice of how to get there? Or what to do once you've arrived?"

"It is my choice not to go there at all," Scarlett snapped back.

"Then you are prepared to accept the consequences of that choice and all those that choice will affect?" Juliette asked, pushing herself up to a standing position. She stood, looking down at Scarlett now.

The balance. Juliette had always been the balance between Nuri's innate wildness and her own lethal intensity.

"Talwyn is more suited for this!" Scarlett answered, rising to her own feet. "She was raised here. She has trained for this. She is prepared for this."

"She cannot do so alone, although she wishes she could. You and she are very similar, you know," Juliette said, her tone turning bored as she turned and began wandering around the cavern.

"I am nothing like her," Scarlett spat. "She is not my family. *You* are my sister. Nuri is my sister."

"Talwyn is not as she appears," Juliette replied with a knowing smile, "but, like you, she cannot complete her tasks alone. Like you, she has done what she has needed to survive. In the end though, you will need each other."

"I need no one," Scarlett seethed.

"No, you do not. However, wouldn't it be nice to have someone with whom your soul can rest and you can take a breath?" Juliette replied, her knowing smile turning into a smirk. When Scarlett only glared at her, she continued. "Should you choose not to fulfill your purpose, you choose to turn your back on those who cannot defend themselves and sentence them to my same fate."

"I cannot do this!" Scarlett screamed at her friend.

"Why?" Juliette insisted, coming right up to Scarlett's face. "You can do anything! Overcome everything! Why does this scare you?"

"Because I do not know who I am any more!" Scarlett cried. "How can I lead an entire kingdom if I do not even know who I am? How can people be loyal to a queen who doesn't know her own self?"

Juliette gave her a small smile, like she had been waiting for this exact moment. As if she'd known these were the words that needed to be said. She reached over and cupped Scarlett's cheek with her hand. "I suppose, my dear sister, *who* you are depends on who you *want* to be."

Juliette moved away from her then and strode to the center of the cavern. "My mortal death started a chain reaction you have yet to discover, but there were plans in motion long before we entered this world. What would you give to have that night play out differently?"

"Anything," Scarlett whispered, watching Juliette carefully.

"Would you sentence others to my same fate when you have the ability to change it?" Juliette hissed the last words with so much venom Scarlett winced and sank back to her knees.

The cave plunged into darkness, and she heard Juliette whisper, her voice sounding as if it were all around her, *"Who do you desire to be?"*

Scarlett felt her magic sputter to life. She felt the fire and the ice flood through her bones, her being. She raised her palms and flames of white encompassed the room. Shards of ice hovered above the fire, refracting glittering light along the walls. Then she sent her beloved shadows into them all.

Juliette appeared before her once more and clasped Scarlett's hands in her own, whispering again, "Who are you?"

Scarlett fixed her eyes on Juliette's, on those beautiful amber eyes. She felt the ice and flames swirling as one in her own eyes. "I am someone who has faced the darkness and found the beauty it had to offer. I am someone who can create stars in the void when the light has gone out. I am someone who cares for those the realms have forgotten. I am someone who can bring beauty from brutal ashes. I am a fucking Queen."

"Yes. Yes, you are, your Majesty," Juliette replied. She stood slowly and bowed low.

Scarlett swallowed hard as she took in her sister, whom she still blamed herself for losing. She pushed the ache in her heart down, down, down.

"Do not do that," Juliette said softly. "You cannot run from grief, just as you cannot run from what is your very being."

"I do not know what to do," Scarlett answered quietly.

"You do not need to know all the answers right now. You only need to get up and take the first step." Juliette's voice brushed down her soul, and she held out a hand to Scarlett. "You were never meant to do life alone. No one is."

One step. She could do that. She could take one step up out of this last pit. She could climb one step out of this hell that seemed unending and unyielding.

Juliette's smile was wide as Scarlett took her hand and stood.

CHAPTER 39
SCARLETT

The cave illuminated, and Scarlett blinked back at the sudden brightness. Gone were the rocky walls and dirt floor. A beautiful, ornately decorated apartment of sorts lay before her. Plush rugs were under her feet, and a large four-poster bed was along the far wall. To the right was a long glass table and atop it was a bowl of silver liquid.

There were windows all along the walls now, looking out into clouds. High above the ground, then. Not in some dirty, musty cave. Various doors led from the room to the gods knew where.

She turned unimpressed eyes onto Juliette.

"What?" her sister asked innocently. "If you honestly thought I was going to live in a dirt cave, you never really knew me at all."

"You live in a magic cave?" Scarlett asked doubtfully.

"The cave is just an entrance," Juliette said with a wink.

"So where are we actually, then?" Scarlett asked as she made to move to the windows.

"That is not to be revealed to you right now," Juliette answered, striding for the glass table.

"So because you are an Oracle, you now speak in ridiculous riddles?" Scarlett scoffed, following her.

Juliette laughed, and Scarlett marveled as the familiar sound washed over her. "Wait until you meet Princess Ashtine," Juliette replied with a smirk. She had reached the table, and she looked down into the silver pool before her.

"You are the daughter of two powerful beings who sacrificed much to save our world," Juliette said, as if reciting a lesson. "Now a king returns to take the throne, and all the worlds hold their breath as the stage is set."

"Wait, *two* powerful beings? You know who my father was?" Scarlett asked, coming to a halt beside Juliette.

"I know much, Scarlett. Things I cannot reveal to you, but I can guide you to the truth."

"Why can you not just tell me?" Scarlett demanded. "Who is my father?"

"The question you need to be asking is who is your mother? Answer that question, and you will answer the first."

"My mother is Eliné. That does not answer the first question. Sorin does not know who my father was as her companion was killed by Deimas and Esmeray."

A map of the continent appeared on the table beside the bowl. "Your answers lie across the seas, sister. In a land locked away by ancient magic."

"Avonleya?"

"Indeed. The Fae Queens hid keys. If found and used, the keys will allow the bearer to enter the land." Juliette turned to face Scarlett once more. Her face was all business now, like it would get when they were planning missions. "You are the only one who can find the keys. It is why you were kept hidden. It is part of the reason you are considered a weapon."

"Why me?"

"Because Eliné is the one who hid most of them. Queen Henna disguised the seven keys, and her daughter can restore them. Eliné entrusted one to each bloodline. Queen Selinya hid the other two, but you can find them."

"Queen Selinya? Who is that?"

"Keep digging through those books you've found, Sister. You are close to uncovering everything," Juliette said with another knowing smile.

"How about you just fucking tell me?" Scarlett grumbled.

"You will, of course, also need the lock."

"The what now?" Scarlett asked, looking up.

"The keys have to unlock something, do they not?" Juliette's eyes were twinkling as she continued. "Before you leave here, tell the High Witch that you are the one she has been waiting for."

"What does that mean?"

"She will know."

"Could you be any more obscure?" Scarlett sighed with a glare.

"Oracle perks, I suppose," Juliette answered with a half smile.

"And how am I to find these keys? I do not even know what they look like," Scarlett said as she studied the map before her.

"A child of each possesses them on a chain of wind-kissed stone," Juliette answered.

Scarlett rolled her eyes. "Here I thought we were on the same side."

Juliette gave a soft laugh once more. "The Oracles have long been outside of any reigning power's jurisdiction, but they have always had a strong relationship with Eliné."

"I can come see you? Visit you often?" Scarlett asked quietly, keeping her eyes on the map.

"I may not always be able to give you answers or counsel, but as your friend, yes. I am always with you. Always on your side," Juliette answered. After a moment of quiet between the friends, she clapped her hands twice and said, "I will give you three gifts before you leave today. One, regarding the keys, you will find that the keys have always been trying to get home."

"What does that mean?" Scarlett ground out from between her teeth,

"Two," Juliette said with a smile. "An Artist must give you the twin flame Mark."

"The Artists are from the Earth Court," Scarlett said slowly.

"Yes. You would definitely want a highly skilled Artist for that

Mark…unless you know an all-powerful Seer." The wicked glint in her eyes sparked a star to life in Scarlett's chest.

"You can give me the Mark?"

"If you are choosing it. If you are accepting the bond that has always existed there, yes. It would be my honor to give you the Mark, especially since it will save his life."

"What does *that* mean?" Scarlett asked, her attention snapping to her friend.

"When he took that Mark without a companion Mark, he took a great risk. Because there is no companion for that offering to latch on to, it drains his own magical reserves. When those are gone, it will begin to drain his very life force. Sending the Ash Rider to you cost the Prince of Fire greatly."

"How did he find me?"

"There is not time, Scarlett. He fades as we speak," Juliette said, grasping her left hand. "Interesting."

"What?" Scarlett asked, looking down at her own hand.

"He protects you. Even now. He weakens hour by hour, but he continues to protect you. He weakens to keep you safe, to keep your location a secret from them." Juliette's eyes met her own. "I need you to take down his enchantments, or I cannot Mark you."

"I cannot undo something I know nothing of," Scarlett protested.

Juliette put her hands on either temple and closed her eyes, then lowered them back down to her sides. "You must remove the shields and enchantments, Scarlett. Only your power can cleave them"

"I can't. I did not put them there," Scarlett cried.

"No, you did not. Your twin flame did," Juliette replied simply. "Now remove the shields."

"I don't know how," Scarlett snapped.

"Of course you do," Juliette said with a dismissive wave of her hand. "If you do not remove them, we are done here."

Scarlett glared at Juliette, then closed her eyes. She took a deep breath.

In and out. In and out. In and out.

She stilled, reaching for the recesses of her mind, where she reached for her magic, and she found them. She saw the flames that surrounded the edges of her being. The flames were warm and safe. The flames were home. She placed a mental hand against the flames. She felt them struggle as if someone were trying to keep them lit. *I'm okay,* she whispered gently to the flames. *I'm safe.* The flames sputtered, and she sucked them into her palms.

And then she saw it. She saw an endless abyss of power. Her power. Golden flames and ice and water and ashes swirled in it, but also glittering white flames of pure white.

And shadows. Her shadows danced and flitted among it all.

Unending.

Unrelenting.

Wild and vast and deep. The deepest recesses of her own self. Beyond herself even.

She opened her eyes to find a Mark flaring on her left hand. "The third gift..." Scarlett swallowed.

Juliette smiled. "By finally accepting who you are as a whole, the light and the dark, by not trying to cage parts of yourself, you will find your magic is a song in your very blood, sister. You will find the control you have sought for months. Now go. Save your twin flame, and then it's time to let that wildfire burn."

Scarlett turned towards the way she had come and found Shirina sitting by the entrance, those silver eyes glowing bright. Then, in a flash of white light, the panther was gone.

"One last thing, your Majesty." Scarlett turned back to Juliette, who was standing near a window, looking out. "Those who can walk among the worlds brought a book with them in the beginning. You would do well to find it."

"How am I to find such a thing?" Scarlett demanded.

"Keep down the path you have already discovered. Now go."

"Damn Oracle with her cryptic riddles," Scarlett muttered under her breath. She could hear Juliette's ringing laughter as she practically ran down the passageway.

She burst out of the cave and into the daylight. The sun was high in the sky. She must have been in the cave for hours. Hazel stood exactly where Scarlett had left her and bowed low as Scarlett emerged. "Your Majesty."

Rayner shot to his feet from the rock he had been sitting on and rushed to her side. "Are you all right?" His eyes were scanning her up and down.

"I am fine, Rayner, but Sorin is not. We need to go," Scarlett said, taking the sword he extended to her and sheathing it to her back.

"I cannot take you with me," Rayner said, shaking his head.

"What do you mean? How will I get home?"

"How did you get here?"

"Shirina brought me, but she is gone. She left while I was still with Jul— the Oracle," Scarlett cried, panic entering her voice. She looked around, desperately searching for help, and her eyes settled upon Hazel.

"The Ash Rider is correct," the High Witch said sternly. "He cannot ride with a passenger. You, however, can Travel with one, likely several."

"But I don't know how to Travel. I haven't learned yet," Scarlett said.

"You've never Traveled before?" Hazel asked with a raise of a brow.

"Not on purpose, no. I don't know how."

"Of course you do," Hazel replied harshly. "Did the Oracle not give you back your magic? Did she not release your power for you?"

Scarlett whirled back to Rayner. "How do you Travel in the smoke? Tell me what I need to do."

Rayner shook his head. "I do not think it is the same, Scarlett."

Scarlett closed her eyes, reigning in her breathing. She could do this. She had to do this.

She heard Hazel clear her throat. "Be sure and take the male with you," she said with a nod towards Rayner. "We do not look kindly upon males who are unattended in our lands."

"Understood," Scarlett answered. "Thank you. For everything. I will return the clothes."

"They are yours to keep."

As Hazel turned to leave, Scarlett remembered what Juliette had told her. "Wait!" she cried. Hazel stopped and turned back to her. Scarlett closed the few feet between them quickly. "The Oracle said to tell you that I am the one you have been waiting for." Hazel's violet eyes widened in surprise. "What does that mean?" Scarlett pressed.

Tears welled in the Witch's eyes, and Scarlett stepped back, stunned. "It means," Hazel said, her voice softer than it had been all day, "that you know my son and that it is time for him to return."

"Your son? But Witches don't—" she stopped herself before she finished what she was going to say. The Witches despised men. Male children were looked at as a curse, not a blessing.

"You are right," Hazel replied, as if she could read her thoughts. "We do not. But when he was born, I could not kill him. He was my child. My son. I enlisted the help of Queen Eliné, and she helped me smuggle him to another land. Where he went, neither of us knew. We couldn't know, to keep him safe. But the Oracle told me that one would come who would know him, and when she came, he could return."

"I don't know your son, though," Scarlett said gently.

Hazel stepped closer to Scarlett. She was so close she could smell a dozen herbs at once on her. "The Oracle is never wrong. If she says you are the one, then you know him. Think, your Majesty. Your paths are intertwined. They crossed at some point. He is powerful. More powerful than any of my sisters. It was why I had to send him away."

"But I grew up in a land with no magic. I grew up in the human lands. Magic doesn't exist there," Scarlett protested.

"Magic is not readily found there," Hazel corrected. "But there are exceptions to every rule if the give is great enough. You accessed your magic there, did you not?"

"Yes, but no one else..." she trailed off. There *was* someone else. Someone who had created powerful wards. Someone who was being given a tonic to help him access his magic. "Cassius," she breathed. "Your son is Cassius."

The tears spilled from Hazel's eyes. She took Scarlett's hands in her own and squeezed them. "He is well?"

"He is my soulmate," Scarlett answered, tears spilling down her own cheeks. "He saved my life, in more ways than one."

"Go. Aid your twin flame. Then bring my son home," Hazel said. She turned and walked down the path they had climbed up a few hours earlier.

Scarlett turned back to Rayner. "Where is Eliza? We are going to get her and then we are going to Sorin and Cyrus."

"She awaits our return in your quarters," Rayner answered.

Scarlett grabbed Rayner's hand and closed her eyes. She thought back to the cellar in the Lairwood House, how Sorin had instructed her to focus so intensely on the beach, picturing every detail. On the edges of her mind, she saw the room. The room she'd been sharing with her twin flame for weeks. She could see the room as if she were looking through a smoke screen. She heard the words Sorin had whispered to her. *You need to take a step. Do not think. Just do it.* She sucked in a breath and took a step forward, as if creating a rip in that screen, in the world, and when she opened her eyes, she found herself looking into Eliza's grey ones.

Eliza's eyes were wide with shock, but Scarlett only said, "You knew?"

At the confusion that flitted over Eliza's face, Scarlett held up her left hand. Eliza's eyes widened more as she took in the Mark. "Who Marked you?"

"That is irrelevant. You knew. How long have you known?" She tried and failed to hide the hurt in her voice.

"We all knew," Eliza replied. "I Marked him. The others saw the Mark when he returned."

"When did you Mark him?" Scarlett demanded.

"Before he came for you in the mortal lands. It was how he knew where to find you in the house."

"Why didn't you say anything?" Scarlett demanded.

"It was not our place. It was between you and him. He was adamant that he did not want to make the choice for you. You needed to make it on your own. You need to speak the claiming words to start the Trials," Eliza said as she stepped back from Scarlett.

"What?"

"The Mark is not completed until you have spoken the Claiming Rite to initiate the Trials."

"What are they?"

Eliza told her what they were, and Scarlett's lips formed a thin line. "I shall say them when I am damn well ready to say them. For now, we must go."

"But he will not...recover until you speak it," Eliza argued.

"Then we better hurry," Scarlett purred, narrowing her eyes at the general. She grabbed Eliza's hand and looked over at Rayner. "You will carry yourself?"

"The queen will not permit me to enter on my own. She will have wards. I do not even know if you can get in," Rayner answered.

"She is no longer the only queen, and she will not keep me from him," Scarlett answered, a maniacal gleam in her eyes as she grabbed Rayner's hand in her other.

"Where are we going?" Eliza asked.

"First, we are going to get my Court. Then we are going to find some damn keys," Scarlett answered as she peered through that screen in her mind, searching.

"And then?" Eliza asked, her voice hushed, as if she were seeing Scarlett, really seeing her darkness that she kept so locked up, for the first time.

"Then we are going to set the world on fire," Scarlett answered.

The Mark may not have been complete, but she could still feel that bridge between their souls. The one that had been there since she first saw him in a training barracks in Baylorin. She mentally ran along that bridge now, and she saw him sitting at a giant polished oak table. Talwyn was at the head of it, her face as cool and calculating as always. To her right was a male with black hair and bronze skin, a crown of autumn leaves and vines above his head. To her left was a female with silver hair like Scarlett's own. She was lean and gorgeous, one of the most striking people Scarlett had ever seen. The silver hawk, Nasima, sat upon her shoulder. Briar was on the side with the male, and his face was grave. She had never seen him without his flirty smile in place. A male, whom Scarlett assumed was his Second, was seated beside him and looked almost identical to him. Across from him sat Sorin with Cyrus. Sorin was pale, and the crown atop his head was dimmer than it had been this morning, but you wouldn't know he wasn't at his strongest. Not if you didn't know what to look for.

Scarlett grabbed hold of that bond she'd been so adamantly ignoring, and she stepped through a rip in the world.

CHAPTER 40
SCARLETT

There were gasps of surprise and the scraping of chairs as nearly everyone around the table shot to their feet when Scarlett, Eliza, and Rayner appeared in that room. Nearly everyone. Talwyn and the silver-haired female stayed sitting. Scarlett felt multiple powers spearing toward them all at once. Rayner and Eliza shielded with their flames and smoke, but Scarlett's own white flames shot up like a wall between them and the others in the room.

"Starfire?" the silver-haired female asked. She didn't seem surprised, but rather an air of curiosity was in her tone.

Scarlett cast them all a wicked grin as she threw her shadows into the flames, turning them black.

"Interesting," the silver-haired female said, cocking her head to the side as she studied the flames.

"How dare you come here without being summoned!" the male with the black hair roared, coming towards them.

Scarlett merely blinked, and her shadows had him bound and gagged and kneeling on the floor.

"Scarlett?" Sorin said her name in shock, his eyes wide with terror. He made to come to her but was stopped by Talwyn.

"Stay where you are, Prince," Talwyn said. Her voice was even and calm, like this happened every day. Thick vines appeared, ensnaring Sorin to his chair.

Scarlett smirked at her. With half a thought, she had those vines frozen and shattering, just as she had done to those tree branches all those months ago in the clearing in Baylorin. The Court Royals and their Seconds were all shielding as the frozen shards sprayed around the room. Then she leveled a deadly glare at Talwyn. The male who had been advancing on them raged around his bindings as Scarlett took a step towards his sovereign.

"Dismiss them," Scarlett ordered, her voice lethal.

"Leave us," Talwyn said, her voice cool, commanding. With a wave of her hand, every single other person in the room was gone except for Sorin and his Inner Court. "You have something to say?" she purred at Scarlett, but Scarlett's attention had turned to Sorin, whose golden skin was so, so pale. She could *feel* him. Everything. The fracture not only to his power but to his soul. The breaking of taking a twin flame Mark without having it returned. She ignored Talwyn completely, taking a step towards him. The Mark on her hand tingled, as if it anticipated what was about to happen.

"You told me to figure out what I was."

She took another step towards him and lifted a hand. In it, flames of purest white hovered.

"You told me to figure out what I was to the realms."

Another step had her lifting her other hand where water and ice swirled in an orb.

"You told me to figure out what I was to you."

Sorin was so still, as if she had frozen him when she'd frozen those vines. When she took the last few steps to close the space between them, he stood. She took in those golden eyes, his dark hair. She noticed his crown of flame still glowing atop his head, and with a smirk, she lifted her palms. The flames and water and ice jumped above her head, weaving amongst themselves to form a crown of ice and water, the flames creating a burning jewel in the center.

He gaped as the crown settled down onto her silver hair. She sent tendrils of her shadows snaking up the crown, winding their way around the ice and sparkling like black diamonds. And then, just because she could, she sent shadows dancing among the flames of his own crown.

He stared at her, and she could see the question in his eyes. "I have so many treats to give you should you speak the question on your tongue," she said, her voice low and full of promise.

Sorin swallowed. "What are you to me?" His own voice was hoarse, hardly more than a whisper.

"You came for me, and I have come for you." Sorin's eyes widened as she held up her left hand. Then she spoke words she had said before, but not in the Old Language. They were words her soul had known before she had. "I am yours, and you are mine. I choose you, above all others. Always." Scarlett gasped slightly at the burning that seared through her hand as the Mark flared gold then stood black as night against her skin. "You are my home, Sorin Aditya. I want no one else. I want it to always be you."

Sorin took her face in his hands and kissed her. Deeply. Thoroughly. A claiming. Caring as much as she did that they had an audience, which was not at all. She pulled back and brought a hand to cup his cheek.

I am yours and you are mine. She heard him echo the words into her own mind as he gazed into her eyes. She watched as his own eyes flicked up to her crown of starfire, and he crooned, *Princess of Fire.*

About that...

Sorin's brows rose in question, and she turned to face Talwyn.

The queen's long mahogany hair flowed around her on that phantom wind that seemed to always accompany her. She still sat in her chair at the head of the table, her face unreadable. She propped her head on her hand as if bored when Scarlett said to her, "I am also the daughter of Eliné Semiria, and I am her heir. I am a queen in this land, and I lay claim to the Fire and Water Courts that are rightfully mine."

Talwyn's jade green eyes were fixed on hers, and a knowing smile spread across her face. "Of course you are a queen, Cousin."

Scarlett stilled, not sure of what to say. Was Talwyn being sincere, or was it some kind of trick? She glanced at Sorin, who was also staring at Talwyn.

"You willingly acknowledge that she has a right to rule beside you?" he asked. His skin already had its color back. His crown was glowing brightly atop his head.

"Of course I acknowledge it. I sent you to find her," Talwyn answered snidely, rising from her chair. She waved a hand, and the table before them disappeared in a swirl of sand. She strode for them, and Scarlett felt the entire Inner Court fall into line behind her and Sorin.

"You sent me to find a weapon," Sorin countered, a shield coming up around them all.

"I told you that you were *going* to find a weapon. I sent you to find your twin flame," Talwyn corrected. "I had assumed you had found her when you sent Amaré to Briar asking about the Semiria rings all those months ago, but when she returned with you without her Mark, I did not know if it was her. And then there was the matter of the mortal prince that is squatting in your palace. I thought he was brought with because he was her husband. I needed to know, so I came to him to try and learn the truth."

"You kidnapped him!" Scarlett growled, orange flames appearing at her fingertips.

Talwyn sneered at her and a gust of wind had her flames extinguishing.

Scarlett felt her mouth twist up in a fiendish grin as she sent her shadows slithering across the floor to her cousin. Then she shaped those shadows into actual snakes. With tongues of fire. And scales of razor sharp ice.

"Scarlett…"

She could hear the awe in Sorin's voice.

"So many treats, Prince," she crooned.

Talwyn stilled, but she did not back away from the shadow snakes that hissed from the floor, rallying to strike at Scarlett's first thought.

"I did not know it was truly her until the day I surprised you both in the courtyards and saw your Mark but without a companion." Talwyn's eyes were on Sorin, and they narrowed in disgust as she said, "Only you would do something so reckless and stupid. I had hoped she would discover it while you trained her. I had hoped that you would help her see it, that your useless Inner Court would step up and do their godsdamn jobs and tell her." She threw a glare at the others when she said it. "But it was taking too long. Things are happening too quickly across our borders, so I summoned you here with the other Courts. We needed to plan, and I needed you away from her. When I felt you enter these halls with Cyrus, I sent Shirina to take her to the Oracle." Talwyn stopped on the other side of the shield, her jade eyes shimmering. "Welcome home, Scarlett."

"You lie," Sorin breathed.

"Do I?" Talwyn countered, raising her brows. "Ask her."

Sorin turned to Scarlett. "Shirina? That is how you got to the Witch Realm?"

Scarlett nodded. "Yes. She took me to the High Witch who took me to the Oracle."

Sorin blinked in surprise and horror, glancing behind himself to Rayner who nodded confirmation. His eyes settled back on Scarlett as he asked, "You met the High Witch?"

"I do believe the Oracle also told you of some keys?" Talwyn chimed in again, an arrogant smirk in Sorin's direction.

Scarlett looked from Talwyn to Sorin. He was waiting for her to answer. Scarlett felt as though she were being forced to choose a side when Juliette had made it sound like they'd all be working together.

"Yes, she told me of the keys," Scarlett sighed.

"Who can find them, Scarlett?" Talwyn taunted softly.

Scarlett glared at the queen. Turning back to Sorin, she said through her teeth, "I can. Eliné hid them, so I am the one who can find them. Henna disguised them so Talwyn can restore them to their true form."

"So in a way, Prince of Fire, you finding your twin flame indeed found me the weapon I sought. The weapon that will aid me in finding the Avonleyan Keys, which will get us inside of Avonleya to seek our true revenge." Her jade eyes were glowing brightly as she held Sorin's stare. Scarlett looked back and forth between them.

"The Oracle also told me that the two of you would willingly help with the tasks that lie ahead," Scarlett ventured.

"What tasks?" Cyrus asked from behind them.

"Oh, you know. Keys. Answers. Blood magic," she said, waving her hand dismissively. "All the fun things."

"Of course I will help you," Sorin interjected, still glaring at Talwyn.

"Yes, but we will need Talwyn's help, Sorin. She is the only one who can restore the keys, and if you two cannot at least tolerate each other, it will not help matters."

"We all have our roles to play in this," Talwyn said, turning and walking back to her chair. She sat down, leaning back comfortably and crossing her legs one over the other. "Sorin and I do not agree on many things, but I do not hate him entirely."

Sorin snorted a laugh. "It appears we are getting lots out into the open today, Talwyn. Let's not fabricate more lies now."

Talwyn's voice was hard as she replied in that cool, calculated voice of hers. "I have known you my entire life, Prince of Fire. You were by my aunt's side every single day. I would pray to the Fates that if I could not have you by my side when I was queen, that I would have someone just as loyal. No, I did not start to hate you until you left me alone. A child on a throne. Even now, years later, I cannot find it in myself to entirely hate you, if only because I once loved you so fiercely."

Scarlett looked between Sorin and the queen. She couldn't quite read his face. It was a mixture of regret and disbelief.

"You sent me from your side," Sorin snarled. "I *was* there for you. You sent me from your side and replaced me with Luan."

"You begged to leave my side and retrieve Eliné," Talwyn snarled. "You led that mission yourself and lost more than a queen in the process."

Scarlett could feel the hurt and betrayal emanating off of Talwyn.

"I know you, Sorin," Talwyn continued. There was no kindness in her voice. "You are the one who taught me how to watch others. To learn their tells and weaknesses. I was your last remaining connection to Eliné. You had watched me grow up. You had trained me. In many ways, you were more my father than my own ever was, even with the short time I had with him. I had barely lived. I *have* barely lived, not compared to you and many of the others. And now I was expected to rule in a realm, in a world, I knew very little of, and you begged to leave my side to retrieve her. You left me and lost what I valued most in the world."

Scarlett had no idea what she was talking about. Her mother? Did she blame Sorin as he had blamed himself for her death for so many years? Sorin said nothing as he stared at Talwyn.

"Sorin is not responsible for Eliné's death," Scarlett said slowly, glancing between the two of them.

Talwyn huffed another humorless laugh. "My aunt chose her own fate when she left in the middle of the night for her own reasons. However, her Second chose to try to retrieve her and lost so many on a fool's errand. He *is* responsible for those lives, Cousin. Those losses are his fault. Those losses are his failures."

She felt Sorin's guilt down their twin flame bond. She felt him inwardly flinch at her words. Was she referencing Thia? If Cyrus could forgive him for that, who was she to hold such a grudge?

But before Scarlett could voice her questions, Talwyn said, "I will not deny that our personalities and styles of ruling clash on more than one level. I will not deny that how I do things is very different from how Eliné did things. We will likely continue to fight each other in many areas, but not in this. Not when it matters. Not when the entirety of the world is at stake."

A swirl of sand appeared near Talwyn's head, and she reached up and plucked a note from the center, just as Scarlett had seen Sorin do with the fire. Talwyn read the note once and stood from her chair.

"You all must leave. Azrael is returning." Talwyn waved her hand, and the table reappeared, complete with papers strewn about. "Who else knows who Scarlett really is?" she asked of no one in particular.

"The people in this room, and Briar and his Inner Court," Sorin answered. "And apparently the High Witch."

Scarlett did not interject to mention the fact that Mikale, Nuri, and Cassius also knew who she really was.

"Let's keep it that way for now," Talwyn said, coming to stand before them once more.

"Azrael does not know?" Sorin asked incredulously.

"No," Talwyn confirmed. "I have told no one of what I suspected, not until I was sure you would indeed find her. Not until she had accepted her place. Let's keep it quiet a while longer, if you please. It will likely be to our advantage in the end. Now go. He approaches."

"I do not know if I believe you, Talwyn," Sorin said, a fire portal appearing behind the Fire Court.

"I understand," Talwyn said, "but I do believe I told you that the Fates would place us on the same side." Her arrogant smirk of victory had returned. "We shall speak soon, Prince."

As she said it, an unexpected gust of wind swept through the room, pushing them all out into the open portal except Scarlett. The portal snapped shut behind them, and the two queens stood facing each other.

"What else did you learn? What else did the Oracle reveal to you?" Talwyn demanded.

"You show me yours, and I'll show you mine," Scarlett crooned in reply.

"This is not a game. You accepted that throne and became a part of something. You have responsibilities to your people," Talwyn retorted.

"Yes, I did. I became a part of something I think is much bigger than you realize," Scarlett replied, picking up a stack of papers from the table. She skimmed the first page. Reports from the mortal lands.

"Explain," Talwyn said with venom in her tone.

"I don't trust you enough to explain myself to you," Scarlett answered casually.

"What about working together?" Talwyn snapped. "Did you not just preach to your twin flame that we were going to need each other?"

"I did, but loyalty and trust are not things I just give blindly." Scarlett flipped the page of the report. This couldn't be right.

Talwyn took a step towards her, but one of Scarlett's shadow snakes rose up before her, and she froze.

"Nice pets," Talwyn said snidely.

"I thought so," Scarlett retorted, flipping another page of the report. "So much more effective than wolves." She leveled a cool stare at Talwyn. "Although, they can really become anything I need them to be." The shadow snakes twisted and writhed until three wolves stood before her. Their eyes swirling with flames.

"It would appear you've learned some new tricks," Talwyn said through clenched teeth, her eyes on the shadow wolves. "But have you mastered your magic enough to wield it when it matters?"

"Step closer and find out," Scarlett purred.

"My Second is nearly at these doors," Talwyn snapped, thrusting a hand towards the double doors at the end of the room. A gust of wind barreled into them, keeping whomever was on the other side from entering.

"Talwyn," a deep male voice snarled from the other side.

"Your twin flame?" Scarlett asked, sniffing once.

"No," Talwyn answered, her eyes hardening. "Do you need a portal to get out of my face?"

"No, no," Scarlett drawled. "Until next time, Cousin."

Then she stepped through a rip in the world, taking her shadow wolves with her.

CHAPTER 41
SCARLETT

S carlett stepped into Sorin's private quarters to find the others bickering amongst themselves, apparently about how to get back to her at the White Halls.

"Honestly," she drawled, as her shadow wolves prowled around her. "I've put on such a spectacular display of magic and power today, how could you possibly be worried about me?"

"Really? Wolves?" Cyrus asked with an unimpressed glance as they all turned to face her.

"Would you prefer something with a bigger bite, Darling?"

As she spoke, the wolves merged until a dragon filled the space behind her. Its eyes were glittering ice, and it spewed flames from its mouth as it huffed and curled protectively around her. She reached up and stroked its head, and it set its massive snout on her shoulder, smoke furling from its nostrils.

A mad grin spread across Cyrus's face, but before anyone could say anything further, Sorin growled to his Inner Court, "Go find something else to do."

Eliza and Cyrus were already halfway to the door before he finished speaking while Rayner disappeared in smoke and ashes.

Sorin turned to Scarlett, and she recognized the hunger that filled his eyes. The same primal lust she'd seen the night before at the dance club lined his features. His eyes went slowly up and down her body, and her shadow dragon dissipated behind her as he purred, "That seems like it will be extremely inconvenient to take off."

Scarlett looked down and realized she was still wearing the witch clothing. She crossed her arms across her chest and replied shortly, "It was what the High Witch gave me to wear when I showed up on her doorstep in my nightclothes."

"It is what they wear for flying," he replied.

"Flying?"

"Yes," he said as he prowled over to her. He reached for her waist, tugging her closer. "I do not want to talk about the Witches right now." His voice was thick. So much desire filled his face, his *scent*, that he had missed her own change in mood.

He was home. He was safe. And now that the utter fear for his life had dispersed from her veins, there was a fury at being kept in the dark. Again.

As Sorin leaned in to kiss her, she said, her voice low and sultry, "Then let's talk about how long you've known I'm your gods-damned *twin flame*."

Sorin took a step back like she'd shoved him. His eyes went from want to dread. He ran his hands through his dark hair, letting out a sharp breath. "I did not... You told me you did not want the Fates deciding your future. The Fates determine your twin flame, Scarlett. I wanted you to have the choice."

"How long have you known?" she repeated, her voice quiet with rage.

"So because the Oracle told you I am your soul destined, you accept it? Because the Oracle told you that you are a queen of this realm, you are suddenly fine with it?" He retorted. The embers in the fireplace roared to life as he released some of the ire roiling with his frustration.

Scarlett smirked at him and added her shadowfire to dance among his flames.

Then ignored the unexpected rush of having her magic inter-mingle with his and what that did to her body.

"She helped me realize that just because the Fates decide some-thing, it is still mine to choose. She helped me realize that if I choose it, I still direct my own path. I define what it means to be a queen in this realm. Not the Fates. I define what it means to be your twin flame. Had you told me, it would still have been my choice to choose it." She took a step towards him. "How long have you known?"

He studied her hard. "A part of me wondered the night you fought with Nuri. I suspected in the days we spent at my apartment after the beach. I knew the moment you walked out to go to Mikale."

"And you didn't think I deserved to know?" Her voice was shrill now.

"You wanted to make your own path!"

"You took my choice from me by not giving me the choice!" Her shadows were swirling around her with agitation, and she fought to keep her magic under control with her rising emotions.

Sorin stalked towards her, closing the small distance still between them. "I left it to the Fates. If you felt it, if you accepted it, I would be eternally grateful. If not, I would have accepted that, too, and been grateful for what you did offer me these past few months."

"If I had not taken the Mark, what would have happened to you?" Scarlett demanded. Frost coated the windows as she worked to control her own frustration and anger.

Sorin didn't seem to notice as he sighed. "Taking the twin flame Mark without a companion is offering a piece of your soul up for anyone to find. It is drawn to its twin flame, but if it is not accept-ed..." He paused, running his hands through his hair again. "It continues to try to find its mate and drains its owner of their power. It weakens them until they have depleted their magical reserves or until something else finds it."

"And then it drains your very life force," she snapped.

"If you knew, why did you ask?"

She ignored his sarcasm. "You would have lost all of your power? You would have left your Court, your people, defenseless?"

"It was the only way I could find you in the Lairwood House." His face had softened, but his voice was still edged with frustration as he spoke. "The connection from the twin flame bond—it allows us to find each other, Scarlett. It is a supernatural linking of our souls. It is why we can speak into each other's minds. We can feel each other's fear and sadness and joy."

"It's how you knew I was in the Witch Realm," she said, as so many things suddenly made sense. How she felt like he could sometimes hear her thoughts. How he always seemed to know where she was. How he could reach her when the darkness was suffocating.

Sorin nodded. "Yes. It was not a full twin flame bonding, but a fractured one I suppose. I panicked when I felt your terror. I wanted to come to you, but I could not let Talwyn see I was weakening, even though she suspected. Had I left, she would have followed, and I did not know what was happening. I did not want to make things worse, so I sent Rayner."

"You risked *everything*. You risked your Court," she said, her tone still severe.

Sorin took her face in his hands. "Yes," he snapped, his tone full of uncompromising will. "And I would do it again. I told you the day I pulled you from that hellhole that I would cross deserts and oceans and lands and realms to get to you. Then I told you in a dark forgotten library passage there will never be a world where there is not a you and me because should you be ripped from me in this world, I will cross them all to find you. I have told you in every possible way I could without coming right out and saying the words."

"You should have just said them," she cried. "You said you had told me everything. I specifically asked you!"

"You deserved to have the choice, Scarlett," he answered, searching her eyes, his own seeming to plead with her to understand. "I did not want you accepting the bond because it was shoved on you, or you thought you had to save me."

"But I needed to accept it to save you!"

"I wanted you to accept the bond because you *chose* it. Not because my life depended on it. I wanted you to accept the bond because you *wanted* it. Because you chose *me*, not the bond."

"I would have chosen you," she said, tears welling in her eyes. "I would have chosen you the day you kissed me in the archery grounds. I would have chosen you the night we danced at the Pier. I would have chosen you when I saw the pride in your eyes when I wielded my magic in the courtyard for the first time. I would have chosen you the moment you showed up in that room to rescue me."

"You do not need rescuing, my Love. You never have," he said softly, reaching up to brush back stray hair.

"You're right. I don't," she snapped, stepping out of his reach. "I take care of myself. Every damn day. I have for years. Apparently I still am. I thought I had found some place to breathe, even if just for one second. I thought I had found a place where I could depend on someone other than myself. I thought I had found home."

"You have found that," Sorin argued. "This is your home. This is your family."

"I didn't realize families kept something like *this* from each other," she replied sarcastically.

"Scarlett, that is not fair," Sorin protested.

"Not fair?" She stalked back to him, poking him hard in the chest with her finger. "What's not fair is that every single one of you knew I was your twin flame and no one bothered to let me in on the secret."

"*You* wanted to make the choice, Scarlett. You wanted to decide your own future," Sorin shot back.

"Back to this again?" Scarlett screamed. She raked her hands through her own hair, forgetting it was in a braid. She swore as her fingers caught in the plaits and yanked the tie out, shaking her hair free. "*You* took my choice away by not telling me!"

"No. I. Didn't," he ground out through his teeth.

Scarlett froze. "What do you mean no you didn't? The minute you chose not to tell me, you took away my choice."

"You could have chosen at any moment," Sorin said. His voice was as lethal as when they had fought that morning. "At any point in time you could have chosen this. You could have chosen us. You told me you chose me. All you needed to do was choose *us*. You did not need to wait for me to tell you anything. You have never waited for permission for anything before, so why this? You do not get to blame me for pushing something away because you were too scared to acknowledge it was there."

Scarlett stared at him as emotions warred inside her. She could feel her eyes turn to flame, and Sorin's did the same. Flames appeared in one hand, and ice crackled at her fingertips in the other. Her shadows swirled around her, a twister of black. She closed both her fists, pushing that magic down, down, down.

After several moments of thick tension, she said, "We are done here." She turned to leave, not sure where she was going to go. She didn't care. She took a step through that smoke screen, through that rip in the world in her mind, and as she did, she felt Sorin grip her elbow.

She stumbled when her feet sank into sand, and Sorin caught her, keeping her upright.

"Let go of me," she seethed, whirling to him.

But Sorin caught her shoulders and held them tight. "No."

"Let go of me," she said, her voice viciously low. She made her skin bitterly cold, and she felt Sorin's hands warm as they held her.

"No," he repeated through gritted teeth. Her shadows wrapped around his wrists and arms, biting into his skin. "You do not get to walk away from us. We promised each other. We do not shut each other out. Not any more."

"Let me go!" she screamed. Tears escaped down her cheeks, and she slid to the ground as all the emotions and events of the day pressed in on her.

Sorin slid down with her, pulling her to his chest. He wrapped his arms around her while she cried into his shoulder. He stroked her hair, and she felt him press a kiss to the top of her head. He brought her hand to his chest, letting her feel his breaths. In and out. In and out.

When her breathing had evened out, he gently pulled her away and forced her chin up with his finger. He looked at her as if he could see her soul. His voice was soothing but filled with resolve.

"I will never let you go, and I will always come for you. Whether you are in the human lands, the Witch Kingdoms, or some sandy desert, I will come for you. Not because you are my queen. Not because you are my twin flame. I will always come for you because I choose you, Scarlett Monrhoe. I choose every flame, every drop of water, every shard of ice, every bit of darkness. I choose each smart ass comment and each middle finger you throw at me. I choose every way we challenge each other. I choose every night of dancing and scandalous dresses. I choose every morning of waking up next to you and watching you master your magic. I choose *you*, and I will always choose you. I am yours, and you are mine. In this life and every life after."

More tears slipped free. She tried to turn away from him, but he held her there, golden eyes locked on hers. "I don't know what I am doing. With any of this. I don't know what I'm supposed to do," she whispered.

"That has never stopped you before," he replied, leaning in and kissing a tear away on each cheek.

"I am a mess, Sorin. I am still darkness and shadows and—"

"Scarlett, I love you like the stars love the night. All the way through the darkness," Sorin said gently. "You are not alone, and never will be again. You get all of me, and I get all of you. We do not shut each other out. We do not get to tell each other to leave. There will forever be a you and me."

Scarlett shifted into his lap, bringing a leg around each side of him to straddle him, and hooked her legs around his back. He grasped her hips, pulling her close. She looped her arms around his neck. "I choose you, Sorin Aditya. I choose every ember and wisp of smoke. I choose every snarky comment about my cranky mood, and every teasing remark about my love of books and shoes. I choose every time you challenge me and call me on my own bullshit. I choose falling asleep next to you every night and kissing you good morning with each sunrise. I choose to follow you to the ends of this realm and every other realm known and unknown. And after we fade, I will follow you to whatever life is next. I choose you, and I will always choose you. I am yours, and you are mine. In this life and every life after."

Sorin's own eyes glimmered with unshed tears as he brought his lips to hers. The kiss was gentle and perfect, encompassing everything they were to each other.

I love you, he said down the bridge between their souls.

Always, she replied, bringing her lips back to his.

Sorin pulled back and, looking into her eyes, he said, "The desert? Really? I hate sand."

Scarlett rolled her eyes as he helped her up. "Gods, you're such a baby. You didn't seem to mind it on the beach that night." She brushed off her rear and the front of her witch-leathers. Looking around, she said, "Where are we anyway?"

Realization seemed to dawn on Sorin as he muttered, "Shit."

Sorin was staring over her shoulder, and Scarlett turned to find the male with the black hair approaching. His skin seemed even darker under the hot sun. He was flanked by two sentries, and his face was a mixture of smugness and fury. He stopped a few feet away from them, looking them both up and down. He pulled a sword from its sheath on his back and leveled it at Sorin's heart.

"I do not believe you were invited to these lands, Prince of Fire," the male said, his voice filled with calm rage.

"Believe me, I would never come here willingly," Sorin remarked flippantly. "How anyone could like having sand up their ass all the time is beyond me, although it seems fitting for you."

The ground beneath them trembled, and Scarlett felt Sorin place a hand on her back to steady her. "You do not get to come to *my* Court and be disrespectful, Aditya," the male spat.

Scarlett glanced at Sorin. He was picking at invisible grains of sand on his tunic, still in the elegant clothes he'd worn to the meeting with the other Courts and Talwyn.

"Azrael, I can disrespect you anywhere. I would not travel all the way here just for that," Sorin replied, his tone bored.

A sharp wooden stake appeared in the male's other hand, and

Scarlett threw Sorin an incredulous look. "He has been here less than a minute, and you have already pissed him off?"

"He's a prick. He is always pissed off," he drawled.

"You are such a child," Scarlett replied, rolling her eyes.

"I am a child? You just dragged me to the middle of a desert to avoid admitting you are madly in love with me."

Scarlett stuck out her tongue at him.

"I am sorry to interrupt whatever...*this* is," the male cut in, annoyance in his tone and all over his face as he looked between the two of them. Then to Scarlett he said, "But who are you?"

Scarlett glanced at Sorin again, but he was glaring back at the male before them. "Sorin, who is this?" she asked instead, looking the male up and down with an unimpressed sweep of her eyes.

The male huffed a laugh of disbelief.

Sorin sighed and, sounding as if he would rather be anywhere but here, said "Scarlett, this is Talwyn's Second in Command... whom you bound and gagged with your shadows earlier today, by the way."

Scarlett looked the male up and down again. "You are the earth guy?" Eliza had told her about the feuds between the Fire and Earth Courts. How had she managed to travel *here*? She was sure Sorin was going to literally combust into flames at the laughter she could feel him holding in. The male before them snarled with rage.

"I am the Prince of the Earth Court and the Second in Command to the Queen of these lands," he spat. "You two do not have permission to be here, and as such, I have the authority to bring you in for questioning."

Vines appeared at Sorin's wrists, binding them together. Sorin seemed none too concerned as he gazed at the prince unruffled.

That is until the same appeared at Scarlett's wrists, snapping them together.

A ball of flame appeared at Sorin's shoulder, and he snarled, "Release her, Luan."

The prince shot a superior look at him as he wondered aloud, "Who is this female that keeps appearing at your side, Sorin? It is almost as if you came home with a—" The prince stopped short as his eyes fell upon the Mark on her left hand. They darted to Sorin's left hand and then to his face. The prince seemed to have panic tinging his tone as he said, "She is your twin flame."

Sorin's smile was savage and cruel as he growled, "She is. Now release her."

Why does he seem nervous about that?

"Because," Sorin answered her out loud, apparently having heard her question, "Fae can be…territorial."

"Well, clearly," Scarlett retorted with a roll of her eyes. "He seems very upset that we are standing in his sand."

The Earth Prince growled low in his throat, but Sorin's answering snarl was louder and much more threatening. "We are not just territorial with our lands. I have told you we get very protective of our people, our loved ones. It is a little more intense when it is our twin flame."

Scarlett groaned. "You mean to tell me you're going to be even more of a mother hen now?"

"There have been many brawls when it comes to protecting lovers, especially twin flames. I do believe a palace was destroyed once because another male smiled at one's twin flame shortly after the connection had been Anointed."

"It sounds like Fae males need to grow up and use their big boy words," Scarlett mused, huffing a laugh. But then tree roots appeared around Sorin's wrists, reinforcing his restraints, and blinding rage roiled in Scarlett's veins.

Sorin's eyes shot to her with an amused smile. "Interesting tidbit— females can get just as territorial over their lovers and families."

"Lover? I do believe you turned me down last night," she crooned back.

"A mistake I will not be making again."

"Enough of this," the prince before them said. "I do believe there is a tower at the palace that can hold the two of you until I have had a chance to confer with the queen and verify your stories, but who knows how long it will be before I can see her. A few days perhaps?"

A tower? Scarlett felt her heartbeat thunder at the word. Her breathing went ragged. He was going to lock them up?

"Easy, Love," Sorin murmured soothingly.

"Escort them if you will," the Earth Prince was saying to his two soldiers, a sand portal appearing behind him.

"No!" Scarlett cried out. She looked desperately to Sorin, whose eyes were on her. "Do something!"

He held her gaze, his eyes intense and swirling with so many emotions she couldn't process them all. "You do not need rescuing, Love. No one can lock you up. No one. No one puts you in a cage."

With an icy flare, the tree roots around Sorin's wrists froze and shattered. Starfire followed, dissolving the vines binding their wrists. The Earth Prince cried out in rage and swung with his sword, but it was met by Scarlett's own, her shadowfire wreathing its blade.

"The Spirit Sword," he breathed, taking in the blade she wielded. His eyes were blazing with fury as he enveloped them in a swirling sandstorm. Scarlett's shield flared to life, and she felt Sorin's do the same beside her. Grains of sand sizzled as it whipped around their flames.

"That sword belongs to the queen," the Earth Prince seethed.

"And the queen wields it," Scarlett snarled back. "Talwyn knows I have it, and she knows it is mine to possess."

"Impossible," he shot back. "It is her birthright."

"It is my own birthright as much as it is hers," Scarlett replied. The crown she had summoned earlier appeared on her brow.

The prince's sandstorm diminished as he beheld her, bedecked in witch flying-leathers and a crown fit for a queen. She felt Sorin place a hand on her back. "We are fine, Love. We are safe."

"Who are you?" the Earth Prince snarled.

"Scarlett M—" she paused and looked down at her ring. A smile filled her face, and her shadow dragon formed behind her and Sorin. With a roar, it spewed a ring of fire around them. "Scarlett *Semiria*, Queen of the Western Courts, and a queen of this realm."

Sorin ventured, his voice calm but assertive, "There is much you do not know, Azrael. I suggest you speak to Talwyn."

"Talwyn would never keep such things from me," the prince

spat back, but Scarlett could see the doubt in his eyes as he backed away from them, from *her*.

"The queens keep their secrets, even from us," Sorin replied. His tone had softened a touch, like he knew the blow the prince was feeling at being left in the dark.

"I am not you, and she is not Eliné," the prince shot back.

"Go talk to Talwyn," was all Sorin said.

Scarlett felt a fire portal flare open behind them, and Sorin took her hand in his, tugging her gently backwards through the ring of flames. The Earth Prince was still staring at them when the portal snapped closed.

"Earth guy?" Sorin asked, turning to look at her. "You called Azrael Luan the earth guy." He laughed out loud, rich and deep.

Scarlett glared at him and waved him off. "I was flustered. I hate not knowing everything I should." She huffed a sigh of frustration, blowing a stray piece of hair from her eyes. Then she looked around.

They were standing in the middle of what appeared to be a mid-sized home. She stood in a great room. A moderate kitchen was to the right, with an island in the center of it. There was no separate dining room, and the counter was piled high with fresh groceries. Overstuffed chairs and chaise lounges were scattered around a fireplace that roared to life to her left. Bookshelves filled with books lined both sides of the fireplace. There was a hall that led to a staircase along the back wall. She turned to look out a window and found snow-covered mountain tops staring back. Large evergreens stood stark against the backdrop of the mountains.

She whirled to Sorin, who was watching her with anticipation, his golden eyes so full of joy and love. "Are we at your mountain home?" Scarlett breathed, stepping closer to the window. There was nothing else around for miles. Not that she could see, anyway.

"*Our* mountain home," Sorin said, coming up behind her. "You get all of me, and I get all of you. No one else is allowed in. Ever."

"Never?" Scarlett asked, with a raise of her brows.

Sorin slid his arms around her waist as he said, "Never. I guess Cyrus has been here once. They have tried. Eliza has come banging on the door more than once, cursing me soundly when I refuse to let her in."

"How often do you come here?"

"When I need to get away. When I need to think. When I need to drink and brood."

"So when you need to throw a temper tantrum?"

"When I need to be alone with my twin flame." His voice had dropped low, guttural.

Scarlett turned in his arms, and the look on his face was pure hunger, his eyes glazed with thick desire. "Hmm. The palace isn't big enough for us to get some privacy?"

"Not for the sounds you will make this evening, Princess," he growled as he brought his lips to hers. Scarlett's toes curled in her boots at the promise those words held. Her twin flame. The one who came for her. The one who wouldn't let her go. The one who claimed her. She wanted to give him everything she had.

The kiss was slow and gentle at first, until she felt the connection between them practically vibrating. Then she couldn't get enough of him. She needed to touch him everywhere. She needed him to touch her everywhere. It was as if that bond snapping into place made her need to connect with him in every possible way. She pulled back and purred, "You're right. These witch-clothes are extremely inconvenient."

Sorin gave her a devilish grin, and flames licked along her body, up her legs and torso, across her arms, and when they had disappeared she stood in the red dress she'd worn the night of the party on the Pier last summer.

"This one?" Scarlett asked, raising a brow in surprise.

"My Love, the ways I have imagined taking *this* dress off of you since that night are impossible to count," he whispered into her ear, and she felt her core heat and her skin tighten in all the right places. She reached up to remove the crown that still adorned her head, but he hissed, "Leave it."

He brought his lips back to hers, and this time the kiss told her exactly what he wanted. She pressed herself against him, and she could feel him hard against her. His tongue slid across her lips, and she parted them instantly. He swept in, sliding against the roof of her mouth, her teeth. He nipped her lower lip as he pulled back just far enough to look into her eyes, and beneath the predatory lust, there was a glimmer of concern. "You are ready for this? I will understand if you are not." He stroked a thumb across her cheekbone.

"Now, Prince, there was mention of worshipping me, and I do like to be adored," she crooned.

That grin on his face turned downright feral. "Thank the gods." He kissed her again, then began trailing kisses along her jaw. "Princess, I do not even know where to begin," he murmured, his teeth grazing the shell of her pointed ear.

Scarlett couldn't help it. A low moan escaped her as she tilted her head back against the window behind her, giving him better access to her neck. He chuckled darkly in approval, and the sound skittered along her bones. He kissed and licked down her throat, down to her collarbone. Lower. And then he stopped. Scarlett whimpered in protest.

Sorin braced a hand beside her head against the window as he brought his face close to hers, running his nose down the length of her own. "Such new sounds from you, Princess," he teased. She felt his other hand behind her then, reaching for the buttons on her dress.

She couldn't think of any smart ass comment as his fingers grazed her bare skin. Every bit of her attention, every thought, was focused right there. She reached up to help with the skin tight dress, but Sorin hissed at her again and she froze. "Let me do it," he growled into her ear.

She buried her hands in his hair as he returned to her neck, sliding her dress slowly down. Finally, that dress fell to the floor, pooling around her feet, and Sorin stepped back, taking her all in. His eyes were heavy lidded as he purred to her, "I do not know which part to worship first."

She reached for him, ready to undo those buttons and show him exactly where he could start, but he clicked his tongue. Grabbing her wrists, he pinned them against the wall near her head. He kissed each wrist, seeming to remember where those bruises had been from another man who had done the same but with such cruelty. "What kinds of things will you let me do to you, my Love?" he murmured.

Her knees were weak and her whole body was trembling as he kissed her lips, her neck. He reached her breast, and she arched into him. He circled her right breast with kisses while his left hand trailed down to her left breast. As he took her right nipple into his mouth, he palmed her left breast, and she moaned. Still, the kisses trailed lower. Down her torso. Down to her navel. Lower. Lower. Until he knelt before her. Until he knelt before his queen. Until he knelt before his twin flame.

There was wicked dominance on his face as those kisses moved to her inner thighs, circling the spot she wanted him most. She thrust her hips forward in demand, but he only chuckled, trailing a finger lazily around that spot, taunting her. She whimpered again, not caring that she was begging. "Sorin. Please."

He laughed low. "I guess you *do* have manners."

Before she could reply, his tongue dragged across the apex of her thighs, and she cried out. His hand gripped her hip, pinning her to the wall. He took his time with sweeping strokes of his tongue. Scarlett gripped his shoulder, her nails digging in. She moaned when he slipped a finger inside her, then two. She felt release building as he worked those fingers in her, his tongue continuing its ethereal work on that bundle of nerves. Harder and faster he pumped those fingers until he took her over the edge, continuing to stroke her through it all. White starfire flames exploded around her with crystallized ice diamonds dancing among them. She didn't care. The entire house could have burned down around them, and she wouldn't have had one fuck to give right now.

She reached for him as he stood, a satisfied, smug male smile on his face. She wanted that shirt off of him. Those weapons. Those pants.

"Gods, Scarlett." His tone was raspy and ravaging as he ran his tongue across his glistening lips. "You taste divine."

Her mouth crashed into his, their tongues dancing against each other as she tasted herself on him. He hoisted her onto his hips, his hands squeezing her ass. She wrapped her legs around him tight. Her mouth was still on his when he started towards the hallway, then through a fire portal. Her long hair was a mass around them both. She kissed down his neck and throat while her fingers undid the buttons on his tunic as quickly as she possibly could.

Sorin stepped them into what she assumed was his bedroom. She didn't care. He could have just laid her down on the floor of the sitting room and taken her right there.

It was easily as big as the kitchen and sitting area put together. A large bed was before them, with a giant soaking tub underneath the window on the far wall. A fireplace was opposite the bed, a grey sofa before it. He set her on the bed, shrugging off the shirt she had managed to unbutton. She reached for him again, undoing all the buckles as daggers and swords thudded to the floor. She made short work of his pants, and her mouth dried out as he sprang free, long and thick. He quickly slid them off, and she reached for him again. He was hard as granite in her hand, and she brushed a thumb over his tip. He groaned low, his cock twitching in her hand. She grinned up at him with wicked delight as he made to move over her.

"But I have so many uses for my tongue," Scarlett protested, her voice sensual.

"Later," he growled.

Scarlett wasn't about to argue. She slid back on the bed as he crawled onto it, hovering over her. He kissed her breasts, nipping and licking her nipples. Scarlett fisted her hands in his hair, bucking her hips up in demand. Sorin laughed low. "But I have so many other ways to worship you, my Love."

"Later," Scarlett gasped between her panting breaths.

Sorin dragged himself slowly along her entrance. Scarlett whimpered, dragging her nails down his back, trying to pull him closer to her. With a wicked grin, he did it again. The third time, Scarlett ground out "Enough." She tried to sound as demanding as she felt, but it came out as a plea. She was growing impatient. She *needed* him in her. Now.

Sorin gazed down at her, pure love and adoration in his eyes now. Scarlett cupped the back of his neck with one hand. With the other she brushed a lock of that soot black hair from his brow. Looking into his eyes, straight into his soul, she whispered, "I love you, Sorin, and I choose *you*."

The words snapped something in him. He pushed into her slowly, inch by inch. She moaned as he filled her. She clenched his muscled biceps when he was seated to the hilt and stilled, letting her adjust. "I love you, too, Scarlett," he said, his own breathing as shallow as her own.

She writhed beneath him, begging silently with her hips for any type of movement and friction, and with a look of pure possessiveness, Sorin finally obliged her. He slowly pulled out a few inches, and Scarlett squeezed those muscled arms she was gripping as he thrust back in. Slowly, he did it again and again. She pulled herself up to him, kissing his neck, along his chest. She gasped when he started to go faster, harder.

"Scarlett," he groaned, and she moved her hips in rhythm with his. She dragged her nails down his back again as pleasure seeped into every part of her. The connection between them was vibrating wildly. It was a hum in her veins. It was tangible, like she could reach out and touch it. It wove between them, intertwining around them, joining every facet of their beings and souls.

Their powers tangled around each other as if they, too, were connecting. She could feel them, flames dancing with ice, ashes swirling with water. Where they mingled, they glowed, and an aura of flames surrounded them. Her shadows swirled amongst it all.

She gasped his name as release barreled through her again, and he kept moving in her, drawing out her pleasure. Only when she had neared the end of her own release, did Sorin find his, groaning her name into her neck as he spilled himself inside her.

Sorin rolled off of her, panting as hard as she was. She nestled into his side, resting her head on his chest as he stroked her hair. After a few moments, when their breathing had calmed, Sorin said gently, "You are…all right?"

Scarlett lifted herself up to look into his eyes, where she found home staring back at her. She stroked a finger down his cheek and pushed herself up to brush a kiss to his lips. Then she said with a sensuous grin, "Prince, anytime you feel the need to worship me like *that* I will be most willing to accept your adoration."

Sorin's face was dead serious as he cupped her cheek with his hand and said, "Love, I plan on worshipping you in every possible way for the next thousand years and even that will not be enough."

Sorin brought his lips back to hers. She hauled herself on top of him, deepening the kiss. She pulled back just enough to murmur onto his lips, "Let's do that again."

A wicked grin spread across his face. "Princess, it would be my pleasure."

CHAPTER 42
SORIN

The window over the huge bathing tub told him it was well into the night as Sorin lay beside Scarlett, making lazy strokes from between her breasts down to her navel and back up. He took in that naked female laying beside him, her wild mass of silver hair splayed around her like metallic paint splattered onto a canvas. The crown she'd summoned for herself lay on the bedside table near them. She'd removed it after he'd flipped her onto her stomach, and it had fallen to the side. She had simply plucked it from her hair, throwing it to the ground as he had given her what she'd begged for.

Repeatedly.

He had retrieved the crown from the floor as he had headed down to the kitchen to get them some wine. When he'd returned, she had taken the glass from his hand, downed the entire thing, and dragged him back down onto the bed with her. Sorin had experienced her wildness in her training. He had watched her wildfire prowl beneath her skin on a daily basis. Her letting herself be free in bed with him? She was a whirlwind he would never get enough of.

He would never forget his terror when she appeared in the council room at the White Halls. That terror had quickly been

374

replaced by utter admiration as he beheld her decked out in witch-attire, as Death's Maiden stared down the Fae Queen and bound Azrael Luan with her shadows. Then those eyes had turned to him. When she had held up her left hand with the Mark, her knees had nearly buckled. When she spoke the Claiming Rite, he felt like he could take a full breath, like his lungs had been incapable of fully inhaling since he took his own Mark months ago. In a matter of moments, his power had come roaring back to its full strength.

Then this amazing female beside him claimed her throne and stepped into a role she had been destined for. How she had finally accepted that was a story he was anxious to hear.

Now, however, she was tracing the dark ink that adorned his chest, his Marks signaling various loyalties and pacts made. He hissed as the tip of her finger turned icy cold against his skin. She just laughed at him, a silvery lilting sound that was more beautiful than her piano music. "Cruel, wicked thing," he crooned against her temple, pressing a kiss to it.

Her attention had turned to his twin flame Mark, and she held up her own left hand, comparing the two. "Why has it grown?" she asked.

Indeed, the Mark had once flowed from the back of their hands down their thumb and index fingers. Now it had progressed to their middle fingers as well. "They are the Trial Markings." She frowned at him as she contemplated his answer. "Do you remember on the beach when I first told you about the twin flame? I told you the connection had to be tested."

"Five trials," she said quietly, holding her hand in the air above her head, studying it.

He nodded his head. "Yes. They can be done in any order and at any time, except for the first and the last ones." With his own finger, he touched the tip of her thumb. "The first is The Claiming. When you accept and acknowledge that the twin flame bond exists. Speaking the Claiming Rite initiates the Trials and offers up a piece of your soul to the other. The second," he said, moving to her pointer finger, "is The Rescuing."

"When you rescued me from the Lairwood House," she said, looking back at her hand.

"Yes and no," Sorin answered. "That was my rescuing of you, but also when *you* rescued *me* by accepting the Mark and restoring my weakened magic and life force." She looked at him in surprise, and he chuckled. "I can't be doing all the work, Princess."

"I am a Queen, you know," she retorted, flicking his nose.

"Would you rather I call you your Majesty?" he teased with a raised brow.

"No, no," she said, waving her hand in mock dismissal. "I don't want you to feel outranked. I know how territorial you Fae males are." Sorin snorted, nipping at her earlobe. "We had those two before," she continued. "What is the new one?"

Sorin gave her a feral grin. "The Joining."

"Hmm," she mused. "Shouldn't we have several new Marks by now then?"

Sorin barked another laugh, brushing a kiss to her lips. His equal in every way. His mirror. Someone he thought he'd never have. "The Joining is physical, yes," he said. "But it is also the joining of our souls and our magic."

"And the fourth Trial?"

"The Sacrifice," he explained. "It will test what we are willing to give for each other, for our bond."

"What of the fifth?"

"The final Trial is The Anointing and can only be given after the other four have been received," Sorin answered.

"How do we get it?" She was still studying her Mark.

"When we have the first four Trials completed, the connection must be anointed by a Seer who can confirm and bless the bond."

Her eyes jumped to his. "A Seer? We must go to the Oracle?"

"There are plenty of Seers in the realms. The Oracle is simply the most powerful, the most ancient of them, but any Witch would have some sort of Seer gift, even if it is not their dominant one," Sorin explained. His fingers had begun roaming over her again. He couldn't help it. He needed to touch her, feel her. He needed his scent all over her. He had downplayed how possessive males became of their lovers when he had spoken of it in the Earth Court. It only got worse if they took a wife. And if they found their twin flame? He was not looking forward to being around others for quite some time, not even his family.

Scarlett frowned at him. "So we must go back to the Witch Kingdoms?"

"We could," Sorin said, his tone considering. "Or we could use the Witch that already serves in our Court."

Scarlett's eyes widened. "A Witch lives here? In the Fire Court?"

"A select few do, yes," Sorin answered with a smile. "If they enter into a covenant with a prince or princess of the Courts." He pointed to a Mark that was inked on the inside of his right forearm, just below the crease of his elbow. It was a black whirl of stars and moons. "You will find a similar Mark on Beatrix, our Healer."

"Beatrix is a Witch?" She was tracing the Mark he had shown her now.

"All Healers are Witches. Beatrix's dominant gift is healing, and she is one of the most skilled in all the realms, but she possesses the other Witch gifts of prophecy and apothecary as well."

"So we get this last Trial done, we go see Beatrix, she anoints our connection, and then what? Will we be married?" Scarlett mused.

"I suppose, for all intents and purposes, yes, but the twin flame bond is deeper than any marriage bond," Sorin said, watching his own finger tracing around her nipples.

She huffed a sarcastic sigh. "These Fae customs are so complicated. In the human lands, they just exchange rings."

"My Love, if a ring will make you happy, we can do that, too. If you want a grand ceremony and party, then we shall have one. If you want to shout it from the rooftops, I shall find the tallest building," he said, leaning down to kiss where his finger had just been tracing.

"Gods, no," Scarlett said, with a shade of disgust in her tone, running her fingers through his hair. "A ring shall do just fine. In the meantime, though, before we're Anointed or whatever, what will we be?"

"Beatrix can still sanctify a marriage so that it is official for... political purposes, until the twin flame bond is Anointed," Sorin answered.

"Hmm," she hummed, her attention having returned to her own Mark. Her lips were pursed and quirked to the side. He could tell she was thinking deeply about something. "That would probably be a good idea."

"Why?" he questioned, his fingers now lightly grazing up and down her hip and thigh.

"Do I need a reason to want to marry you?"

"No, but you always have a reason," he returned with a knowing glance. Her eyes were different. The icy blue was paler, almost silvery.

"Maybe I just want to be able to call you husband."

"That would certainly be a step up from all the names you usually call me," he retorted.

"Careful, Prince," she crooned sensuously, "we may be twin flames, but I will still throw down with you."

Sorin chuckled, brushing another kiss to her lips. She hissed at him, but kissed him back. "You produced white flames today. On purpose," he said, pulling back and looking into her eyes once more.

"I did. I... The Oracle helped remove some obstacles that..." She sighed, and it made him wonder what exactly had happened with the Oracle. "She answered some questions, but it also created about a hundred new ones. And she did help me overcome some things that were keeping me from accessing my full well of power."

"Your power will already be feared among the rest of the world, but when our magic is bonded..." Sorin couldn't help the shudder that went through him. He had felt it. He had felt their magic playing and joining and intertwining while they'd been doing the same with their physical bodies. Thinking out loud, he mused, "If we ever have children, their power could be extraordinary."

Scarlett went rigid beside him. "Do you take a tonic?"

"Yes, Scarlett," he answered softly, stroking a finger down her cheek. "I take a monthly aid."

She ran a hand down her face. "Thank the gods." Her eyes

closed for a moment before she opened them and met his gaze. "Sorin, children... I..."

"Relax, Love. That is a discussion we can have down the road."

"Far down the road," she said pointedly.

"When you are ready," he confirmed.

"I mean, I know you said it is difficult for Fae to conceive children, and my cycle has never been exactly normal—"

Sorin brushed a kiss to her mouth, silencing her rambling. "Scarlett, I did not bring up children as a way of saying I wanted them right now. Yes, children are rare for Fae, and should we have them someday, they will be a blessing, but not now. Right now, I want you all to myself." He felt the tension ease from her muscles some. "As for your cycle..." Her eyes flew back to his, widening. "It was not normal for mortals, I suppose, but I am guessing you experience it every season rather than every month."

"Oh my gods." Her hands came up and covered her face, but he could see the slight flush to her cheeks. "I do not even want to know why you know about Fae menstrual cycles," she muttered from beneath her hands. Sorin laughed, and she slowly lowered her hands. "Seriously. Why do you know that?"

"I did have basic anatomy in my lessons, Love," he laughed. "But Talwyn wasn't lying. I did help raise her in many ways. You learn things, even if you do not want to, when you are put in that situation."

"That's weird," she muttered again.

He felt her finger begin tracing his Marks once more, and he didn't think this would ever get old. These completely normal moments with her in his bed speaking of random things. When he wasn't a prince and she wasn't a queen, and they were just...together.

"What are you thinking?" she asked, drawing his attention back to her.

"That you are perfect. This is perfect," he answered softly.

He felt her hook her finger under his chin and pull his mouth up to her own. He scented her desire a moment later. He was about to appease her once more when he felt a slight tug on his mind. Inwardly, he groaned.

Scarlett's eyes snapped wide open. "What was that?"

He shouldn't have been surprised she felt it, too. Their twin flame bond was almost completed, but that she had felt the tug still caught him off guard. "Your cousin summons me," he answered grimly.

"Talwyn? Why?"

"I would venture to guess it has something to do with our little discussion with Azrael earlier," he muttered.

"But you do not have to go, right?"

"Technically no, but…" he trailed off.

"But you want to go?" she said with a small smile, angling her head. She kept it off her face, but he felt the small hurt down their bond.

"My Love, what I *want* to do is stay here for the next week and fuck you in every room and on every surface of this house," he purred, bringing her eyes back to his.

"Then what is stopping you?" she crooned back, her hand sliding down his chest, down his abdomen.

At the same moment, a flame appeared near his head. She paused her descent as he reached up and plucked the note from the fire message, skimming it quickly. "According to Cyrus, she sent word she will be at the Fiera Palace at dawn." Then he added, "She tends to throw quite the fit when she does not get what she wants."

Scarlett rolled her eyes, grumbling, "It seems to be a Fae trait."

"You do know you are Fae, my Love, do you not?" he asked in amusement.

"I know, but I wasn't *raised* Fae. It's different. I learned to use my words when I am upset."

"You learned to use daggers and violence," he said pointedly.

"Semantics," she replied with a fiendish gleam in her eyes, rolling onto her side to face him. Her bare breasts rubbed against his chest as she gave him an enticing smile.

"Your wickedness," he ground out, "rivals the Witches, Princess."

She laughed, low and seductive. "Stay, and I will show you just how wicked I can be." But then, "Are you serious?" She flopped back onto her pillow.

A mass of snowflakes had appeared near Sorin's head now, and he winced slightly. "I tried to warn you." He reached up and pulled a note from the flurries, this one from Briar. Apparently, Talwyn had summoned him as well. Of course, he didn't know Scarlett had claimed their Courts, and thus their allegiance was now to her. He sighed. "May I make a proposal?"

"Do I have a choice?"

"You always have a choice," he answered gently. He leaned down and brushed a featherlight kiss to her lips. "Let's go home *and*," he continued over her groan, "let's find Beatrix, have her sanctify a marriage, and see what Talwyn has to say. Then we can spend the next few days here, all by ourselves."

She seemed to consider, then said, "The next week. I rather like your earlier idea."

"Deal, Princess," he replied, leaning in to kiss her again. Then he slid from the bed before he, or she, could take things any further. "Get ready, Love," he said over the protesting curses she was muttering under her breath. As he said it, the tub near the window began to fill with steaming water.

Scarlett sat up while he walked around the end of the bed. "Get ready here? All I have is that red dress. I have no idea what you did with my witch-clothes."

He took her in, sitting naked amongst the mess of sheets and goosefeather down comforter. It took all of his self-control not to get right back in that bed with her. "Check the armoire," he said, sliding on his pants and walking to the bedroom door.

"And where are you going?" she asked, her eyes narrowing.

Sorin stopped at the threshold and looked over his shoulder. "I am removing myself from temptation."

Her answering scowl had him hiding a smirk as he walked out of the room to leave her to get ready.

CHAPTER 43

SCARLETT

S carlett casually sat at the large table in the formal dining room at the Fiera Palace. Eliza was next to her, her arms crossed across her chest, scowling at no one in particular. Cyrus and Rayner were standing along the wall, keeping a wary eye on Sorin. Sorin was leaning against the wall nearest her, and she could feel his struggle down the connection. She felt the primal rage when Rayner had told her good morning as they walked into the dining room. She had simply patted Sorin's arm, kissed his cheek with a smirk, and walked to the table. His Inner Court, however, had instantly noted the change in mood, the shift in scents, and since that time, they'd all been on edge. Briar was also already there, sitting at the opposite end of the long table, an amused smile on his lips as he watched Sorin. They had already explained what had happened after he'd left the White Halls yesterday afternoon.

Scarlett and Sorin had bathed and gotten ready up at the mountain chalet. Sorin hadn't been lying when he had told her to check the armoire in the bedroom. It was full of dresses, tunics, pants, and other clothing. She also discovered her witch-suit and witch-leathers, which she found she much preferred to the Fae-leathers. The lightness of the witch-leathers allowed her to move more easily. She had dressed while Sorin had bathed quickly, pointedly throwing up a shield of flame anytime she tried to get closer than ten feet to the tub. She had stuck her tongue out at him as she slipped into black pants and a sage green tunic with rose gold beading.

Sorin had portaled them to their quarters. Then they had silently made their way to Beatrix's office. The Healer, who was up working in the middle of the night, looked up when they entered the room, a smile forming on her lips. Scarlett, not really remembering any of her interactions with the Healer, had been shocked that she had graying hair and the start of aging skin. She looked like a mortal woman who was in her early sixties, not an immortal Witch. She had come to Sorin and embraced him like a grandmother embracing her grandson. With her Fae hearing, Scarlett had heard Beatrix whisper to him, "I told you the Fates would find a way, Prince," and, as Sorin pulled back, she could see tears glimmering in his eyes.

Beatrix had sanctified their union, and afterwards, as they were walking back to their chambers, she had asked Sorin, "I thought Witches were immortal like Fae?"

"They are, but even we fade in time. Compared to mortal lifespans, though, yes, we are immortal," Sorin answered, her hand clasped tightly in his.

"But she looks…older?"

"Witches do not have a Staying like Fae do. When Fae reach a certain age, we enter a Staying, where our bodies stop aging, usually in our early twenties. Witches continue to age but very, very slowly," he explained.

"How old *is* Beatrix?" she had asked, peering up at him.

Sorin shrugged his shoulders. "I have known her my entire life. She was in service to my father when I was young and looked exactly as she does now."

Scarlett had nodded, then had suddenly realized they had not returned to the private living wing of the palace but were standing at a door on the main level. "Where are we going?"

A sly smile had spread across his face. "Consider it a marriage gift."

"I do love gifts," she had said with mock wistfulness, watching him draw a symbol with flames on the door.

The door had opened, and Sorin had led her down several sets of stairs. At the bottom was a stone wall. He had taken a dagger from his belt and pricked his finger, drawing the same symbol on the wall with his blood, and with a grinding groan, the stone had slid to the left revealing a large chamber that had apparently been carved deep into the side of one of the mountains. Inside, though, Scarlett had gasped when Sorin led her in and illuminated the room with flames. Jewels lined the walls from tiny to larger than eggs. Trunks of gold, silver, and other precious metals lay all over the floor. On the back wall, each in its own compartment, were various crowns, and she saw the one she had created for herself in the very center.

She had turned to Sorin with a raised brow when she saw it, and he had simply said, "For safekeeping," with a wink. Then he had led her to a stone table. As they had approached it, she had realized it was not a table at all but a case with a glass top and inside were rings of every shape and size and varying metal. Rings with diamonds and rubies and emeralds and sapphires. She had inhaled sharply as she took them all in.

"Pick whichever one you like," he had whispered into her ear from behind her.

"Sorin, I couldn't possibly," she had breathed, bringing a hand to her throat as she took in the rows and rows of gleaming rings.

"Of course you can. They are as much yours as they are mine," he'd answered, pressing a kiss to her temple.

"They are your family riches," she'd argued.

He had turned her gently then, bringing his brow to hers, and whispered, "*You* are my family, Scarlett. You are my wife. You are my twin flame. What is mine is yours, as if it has always been yours."

She had kissed him, tenderly at first, and then it had turned passionate, and he had taken her right there in that room of treasures and jewels, bending her over that case of rings.

She smiled at the memory as she played with the ring that now adorned her left ring finger. It was a band of gold with a large diamond flanked by two smaller rubies on each side of it. Sorin had chosen a black gold ring with three black diamonds embedded into the band.

Sorin's eyes slid to hers as he ground out down the bond, *What are you thinking about?*

Oh, just a few more uses I thought up for my tongue, she purred back.

"You two," came Eliza's voice from beside her as she sniffed the air, "need to keep it in your pants for the next few hours. Then you can go fuck like rabbits until you can't move."

Cyrus huffed a laugh from behind them, but before Sorin could respond, they all felt that icy wind cross their wards. The males in the room instantly straightened, Briar rising to his feet. Eliza's hand slid to her dagger at her waist. Scarlett merely picked up a muffin from the food spread before them and took a bite.

A few minutes later, Talwyn prowled into the dining room, Azrael Luan beside her. Talwyn was in her usual brown pants and white tunic, her weapons in all the usual places. Scarlett locked eyes with Azrael as she said sweetly, "Welcome to my home, Earth Guy. Muffin?"

Azrael sneered at her, and out of the corner of her eye, Sorin lurched from the wall. Cyrus clasped a hand on his shoulder, holding him back.

Relax, Prince.

Do not bait him right now, Scarlett. I beg of you.

"I see the twin flame bond has settled into place," Talwyn said coolly, her eyes falling to Scarlett's left hand. "Not yet Anointed, but married?" Surprise colored her tone as she looked to Sorin.

"A few hours ago," he ground out.

"And why are we meeting in the dining room and not your council room?" Talwyn asked.

"Because," Scarlett cut in, "you called a meeting as the sun rises, and I get cranky if I don't eat, so I wanted breakfast." In emphasis, she popped the last of the muffin into her mouth.

Talwyn studied her, as if sizing her up for the first time. "No weapons today, cousin?"

A wicked grin spread across Scarlett's face. "I do believe my *husband* could rip out a throat with his bare hands if someone so much as looks at me wrong right now. I do not need a weapon."

Talwyn's eyes went back to Sorin. "Indeed."

Cutting in to smooth the tension, Briar asked, "Is Princess Ashtine not joining us this morning?"

Scarlett hadn't realized they were indeed missing one of the Courts. She assumed she was the silver-haired beauty that Scarlett had seen at the White Halls.

"She will be here momentarily. She is gathering information for me on something," Talwyn replied shortly. She took a seat across from Scarlett, picked up a pastry, and took a bite. Every other Fae in the room went still. "I do eat, you know," she snapped at them.

"Sit down, you male pricks," Scarlett said, waving her hand at the various chairs around the table. "Eat something. There's no reason we can't talk and fill our stomachs."

The males all glanced at each other, then took stiff walks to the table. Sorin sat to Scarlett's right, Cyrus taking the seat next to him. Rayner moved to Eliza's left. Azrael slid into place next to Talwyn, across from Sorin. Tense silence settled over them all. Scarlett sighed loudly, looking at Talwyn. "Do we need to go around and introduce ourselves, or do you just want to tell us why we urgently needed to meet this morning?"

A thin, unamused smile formed on Talwyn's face as she angled her head slightly and said, "You are not one for decorum, are you?"

"They tried to instill it in me in the human lands, but no, I am not," Scarlett answered, her tone slightly domineering.

"It has been a long night, Talwyn," Sorin sighed from beside Scarlett, his hand coming to rest on hers. He sounded wary and tense. "Let's get on with it."

"Fine," Talwyn said, her lips pursing as she clearly worked to keep her temper under control. Her jade eyes narrowed. "What part of keep this to ourselves yesterday afternoon did you lot not understand?"

Scarlett glanced to Azrael who was glaring at her and Sorin, but who was also purposefully not looking at Talwyn. She could only assume they had argued.

"It was not intentional, Talwyn," Sorin answered, "but to be honest, he should know. So should Ashtine."

"I do know," came a soft feminine voice at the entrance to the dining room. That beautiful female strode into the room, full of grace and perfection. Her long, silver hair flowed behind her on phantom winds like Talwyn's did, and her silver hawk rested on her shoulder. All the males in the room rose to their feet as she entered and didn't return to their seats until she sat across from Briar, her silver eyes settling on him. She had no Second or guards with her.

"Princess Ashtine," Briar said, his eyes on hers as well, "meet Queen Scarlett. Queen Talwyn's cousin."

"It is a pleasure," Ashtine said. Her voice was warm and mystical all at once. "You have caused quite the stir among the winds."

"Speaking of the winds, Ashtine," Talwyn cut in. Scarlett nearly started at her tone. It was not the cool, icy tone used with Sorin or Briar, but one of respect, almost reverence. "What did you learn this morning?"

"Sorin was not mistaken, Talwyn," Ashtine replied, her eyes going to her queen. "They are not mortals. It is as if they have found a way to glamour themselves."

"You were in the human lands?" Scarlett asked quickly. "Where?"

Ashtine's kind silver eyes settled on her, and Scarlett had to work not to squirm under her gaze. There was something other about the princess, and she couldn't quite place it. "I was at the home of your previously betrothed."

Scarlett felt her face pale. "You were at Mikale's?"

"Sorin told us at our meeting yesterday morning that he suspected he was not mortal. I sent Princess Ashtine to see what she could discover," Talwyn explained.

With her eyes still on Talwyn, she said to Sorin down their bond, *You told them about Mikale?*

Nasima told Ashtine about that day in my old apartment. Ashtine has been keeping an eye on things. They know nothing else. He squeezed her hand gently in emphasis.

"But how did they get to the mortal lands?" Cyrus asked, breaking the silence that had ensued.

"That is the question, isn't it?" Talwyn replied thoughtfully.

"What is he if he is not mortal? Have others been found in the other lands?" Briar asked. His usual bright eyes and lighthearted manners had been replaced by an intense resolve. The look of a prince set on protecting those in his charge.

"Rayner has not seen nor heard of any," Sorin answered, glancing to his Ash Rider.

"Nor have I," Princess Ashtine chimed in, "but that does not mean it has not happened. There are powerful spells and charms out there. After all, I did not know about Scarlett thanks to powerful old magic. Your mother did her work thoroughly it seems." The princess's eyes were still on Scarlett, a look of curiosity on her face, as if Scarlett were a puzzle she could not figure out but delighted in the challenge.

Scarlett sat quietly, watching the others exchange thoughts and ideas, taking in their facial expressions and tones.

"If they have come from other lands, perhaps it would be wise to invite the leaders of the territories to a summit, Talwyn," Sorin suggested. "They should be put on alert. Maybe there are already others among their lands. They could be preparing."

"It has been centuries since all the leaders have convened in one place," Azrael drawled. "You cannot honestly think they would all come?"

"If the queens summon them, they will come," Sorin argued.

"Hazel seemed agreeable enough," Scarlett cut in, only half listening to what they were saying around her. She was lost in her own thoughts of things she'd discovered about Mikale and Lord Tyndell. "I'm sure she would come."

The room went silent, and every set of eyes turned to her. It took her a moment to realize it. Sorin was watching her closely, as if he knew she was not completely present.

"I do not think," Talwyn said slowly, her words clipped, "that the High Witch's name and agreeable have ever been used in the same sentence."

Scarlett wasn't sure what to say. Hazel hadn't exactly been welcoming, but she wasn't nearly as terrible as the Witches had been made out to be. Finally she said, "If you want a meeting with the leaders of the realms, Hazel will be there. We have a…mutual need of each other at the present."

Talwyn's brows rose high. "Pray tell, what is that?" Her voice was calm, but Scarlett could hear the effort in it. It seemed she was not too keen that she had somehow managed to get on better terms with the High Witch in one meeting than she had in her years as queen.

Scarlett, however, was not ready to reveal what she had learned of Cassius. They didn't even know who Cassius was. She didn't feel right telling all of them before she told Cassius himself. Besides, she was certain her cousin had secrets of her own she was keeping from her. Despite her claims in that council room yesterday, this was, in fact, a game. It was all a game of gleaning information and revealing it at the proper time, so she answered with a shrug, "That is business between me and the High Witch, but she will come if asked."

Talwyn glared at her, and she felt Sorin throwing her a sidelong glance.

Princess Ashtine cut in with her mystical, silvery tone. "I agree that it would be fruitful to hold a summit. However, we also need to attend to the mortal lands immediately. Every resource needs to be put to use to figure out what they are and what they want."

"I would assume," Azrael said, "they are there for their weapon." As he said the last words, his eyes narrowed at Sorin, his lip curling into a snarl.

Sorin ignored him completely, instead looking at Talwyn and saying with casual arrogance, "Leash your dog, Talwyn, or did you not fill him in on everything you told us yesterday?"

Scarlett felt a whip of wind in the dining room, Talwyn's jade green eyes flaring as she replied, "Hold your tongue, Prince of Fire."

"Enough," Scarlett said. She didn't yell it, but her voice was firm enough that every single person turned to her. "I know there are scores to settle and old feuds that I know nothing of. Frankly, I don't give a shit. I have matters to tend to in the human lands and need to return. The Crown Prince needs to return home as well. I will look into things while there. In the meantime, call the summit. I can return for it if it falls before I am able to complete my business there."

"No," Talwyn said. There was no room for debate, no room for discussion in her tone.

Scarlett heard Sorin suck in a breath beside her.

Scarlett... came down the bond, but she somehow threw that connection from her mind, blocking him out.

"Shit," she heard him mutter under his breath.

"What did you say?" Scarlett asked slowly, coldly.

"I said no," Talwyn replied, enunciating each syllable. "You have just returned. You have only started to master your gifts. Until you do so more fully, you must stay here."

"I am not your subject," Scarlett replied. Her voice was as sharp as the edge of a dagger, and Talwyn stilled. "In fact, as of yesterday, this entire side of the table is no longer under your jurisdiction. You do not get to give me or them orders, cousin."

"You do not understand the gravity of all of this, Scarlett."

"I think you will find I understand a lot more than you think I do."

"Enlighten me then, *cousin.*"

"I do not need to prove myself to you," Scarlett hissed.

"No, but you do need to prove yourself to your people. To your Courts," Talwyn purred.

"She needs to prove nothing to us," Sorin snarled.

"The rest of her people do not get the pleasure of being between her legs, Prince of Fire. She certainly does need to prove herself."

Scarlett felt the flames flicker in her eyes. Everyone else in the room had gone silent as the two queens stared at each other, letting the power struggle play out. "You do not," Scarlett began, her voice quiet with rage, "get to invite yourself into *my* home, insult me, my Courts, my family, and my husband and try to give me orders."

"This is not your home," Talwyn spat back. "Your home is in the Black Halls."

"*This* is my home, and *this* is my family," Scarlett answered, gesturing to the people along her side of the table. "I am going to the mortal lands. I have friends there who need me and other matters to tend to. I depart tomorrow. If you need me to speak to Hazel before I go, send word." Scarlett stood to leave the room.

"Are you dismissing me?" Talwyn asked, shooting to her feet. Incredulous anger rang in her voice and colored her face. Azrael was on his feet as well, a tentative hand on Talwyn's arm.

"I guess I am," Scarlett replied with a shrug, and she strode for the doorway. Before she crossed the threshold, she looked over her shoulder at Talwyn simmering with rage and said sweetly, "You may see yourselves out. Princess Ashtine, it was a pleasure to meet you."

"We are not done here," Talwyn seethed, starting towards Scarlett.

Between one breath and another, panthers made of shadows appeared between them, growling and snapping teeth of razor sharp ice. "Oh, I think we are."

Scarlett left the dining room. They were on the main floor of the palace, and she strode for the main gates. As she was nearing the bridges, she heard her name being shouted. Callan. They had not spoken since their argument in the gardens. That seemed like ages ago. She closed her eyes and kept walking. She couldn't deal with him now.

She slipped from the doors, walking until she was standing on the banks of the river that ran through her home. She knew Callan had tried to follow her. Her shadow panthers had snarled warnings at him that had kept him from following further. As she stood there, she peered through that rip in the world, aching to step through onto a beach that meant so much to her. But she couldn't. Not yet. She couldn't go back to Baylorin alone, not even for a moment, just to breathe in that sea air.

She felt him rather than heard him come up beside her. He didn't say a word. Just stood beside her. "I can see it," she said. "I can see that beach as if looking through a window. I am ready to go back."

"I know you are, Love," Sorin said gently.

"We've left them there too long. We should have gone back for them weeks ago. Who knows what he's been going through." After a pause, she added, "I miss him, Sorin."

Sorin was silent for a long moment. He knew who she was talking about. He gently took her hand as a fire portal appeared to his right. She saw a beach through it, and she dug in her heels as Sorin tugged her gently towards it. "We can't go. Not quite yet. I need to plan. I need to—"

But Sorin scooped her into his arms and stepped through the portal while she was still speaking. They stood on a beach in the warm sunshine. It wasn't her beach, but it was nearly as breathtaking, maybe even more so.

The water was a clear turquoise blue. The waves gently crashed onto the sand. Crabs scuttled to and fro, and she breathed deep, so deep, letting that ocean mist fill her lungs. The water seemed to sparkle and shimmer as Sorin lowered her to her feet, then wordlessly knelt before her and removed her boots.

She stepped into the water, hissing slightly at the cold, but then she closed her eyes and let the events of the last few days wash over her. She felt flames lick along her body and her pants and tunic were replaced with a sleeveless lightweight dress, white and flowing, a gold roped belt slung low on her hips. Wherever they were, the winters did not bring the chill and snow as it did in the mountains.

She had no idea how long she stood there, sorting through everything that was to come, as plans took shape in her mind. Time seemed to have paused for a moment while ideas formed, and she sifted through information. After a while, she heard from behind her, "Your twin flame may be a son of Anala, my queen, but your heart beats for Anahita."

Scarlett turned to find icy blue eyes, the same color as her own, fixed on her. A knowing smile played on his beautiful face. "And where is my husband?" she asked with a raised brow, looking around. Sorin was nowhere to be seen.

Briar chuckled. "Since he is feeling a little...overprotective right now, he is up at the House of Water."

"I hope it is all right that he brought me here," Scarlett said, her eyes going back to the horizon where the sea stretched far and wide.

"This is your kingdom. You may come here whenever you wish," Briar said simply, stepping to her side.

"No," Scarlett replied with a shake of her head. "I did not come here to take over or claim any lands. This Court is yours, Prince."

"Even then," Briar said after a pause, "you are free to come here whenever you wish."

"I do my best thinking by the sea," Scarlett mused, not really to Briar, but just to say the words aloud.

"As do I," Briar said. "It is as if the tide and surf wash everything else away so that what I need to see, what I need to do, is crystal clear before me."

Scarlett turned to Briar as he spoke and found his eyes watching the distant horizon, too. Her heart, her soul, was Sorin's, but even as her twin flame, he would not understand her draw to the sea, to the water. But this male beside her? He knew exactly what sandy beaches and crashing waves elicited from her. "You remind me of my dearest friend in the mortal lands," she mused, turning back to the sea once more.

"Oh?" Briar asked. "A good thing, I hope. Other than the fact that I seem to remind you of a mortal woman."

"My dearest friend is male, you twit," she said, giving him a light shove. "His name is Cassius. He saved my life." And after a long pause, she added, "And he is not mortal. He is the High Witch's son."

Briar was quiet for a long moment before he said, "You know, Sunshine, you certainly add some new type of excitement every time I see you."

Scarlett huffed a laugh under her breath with a wince. "I hope Sorin feels the same when I tell him."

"He does not know?" She could hear the surprise in his voice.

Scarlett sighed. "So much has happened since I saw the Oracle. Other things were more pressing. It just hasn't come up again. Until now." Briar merely nodded once. They stood in silence for several more minutes, then Scarlett said quietly, "Thank you, Briar. For not leaving me out here alone."

"It is my pleasure." His voice held complete sincerity, absent of its usual flirtatious tone and carefree attitude. He reached over and gently squeezed her hand.

She glanced at him from the corner of her eye. "Sorry my shadows bit at you."

Briar barked a laugh. "Do not tell Sorin I just held your hand, and we will call it even."

"Deal," Scarlett said, laughing. "I suppose we should join the others. I do believe Sorin will curse me soundly when I tell him I need to go see the High Witch, and I don't think she will be particularly fond of his presence if he joins me."

Briar laughed again, turning with her. "I think that is a good assumption considering you seem to view the High Witch very differently than the rest of us." With a teasing sigh and a wink, he added, "Although I do enjoy watching you two square off. I will be on your side if you prefer. Just to see Sorin squirm a bit more."

"Pot-stirrer," Scarlett laughed as they walked a little ways up the beach.

"Sorin needs someone to challenge him every once in a while. He is used to getting his way," Briar smirked from beside her. A second later, a portal of water appeared before them.

Scarlett snorted. "Now you're making him sound like Talwyn."

"Sunshine, you have no idea. There is a reason they butt heads the way they do," Briar muttered grimly, and they stepped through the portal.

CHAPTER 44

SCARLETT

S carlett stepped into a bright meeting room. The ivory marble stones of the House of Water were smooth as glass, polished and gleaming, and there were large windows every few feet, most thrown wide open, letting in all the sunlight and the smell of the sea beyond. There was an expansive balcony with a perfect view of the harbor and the crystal clear blue sky. Large ivory pillars were interspersed throughout the room with sea blue gossamer curtains flowing gently in the breeze. She had to admit, it did rival the Fiera Palace for beauty.

She was about to ask Briar, who was still beside her, if there were ever clouds in the sky here, but the room had gone completely silent when they had appeared. Everyone in the room had stood.

And bowed to her.

She felt her cheeks flush as she said quietly, "Please. Don't."

Sorin was at her other side in an instant. "There are battles coming, Scarlett. There are choices to be made and loyalties to be given. We give ours to you."

Scarlett swept her eyes over those in the room. Cyrus, Rayner, and Eliza were there, but they were among Briar's Inner Court. She had seen the one male once or twice. She assumed he was Briar's Second, but the others she had never met.

"Then thank you. I am humbled by your choice." She rose on her tiptoes to kiss Sorin on his cheek as she said down the twin flame bridge, *But you, my Love, never bow to me. We are equals.*

What is worship but bowing before my queen? he purred back, a sinful glimmer filling his eyes.

Scarlett smirked at him. *In the bedroom, you may bow all you'd like.*

Briar coughed beside her, and she turned to find him with a knowing grin on his face. She winked at him as she said, "I do suppose you should introduce me to your Inner Court, Prince."

Cyrus, Rayner, and Eliza had all returned to their seats, but Briar's Court seemed to straighten even more. They all had the same dark skin as Briar, obviously obtained by spending every day in this beautiful sunshine. The male she had seen before looked remarkably similar to the Water Prince. He had the same icy, blue eyes and hair so blonde it was nearly white. Even his build was similar. The only real difference seemed to be that he was an inch or two shorter than Briar. "This is Sawyer, my Second," Briar said when they came to stand in front of him. "And my younger brother."

"Brother?" Scarlett asked, the surprise evident in her voice as she whipped her head to Briar.

"Indeed," he said with a nod. "Although not quite as handsome, wouldn't you agree?"

Scarlett laughed, turning back to Sawyer. "I am so sorry you had to grow up with this as a role model," she said, jerking her thumb at Briar.

Sawyer seemed unsure whether he should laugh with her or stay at attention. Briar clapped him on the shoulder. "Relax, Brother. I told you she is a delight, especially when she squeezes Sorin's balls."

A familiar twinkle entered Sawyer's eyes at that. A twinkle that told Scarlett Briar and Sawyer were similar in more ways than one. She laughed again as they moved towards the other male. His hair was a sandy blonde color, and his eyes were a heavenly shade of turquoise. He was muscular and had a hard look about him. "This hard ass is the Commander of my armies, Nakoa," Briar said.

Nakoa gave a nod of his head to Scarlett, and Sorin chimed in down the bond.

He is also Eliza's occasional lover.

It took every bit of self-control not to react to that bit of news. Eliza had never told her she had a current lover and certainly not that said lover was the Commander of the Water Court's armies.

They often work closely together to train our armies. Nakoa actually trained Eliza when she became more skilled than most here.

She tucked that information away as she followed Briar to the female next to Nakoa. All these little tidbits of information. Sorin needed to fill her in on *everything* if she were to actually lead these Courts.

The female before her now was beautiful. Not the stunning, ethereal beauty of Princess Ashtine, but a graceful, simple beauty. Her light golden hair was braided down her back, but she didn't have the blue eyes of the others. Hers were a soft gray, like the color of stormy skies over the sea. "This is Neve, my Third."

"I have heard much about you," Neve said, giving a slight bow of her head.

"Don't believe a word this one has to say about me," Scarlett scoffed with a smile. "He's still irked I threw fire at him."

Neve laughed with a smile that filled her eyes. Turning to Briar, she said, "She is as enchanting as you described, Prince."

"I do not think I could ever do her justice. There really is no way to quite describe Queen Scarlett," Briar replied with a wink.

Scarlett stuck her tongue out at him as she interlaced her fingers with Sorin's, and she let him lead her back to the head of the table. Tea and sandwiches, along with fruit and cheese, appeared on the table, and they all took seats. Sorin took the seat to her right, and Briar took a seat to her left.

"Right then," Scarlett said, holding her chin a bit higher. "I don't know how Talwyn ran things. Honestly, I don't care. I don't care about ranks or titles. In this room, in these Courts, we are all on the same playing field. You are free to speak and share your thoughts. We make decisions that concern these two Courts together."

She could feel pride emanating from Sorin and Briar beside her. The Fire Court's eyes held only respect. Nakoa's eyes were slightly doubtful, but that was to be expected when he'd only just met her.

"I am assuming you two were filled in on the happenings this morning from Sawyer?" she asked, addressing Nakoa and Neve.

A feline smile spread across Neve's lips. "Oh, we watched. You really handled her quite spectacularly if I do say so myself."

The confusion must have flitted across Scarlett's face because Sorin said beside her, "Remember when I told you of Water Gazers?"

Understanding flooded through her as she turned to Briar. "You created a water mirror for them? Where?"

"My crystal clear water glass, of course," he said with a wink.

"Wonderful," Scarlett breathed. "Less to explain then."

"You honestly think," came Sawyer's voice next to Briar, "that the High Witch will come to a summit?"

"The High Witch doesn't give a fuck about the rest of the world," Nakoa said coolly from down the table, and in that instant, Scarlett saw exactly why he and Eliza were casual lovers.

"I didn't say she would be enthused by the idea," Scarlett retorted. "But, yes, she will come."

"What makes you so sure?" Nakoa shot back, his turquoise eyes full of challenge.

She felt Sorin suck in a breath beside her, as she'd often heard Cassius do when someone challenged her. A smug smile formed on her lips, and she propped her head on her hand as she replied sweetly, "Because I know where the High Witch's son is, and she has asked me to bring him home. She owes me a debt."

The entire room went still and silent, except for Briar to her left, who chuckled. "I swear to Anahita, Scarlett, sometimes I think you hold back information just to reveal it at the time it will cause the most dramatics."

But some of the others did not seem nearly as amused. "The Witches do not allow their sons to live," Nakoa sneered. "At least not powerful ones, which I would expect a High Witch's son to be."

"Oh, he is," Scarlett said, her eyes settling on Sorin, who was watching her carefully. "He is incredibly powerful. He created wards in the human lands with very little training."

Understanding dawned as he breathed, "Cassius."

She nodded at him as she continued. "We need to get him out of there. We leave in two days, but before we go, I need to visit Hazel."

Sorin's eyes widened as Cyrus exclaimed from his side, "You're going back to the Witch Kingdoms? We just got you out of there!"

Scarlett's eyes slid to Cyrus. "Rayner will tell you the High Witch was perfectly agreeable when I was there before. I really do not understand why there is so much fear of them." She reached casually for a cucumber sandwich and took a bite, while every one of the Fae in the room looked at her with disbelief.

It was Sorin who cleared his throat and ventured, "Scarlett, the Witches are notorious for swinging swords first and asking questions later. They do not hesitate to kill for the slightest offense. Not to mention they are incredibly powerful. The fact that you entered their lands without permission and left without even a scratch is unheard of. They have sent heads back without the bodies to prove outsiders are not welcome. I truly do not know how you did it."

"But she didn't even threaten me. She wasn't exactly pleasant, but she escorted me to the Oracle herself," Scarlett argued, taking another bite of her sandwich.

"Yes, but she addressed you as Majesty," Rayner cut in with his quiet, calculating voice. "She appeared to have already known you were a queen before you had even accepted it yourself. She would be a fool to attack a Fae Queen."

"Then I shall be safe this time as well," Scarlett countered.

"You cannot just go to the Witch Kingdoms, Scarlett. Going there requires weeks of correspondence and arrangements being made," Sorin said.

"I do not have that kind of time," Scarlett answered calmly. "She will see me."

"It is just not how things are done," Sorin countered.

She could hear the exasperation and frustration in his voice. She didn't care. She carefully set her half-eaten sandwich on a napkin before her, then she slowly met his stare. "I am not asking for your permission, Sorin." Her voice was low and sharp. The others in the room had fallen silent.

"What happened to everyone in this room having a say?" he bit back through gritted teeth. Turning to the rest of the table, he asked, "Who here thinks this needs more planning?"

"The Witch Kingdoms are unreliable and perilous," Eliza cut in. "It would be incredibly risky to go without an invitation."

"I am going," Scarlett said, finality ringing in her tone. "Yes, everyone here has a say, but everyone here is also free to make their own choices, including me."

"Then why even have this council?" Sorin seethed.

"Sorin, I cannot leave him there any longer! I need you to come to Baylorin with me, and I need you to be able to access your magic. The High Witch may be able to help with that." She stared into his golden eyes. She could feel everyone's eyes on them. "I do not make this choice to be brash and naïve. I make it because I need you with me when we go get Cassius… And when we face Mikale."

She had never spoken so plainly. She had never spoken so boldly of her needs. The Assassin Lord had drilled into her that to need was to show weakness. Never reveal your weaknesses. Better yet, don't have any. But she knew she could not face Mikale alone, not again. So she laid herself bare before him. She needed him, and she needed Cassius.

Sorin breathed out a heavy sigh. "Then I am going with you to the Witch Kingdoms."

She threw a knowing look at Briar, who was trying his best to hide the smile that played at his lips as he sat quietly beside her. "The Witches hate males, and I can't entirely say that I blame them when you get so fucking overprotective," Scarlett grumbled, crossing her arms and sitting back in her chair. At the narrowing of Sorin's eyes, she added, "I'll take Eliza and Neve with me if it will make you feel better."

"No," Sorin answered flatly.

"No?" Scarlett asked, with a tilt of her head.

"You are free to make your choices, my *Queen*, and so am I, according to what you just said. I will either go with you, or I will go on my own."

"Then I guess we are going on an adventure," Scarlett replied sweetly.

CHAPTER 45

CALLAN

Callan sat at their usual table in the library, waiting. She hadn't come to sit with him yesterday, and it appeared she wasn't going to be coming today either, seeing as it was nearing the time she usually left to get ready for dinner. Tonight was supposed to be their weekly dinner, but he wasn't holding his breath that she would show up at this point.

He had not seen her since their argument in the gardens. Well, that wasn't true. He had seen her that morning striding for the front gates. He had called after her, but she had hardly paused. And when he had tried to follow, terrifying panthers of shadows had snarled and snapped at him before they continued trailing her out of the palace.

Of course, Sorin had been allowed to follow her.

Callan ground his teeth together at the thought. He was always allowed near her. He was always allowed to brush her fingers or stroke her hair. Meanwhile, he had to evaluate every gesture and word these last few months.

Apparently, it didn't even matter anymore. She wasn't planning to stay in Baylorin. She was going to leave after she saved the orphans. And she would. She would save them all, and then she would disappear. Not into shadows, but into flames and ashes. Into the arms of a Fae prince rather than a human one.

Callan slammed the book shut that was before him, swearing.

"I didn't know you knew such language, Princeling," came a feminine drawl from behind him.

He turned in his chair to find Eliza smirking at him. She was in her usual attire, bedecked in her weapons. "What do you want?" he snapped.

"You are in a mood today," Eliza replied, sliding into the chair Scarlett usually occupied.

"Why would you deign to notice?"

Eliza clicked her tongue. "While your temper is cute and all, I reside with a prince whose temper literally elicits fire, so you don't really scare me."

"Is there a reason for your visit this afternoon? Or is it just to tell me about the amazing Fire Prince?"

Eliza studied him a moment before she asked cautiously, "Have you spoken to Scarlett today?"

"No. I tried to follow her, to speak with her, and she sent her panthers to stop me."

"Yes, those are new and quite terrifying," she mused with a grin of delight.

Callan shook his head. "You would get along well with those of the Black Syndicate."

Eliza's eyes snapped to him. "What would a prince know of the Black Syndicate?"

Shit. That was a secret that apparently had not been shared with Sorin's Inner Court. How much did they even know about Scarlett's past?

"I know the same as everyone else. It is where the darkest and foulest criminals and beings are trained and come from."

Eliza gave him a suspicious look. "Do you know anyone from the Black Syndicate?"

"Do you?" he countered.

"No. Your turn," she said with narrowed eyes.

When he did not reply, her eyes grew wide. "You do. You do

know someone from the Black Syndicate. That is a tale I would love to hear."

"Maybe someday I will share it with you," he replied coolly.

"Color me impressed, Princeling," she said as she shuffled through the books on the small table. "What exactly are you researching these days?"

"Those are Scarlett's," Callan answered tightly. "I have been reading up on the various territories."

"Learn anything interesting?"

"Yes."

When he didn't elaborate, the general lifted her eyes to his. "Anything you'd like to share?"

"Anything *you* would like to share?"

Eliza gave him an amused smirk, and she sat back in her chair, crossing her arms. "What would you like to know?"

"Does it matter? You will not answer my questions anyway."

Eliza gave a soft laugh. "I tell you what, Princeling. I shall give you a free pass. I will answer three questions today. As long as it will not reveal any secrets of my prince or queen or endanger this Court."

"No making me dig in a book first?"

"Would you like to dig in books first?"

Callan narrowed his eyes at Eliza, waiting for the other shoe to drop. Everything with the female had always been a trap or a test. "Is Scarlett avoiding me?"

"I don't know."

"Bullshit. You are friends. I saw you embrace her after her argument with Sorin."

"That was not an argument," the general replied as she reached for another of Scarlett's books. "That was a fight. A gigantic fucking fight."

"And they have…resolved their issues?"

She smiled slightly. "One could say that."

"Where is she today?"

Eliza flipped a page of the book she was looking at. "Today? She has been quite the traveler today."

"What does that even mean? She has gone down to the city? Is that where she was heading when she walked by the bridges?"

"No. That was not where she was heading, and the city is one place she has not been today."

"I thought you were going to answer my questions," he ground out.

Eliza flicked her gaze to him briefly before returning her attention to the book before her. "Today, human prince, Scarlett has been in the highest peaks of this mountain range, the formal dining room of this palace, the House of Water in the Water Court, and at this very moment, is in the Witch Kingdoms."

Callan nearly fell out of his chair. "She is where?"

"Was something I said unclear?"

The Witch Kingdoms. He had read about that territory. He wasn't sure which was more terrifying— the Witches or the Night Children. Having had the displeasure of interacting with Nuri a few times, he honestly couldn't say.

"Why would she be in the Witch Kingdoms?" he said slowly.

"She went to visit the High Witch."

"Why would Sorin let her go see the High Witch?"

At that question, Eliza stilled and slowly brought her eyes to his. "Sorin does not *let* her do anything."

"Did he at least go with her?"

"Yes. *That* was an argument, but she eventually relented."

"Thank the gods for that," he muttered.

"I've answered several questions for you today, Princeling. Now it is your turn," Eliza said, returning to the book before her.

"I did not agree to such terms."

"Then only answer if you wish. How long will you pine for her?"

"What?" he balked.

"Was my question confusing?"

"No."

Eliza waited, flipping pages slowly.

Callan sighed. "I cannot help that I love her. I cannot help that, despite having tried to move on, no one comes close to her. I cannot help that a part of me will always hope she will come to my side and become my queen."

"And what will it take to quell that desire?"

She did not look at him at the question. The general just continued to flip pages of that damn book.

"I suppose," he said through gritted teeth, "that should she marry another than my hopes will die."

"Where does she find these books?" Eliza asked suddenly, sitting straighter.

"I do not know. She has them with her when she arrives, but the last time… We went for a walk in the gardens and argued. She apparently did not come back for them," Callan answered.

"She has had a busy couple of days," Eliza murmured, half-listening as her eyes flew over the pages before her.

"What has happened?"

Eliza stood, her eyes still on the book. "If I know her at all, she will seek you out soon and explain everything. You truly do not know where she found this book?"

"No," he said slowly. "Why? What is it about?"

"Blood magic. Old, ancient, powerful blood magic." When she lifted her eyes to Callan's, her gray eyes were a storm of shock and terror. "She knows far more than she is letting on. She knows where they're coming from," she whispered, more to herself than him.

"Where who is coming from?"

"I must go, Callan. I am so sorry. I will find you later."

Callan could, once again, only stare as another female left him standing alone in the dark.

CHAPTER 46

SORIN

S orin gripped Scarlett's hand tightly as they stepped out of the air into the center of a tree grove. The skies were grey and stormy like they always were in the Witch Kingdoms. Every one of his senses was alert, and his fire crackled just below his skin. When they were alone, he had tried again to convince Scarlett they needed to wait to come back here, but she had insisted. They had instructed Rayner to send word if the summit day and time were set, and they would deliver the request to the High Witch while they were here.

He looked to his twin flame who stood beside him, bedecked in the witch-suit and witch-leathers that she had been given when she was here yesterday. How was that only yesterday? The witch-clothes seemed oddly fitting for her, though. The winds rustled and the hair on the back of his neck stood up. He thought of telling Scarlett again they should go and come back at another time, but the High Witch likely already knew they were here. The enchanted trees of the realm were as beautiful as ever…and delivered messages on the winds.

"Come on," Scarlett said grimly, starting to walk towards the castle that loomed before them.

Sorin tugged her to a stop with the hand he still gripped. "Come on where?"

She looked at him as if he were dimwitted. "To the castle, of course."

"We are just going to walk up to the castle doors?"

"How else will we find Hazel?" Scarlett asked, annoyance in her voice.

"She will find us," Sorin murmured, glancing around the clearing. Everything was still now. Even the winds had quieted. He strained his hearing.

"We don't have time to wait for her to find us," Scarlett hissed in a whisper.

"Then I apologize for keeping you waiting."

Sorin froze at the icy voice that came from behind them. He fought the protective urge to push Scarlett behind him as he slowly turned to face the High Witch. She wasn't alone. They were surrounded by Witches, all with black ashwood arrows aimed at their throats, as they stepped from the trees. It was the same way they were always greeted when they entered the Witch lands.

Do not shield, he warned Scarlett.

Why would I not shield against arrows?

Witches are powerful enchantresses. Those arrows will penetrate a shield easily, and they will view your shield as an attack and permission to kill.

You cannot be serious?

Sorin did not respond, and he felt Scarlett stiffen beside him, moving imperceptibly closer to him.

"Your Majesty," the High Witch said coolly with a low bow. The Witches surrounding them did not move. "You have come here twice in two days. Both times without invitation or warning."

The accusation and threat were clear in her tone.

He saw Scarlett raise her chin as she said, "Yesterday I was brought here by Shirina. Today I come of my own accord."

"Is it not rude to invite yourself into someone's home?" the High Witch asked in that ruthless, calm voice of hers.

"I apologize for the lack of propriety," Scarlett replied, "but I come on urgent matters that could not wait."

The High Witch was quiet, her eyes fixed on Scarlett, contemplating. Then they dragged to Sorin, who stared right back into those violet eyes, unwavering. "I see you have saved your twin flame," she said to Scarlett, her eyes still on Sorin. Witches rarely spoke to males. Not unless there was no other option. "I will meet with you, but not with him present. Males have no place in this meeting."

"She will not meet with you alone," Sorin snarled, his lip curling back.

"Do not speak to her," growled a black-haired, dark-skinned Witch to his right.

"Do not be rude, Arantxa," the High Witch said smoothly.

"While he is my husband and twin flame, he is also my Second and must be there as well," Scarlett interjected. "I cannot complete the task at hand without him."

The High Witch's eyes snapped back to Scarlett, and those violet eyes narrowed. "Stand down," she said shortly to the Witches, and they did so immediately. "Arantxa and Jetta, accompany us to the castle. The rest of you return to your kingdoms." There were flashes of light as the other Witches disappeared among smoke. "Come with me," the High Witch said, brushing past them. They fell into step behind her, Arantxa and Jetta taking up the rear, arrows still strung on their bows and at the ready.

They reached a room in the castle, and before they entered, the High Witch said, "Arantxa and Jetta guard the doors. No one comes in."

"You are going to meet with them alone? Here?" Arantxa blurted out.

"Are you questioning me?" the High Witch asked viciously.

"Of course not, Lady," Arantxa replied, bowing her head.

Sorin and Scarlett followed the High Witch into... Well, Sorin wasn't quite sure how to describe the room. It was unlike any other room he had ever seen in the Witch Realm. It was almost warm and inviting.

Almost.

There was a hearth on one wall with a sofa facing it. Bookshelves lined either side. On the other wall, there were a couple of comfortable looking chairs with a table between them. At the other end of the room, though, were bottles and cauldrons. Spices and ingredients lined shelves upon shelves along the back wall. It was almost as if it were a lab of some sort. The scents of rosemary and thyme and sage filled the air.

"This is your alchemy room," he breathed before he realized he was speaking. A Witch's alchemy room was sacred to her. It was a private area where others were rarely allowed, save for lovers. It was her sanctuary to hone and practice her craft.

"Yes," the High Witch snapped. She had tossed her cloak along the back of a chair and was back by the cauldrons, stirring one. "Very few others have been in this room, and only two others who were not Witches."

"My mother," Scarlett supplied, examining the books on the bookshelves.

Sorin's head snapped to Scarlett. "What?"

Scarlett winced at the realization that this was yet another secret Eliné had kept from him. A mixture of anger and sorrow filled him.

"Eliné was sworn to secrecy, Prince," the High Witch said tightly from across the room. "She was bound by ancient magic to never breathe a word of what happened when she was here."

"She was here more than once? With you? Alone?"

The High Witch cocked her head to the side, examining him. "I never understood why it bothered her so much to keep things from a male, especially a male who was not her lover. But seeing you here now, I suppose I can see it on a small scale."

"We rarely had dealings with the Witches while Eliné was queen. How often could you have seen her?" he demanded.

A smirk spread across the High Witch's face. "The *Courts* rarely had dealings with me, Prince. Eliné and I were close friends, sometimes closer than friends. She handled any affairs of the Witch Kingdoms personally." Before Sorin had a chance to reply to that, her eyes slid to Scarlett. "You are completely off your tonic now, I assume, judging by your ease of Traveling these days?"

Scarlett was leafing through a book she had plucked from the shelf, but she looked up with a curious expression on her face. "How do you know about my tonic?"

"I was the one who created it for your mother," the High Witch replied simply, sprinkling some sort of green powder into one of the cauldrons.

"You knew she was expecting a child?" Sorin asked incredulously. "You have known of her existence this whole time?"

Hazel studied him intensely for a long moment, as if debating if she should say anything further. "The queen was born here. I delivered her myself."

Sorin felt like he had been punched in the gut, the air sucked from his lungs. "How long?"

"Until they departed for the human lands shortly before she turned three."

"Three years? She lived here? While Talwyn struggled on the throne? For three years?"

"This is why I did not want you present in this meeting, Prince," the High Witch snarled through gritted teeth.

"It is how you knew who I was when I was here yesterday?" Scarlett asked softly.

"You look just like your mother," the High Witch said. "I nearly called you her name when I first laid eyes on you."

"Who is the other you've allowed in here besides my mother?" Scarlett asked, returning to skimming the book in her hands.

"Eliné," the High Witch answered, moving down her table to another cauldron.

Sorin was about to question such a bizarre answer when Scarlett stepped forward, gently closing the book in her hands. "Who is my father?"

"I do believe the Oracle told you the question you should be asking that will lead to the answer of that one," the High Witch replied, stirring a cauldron clockwise.

"Indeed," Scarlett murmured. She stepped forward again. "Hazel, please." A soft, sorrowful smile filled Scarlett's face. Sorin braced himself for the rage of the High Witch at being addressed by her name and not her title, but it never came. Instead, the High

Witch's features seemed to almost soften. "Sorin knows Cassius as well. They are friends. In the human lands, men are superior in every way. I will need him to help me get Cassius out."

Those violet eyes narrowed as the High Witch said, "You fear for his safety?"

"Yes," Scarlett answered quietly.

"If you have stopped taking the tonic, you can access your powers in any land, with or without that ring on your finger. You and your blood kin are some of the most powerful beings at this moment in time. You will not need the prince."

"I will, Hazel. I have a history there, and it is not a pleasant one. Furthermore, I have more than the task of retrieving Cassius while I am there, although that is the most pressing. In fact, I will need more than Sorin, and that is why I am here," Scarlett replied. Sorin resisted the urge to step to her side when she moved even nearer to the High Witch. "I would like to bring Sorin and his Inner Court with me to Baylorin, and I need them able to access their magic while there."

The High Witch turned back to her various concoctions and stirred one, bending down to sniff it. "There is a tonic that can do it, but it is much like the one you took, Young Queen. The body will become dependent on it and go through withdrawal if it is not taken. You will need to learn to brew it, and upon returning, they will not feel well. I trust you remember the process of expelling the tonic from your body? This one will be worse. The cost of gaining power is greater than the cost to deny it."

Scarlett glanced at Sorin with a grimace. "I understand. They will be able to choose when and how often to take it, but I am not an apothecary. Can you not make several doses to take with us?"

"Do you know precisely how long you will be gone? Exactly how many doses you shall need?" the High Witch asked, turning to the shelves of ingredients behind them. She reached up and pulled down several bottles of crushed herbs and powders.

"Of course not," Scarlett answered.

"Then that is not possible, is it?" The High Witch turned back to face them once more. Her violet eyes settled on Sorin, and to his surprise, she addressed him directly. "How much history does she know, Prince?"

"History of her lineage or history of the Witches?" he countered.

"Are they not linked?" she replied, her lips forming a thin line. When Sorin did not respond, the High Witch sighed sharply. She waved a hand, and a book floated from the bookshelf to them. Scarlett held open her hands as the book settled into them, flipping to a specific page. Sorin looked over her shoulder at an illustration of the various territories.

"As I am sure you are aware, the Avonleyans gave the Fae their magic in exchange for being a source of power to them," Hazel began.

"Yes, Sorin told me that much. He also told me that the Night Children are descended from the Avonleyans," Scarlett conceded.

"That they are. The Night Children may not have magic, but they are as strong as an Avonleyan and Fae in every other way, and become even stronger when they drink from either, which is why many sided with Deimas and Esmeray in the war. But, before the Great War broke out, the Avonleyans worried about their Fae kin on this continent as the Night Children grew restless, so they provided guardians for them."

Scarlett's head tilted to the side in question.

"The Witches and Shifters were created after a powerful Sorceress was captured and stripped of her magic as penance for her crimes. Her magic was gifted to the Witches and Shifters. The Witches were bonded to Queen Eliné, and the Shifters were bonded to Queen Henna. To maintain their dominance, however, the Avonleyans also granted such gifts to the Fae Queens, respectively."

Sorin's eyes snapped up to the High Witch. "Are you saying Scarlett possesses the powers of the Witches?"

"Can Queen Talwyn not shift and transform energy and physical matter?"

"My mother was a renowned Healer in the mortal lands," Scarlett whispered, studying the text before her.

"Eliné was very skilled in the craft," Hazel replied.

"You knew?" she asked, lifting her eyes back to the Witch's.

"We kept in touch. When she left here with you, two others went with her."

Scarlett's head cocked slightly to the side. "One has returned?"

"Yes. She is his cousin."

A look passed between the queen and the High Witch that Sorin could not read, and he had no idea who was being referenced.

"Here's what I do not understand," Scarlett mused after a moment. "Why did the Avonleyans give others their power at all? How did they even do that?"

"An excellent question, your Majesty," Hazel answered. "And one you would do well to figure out."

"You don't know, or you won't tell me?" When her question was met by silence, Scarlett asked another. "Do you know what Deimas and Esmeray sought so greatly across the sea?"

"What does anyone seek that could cause such a war? That could change the course of an entire world?" Hazel countered. "Power, of course."

"But the Avonleyans had dispersed much of their power by that point," Scarlett argued.

"Much, yes, but not all."

"You're as helpful as the Oracle," Sorin heard Scarlett mutter under her breath.

Silence fell in the alchemy room. The High Witch turned to her wall of ingredients and began pulling more bottles and pouches from it. Sorin's eyes were on Scarlett, though. Her head still down, studying the book.

Are you all right?

She lifted her eyes to his when she felt him and gave a subdued smile. *Yes? No? I don't know.* She sighed. *I'm just trying to figure some things out.*

Sorin moved closer to her and pulled her to him, kissing the top of her head. She settled into his side, and he breathed in her scent.

Thank you, drifted down the connection.

For what?

For insisting on coming with me.

Sorin flicked her nose playfully as he stared into those beautiful eyes of hers, getting lost in the ever-changing blues and golds. *I will cross the realms for you, my Love.*

There was a tinkling of vials. He had forgotten where they were, who they were with. Scarlett smiled sheepishly, a slight flush tinging her cheeks, and returned her attention to the High Witch. Hazel was studying them, a look of curiosity on her face. "I have only seen a true twin flame bond a handful of times," she said when they strode towards her. "Who sanctified your marriage?"

"A Healer in my Court," Sorin answered. "Beatrix."

"Ah," Hazel said, beginning to line up vials. "She is one of our Sages."

"What is that?" Scarlett asked, watching the High Witch closely.

"The Sages are the oldest of the Witches. They are wise and keep our history. We go to them for advice and instruction when needed."

"Do the Witches believe they have a twin flame?" Scarlett asked, walking to the work table.

"Some do," the High Witch answered, organizing more supplies atop the work space.

"And you?" Scarlett pressed.

"What difference does it make?" the High Witch snapped.

Scarlett shrugged. "Hoping something beautiful exists for you seems far better than believing it doesn't."

"Hope is for fools," the High Witch remarked.

"Hope is for the dreamers," Scarlett answered, picking up one of the vials from the table to examine it. "And you must be a dreamer."

"And why would you assume that?"

"Because you sent your son away to save him in the hope that he might have something different, something better than what you could provide him here. That sounds like a dreamer to me," Scarlett answered, meeting the High Witch's violet stare once more.

"I suppose it does," Hazel answered, and Sorin could swear a smile tugged at the corner of the Witch's thin lips.

Sorin could only watch in awe at this female beside him,

conversing so casually with the High Witch of the Witch Kingdoms. The last time he had seen the High Witch, he had come with Talwyn. To say the encounter had been confrontational was an extreme understatement. They had lost two soldiers on that visit, and the High Witch had all but thrown them out of the castle. Talwyn, in true fashion, had been livid, and relations with the Witches had been strained ever since.

Silence had fallen while Hazel worked, tossing various herbs and powders into a cauldron before her. It was just beginning to boil when Scarlett said tentatively, "Hazel."

"Yes?" the Witch replied, her voice tight, as if she were trying to be pleasant.

"If I bring Cassius here, he will not be welcome."

The High Witch froze. "The Oracle said when you arrived, it would be safe for him to return."

"I know what the Oracle said. She said it would be safe for him to return, but to return *here*, though? How will you explain him to your people?"

"That is not your concern," Hazel snapped, and Scarlett winced.

Sorin felt her brace herself as she said, "It is my concern. I will not bring him here if he is to be ostracized because he is a male. He was an outcast on the streets and has had to prove himself over and over again. I'll be damned if he receives such treatment here."

Hazel dropped the vial she was holding, and it crashed to the floor, shattering everywhere. "He grew up on the street?"

"He was an orphan, Hazel. He grew up on the streets until the Assassin Lord took him in and trained him. Then Lord Tyndell discovered him and brought him up in his home alongside his children. Even now, he is treated differently because he does not have noble blood. Do not make him come to a place where he will continue to be treated as such simply because he is male," Scarlett said gently, going around the table to pick up shattered glass.

"Did Eliné know him?" Hazel whispered.

"She did. She did not tell any of us who or what he is, but yes.

She knew him and loved him as if he were her own," Scarlett answered tenderly.

"I cannot leave him there any longer," the High Witch said, gripping the side of the table. "Every day I think of him. Every day I wonder if he is still alive, what he looks like. Every day I wonder who he is."

"I cannot leave him there any longer either," Scarlett replied, standing and cupping the glass shards in her hands. She stood toe to toe with the High Witch now, and Sorin tensed at her closeness. He had been so worried about realm politics and the proper way to do things. He had never let himself consider that maybe it wasn't the *best* way to do things. That just because things had been done that way for so long didn't mean they needed to continue on that way.

"He is kind and loyal and funny, despite growing up on the streets," Scarlett was saying to the High Witch.

"You care for him?" the High Witch said, raising her brows.

"My relationship with Cassius is one that cannot be put into words, my Lady. Our paths are intertwined. Sorin says he is my soulmate," Scarlett said. It was the first time Sorin had heard her address Hazel with any sort of reverent title. Flames flickered to life in her palms, melting the glass shards she still cupped into nothing. "I would give my life for him, and he would give his for me. Let me bring Cassius to *my* home, where you are welcome to visit him anytime until he can truly come home."

Sorin held his breath as the High Witch studied his twin flame. Fierce defiance sharpened her features, but also a longing just as powerful. "A queen would give her life for the son of a Witch?"

"Cassius is your subject and your son, and I will do as you wish, but please, Hazel," Scarlett begged, taking the Witch's hands in her own. "Please do not make him return to a place where he will be treated as less than. He has faced enough of that where he is now."

The High Witch held Scarlett's gaze a moment longer before she dropped her hands and turned back to the work table. "Do what you think is best, Child," she said, beginning to hand Scarlett herbs and bottles. "I am beginning to suspect that Cassius is much more than just your soulmate, and if I am correct, he will desire to be by your side rather than my own anyway."

Scarlett froze, her eyes snapping to the High Witch. "Cassius and I are not— We have never been—"

A faint smirk tilted the High Witch's lips. "I know you are not lovers, your Majesty." She glanced at Sorin. "If that were the case, I think your twin flame would be a much bigger threat to my son than my own people."

Sorin gritted his teeth at the mere idea of another touching Scarlett in such a way. He knew it wasn't logical. He knew what the relationship between Scarlett and Cassius entailed, but the newness of the twin flame bond flared through his body. He fought to keep back a snarl, and Scarlett shot him an amused look of knowing, clearly feeling his struggle.

I am finding a necessity arising, my Queen.

Scarlett's eyes widened slightly, and her cheeks flushed. It was his turn to send her an amused smirk.

Scarlett swallowed thickly, returning her attention to the High Witch and fumbling her words. "If you believe we are not lovers, then what do you think he is to me if not my soulmate?"

"Another excellent question, your Majesty. If I am correct, your destinies are indeed intertwined in ways you cannot even begin to fathom."

"Let me guess, you're not going to expand on that statement?" Scarlett grumbled, tossing powder into the cauldron at the High Witch's instruction.

If Talwyn had spoken to the High Witch like that, Sorin was fairly certain there would be bloodshed. Then again, the High Witch would have never let Talwyn into her alchemy room. Yet here was Scarlett, conversing with her as if they were long-lost friends. How bizarre the last few days had become. So many things he had thought were true and right had been tipped on their side and set alight by the mere act of a girl accepting a throne.

"If I were to expand on my statement, it could change things. The Fates would be displeased. You will know when you are meant to know," the High Witch replied simply.

"For the love of the gods," Scarlett muttered.

"For the love of the gods, indeed," the High Witch answered.

It was an odd retort, and Sorin wondered what she meant by it, but before he could question it, the High Witch began snapping detailed instructions at Scarlett about how to brew this tonic and all thoughts left his head as they got to work and began to put a plan into motion.

CHAPTER 47
SCARLETT

"I am not sure how excited the others are going to be to learn they are going to the human lands," Sorin said to Scarlett as she removed her witch-leathers in their rooms.

"They need a little more adventure in their lives. They're too pampered up here in this giant palace," Scarlett said dismissively, walking towards their enormous closet. She heard Sorin chuckle, and she poked her head back into the room. "I never did ask Hazel about these witch-suits."

After they had agreed that Cassius would come here instead of to the Witch Kingdoms, Hazel had set about showing Scarlett how to make the tonic. It was all common ingredients that could be found nearly anywhere.

"Tonics and elixirs are not so much about magic as they are about combining the right ingredients at the right time and under the proper conditions. But even more than that, it is knowing which ingredients do what to the body and how. Nature has provided everything one would need for healing and nourishment," Hazel had told her. "When you return, I will teach you properly. And Cassius."

She had sent them on their way laden down with several of the ingredients to get them by until they could purchase some in Baylorin. Shortly before they'd left, they'd received a message from Rayner that the summit time and location had been set. Hazel had agreed to attend, albeit reluctantly, only with the absolute assurance that Scarlett would be there and that she would not have to deal directly with Talwyn.

"What do they fly on? Broomsticks?" Scarlett now asked Sorin, leaning against the doorframe to the closet, unwinding her hair from its thick braid. She was exhausted after not sleeping the night before. The sun was nearly set, and she was looking forward to a hot bath and sleeping past sunrise tomorrow.

Sorin burst out laughing. "Broomsticks? Why would they ride around on broomsticks?"

She scowled at him. "That's what is said about Witches in the human stories."

Sorin only laughed harder. "You cannot be serious?"

Scarlett glared at him, but a small smile formed on her lips. She'd never seen Sorin laugh so hard. She'd never seen him so... happy, despite having to return to the human lands tomorrow.

After he had gotten his laughter under control, he crossed the room to her, unbuckling his own swords and daggers. They hadn't told anyone they'd returned, although she guessed his Inner Court likely felt them through the wards. They were not wanting company at the moment, though. No, all she wanted was a bed to sleep in.

"No, my Love," he said, walking by her into the closet, "the Witches do not ride around on broomsticks. They fly on griffins."

"On what?" Scarlett asked, turning to face him.

"Griffins," he answered, like she should know what he was talking about. He peeled his tunic from his chest and tossed it to the laundry bag in the corner. Noting the confusion still on her face, he said, "You know, half lion, half eagle beasts. Griffins."

This time, Scarlett burst out laughing. "Oh, come off it," she said between giggles. "What do they *really* fly on?"

An amused smile was on Sorin's face now. "The Witches fly on griffins, Scarlett. I swear it."

Scarlett stopped laughing, her eyes widening. "I want to see one."

"We do not have them here. Only the Witches have managed to tame them, if you can even call it that," Sorin replied. "When the territories were isolated, all the griffins were sent to the Witch King-doms because they were the only ones who seemed to be able to do anything with them."

"I won't believe you until I see one," Scarlett replied matter-of-factly, striding past him and bending down to unlace her boots.

"You will believe they fly around on broomsticks before you will believe they fly on griffins?" he asked. She felt him come up behind her.

"I suppose that's a valid point," she conceded as she stood once more. She turned to face him, reaching up a hand to his cheek. There was slight stubble there, and it rubbed at her fingers. "I am sorry my mother kept so much from you."

Sorin's eyes darkened a touch, and his own hand came to cup her face. "The thing that haunts me most about the things your mother kept from me is not the threat of what lies in the mortal lands, or the fact that she was with Hazel for nearly three years. It is that I could have found you so much sooner. I could have found you before…"

Scarlett's heart clenched as she felt his pain and regret. "Sorin, do I wish I had not experienced some of the atrocities I have? Yes, but somehow it all led me here. Somehow, it all led me to you. Even when I lay on a stone floor in a cold manor house believing all hope had been lost, it still led to you. It still led to us. I do not know that I believe in the Fates as you do, but I have to believe that something beautiful always comes from the heartaches we experience. I have to carry that hope that it's not all for naught."

A soft smile spread across Sorin's face as she stared into his golden eyes. "Hope is for the dreamers, Princess." He leaned in and kissed her softly.

"Darkness is for finding the stars, Prince," she murmured onto his lips.

Then he pulled back and said, "But can I make a request?"

"Hmm?" Scarlett murmured, still tasting him on her lips. Maybe the bath and bed could wait a little longer…

"I need to know that we will not keep things from each other. We cannot keep the secrets your mother did," Sorin said tentatively.

Scarlett snapped from her thoughts at his words. "I do believe, Prince, *you* kept dozens of secrets from *me* about my very existence." She stepped back from him slightly, her hands going to her hips.

"Valid point," Sorin said, crossing his arms across his muscled chest. She tried not to stare as those muscles rippled with his movements. "But to be fair, had you been more forthcoming about things when I met you, I would have figured out who you were a lot sooner, and it would have saved you a lot of trouble."

An unimpressed smirk formed on Scarlett's lips. "Are you suggesting I should have just shared intimate details about myself with a complete stranger who clearly disliked me when I first met him?"

Sorin sighed with acquiescence. "My darling, tenacious wife, from this point forward, there are no secrets between us. No hidden plans to surprise one another in other lands."

"Sorin Aditya," Scarlett said, stepping back to him and looping her arms around his neck. "I trust you with everything I am. After today, there is nothing I will keep from you. I swear it on the Fates."

"You do not believe in the Fates," Sorin said pointedly.

"Fine, I swear on my life," she answered with a roll of her eyes. "Is there anything else *you* need to share with me?"

"Not so much a secret, but something you need to know about me and Talwyn," Sorin ventured cautiously. Scarlett threw him a suspicious glare and stepped back once more. She leaned against the wall, crossing her arms across her chest, waiting for him to continue. He took a deep breath and leaned back against the dresser behind him. Bracing his hands on it, he said, "After your mother left, I went to see the Oracle. To see if she could tell me where your mother had gone." Scarlett's brows rose in surprise, but she said nothing. "I went to the Witch lands uninvited and begged the High Witch to take me to the Seer. I did not care if she killed me. I almost wanted her to at that point, but after I spent three nights in their dungeons, she took me there herself. Now I realize it was likely because your mother was there that I was spared."

"Cyrus didn't know you went? Or Briar?" Scarlett asked quietly.

"No one," Sorin said, shaking his head. "The Oracle, of course, did not tell me where Eliné had gone or why. She cut my palm and dripped my blood into a scrying bowl. After peering into it for a long while, she told me something that… I cannot even begin to describe how I felt. Terrified? Enraged? She told me that the daughter of a queen was my twin flame."

Scarlett's eyes widened. "You thought your twin flame was Talwyn."

Sorin shook his head. "I could not even fathom such a thing. I could not imagine ever loving her like that. I had watched her grow up. I loved her as my dear friend's daughter. Nothing more. The idea of her being my twin flame was horrifying. Even worse, Talwyn believed she had found her own twin flame. His name was Tarek. They had taken the Mark and were in the Trials. The rift between me and Talwyn? It is a great deal my fault. After visiting the Oracle, I did not know what to think. I believed her Trials would fail, and I hated that she was the person I thought I was supposed to love on such a level. I knew she would hate me if I ever told her. She loved Tarek with her entire being."

Scarlett's thoughts were racing as she replayed all the various interactions she'd seen between Sorin and Talwyn. "In the court-yard, she asked if your love for her died with my mother?"

"Of course, I knew by that point that *you* were whom the Oracle had meant, but yes. I completely understood why she said such things. I have never entirely hated her, but I have hated what I thought she was to me. Then we went on that mission to rescue your mother." Sorin ran a hand through his hair. "Gods, Scarlett, you may not blame me for the death of Eliné, but Talwyn does. And she blames me for the death of her twin flame because Tarek was on that mission as well. Talwyn had sent two with me, trusting that I had found her, and he was one that was… There is so much hurt and anger and conflict that could have been avoided. Things could be so different…"

424

Silence fell between them in that closet as he trailed off. Scarlett studied him, the sorrow and shame that lined his features. She swallowed thickly as she stepped to him. "An ancient immortal once told me that we make bad calls, but we can't change them. You deal with it. You learn from it. You become humbled by it. But you do not let it define you. You let it shape you." She ran her fingertips lightly along his cheek and down his jaw. "Just as I do not wish away the experiences that forged me, you must not wish these things away. They led us here. To this place. To each other."

"Careful, Princess," he said with a small smile. "It is starting to sound like you believe in the Fates."

Scarlett wrinkled her nose at the idea, and he laughed.

"We will go and get Cassius and find these keys and deal with Mikale. Then we will deal with my cousin," Scarlett replied softly, stroking her thumb along his cheekbone once more. Sorin's own hand came up and cupped her neck as he leaned down and kissed her. After a moment, she pulled back and, looking into those golden eyes, she said, "Rayner said that no one knows what the Oracle actually looks like. That she appears differently to everyone."

"That is true," Sorin replied.

"What did you see?"

"I saw you," he replied softly.

"What?"

"I thought it was Ashtine, actually. The silver hair, I suppose." He twined a lock of it around his finger. "Looking back, though, it was you. It has always been you," he said. She brought her lips back to his, and he deepened the kiss. She slid her hands along his bare chest, and his fingers fisted into her hair as he pulled her against him. "Again with this damn witch-suit," he murmured onto her lips.

She laughed, stepping back and disentangling herself from him. "I need a bath anyway," she said sweetly, tugging the witch-suit down her shoulders as she walked away from him.

"Still so wicked," he said, clicking his tongue.

She only laughed as she began heading to the bathing room, where she knew a steaming bath was waiting for her.

"In the interest of not keeping secrets though…" she trailed off, pausing by the closet door.

"What?" Sorin asked, his eyes narrowed at her.

"The Oracle is Cassius's cousin."

"What?"

The shock on Sorin's face made her grin like a mad woman. Maybe Briar was right. Maybe she did enjoy the grand reveal a little too much.

"That is not possible. The Oracle is centuries old. Cassius is…not."

"The Oracle, it seems, is replaced every millennium or so. When a new all-powerful Seer is born."

"And you think the Oracle is Cassius's cousin because…?" Sorin asked, doubt creeping into his eyes.

"Hazel told me tonight."

"When? When did those words cross her lips?"

Scarlett rolled her eyes. "She didn't come right out and say it. Two went with my mother to the human lands. Sybil and Juliette. When I saw the Oracle, it was Juliette. When I—" Scarlett swallowed. "When she died, it apparently released her essence or something, and she was able to return here and replace the previous Oracle. She had visions. In Baylorin, before everything. It's how she knew about me. Who I was. She shared the visions with Nuri. It's how Nuri knew."

"If Cassius and Juliette are cousins, that would make Sybil…"

"The High Witch's sister," Scarlett finished.

Sorin just shook his head and muttered, "I am going to bed."

Scarlett laughed as she made her way to the bathing room.

She emerged a half hour later, clean and exhausted, and more than ready to sleep and sleep and sleep.

When she approached the bed, though, Sorin lifted his head from his pillow. "Your shadows," he said softly.

She paused, smiling faintly as she pulled back the covers on her side. "What of them?"

"They are gone." He was staring at her in fascination.

426

She smirked, and a whorl of shadows snaked across the bed, caressing his cheek, before fading away into nothing once more.

"How?"

She had realized her shadows had disappeared while she had bathed in the mountain chalet early that morning. She could feel them hovering just beneath the surface, but they were no longer visibly swirling around her unless she commanded them to do so.

"I love my darkness, Sorin. It is beautiful, and I do not wish it away, but I only need it when I lose sight of the stars."

"You found the light?" She could see a soft smile on his lips as she blew out the candle beside the bed.

"I learned where to look."

"Oh?" he asked, propping himself onto an elbow to look down at her as she nestled in beside him.

"The brightest star always leads home."

CHAPTER 48

TALWYN

T alwyn Semiria stood in her chambers in the White Halls. She hadn't slept in days. Every time she closed her eyes, her dreams were filled with omens and terrors. Her chambers occupied the highest tower of the Halls. She had windows on all sides so she could see every direction. She looked out the northwest window now, towards the Fire Court. Things had not gone according to plan. No, things had not gone well at all.

When Talwyn had sent Sorin to the mortal lands to find his twin flame, her cousin, she had expected them to return and Scarlett to come here, to the White Halls. Then she had expected Scarlett to take up her place in the Black Halls to the south. She had expected there to be some sort of natural family kinship, some sort of immediate bond. Instead, there was fear that had turned to utter contempt.

Sorin had kept Scarlett from her. First, he'd kept her hidden, and now she resided with him. She knew they were twin flames, but she had still expected them to come *here*. Scarlett was a Queen of the Fae Realm. She should be in the Black Halls, not squatting in the Fire Court.

There was a slight breeze, and Ashtine stepped into the room. Talwyn turned to her friend with a frown. "You bring news?"

Ashtine crossed the room and sat gracefully in a chair near the window. "You were right," she replied in her mystical voice. "The mortal kings are gathering their forces to them, but where they are planning to position them I have not heard. Even the winds do not know."

Talwyn didn't reply, returning her attention to the window. There had been no signs of the immortals posing as humans in any of the other realms. Ashtine hadn't discovered any at least. Then again, they hadn't known they were in the mortal realm until Sorin made the claim at the meeting the other day. In a few weeks, if the other leaders agreed to attend, she would lead a summit, and hopefully they'd all realize the threat.

She had been shocked when Scarlett had sent word that Hazel would be attending. The High Witch had been a nightmare to work with. So much so, in fact, that she'd sent Briar or Azrael to deal with her the last few times. The soldiers she'd lost to the ruthless Witches still made her see red.

"I cannot possibly let her go back there right now, Ashtine," Talwyn said softly. "Not with so many unknowns there. She is not ready to face those."

Ashtine was quiet, contemplative. They had grown up together. Both young princesses, Ashtine of the Wind Court and Talwyn here. Ashtine's mother had been killed with the other Royals by Esmeray, and their friendship had only gotten stronger when Talwyn's mother was later killed. While Talwyn was quick-witted and fast to act in dire situations, Ashtine tended to sit back and take things in, likely because she was a Wind Walker and spent much of her time listening among the winds.

"I do not think you will be able to stop her," Ashtine finally replied. "She seems incredibly adamant about going back."

"Just because she is adamant does not mean it is the right move," came a male voice from the doorway.

Talwyn turned to find Azrael, stone-faced and somber.

"Precisely. I know these realms. I know how they work. I know the histories. She has barely scratched the surface," the queen replied.

"That may be true," Ashtine cut in. She was one of the few people who ever dared to interrupt her, and when she did, she spoke as if she didn't even realize she was doing it. "But she was raised in the human lands. She knows more about that realm than any of us. If she had to go to another realm, it is the one she should go to."

"But she does not *have* to go to another realm," Talwyn snapped.

"I cannot believe Aditya is letting her go back. You would think as her twin flame he would want to keep her from such dangers," Azrael said sourly, crossing the room to join them near the window. He said Sorin's name as if he were saying a vulgar word. Although to him, Sorin's name was such a word, Talwyn supposed.

"I would venture to guess that no one *lets* Scarlett do anything, and it is precisely because he is her twin flame that he is going with her," Ashtine replied simply.

"And leaving his Court behind after he just returned," Azrael grumbled under his breath.

"Briar will watch over it," Ashtine answered.

"Briar? Why not Cyrus?" Talwyn asked, her head snapping to her friend.

"Sorin's entire Inner Court is going," Ashtine replied. "Did you not know?"

"He will leave his entire Court defenseless?" Azrael demanded, his voice rising in disbelief. "You cannot allow this." He directed the last words at Talwyn.

Talwyn had turned back to the window, her eyes looking north-west again. "I do not have a choice, Azrael. She has claimed her Courts."

"And you just let her come in and take half of your lands?" Azrael snapped.

"They were never *my* lands to begin with," Talwyn retorted. Silence fell in the room. Then Talwyn said to Azrael, "Scarlett sent word that Hazel would attend the summit. Have we heard from Rosalyn or the Shifters?"

"Arianna and Stellan have said they would attend. I am still awaiting Rosalyn's reply," Azrael answered. He leaned against the wall now, his arms crossed over his broad chest.

"That does not surprise me," Talwyn replied. "Rosalyn has never left her realm. The last time a summit was called, she was not the Contessa."

"The last time a summit was called, none of the current leaders were in their positions," Azrael said grimly.

"And what of the mortal realm? Will they be represented at this summit?" Ashtine inquired airily.

"The mortals are the reason we are having this summit," scoffed Azrael.

"But they are directly affected," Ashtine replied. As she stood from her chair, she added, "I think you will find Queen Scarlett will want them represented as well." She tilted her head to the side, as if listening to something. "I must go." Then she was gone on a phantom breeze that swept through the chambers.

"I hate when she does that," Azrael ground out, still standing against the wall.

"You would think one would be used to it by now," Talwyn replied.

"It does not mean I have to like it when she leaves in the middle of such meetings," Azrael retorted.

"You are especially pissy today, Az," Talwyn said, throwing a glance at him. "You are not still upset about the information I withheld, are you?"

"You should have told me," he growled back.

"I told you, I did not want to say anything until I was sure," she snapped back. "You are just mad Sorin made you look like a fool."

"One would think as your Second you would tell me such things," he replied through gritted teeth.

"One would think as my Second you would stop questioning me," she snarled back.

The two Fae glared at each other for a moment, then Azrael's eyes narrowed. "When was the last time you slept?"

"I am fine," Talwyn sighed, her gaze returning northwest.

"You have dark circles under your eyes. You need to sleep, Talwyn. You have used great amounts of your magic these last few days," Azrael said, his tone softening a fraction.

Talwyn knew the rumors that surrounded them. She knew most suspected Azrael was her lover, and while they had their tumbles, it was more about distraction and release than any type of intimacy. She didn't know if she could adequately describe her relationship with Azrael to be honest, but he'd stepped up. When her aunt had left and Sorin had... She still couldn't say what Sorin had done. She had spoken truth when she'd spat at him that his love for her had died with her aunt that day in the courtyard. When she had been on the throne for less than a year, she was pulled to Shira Forst for the first time. Maliq had been there with Rinji and Nasima, and she'd known at that moment who her innermost circle would be. She'd sent Sorin away and gone straight to Azrael. It had been awkward for a while. She had still been learning. Azrael had been running his Court for decades. He'd had to adjust to Ashtine's odd tendencies.

But when Tarek had been killed, she had nearly lost her mind. Sorin had been too busy consoling Cyrus, and Ashtine didn't do relationships like normal people. Not knowing where else to turn, she'd gone to Azrael. The Earth Prince had merely blinked when she had stepped from the air into his Desert Alcazar. She had collapsed to the floor, sobs wracking her body. First her aunt had abandoned her, then Tarek had been ripped from her. And Sorin? He had been responsible for all of it. Azrael had immediately ordered everyone from the room. He had silently put his arms around her and held her while she cried. No words were ever spoken. She had cried herself to sleep and awoke in his bedroom chambers. He had been sitting at a desk across the room, going through various papers. As she sat up, he turned to her, and all she had said was, "We have work to do, Prince."

Since that time, they have been what they are. Since that time, he had come to know her better than anyone else, and not because they shared a bed every now and then. He knew when to push her and when to let her be. He knew the ins and outs of her moods. He had taught her the intricacies of her earth magic. He had helped her hone her Traveling skills, as he was the only other known Traveler in the Courts.

"What I need is a distraction," she said, finally turning to face him fully. She gave him a feline smile, but it did not reach her tired eyes.

Azrael merely gave her a pointed look and said again, "You need sleep." He jerked his chin to the bed across the room. Talwyn scowled at him, crossing her arms across her chest. Azrael studied her, his face turning contemplative. "Why won't you sleep, Talwyn?"

"There is much to be done," the queen said, waving her hand in dismissal and turning to leave her bedroom. Quicker than she could detect, Azrael closed the distance between them and gripped her wrist.

"Bullshit. Why won't you sleep?"

Those muddy brown eyes bore into her jade ones, and she glared at him. In a venomous whisper she hissed, "Because my dreams are not pleasant, and I fear they are not dreams at all."

Azrael pulled her to him, and she stiffened at the closeness. He began rubbing up and down her back, and seconds later she found herself relaxing into him. Her eyes grew heavy. "You will stay?" she asked softly after a moment.

"I shall not leave your side," Azrael replied, leading her to the bed. She was wearing black pants and her usual white tunic. As she crawled onto the bed, Azrael kicked his boots off and slid onto the other side of the bed, propping pillows behind his back. He pulled a book from a swirl of sand, then he said, "And when you wake, if you still need a distraction, I will be happy to oblige."

"Idiot," she muttered as he settled himself beside her. She was quite certain the otherwise always serious male only made jokes around her.

After a long silence, she said, "Sorin will keep her safe, right?"

"Sorin will give his life to keep her from harm, Talwyn. He is her twin flame," Azrael replied, his tone steely and tight.

"That's what I am afraid of," she replied.

She felt Azrael's fingers on her forehead as he began making long, relaxing strokes down her cheek, through her hair. "That Sorin will give his life for her?"

"That she will give her life for his," Talwyn whispered back as she closed her eyes and entered her dreams.

CHAPTER 49
SCARLETT

S carlett awoke in her chambers to find Sorin still sleeping peacefully, his arm draped protectively over her waist as it was nearly every night he slept beside her. She had fallen asleep quickly last night to Sorin making long soothing strokes down her back and side. Despite the uneventful and deep sleep she'd had that night, she still felt utterly exhausted. She could have slept for the entire day. She studied the sleeping male beside her. His face was softened in sleep, and for just a moment she let herself wonder what it would have been like to be just two ordinary people. To wake up like this every morning and not have a million responsibilities demanding their attention. To wake up and eat breakfast in their bedclothes and not have meetings and people to kill and children to save, but…

Queen.

Prince.

Mortal kings.

Fucking Mikale.

Careful to not wake Sorin, Scarlett sat up thinking she would sneak down to the chamber beneath the library and gather some books to bring with her to Baylorin. She'd need to be fast. Sorin would wake soon.

Silently, she set her feet on the marble floor and hissed at the cold. Fire Prince indeed. A dark shadow drew her attention to the corner where Shirina was sitting, her tail switching behind her, those silver eyes glowing.

Scarlett closed her eyes, inwardly groaning. After the secret chamber, she had planned to meet with Callan this morning to explain everything, and let him know he was going home. She slid gracefully from the bed, grabbing a silk robe from the end and putting it on over her nightgown. She padded silently to the panther, coming to a stop in front of her and crossing her arms. "If I touch you, you're taking me somewhere, aren't you?" she whispered to the giant feline. She had to be nearly twice the size of a normal panther. Shirina just cocked her head to the side as all felines had a tendency to do. "I'm changing first this time, you overgrown cat."

Scarlett quickly changed into some charcoal gray pants and a tunic of the same color with fine silver thread throughout it. She slid on her witch-boots and witch-leathers, strapping various weapons to herself. She slid the Spirit Sword down her back as she came back into the bedroom. Shirina stood when she entered.

Scarlett glanced at Sorin, who was stirring. Oh, he would be livid when he woke and found her gone. Shirina gave a growl, and Scarlett knew it for what it was— a warning that he could not come. At the sound of the growl, though, Sorin's eyes flew open.

"I'm sorry," was all Scarlett had time to say as she reached for the panther.

"No!" Sorin roared, his eyes wide with fury and terror, as Scarlett was pulled through a rip in the world.

SORIN

He couldn't feel her. He threw himself down that bridge farther and farther, but he couldn't find her.

Scarlett!

He screamed her name over and over down the connection. He stormed from their chambers, flames licking at his body as his leathers and weapons appeared on him.

How could he not feel her?

A fire portal appeared before him, and he stepped through directly into the White Halls, right outside the doors to Talwyn's private chambers. Flames wreathed his wrists and trailed behind him. He pounded on the door, yelling her name.

The door opened, and he was face-to-face not with Talwyn, but Azrael Luan.

The Earth Prince gave him a sneer. Sorin bared his teeth and snarled, "Where is Talwyn?"

"Not here," Azrael growled back.

"Then what are *you* doing here?"

"I was meeting with the queen before she had to go," Azrael replied with deadly calm.

"Where did she take her this time?" Sorin spat.

"What are you talking about?" Azrael glowered, stepping from the rooms and closing the door behind him.

"Shirina. Talwyn sent that panther to her once before, and she was taken to the Witch Kingdoms. Where did she send her this time?" Sorin breathed, using every ounce of self-control not to throw the male before him against the wall.

"I do not know," Azrael ground out between gritted teeth.

Sorin huffed a laugh in disbelief. "These damn queens and their secrets." He hurled a ball of flame into the wall of the Halls, leaving a scorch mark against the gleaming white marble.

"Enough, Aditya," Azrael snapped, and Sorin whipped his head to him at his tone. He seemed almost nervous.

"Where is Talwyn?" Sorin asked slowly.

"I do not know," Azrael snarled. "I woke her when Maliq

appeared in the room. She walked over to him and when she touched him—"

"He took her somewhere," Sorin finished. "She did not seem to know where she was going?"

"I do not think she was planning to *go* anywhere," Azrael replied, his voice clipped and short. "She grabbed a dagger from her nightstand, but she was in casual clothing. She did not even have boots on."

The two males walked down the stairs to the meeting rooms. Sorin reached up to send fire messages to his Inner Court and Briar at the same moment Azrael sent sand swirls up to his own Inner Court. Ashtine stepped from the winds a moment later directly into their path.

"This is a sight never before seen," she said curiously, observing the two males. Sorin had always found Princess Ashtine different to say the least, but she was astute and unrivaled in her stealth. As a Wind Walker, she knew the secrets carried on the winds, and his wards were carefully crafted to keep her from hearing things from his own home.

"Do you know where the queens are, Ashtine?" Azrael asked, ignoring her comment.

"I do not."

The three continued down to the council rooms, and when they entered, they found their Courts and Briar with his own, presumably having stopped to bring the Fire Court with him. Nasima flew into the room, settling on Ashtine's shoulder. A moment later, a male stepped to her side from a whirlwind portal. Ermir, Ashtine's Second in the Wind Court. Ermir rarely joined them at meetings. While the princes always attended matters with their Seconds, Ashtine never did. She didn't need to. The winds warned her of threats well before anyone could get near her. The fact that she had summoned him made Sorin's stomach drop.

"What is going on?" Briar asked, as the whirlwind snapped shut. He addressed the room, but his eyes were fixed on Ashtine.

"The queens are missing," she replied simply, as if the matter required no further explanation.

"What do you mean they are missing?" Eliza snapped from beside Cyrus. Eliza had little patience for anyone, let alone Ashtine and her peculiarity.

"She means," Sorin cut in before Ashtine could give a reply that was sure to piss Eliza off even more, "that the queens were taken somewhere. Shirina appeared in our chambers about twenty minutes ago and took Scarlett somewhere."

"And Maliq did the same to Talwyn," Azrael added.

"The Witch Kingdoms?" Cyrus asked, raising a brow.

Sorin shook his head, "I cannot feel her there."

"You have heard nothing?" Briar asked, again addressing Ashtine.

She tilted her head as if listening to something, then replied, "Nothing. The winds do not know."

"They cannot have just disappeared," Azrael snarled. He turned to Sorin. "You are the one with the twin flame. Can you not locate her?"

Sorin bared his teeth at the Earth Prince. "I cannot feel her in the territories. I cannot feel her anywhere." His eyes settled on Rayner, who merely gave a nod of his head, and disappeared into smoke, understanding the silent command to comb the lands for her.

"Because they are not in the territories." Ermir's voice was calm and prudent. "Not the lands of this continent, anyway."

Everyone turned to the Wind Court male. Well, everyone but Ashtine, who continued her queer listening to things no one else could hear. She walked to the window, allowing her Second to speak, as though she already knew what he was going to say.

Ermir was one of the oldest of all of them present. He had been young when Ashtine's parents had ruled the Wind Court and had also served in Queen Henna's Inner Court. He had silver hair, the color of Ashtine's and Scarlett's, and he was just as discerning and clever as the Princess.

"Where are they if they are not on the continent?" Azrael demanded. "Why would Sorin not be able to feel his twin flame?"

"Because the Darkness has powers of its own. Powers that can

439

stifle such connections," Ermir replied. His tone was neither grave nor grim. It just was, as if he were stating the weather.

Sorin's blood ran cold at the words, though.

"Are you suggesting they are across the seas?" Briar asked in disbelief.

"Possibly," Ermir said, considering. "Possibly not."

"Where else would there be Darkness?" Azrael snapped.

"Darkness is everywhere, of course," came Ashtine's lilting voice from near the window. "Queen Scarlett walks with it in her wake much of the time."

"I swear to Silas," Azrael seethed. "The two of you need to stop with the fucking riddles and give us answers. The queens of the Courts are missing. We do not have time to sit here and listen to the two of you talk in your Wind Court perplexity."

For once, Sorin had to agree with Azrael.

Ashtine merely studied Azrael, those sky-blue eyes calculating. Ermir had gone silent, stepping to his princess's side, hand within casual reach of his weapon.

Briar stepped before her, his back to the rest of them. "I think what everyone is trying to say, Ashtine, is that time is of the essence here. If the queens are in trouble, we need to know where they are so we can aid them."

A small smile formed on her lips, and as she spoke, her eyes stayed fixed on Briar. "Darkness exists everywhere, in every world, and on every plane."

"Every plane?" Briar pressed. He had always been the one, other than Talwyn, who could speak to Ashtine without losing his mind in frustration. Everyone had gone silent as they let Briar and Ashtine converse.

"You did not think there was only one, did you?" she asked, cocking her head to the side quizzically. When Briar did not answer, she continued, "The planes overlap each other. They are the spaces between the worlds. The planes are how the Spirit Animals can travel among the territories. They travel along the Spiritual Planes. But there are others. The Darkness waits there, in the places between the stars, patiently waiting to be let in when one opens a door."

"So you are saying Shirina and Maliq could have taken them to another plane, and that is why Sorin cannot find Scarlett through their twin flame bond?" Briar asked tentatively.

"If a door was left open, the Spirit Animals would know and would have come to collect one of the beings in this world who can close the door before the Darkness can come through," Ashtine replied.

CHAPTER 50
SCARLETT

S carlett found herself standing on rocky ground amidst a forest of trees. It was cold, and there was a thick fog that made it impossible to see more than three feet in front of her. She pulled a dagger from her hip and looked down at the panther beside her.

"The Forest? Again?" she murmured quietly.

It was silent here. No birds. No other animals. No wind to make the leaves rustle. Just utter, eerie silence. She began walking slowly forward, feeling down that bond for Sorin, but she felt nothing. She tried to Travel as she had done a few times now, but she either hadn't mastered that enough, or she couldn't access that magic here. Shirina was just as silent by her side. At least the panther was here. Although she wasn't entirely sure why she found that comforting. Every time the panther showed up, some startling new information was revealed.

She found a path that wound between the trees and began following it, but the sound of snapping branches and twigs had her whirling to her left. She palmed her dagger as a giant black wolf stepped from the fog along with Talwyn.

"Where have you brought me this time, cousin?" Scarlett asked, her voice low and steely.

"I did not do this, Scarlett," Talwyn replied. She sounded exhausted, as if she hadn't slept in days. "Furthermore, while I know I said I sent Shirina to take you to the Oracle, it was more of a suggestion. She responds to very few."

Scarlett straightened as she took in the queen. She was barefoot, wearing only black pants and a white tunic. Other than the dagger she was holding, she didn't have any weapons on her. She'd never seen her in anything other than her brown pants, white tunic top, and armed to the teeth.

"Maliq brought you here?"

Talwyn merely nodded once. "Although a warning would have been nice, so I could have at least put on boots," she grumbled.

"You grabbed a dagger, but didn't put on boots?" Scarlett asked doubtfully.

"You will come to find that when your Spirit Animal comes to you, it is generally wise not to waste time in accompanying them," Talwyn replied haughtily.

The black wolf had trotted over and sat beside the panther. Jade and silver eyes watched the two cousins.

"What do they want?" Scarlett asked Talwyn.

"I do not know," she answered, her tone slightly resentful.

"I'm assuming we're in Shira Forest?" Scarlett tried again.

"No."

"No?"

"I am unsure where we are," Talwyn snapped, stomping past Scarlett. "I was hoping you would know."

Scarlett turned to follow as she began making her way down the path. "Why would I know where we are?"

"I said I was *hoping* you would know. Apparently, that hope was misplaced. We are here to learn something," Talwyn said. Maliq and Shirina had taken the lead now. "What has the Fire Prince told you of the Spirit Animals?"

Scarlett sheathed her dagger as they continued to follow the animals ahead of them. "That they are a bond between a person and one of the gods. That they are a guide of some sort for those to whom they are bonded."

"Yes and no," Talwyn said, shaking her head. "Yes, they are linked to us and aid us, but they have their own purposes for their true masters."

"The gods," Scarlett supplied dubiously. Their pace had slowed as they'd come to the edge of the trees. There was only rocky waste-land before them now, and they stopped as they stepped from the cover of the trees.

"Yes, the gods. There is something we are meant to learn here. Maliq taking me to the Oracle is how I learned of you," Talwyn replied simply.

"And it is unexpected that Lady Celeste brought you here," said a cool, calculating voice from behind them.

The queens spun around to find the beautiful man standing behind them. His shoulder-length silver hair was tied back, and the eagle perched on his shoulder. He was completely in black, as he had been every other time Scarlett had seen him, and his silver eyes went straight to her.

Talwyn had her dagger cocked to throw as she said with a snarl, "Who the fuck are you?"

"Relax, Fae Queen," the man drawled. "I will not hurt you this time."

This time?

Oh gods. Scarlett flashed back to a dream months ago. A dream where he had been there, and Talwyn had been chained to a wall, screaming in pain. She had screamed Sorin's name.

Talwyn's face was visibly paler as she watched the man, and Scarlett found herself stepping in front of her.

"It's been a while," she said casually to the man. "My dreams are not entertaining enough for you as of late?"

A smile twitched on the man's lips, but never completely formed. "Has it ever occurred to you that perhaps I have other things to do besides make appearances in your dreams?"

"No, not really," she answered.

"Who the fuck are you?" Talwyn demanded once more, stepping back to Scarlett's side. The fear was gone, replaced by lethal rage.

The man merely glanced at her before returning his full attention to Scarlett. "Walk with me, Lady of Darkness."

"Where are we?" Scarlett asked, coming to his side.

Maybe she hadn't actually woken up. Maybe this was a dream after all, and she would soon wake, Sorin beside her.

"This is real," the man said, seeming to read her thoughts. "And you are right. You have nothing to fear from me."

"I have to disagree with that statement," Talwyn muttered, having come to Scarlett's other side.

"*She* has nothing to fear from me," the man said. Then with a shrug, he added, "Others are not so lucky when I need to get her attention."

"You have my attention now," Scarlett said, before Talwyn could retort. "And this is the most chatty you've ever been, by the way."

"We had to…get to know each other first," he replied. "But to answer your original question, we are on a spiritual plane for lack of a better explanation. Think of it as a space between worlds."

"Between worlds?"

"There can be other lands, but not other worlds?" the man asked simply.

"Well, I suppose so…" Scarlett trailed off. Maliq and Shirina had taken up the lead again, and she couldn't help but wonder at the sight of panther and wolf trotting down a path side-by-side. As they rounded a corner, they came to a clearing, and Scarlett halted. It was the clearing where she had seen Callan reading the first time. Her heart stopped and her stomach lurched.

"Are we in Baylorin?" she breathed.

"No. We are in the spiritual plane nearest that land, though. For you to see," he answered. He pointed, and there, in the exact spot the prince had fallen asleep reading, the air seemed to shimmer.

Scarlett walked closer, examining the spot. It was as if there was a true rip in the air. It was how the screens looked when she Traveled. She reached to touch it, but cool fingers stopped her.

"What is it?" Talwyn asked, walking around the glimmer slowly.

445

"Indeed," was all the man said.

An icy wind blew through the clearing. The eagle at the man's shoulder let out a sharp cry, flapping into the air. Scarlett jumped at the sound. The man stiffened and drew the dagger from Scarlett's side. He slashed his palm and then reached for Scarlett's. She jerked back from him, but Shirina was behind her, nudging her forward.

"You must go," the man hissed. "But there is more you need to know. This will help you remember."

Shirina was nudging her hand, and the winds were picking up.

"Fae magic cannot be found here," Talwyn called over the gusts. "I cannot touch my magic here."

"Neither of you can," the man said, reaching once more for Scarlett's hand. He slashed her palm and allowed his blood to mix with hers. Dipping his finger into the mixed blood, he yanked down the collar of her tunic. The Mark was two inverted triangles, with a swirl between them and two stars at either end. It flared bright white before settling in silver white against her skin, just like the stars on her forearm.

"You are doing well, Lady of Darkness," he said. Scarlett could have sworn there was fondness in his eyes. "Finish the Trials, find the keys, and come home."

"Come home?"

But the eagle screeched again, and the man turned to the queens. "You must go. You cannot be seen here."

"Be seen here? In a spiritual plane?" Talwyn asked doubtfully.

"What did you mean 'come home'?" Scarlett demanded again.

But silken fur brushed against her hand, and she was pulled into nothingness.

CHAPTER 51
SCARLETT

Shirina and Maliq brought the queens to a large room, and Scarlett turned in a slow circle, taking it all in. There were windows on every wall, and you could see in every direction. There was a large four-poster bed towards the other end of the room. Half of the sheets were thrown back as if they'd just been slept in. A book was face down and open on a page on the other side of the bed.

Scarlett's gaze landed on Talwyn to find golden light emanating from her palms while she slowly raised them, and she could feel the zing of wards going up around the room. "I suspect your twin flame shall be pounding on the door momentarily," Talwyn said harshly, walking towards what Scarlett assumed was a dressing room.

"These are your private chambers?" Scarlett asked, taking in the bookcase along the wall and the desk neatly organized near it. She walked to the window and looked out to see they were high above the ground in a tower of some sort.

"Yes," Talwyn replied, emerging from the dressing room a moment later in her usual brown pants, white tunic, and boots. There was a swirl of wind around her, and she was bedecked in her weaponry. "If you would bother to reside where you are meant to in the Black Halls, you would find similar accommodations there."

Scarlett ignored the comment as she walked to the bookcase and began running her fingers along the spines.

"Who the hell was that man?" Talwyn seethed, her voice low and dangerous.

"I don't know."

"Seemed like you two knew each other pretty fucking well," Talwyn countered.

Scarlett was about to explain she'd only ever seen him in her dreams when there was a pounding on the door. "Scarlett? Are you in there?"

The door handle rattled, and Sorin banged on the door again.

"I told you. Her wards are up. You will not get in," came Azrael's growl.

"She is fine, Prince," Talwyn called, annoyance ringing in her tone. Turning back to Scarlett, she hissed, "Who is he?"

"I don't know. I've only seen him in my dreams, and he only recently started talking to me. I—"

More banging on the door interrupted her.

"I am fine, Sorin," she called to him.

"I will not believe it until I lay eyes on you," he shot back through the door.

Oh, he was furious all right.

"I think we should focus on what he actually showed us there," Scarlett said, returning her attention to Talwyn. "That glimmer or rip or whatever it was."

"It definitely looked like a rip. Like a Traveling tear but much more powerful," Talwyn confirmed.

"What could tear a plane apart like that?" Scarlett asked as she went back to scanning the bookshelf

"I do not know," Talwyn replied grimly. "And it begs the questions of whether or not there are more of them, and how we are to close them." Scarlett was silent, listening to Talwyn ponder and muse. She was only half-listening at this point until Talwyn said, "You cannot go to the mortal lands, Scarlett."

Scarlett's blood was instantly boiling, rage flashing in her eyes. "This has already been decided, and last I checked, you still do not give me orders," she said, her own tone venomous and low.

"We need to figure out what that rip is and how to close it," Talwyn argued, her tone just as lethal.

"Scarlett…" Sorin's tense voice came from the other side of the door. He must have felt her rush of fury.

"Maybe you can figure that out while I am gone," Scarlett snapped back to Talwyn, ignoring Sorin.

"Your place is here," Talwyn snarled. "Not traipsing around the mortal lands looking for human friends."

Flames of pure white appeared around Scarlett's wrists, and the temperature in the room plummeted. "I did not get the luxury of growing up in these halls, Talwyn," Scarlett said, her voice deathly quiet. "*I* grew up in the shadows and darkness with my sisters." Her shadows seeped into her flames, casting the room into a shadowy glow.

Talwyn's eyes glittered with challenge as her bracelet unfurled and winds blew papers from her desk. "No," she spat back, her tone sharp as a dagger's edge. "You got to run around the human territories without a care for the rest of the world while I was shoved onto a throne to manage a war I knew nothing about."

"Talwyn, take the wards down." This time the voice was Azrael's.

"You are blaming *me* for not being in a land I didn't know I was meant to be a part of? And what war? The war has been over for centuries," Scarlett cried, frost spiderwebbing up the windows. "Do you know what I endured in Baylorin?"

"No, cousin, nor do I really care," Talwyn replied with a sneer. "You apparently have mortal friends worth risking everything to go back for. *I* was completely alone. Your twin flame saw to that."

"Talwyn!" Azrael shouted from the other side of the door. There was a note of panic that Scarlett was surprised to hear from the Earth Prince.

"Oh yes, you were so alone here in these halls," Scarlett retorted bitterly, pulling the Spirit Sword from her back. Flames of white wreathed the blade, and Talwyn raised her whip while pulling a dagger from her side. "You were so alone with a mother and then an aunt while you grew up. With Sorin here and your own twin flame and Azrael. You were all alone, weren't you?"

"Talwyn!" Azrael and Sorin cried together from the other side of the door.

Scarlett felt the wards lower, but Talwyn didn't move a muscle, and Scarlett could appreciate the power and control despite the rage surging through her. The males burst through the door, stopping short as they took in the scene before them.

"Scarlett." Sorin's voice was low, like he was trying not to spook a skittish dog in an alley. "Scarlett, put the sword down. We will go home."

"*This* should be her home. The Black Halls should be her home," Talwyn cried, whirling to face Sorin. "It wasn't enough for you to take my aunt and Tarek from me and then abandon me. You had to take *her* from me, too? How dare you even speak his name, let alone to *her*."

Sorin froze, his eyes wide, his face paling slightly.

Scarlett lowered her blade as she looked between her twin flame and her cousin. The guilt that roiled across Sorin's face was enough to crush her, but to hear Talwyn's own anguish...

"Get out," Talwyn spat, crossing the room to the door. Azrael came to her side, his face hard and unforgiving. "Both of you." She leveled her gaze at Scarlett on those last three words.

"Talwyn." Azrael's voice was grim beside her. "There is a full council room downstairs waiting for information."

Talwyn's jaw feathered as she gritted her teeth. "Fine," was all she said, striding from the room, and Azrael trailing her out. Scarlett could hear her murmuring to Azrael, but even with her new Fae hearing, she could not make out what they were saying.

Scarlett moved to follow, but Sorin stepped into her path, gripping her shoulders. "You are truly all right?" he asked, his golden eyes sweeping her body for any sign of injury.

Scarlett's face softened, and she brought her hand to his cheek. "I am fine, Sorin." She rose up to her tiptoes and brushed a kiss to his lips. He didn't say anything in response as he pulled her to him and wrapped his arms around her. He kissed the top of her head, and Scarlett murmured into his shoulder, "The mother hen thing has really got to go."

She felt him huff a laugh against her hair, and he drew back, looking into her eyes. "I understand that you stepping into the role of queen will require you to do things without me by your side at times, but when I couldn't *feel* you down the bond... Not only are you my wife and twin flame, you are my queen. I will always worry when I cannot be with you. Always."

Scarlett, not knowing what to say, just brushed her fingers along his cheek once more and murmured, "So fussy."

Sorin flicked her nose as she took his hand tightly in hers and let him lead her from the room.

TALWYN

They were only a minute or two behind her, but Talwyn had to swallow down a snarky comment when Sorin and Scarlett entered the council room, hand in hand and eyes on each other. It had been an age since all the Inner Courts had gathered in the White Halls. Had she known that Scarlett was going to be brought to the plane as well, she would have warned Azrael. She would have anticipated the panic of both queens going missing for a period of time.

Talwyn, however, was used to Maliq showing up and taking her to unknown places. Most of the time, no one knew she was gone. Azrael was sometimes there when Maliq would show up, but she had always played it off as though it had been planned. Sorin had likely come straight here upon realizing Scarlett had again been whisked away by Shirina, thinking she commanded the animal to do as before. Sorin's panic would have alerted Azrael. And this, she thought, staring broodingly from the head of the table at all the Fae gathered in her home, is the godsdamn result.

Ashtine was seated to her left, looking at her with that peculiar expression she always had on her face. Talwyn was used to it by now, and it didn't faze her as it did others. Azrael was to her right, as always. When they had walked to the council room, he had only murmured, "You are all right?"

"Fine," she had replied curtly, and Azrael had fallen quiet. He studied her now, his earthy brown eyes seeing right through her walls, and she ground her teeth together. She felt like she was only half present while she and Scarlett told the others about the plane they were taken to and the rip in it that they saw. She waited for Scarlett to mention the man, but she never did.

Talwyn kept the same slightly annoyed look on her face that she always did. Her jade eyes glowed sharply and her lips pursed. No weakness was ever shown. Not in front of the Courts.

"And we do not know how many of these rips there are or where they go?" Neve was asking across the table.

"No," Talwyn replied, her tone clipped. Neve fell quiet, throwing a look to the rest of the Water Court.

"Can it be closed?" came Eliza's sarcastic drawl.

Talwyn gritted her teeth harder. She hated when they were there. At least Azrael's Inner Court rarely spoke a word, letting their Prince handle everything. When Briar and Sorin brought their Inner Courts, they were allowed to speak at will. It's not that she didn't value such input, but there were so many people, so many voices. "I imagine that is why Scarlett and I were taken there," Talwyn replied tightly. Gods, her temper was barely leashed at this point. She needed to get out of this room. Away from everyone. She needed to get out.

"But how?" This time it was Sawyer from Briar's right.

Talwyn felt her lips form a thin line. Everyone was looking at her.

When she had first learned of Scarlett, she had felt a deep sense of relief. She wouldn't have to bear the burden of ruling alone any longer. She had never once felt threatened by the idea of ruling together. And yet here she sat, everyone still looking to her for answers. Here she sat, still a baby in Fae years, ruling entire lands and being expected to know the secrets of the world and its gods. Here she was, shoved onto a throne she wasn't prepared for, with magic she had mastered and somehow still barely controlled at times.

That leash on her temper was so taut now, her power roiling just beneath the surface. Lightning was crackling at her fingertips under the table. She felt a vine wrap around her wrist and glanced down to see little purple flowers sprouting from it. Her eyes slid to Azrael, his eyes slightly narrowed and fixed on her. To anyone else, he looked like he always did— a scowling bastard. But to her, she saw the tensed shoulders preparing to intervene if she lost control.

"I do not know yet," Talwyn replied, the restraint sounding in her voice. "But I have ideas I will be looking into as soon as we are done here. However, I do believe our new queen likely has more insight than I do."

Fuck it. If Scarlett wasn't going to bring up their guide on that little adventure, she sure as hell would.

All eyes swung to Scarlett, who was now glaring at Talwyn from the other end of the table.

"Always so chatty, cousin," Talwyn went on. "And now you have nothing to say?"

Scarlett tilted her head to the side as if contemplating, and godsdamn Sorin stepped in. "Maybe you could explain why you think she knows more than she is letting on?"

Talwyn settled back in her chair and summoned a cup of tea, holding her cousin's stare. She could see the challenge in her eyes, daring her to speak on this further.

She'd faced far scarier things than her.

She took a sip of her tea and said, "We were not alone in the plane we visited. We had a guide. A man that your queen apparently knows very, very well. A man bonded to Altaria."

Sorin's head whipped to his queen. "Who?"

Scarlett's teeth were clenched, and Talwyn recognized that she was working to control her own temper. That her rage was leashed

453

as tightly as Talwyn's own was. She merely sent her a sweet smile and sipped her tea once more.

Scarlett let out a deep breath. "As I have already told Talwyn, I do not know who he is."

"You certainly conversed with him as if you knew him. You recognized him as soon as he made his presence known," Talwyn retorted. If Scarlett wasn't going to tell her what she needed to know to protect her people, she'd get every godsdamn person in this room on her side.

"How many times have you seen him? Who is he?" Sorin demanded, turning back to his wife.

"I do not know who he is," Scarlett reiterated. "He's been in my dreams in the past."

"Mikale?" Sorin asked sharply.

Scarlett shook her head. "No. I mean, he's been in those dreams, too, but as an observer. He's only spoken to me a few times. I do not know who he is," she replied.

"And he is bonded to Altaria?" Briar asked curiously from Scarlett's left.

"I would assume so. They seem to have a connection similar to the one I've seen between Sorin and Amaré."

"What has he said to you?" Sorin cut in.

"Nothing of importance, or I would have told you about it," Scarlett snapped, meeting his stare.

Ashtine's lilting voice cut through the voices. "He has only appeared in your dreams before now?"

Scarlett's gaze flickered to the princess. "Yes. He was there when…when Shirina and I were bonded."

Ashtine merely propped her head on a delicate hand and studied the new Fae Queen.

"How often does he come for you?" Sorin asked, his entire body tense.

"He does not *come for me*," Scarlett drawled. She closed her eyes, pinching the bridge of her nose. There was a flicker of shadows as they coiled around her arms, then they were gone. "He…"

Sorin reached over to touch her hand, and she jerked it back from him. Talwyn's brows rose in surprise at the reaction. She watched as Sorin's lips thinned. "This...man is the one who took you to the rip in the plane? Told you what it was?"

"Yes." Scarlett's voice was hard and sharp.

"And you believe this...dream?"

"Clearly what happened today was not a dream, Prince."

"And you, Queen Talwyn? Do you believe what this man told you both?" Briar asked, his icy blue eyes hard as they settled on her.

"I believe there are beings in the mortal lands that we have never encountered. This plane we were on was layered over Baylorin. I do not believe these two things occurring are independent of each other," Talwyn answered. With the attention on Scarlett for those few minutes, she had been able to breathe and get her irritation under control.

"You think this rip or tear or whatever is part of how they are entering the mortal lands?" Cyrus asked slowly from beside Sorin.

"That is one possibility, yes," Talwyn said, her eyes fixed on the Fire Court Second. She could see the concern there, the one she had been voicing repeatedly these last two days. She narrowed her eyes at Cyrus and purred softly, "Say it, Fire Warrior."

Cyrus winced slightly as every set of eyes slid to him, including his prince and queen. He took a breath and leaned forward to see Scarlett around Sorin. "Until we figure out this rip, until we know how many rips there are and who this man is that keeps appearing to you, maybe it would be wise to remain here and hold off on going to the human lands. Just until that's figured out," he added hastily as flames appeared in Scarlett's eyes. It was the only reaction she made. She didn't move. She hardly seemed to be breathing.

Talwyn locked eyes with her cousin, and she couldn't help the slight smirk that spread across her lips. "You can ignore my warnings all you like, but will you not heed wise advice from your own Court?"

"I do believe at our last little meeting, *your* Court agreed the mortal lands needed immediate attention," Scarlett replied. Her voice was quiet, venomous, lethal.

"Then others can go," Talwyn returned, her own voice flippant and unconcerned.

"They do not know the kingdoms like I do," Scarlett retorted. "It must be me."

"You are not prepared to go. You are not prepared to face what lies in wait for you there," Talwyn seethed back. Her temper was hanging by a thread. She saw Azrael tense out of the corner of her eye. She saw Sorin do the same beside Scarlett.

"Not prepared to go?" Scarlett asked in a voice of darkness. "You do not know the half of what I am prepared for."

"Are you prepared to face unknown enemies and win?"

"Are you?" Scarlett countered.

"No. That is why I am doing the smart thing and staying here," Talwyn retorted in the same venomous voice.

"Well, then it is a good thing I have faced not one, not two, but three Maraan Lords and have lived to tell the tale. One of them was not so lucky. So I suppose I am not so concerned about the enemies since I know what they are," she purred.

Talwyn blinked at her cousin. Maraan Lords? She didn't even know what those were, but Ashtine spoke from beside her. Her face had gone visibly pale. "Where have you faced a Maraan Lord?"

"You know of them?" Scarlett asked instead, her attention shifting to Ashtine.

"Is there still one you go to face?"

"At least two, but I suspect more," Scarlett replied.

Talwyn turned her gaze to Sorin, but he looked as lost and surprised as everyone else in the room did, other than Ermir. How did Scarlett know of such things?

"I am in need of an explanation, Ashtine," Talwyn said, her voice softening as she spoke to her friend.

But Ashtine continued to ignore them all other than Scarlett. "You are certain?"

"Yes. I am learning the Avonleyan language. I am sure."

The Wind Princess's brows rose in surprise. "How?"

A wicked smile formed on Scarlett's lips. "You will find I am quite resourceful." Then her eyes slid to Talwyn. "And that I am more than prepared to face what lies in wait there."

Talwyn was done. She was done trying to win her cousin over, trying to guide her towards the best decisions. She was done holding her tongue, trying to find common ground with the female who was supposed to help fix things, not make them harder. She had not done all she had these last years to have it all end on a foolish girl's allegiance to mortal friends.

Talwyn stood, bracing her hands on the table, leaning towards Scarlett. Her icy blue eyes were still fixed on her jade ones. Azrael shot to his feet beside her, and she saw thin shields of fire and water come between her and Scarlett from Briar and Sorin as they also stood, hands in casual reach of their weapons. "If you are lost, if you are killed, in the mortal lands," Talwyn said, barely more than a whisper, "all hope is lost. This is not just about your little mortal friends, Scarlett. This is every realm, every life, contained in them. This is the entire godsdamned continent. If you are lost, we cannot find the keys. If you are killed, you doom us all, and that, cousin, will all be because of you. You decide if your mortal comrades are worth more than every other soul in the realms...then be prepared to take full responsibility for that choice."

Then she stepped through her own rip in the world. She felt Azrael grip her elbow as she left. She stepped into her bedroom, preparing to put up her wards and turned to Azrael, who still gripped her elbow, his eyes searching hers.

"Distract me or get out," she snarled under her breath.

He roughly tugged her close to him. She bared her teeth, preparing to take all her aggression and rage out in bed, but then he wrapped his arm around her waist, and she felt the familiar sensation of Traveling. She looked around and found herself in the forest. Jonaraja Forest.

"What are we doing here?" she demanded of her Second, glaring at the male as he stepped back and slowly began circling her.

Jonaraja Forest was ancient. It was said to be as old as Shira Forest itself, and it was one of the greatest kept secrets of the centuries and that secret was entrusted to the Earth Court. The trees here were towering and old, and you could feel the ancient powers emanating from them.

This was also where Azrael had trained her. He was older than she was by at least five centuries and had seen the Great War, had fought in it alongside his parents and hers. Azrael had trained her in all the ways that counted. Not just weaponry and combat. He had taught her how to properly Travel. He had taught her how to control her powers. Yes, she could use them when she came to him, but she had never been taught how to truly control them, how to use them in ways that mattered, how to shape them.

"You demanded a distraction," he snarled back.

"I meant in the bedroom, you damn idiot," she snapped back, a gust of wind blowing through the trees.

"Let it out, Talwyn," Azrael said, his tone softening a fraction. "You barely held it together back there. Let it all out."

"I can control it," she snapped back, her breaths becoming short and ragged.

"Maybe, but you do not have to here," he replied, still circling her. "This isn't your typical rage and temper. This has been repressed for so long, I do not know that you *can* control it."

"Enough, Az," she ground out.

"Let it out, Talwyn. Let out all the rage that has been accumulating since she arrived here."

"Stop!" Talwyn shouted, the earth shuddering beneath their feet.

"Let it out, Talwyn."

The winds were whipping around them now, the leaves on the trees straining under the gusts.

Suddenly Azrael was in her face, gripping her shoulders. "She came here, and everyone willingly bowed before her. She did not have to earn any of it. She came home, not alone, but with a twin flame and could not even see it. She came home and will not even reside where she belongs. She came home, trusting Briar more than she trusts you, her own cousin. She came home with friends she is willing to risk everything for, while you have been here, abandoned in your own realm, working tirelessly to keep the entire world safe."

"Stop!" Talwyn screamed. She reached up to push him away from her, but he only gripped her shoulders harder, his fingers digging into her flesh.

"You lost everything because of *her*," he whispered directly into her ear.

And Talwyn lost it. That leash she had been holding so tightly snapped in half. The ground shook beneath them and small boulders that had littered the forest grounds exploded. Lightning flashed in the skies around them, and Talwyn sank to her knees. Her wind gusts had blown in clouds that mixed with the energy she was shaping in the skies. Thunder sounded, and it began to rain, the ground turning to mud beneath her. She sobbed into her hands as power poured from her, bursts of pure magic that would have sundered any other place but this one of magic as raw as her own.

She felt the outpouring weakening after several minutes, and she wiped her eyes, looking up to see Azrael, who had shielded himself, standing over her. She took a shuddering breath. He only reached down for her hand, helping her to her feet. The rain was soaking them both, and her hair was sticking to her face. He brushed some from her eyes, then took her face in his hands.

"*You* are a queen, Talwyn Semiria," he snarled softly. "You have sacrificed much for these lands. You have been forced to grow up faster than any Fae should have to. You have been betrayed and hurt by those you trusted and faced pain and loss. You have deserved none of it. Do you understand?" She felt tears slip down her cheeks again, and Azrael wiped them away with his thumbs.

"She risks it all, everything I have sacrificed for. Everything I have fought to keep safe and protected and the revenge we seek," Talwyn whispered back to him. "The realms, the Courts, believe me to be a heartless, cruel queen. I have never cared. I have never cared what they thought as long as my people and my kingdom were safe. What if it was all for naught?"

"Then we will adjust our strategy," Azrael answered. "We will meet whatever is to come head on, and you will not face it alone."

Silence hung in the air between them. Then Talwyn whispered, "I am scared, Azrael. I am scared I have failed. I am scared of what is to come."

"You have only failed when you give up, Talwyn. Fear is natural, but you do not yield to it," Azrael answered. He pulled her into him, and this time, he held her close to his chest. She could hear his heart beating beneath her ear, strong and steady, as he'd been for her since the day she had shown up in his Alcazar. "For the next few hours, let someone else worry about it, Talwyn. Let someone else make the hard decisions. Let someone else bear that burden," he murmured into her hair.

"It is my responsibility," she replied, not even bothering to lift her head.

"But it is a *shared* responsibility now," Azrael countered. "Let it be so."

"And what exactly am I supposed to do in the meantime?" she sighed, exhausted.

"I can think of a few things…"

She could hear the invitation in his voice, and she lifted her head to look into his eyes. "You have declined my request for distraction twice now."

"Then allow me to make it up to you," he answered, bringing his lips to hers.

His hands slid down her torso, clenching her ass as he hoisted her against him. Her legs came around his waist, and tongues and teeth clashed. "Not in the rain please," she murmured onto his mouth.

"Whatever you say, your Majesty," he answered, and he stepped her through the world right into his private rooms at his Alcazar. He spun, pressing her up against the wall, and she snarled at him, clawing at the various buckles securing weapons to his body. Talwyn unwound her legs, sliding them slowly down his torso and hips as his hands removed her own weapons.

She reached for his shirt, but he caught her wrists, pinning them behind her back and forcing her to arch into him. "Let go of control, Talwyn," he snarled, his canines nipping and scraping along her neck. "It is just us here. Let go."

"This is not distracting me, Azrael," she growled back, tugging her wrists, but he held firm, pressing his chest into hers. The wall was cool, and she could feel it against her hot skin through her shirt as he pushed her back against it. The contrast made her body shiver against him.

"It will be if you would stop fighting me for control," he retorted, shifting her wrists to one hand. His other hand came around and pulled the strings at the top of her tunic, letting the front gap open. He tugged it roughly to the side, his large palm sliding over the band on her breasts, eliciting a moan of need from her.

Azrael's lip curled in a smirk as he pulled his hand back, slowly dragging it possessively down her torso before coming to the buttons on her pants. "What will it be, your Majesty?" he purred, flicking open the first one. "Will you let me distract you properly?"

Talwyn glared back at him, clenching her teeth. "You better make this worth my while," she snarled at him.

He arched a brow at her. "Have I ever disappointed you?" When she just gave him an unimpressed glare, he leaned in close once more, speaking directly into her ear, his low, rough voice sending heat through her veins. "We both know I know exactly how to make this worth your while, Talwyn." He tugged on her wrists that he still gripped in his hand forcing her to arch into him even more and a frustrated growl escaped her throat. "The sounds I draw from you tell me all I need to know," he continued, his other hand flicking open the next button on her pants.

She snarled at him once more, but her body relaxed into him, letting go of all the tension coiling in her limbs. He chuckled darkly as he released the final button of her pants before scooping her up and tossing her roughly onto the center of his bed.

"Shirt off," he ordered, pulling his own over his head. Talwyn quickly shucked off her tunic, taking in the corded muscles of Azrael's chest and arms. "Keep going," he said with a nod at the band around her breasts, his gaze roving over her.

Talwyn grumbled as she unwound the band, her breasts immediately tightening as the cool air brushed over them, the tips hardening.

Azrael stalked toward her, his eyes dark with predatory intent. He slowly crawled onto the bed, coming over top of her and forcing her down onto her back. "Hands up," he commanded, his voice dark and full of a promise that he would indeed make this worth her while.

Despite her best attempts to maintain some form of control, her breathing was shallow as she slowly raised her hands above her head. She felt his magic wrapping around her, vines coiling around her wrists and yanking them higher, securing them in place. She snarled softly at him, baring her teeth. "Do not get used to this, Luan," she growled.

"Mhmm," he hummed darkly. "I think you say the same thing every time."

She opened her mouth to snark a reply, but his fingertips were skating up her sides, over her ribs, and instead a gasp escaped her. His palms skimmed back down the path his fingers had just taken, his callouses rough against her skin, and when they reached the band of her pants he sat back, pulling them down her legs along with her undergarments. He looked down at her, his eyes glazed and pupils dilated.

"I am not here to be *your* distraction," she snarled at him, and he dragged his eyes to hers, a wicked smile pulling at his lips.

"Of course not, your Majesty," he mocked, his hands gripping her knees and pulling them roughly apart. He bent down, kissing and biting up the inside of her thighs as he made his way higher. And her thoughts scattered as the only thing she could focus on was his lips, his tongue, getting closer to that bundle of nerves. And he was taking his sweet fucking time getting there. By the time he made it to her center, she was panting and writhing beneath him, damn near close to begging him.

"You seem very distracted now," he taunted, his breath brushing over her aching core.

"Azrael," she ground out, arching her hips off the bed, trying to get closer to his mouth.

"Stop moving," he purred, and she felt vines snake around her middle, pulling her down into the bed. His fingers squeezed her inner thighs once more as he pushed her legs wider, before he brought his mouth down onto her, and she moaned in pleasure when he finally, *finally*, raked his tongue over those nerves. He sucked and nipped, his hands holding her open for him.

When he slipped his tongue inside her, one hand slid up, his thumb continuing to move in delicious circles. She jerked against the restraints at her wrists, tried to buck her hips, but the vines just tightened. She wouldn't have been able to focus enough to use her own magic to break the binds if she had wanted to. Every nerve was firing in her body as he brought her closer and closer to the edge. She was panting when two fingers replaced his tongue, and he looked up at her, the look in his eyes saying he knew exactly how close she was. With a wicked grin against her flesh, his tongue found that bundle of nerves one more time, and she shattered around his fingers, crying out his name and arching off the bed.

Before she had even come down from her high, the vines around her middle were gone, and he was flipping her onto her stomach. She snarled as her wrists and arms twisted in their holds to accommodate the new position.

"Ass up, my queen," he crooned, his hands grasping her hips and hoisting her up onto her knees, not giving her time to carry out the command on her own. His palm dragged down her spine, and she felt him press against her from behind. When he had removed his own pants, she had no idea. He leaned forward once more, reaching around her to grip her breasts in his palms , and she moaned, pressing her face into the crook of her arm and her ass back into him.

One hand toyed with her nipple, rolling it between his fingers and tugging, as his other drifted south, his long digits once again finding that bundle of nerves at her center. She felt her magic rolling off of her, and she tried to find some semblance of control over it. Some way to shape it so she could torture Azrael as much as he was torturing her, but he was right. He knew exactly how to play her body to make her forget her past, her present, her heartache, her responsibilities. The only things that could hold her attention right now were his hands, his mouth, and his hardness pressing against her.

And while she would never admit it out loud to him, she knew that he understood how much she needed this. She needed someone else to take control, to make the decisions. When it was just her and the Earth Prince, no one was looking at her to lead an entire race of people, entire bloodlines. No one was expecting her to have all the answers or know the secrets of the gods and Fates. When he convinced her to give up control, even just for a few hours, she relished the freedom. She craved it, and Azrael gave her the only safe place she had to enjoy such a luxury that she was rarely afforded.

So she gave in to him when he gripped her hips once more and slammed into her in one hard movement. She let herself get lost in the pleasure he was giving her with each thrust he made, each cry he wrung from her lips. And when she came a second time, and he found his own release a few moments later, she let him gently roll her onto her back, the vines around her wrists vanishing. He pressed a soft kiss to her lips, his tongue gently caressing hers, as his hand cupped the nape of her neck.

"Sleep, Talwyn," he ordered softly when he pulled back from her. He reached down and pulled the blankets up over them, draping his arm around her waist and resting his hand on her hip as she settled back against him. Sated and thoroughly distracted, she was asleep in minutes.

CHAPTER 52
SCARLETT

The council room had fallen silent when Talwyn had left, and it remained so now. Scarlett was struggling to breathe at the words Talwyn had flung at her before she left. Nausea roiled in her gut, and she willed herself not to vomit.

Maybe she was being selfish. Maybe someone else should go and get Cassius, but she didn't know if she could bear it. Someone else telling him who he was, who his mother was. She saw Sorin reaching for her hand, but she snatched it back, placing them on the arms of her chair and gripping tightly. Her shadows were prowling beneath her skin, and she was struggling to control them.

"You are at a crossroads, Queen Scarlett," came Ashtine's voice from down the table. There was nothing accusatory or implied in her tone. She was just stating a fact. "Talwyn made some good points. I trust you have some of equal value."

"Aside from the Maraan Lords? I am the only one who can find the keys," Scarlett answered, somehow finding her voice. It was low and quiet, but authoritative.

"And you know how to locate them?" Ashtine asked, tilting her head to the side in that peculiar way of hers.

"No, I am still working on that," Scarlett answered slowly.

Silence fell in the room again.

"My queen has reasons of her own for needing to return to the mortal lands that cannot be shared right now." Scarlett raised her brows in surprise to find Briar speaking to her left. "All the Courts have secrets. Talwyn has secrets. Secrets I am sure would be shared if they could be, but now is not the time. Scarlett is no different. If she makes the choice to return to the mortal realm, I will trust she does so with the best intentions."

"And when will such a decision be made?" It was Azrael's Second who spoke this time. Azrael had left with Talwyn, surprising Scarlett. Now, she supposed, Azrael would want a full report of what was said and decided after they left.

Scarlett made herself breathe. In and out. In and out. She closed her eyes and could see their faces— Drake and Tava and Cassius and Nuri. This may be her home. She may have found a family here, but *they* were still her family, too.

"Maybe it would be beneficial to take an extra day or two to consider—," Cyrus was venturing, but Scarlett interrupted him.

"No. The decision is made. I am going to the mortal kingdoms. I am leaving in a few hours. Talwyn will be here researching this rip or tear or whatever it is. I need to go there to complete my own tasks, especially if there are more rips that we are unaware of. I would venture to guess that in the coming days there will not be any sort of 'good time' to go, so I will go now."

"And should you fail?" Ashtine asked. Again, her voice was not accusatory, not threatening. It just was.

"I won't," Scarlett answered pointedly, fixing her eyes on Ashtine's sky blue ones.

"Perseverance and tenacity will only get you so far. The Darkness will find your weaknesses," Ashtine said.

"I am the Darkness," Scarlett replied in an icy, smooth purr, allowing her shadows to rip free from her. They swirled around her like a vortex, and she let Death's Maiden come out, too— wicked, calm, and lethal.

"It is interesting that such a power returns to the world at this place in time, when the Maaran Lords have emerged," Ashtine said, standing from the table, not at all fazed, and a wind portal appeared behind her.

"Indeed," said a male next to her, whom Scarlett assumed was her Second. "Idle chatter of the breezes."

He certainly spoke like Princess Ashtine.

"What do you mean 'such a power returns?'" Scarlett asked. "And what does it have to do with the Maraan Lords?"

Ashtine merely blinked at her with that peculiar half smile.

"Briar…" Sorin ground out through clenched teeth.

You cannot speak to Ashtine like that. She will not answer.

Scarlett knitted her brows. *Why not?*

The Wind Court speaks in mysticism and riddles. Ashtine is benevolent and wise, but she can be unintentionally infuriating. Briar is one of the few people who seems able to speak with her without losing his shit, other than Talwyn.

"Ashtine," Briar said, stepping to the princess. Scarlett watched as Nasima stretched a wing out and brushed it against Briar's cheek. "Do you speak of the queen's shadows?" Briar asked, reaching to stroke the hawk's silver head.

"Are they shadows?" Ashtine asked in return, tilting her head as though she were leaning into a phantom touch.

"You do not know?" Briar questioned softly.

Her half smile grew slightly, her voice still mystical and lilting. She paused, like she was listening to something, then said, "Shadows? Darkness? Night? One or all or none?"

"None of those are powers of this world," Eliza cut in sharply. Nakoa glared at her, but Ashtine's eyes had shifted to her.

"Daughter of Anala and Silas," she said, again pausing to listen to whatever the winds whispered, "there are many unknown powers of the realms. Many of them slumber. Many have never woken, but this magic has walked these lands before."

"When?" Scarlett asked, unable to help herself.

Briar glanced at her with a subtle shake of his head, a request to let him handle it. "Ashtine." He stretched out an arm, and Nasima flew to him, clicking her beak. "Not when. Who?"

Ashtine brought her eyes back to Briar. "There were four: father, mother, son, and daughter."

How *did* Briar converse with her and not lose his damn mind?

"Which holds the answers we seek?" Briar asked, taking a step closer to her.

How does he know what questions to ask? Scarlett asked Sorin down the twin flame bridge.

I have wondered the same. His eyes were fixed on the two Royals before them.

"Only one knows for sure," Ashtine replied, "but there are many directions for the winds to blow."

"Tell me three," Briar said as Nasima flew back to Ashtine.

"And what shall you give me in return, Prince of Water?" Ashtine replied, the wind portal once more opening behind her.

"What shall be required?"

Scarlett was watching them closely, and her eyes widened at the brief look that entered Briar's eyes. It was gone so quickly, she had to wonder if it had been there at all. But she had seen Nasima and Abrax in the Forest together, as close as Ashtine and Briar were now...

"A favor of my choosing then," the Wind Princess replied, her Second coming to her side along with Azrael's Second.

"Agreed," Briar said. Three swirling lines appeared around his wrist like a gust of wind. A bargain Mark. "Your end of the bargain. Tell me three."

"A watery prison, a locked away king, a world walker's book," the princess replied as she stepped towards the portal.

"Which direction is wisest?" Scarlett blurted.

"That depends on who is walking the path," Ashtine answered simply, stepping through the portal, the two males following. It snapped shut behind them.

Silence settled in the room. Scarlett looked at her Court seated around her and said grimly, "I assume we should not speak privately of these matters in these Halls?"

A fire portal appeared a moment later, and all of them rose and filed through. They stepped into the dining room where they'd met with Talwyn a few mornings ago.

"Translation, Drayce?" Sorin sighed from Scarlett's side. He waved a hand, and flames raced along the length of the table, food and drink in their wake.

"Before we discuss anything else," Scarlett cut in, "how did you learn to speak to her, Prince of Water? Pillow talk?" Her tone was innocent, but the wink and sly grin she threw at Briar was anything but. She was sure she hadn't mistaken that brief look of desire she'd seen in his eyes.

A roguish smile crossed his lips. "We do not do much talking in the bedroom, Sunshine."

Scarlett laughed at his retort. "Fair enough."

"So perceptive, your Majesty," he said, returning her wink.

"Bullshit," Sorin spat, gaping at his friend.

"I am a little disappointed your Court was so oblivious, husband," Scarlett said, perching on the edge of the table and picking up a pear. "His own Court clearly knows." She watched as the Fire Court gaped at Briar and his own Inner Court. Sawyer smirked beside his brother, grabbing a pastry from the spread on the table. Eliza was glaring at Nakoa. "To be fair," Scarlett continued around a bite of pear, "I likely wouldn't have put it together so quickly had I not seen Abrax and Nasima interact in the Shira Forest."

"In all fairness," Cyrus replied, his golden eyes dancing, "you were literally *living* with your twin flame and had no idea, so maybe you're not as perceptive as you think, Darling."

Scarlett scowled and stuck out her tongue at him.

"How long?" Sorin demanded, shock still on his features as he continued to stare at Briar.

"Shortly after Eliné left," Briar answered.

"Why the secret?" Scarlett asked curiously.

"Because relationships outside your Court are highly frowned upon," Eliza said tightly. "Especially for royal bloodlines."

"It is a delicate matter," Briar agreed, his grin becoming a grim frown, "And one to be discussed later as there are more pressing matters at hand."

"Do you know what she meant with her last words?" Scarlett asked.

He shook his head. "She may not even know what she means. She repeats secrets whispered by the winds. She does not realize she is speaking in perplexity."

"A watery prison, a locked away king, a world walker's book," Cyrus said, mulling the words over. "Any ideas?"

No one spoke.

Scarlett sighed from her perch on the table. "Before I left the Oracle, she told me to find a book."

"Why am I not surprised in the least that you have information?" Briar asked, taking a seat at the table.

"What sort of book?" Sorin asked, sliding into the chair nearest her.

"I don't know. An old one, apparently. Likely the same book Ashtine referred to considering the Oracle's words were 'Those who can walk among the worlds brought a book with them in the beginning. You would do well to find it.'"

"And you are just telling us now?" Sorin asked, his brow arching.

"A lot happened with the Oracle and a lot happened after the Oracle. A lot of which *you* benefited from," she added with a pointed look at Sorin's wedding band on his finger. Sawyer stifled a laugh. "So I apologize, *your Highness*, if I didn't realize I omitted something important until now."

"Don't be a brat," Sorin ground out from between his teeth with an unamused glare.

She batted her lashes at him and replied sweetly, "Don't be an ass."

I am going to start keeping a list of every name you call me, Princess.

She smirked. *What are you going to do about it?*

She could have sworn his eyes went a shade darker as a feral smile crossed his face.

"As much as this little show never gets old," Briar cut in, his eyes twinkling, "World Walkers are mythical beings. Most believe them to be nothing more than legends."

"Rayner said many believe the same of the Oracle, and she is real as can be," Scarlett countered, tearing her eyes from Sorin, who was still staring at her with primal greed.

"Let's say that is the book," Cyrus said, "any idea where we start looking for it?"

"A few," Scarlett answered, popping a grape into her mouth.

"Helpful," Cyrus remarked sarcastically.

"It's more than you've offered," she retorted.

"You are ridiculously unconventional," Sawyer observed with amusement.

"Yes, but I keep things interesting," she replied with a wink.

"Would it possibly be in the same place you've found books on blood magic?" Eliza asked casually. She had been fairly quiet up until now, and Scarlett could not quite read the look on her face.

"What sort of books?" Scarlett asked as another grape went into her mouth.

From a flame, Eliza pulled a book and floated it to Scarlett. Scarlett gently took it and stilled. "Where did you find this?"

"In the library. When I was chatting with the mortal prince. He said it was one of yours. One that you have been reading," Eliza said slowly.

"It's history reading. Nothing more," Scarlett said flippantly, sliding the book under the table. She conjured a shadow panther, who took the book gently in its maw and disappeared back into the darkness.

"History reading. On blood magic," Eliza deadpanned, not convinced in the slightest. "It is not something to mess around with, Scarlett."

"Is my twin flame bond not blood magic? My soulmate bond with Cassius?" Scarlett countered. "It is research, General. Nothing more."

She stared down Eliza. They had never argued before, but she could see the skepticism that lingered in her eyes.

"Who do you think a locked away king is?" Neve asked, fixing a piece of cheese to a cracker and taking a bite, breaking the tension.

"No idea," Scarlett answered, hopping off her perch on the table. "But it is something I can contemplate just as well from Baylorin."

"You still plan to return to the mortal lands?" Nakoa growled.

"Of course I do," Scarlett replied. "Why would my plans change?"

"So then you have indeed deemed your human friends more important than every other person on this continent?" he snarled. The male's arms were crossed, and he glared at her with distrust and contempt.

"Watch it, Commander," Sorin snarled softly from his seat, but Scarlett held up a hand.

"No. It is fine, Sorin. He clearly has something he would like to say." She leveled a stare at the male. "Let's hear it then."

Nakoa glanced at Briar, who shifted uncomfortably in his seat, but gave a slight shrug of his shoulders. "Fine," he growled. He uncrossed his arms and braced his hands on the table, leaning across it towards her. "I think you are being foolish returning to the mortal lands when you are untrained and have barely tapped into your magic. We do not know the full scope of what to expect over there or what exactly is getting in through these tears, and it is unwise to send a *queen* into the middle of that without knowing all the facts. Talwyn's points were valid, and you dismiss them as trivial, despite the fact that she has more experience than you, albeit not by much. But she at least was raised to be in her position. There are many issues at hand here, and you can only seem to focus on one. And I cannot decide if that is because you do not grasp the gravity of the other issues, because you do not understand the politics of the realms, or because you are so selfish you simply do not care."

The entire room was still. "Anything else?" Scarlett asked, her voice soft and honed.

"You are a child who is playing queen," Nakoa continued with a lethal growl. "I do not care that you are Sorin's twin flame. I do not care that my own prince has pledged his loyalty to you."

"Nakoa," Briar warned, his tone sharp and reprimanding. Again, Scarlett held up a hand, silencing him.

"You answer to your people," Nakoa went on. "When you claimed that throne, you claimed responsibility for all of them. Your people became more important than your mortal lackeys. At least acknowledge the fact that you recognize that your actions affect us all, and that you do not care, while you sit here and make idle banter before leaving us all to figure out and clean up this mess with Talwyn breathing down our fucking necks."

Scarlett could feel the flames flickering in her eyes as she stared at the male. Her shadows appeared unbidden, and the temperature dropped in the room. "Do not presume things about me, Commander, when you know nothing of who I left behind to come here." Her tone was calm, icy rage.

"Are they more important than the whole of your kingdom and the threat that is gathering on the horizon?" he growled.

"I did not come here for a throne, but I left dozens of orphans behind in that city. Innocent children that I am *responsible* for." Her voice was a whisper of fury. Nakoa's eyes widened slightly, but he held his ground. "Children who were *dumped* there. Children who have Witch blood and Shifter blood and Night Child blood and *Fae* blood running through their veins. Children who are being targeted, abducted, and killed because of it. I came here for them and found much more than I anticipated."

"So it is your habit to leave those in your charge behind?" Nakoa sneered.

A cruel smile spread across her lips.

"Back down, Nakoa," Sorin said, his tone ringing with warning. He stood, preparing to place himself between the two.

Shadows swirled along Scarlett's arms and legs, thick and impenetrable, engulfing all of her, and when they cleared, she stood in her witch-suit and leathers. She was armed to the teeth, as she was when she prowled the night, the Spirit Sword at her back. "I left them in the care of a powerful Witch and Death's Shadow, hidden and warded in the heart of the Black Syndicate, where I was raised and trained and where the darkest of souls watch over them. Forgive

473

me for assuming I could leave two Courts in the hands of full-blooded, lethally trained Fae warriors while I went to aid those innocents in a land where they cannot access their own damn gifts."

No one was daring to move. It seemed no one was daring to breathe.

"You have made your point, my Love," Sorin murmured, placing a hand on the small of her back.

Eliza pushed off the wall she had been leaning against. "You were raised in the fucking Black Syndicate?"

"Eliné was one of the five council leaders of the Black Syndicate. The Assassin Lord oversaw Scarlett's training personally, and she trained alongside Death's Shadow." He hesitated, casting a questioning glance at her. When she didn't react, he continued, "She is one of the Wraiths of Death. She is Death's Maiden." She could feel his eyes on her, but she still stood facing Nakoa.

"Ho-ly shit," Sawyer swore under his breath. He turned to Briar. "Did you know?"

Briar shook his head, his eyes fixed on the wraith that Scarlett had become. "No."

"That explains your fighting style," Eliza murmured, more to herself than anyone in particular.

"I was trained by mortal mercs and thieves, a Witch, a Night Child and a—" she paused, before she pushed on. "And an Assassin Lord, and for all that training, I was still captured. Despite all that training, *children* are still being abducted for purposes I have yet to fully learn."

"Shit," Cyrus breathed in disbelief. "You said you had *friends* in the Black Syndicate, not that you grew up there."

"You never asked," she purred in response.

"She outranks everyone in the Syndicate other than the Council Members," Sorin supplied calmly.

"But since my motives and my devotion are being called into question, despite me being here for those in my charge there," Scarlett said now, "I shall delay my travels two days so that I can assign tasks like a godsdamned babysitter."

A water portal appeared behind Nakoa. "Take a walk,

Commander," Briar ordered, his tone pure Fae primal command. Without a word, Nakoa turned on his heel and disappeared through the portal.

Scarlett turned and looked around the room. A mixture of fear, respect, and awe mingled on the faces that stared back, no one daring to speak. "I'll meet with you all tomorrow afternoon."

With shadows once again trailing her, she stepped through the world without another word.

CHAPTER 53
SORIN

Sorin watched the queen as she released her temper in the courtyard. Her witch-suit was gone. She was clad in her lightweight training pants and a long-sleeve tunic that barely covered her midriff. She held the Spirit Sword in one hand and threw fire and ice at the various wards, dodging and striking as they bounced back at her. Shadows swirled in her wake as she flipped and ducked and twirled, fighting against herself. He had been training her, yes, but he had not realized how much she had been practicing in her own time. How *good* she had actually become. He shouldn't be surprised, really. Downplaying her skills was what kept many from realizing how big of a threat she actually was.

But more than any of that, something had awoken since she had accepted her throne. Some inner barrier she had been keeping in place had been lifted. She had been wading slowly into her power before, cautiously experimenting. But now it appeared she had decided to plunge in and see how deep she could go. She hadn't been resting enough. Diving so deep so quickly was going to have serious consequences, and soon.

The others had dispersed quickly when she had left, Briar leaving to deal with Nakoa.

"The fucking Black Syndicate?" Eliza asked, still in disbelief, her tone accusatory.

"I can guarantee she has been holding back in training with you, Eliza," Sorin had replied. "I saw her fight with Death's Shadow, who is a Night Child by the way, with no magic. Pinned her to the floor with only a dagger, then laughed in delight about it."

"You were right, Cyrus, I might have competition after all," Eliza had said to his Second, a wicked smile crossing her lips.

"You have no idea," Sorin muttered. "That she did not get into a damn brawl with Nakoa is a testament to the control she has learned."

"She is truly Death's Maiden?" Cyrus asked, his eyes conveying the shock he still felt.

Sorin nodded. "Yes. She and the others, her sisters she will call them, tracked down Eliné's assassin…and then she personally took care of him. At the age of sixteen."

Cyrus swore viciously under his breath. "I suppose if she insists on going to the mortal lands, we will indeed have allies."

"She will have some there, but she is not on good terms with the Council and is on even worse terms with the Assassin Lord. The last time they crossed paths, he…hurt her," Sorin said through gritted teeth. If Scarlett would allow it, he would personally see to the revenge for everything she had experienced at his hand.

"Who are the Maraan Lords?" Rayner cut in quietly.

"That I do not know," Sorin replied grimly.

Secrets. She was keeping secrets again. After they had just had a discussion about not keeping secrets from each other.

"She knows more than she is letting on, Sorin," Eliza said. "Not only about the Maraan Lords but this man in her dreams—"

"I know," he ground out, cutting off his general. "I will talk to her."

"She can't keep things from us, Sorin. She can't—"

"I understand," he snapped, cutting her off again. "She is used to doing things herself, especially the last year. It will take her a little time to allow herself to depend on others. She has only known you a short amount of time."

"She has only known you a few months longer," Eliza countered sharply.

"Precisely why I do not know a damn thing about the Maraan Lords," Sorin retorted icily.

Eliza had merely nodded in understanding at that, and they had dispersed, leaving him to deal with the queen.

He had felt her. He had felt every bit of rage and fury, but he had also felt the flinch when Nakoa had flung those words at her. He had felt where he had hit home. He had felt what had brought that darkness surging to the surface, unsummoned by her.

He was about to step forward as he watched her duck a trio of ice daggers when he stilled. In the span of a blink, she had formed those shadows swirling her into a solid punching bag. Flames wreathed her hands, like tape wrapped around them in combat training, and she began punching. One, two. One, two. One, one, two. Over and over again, her shadows holding strong as she hit and hit and hit.

Stop gawking and draw your sword or leave, Prince, echoed down their bond.

One, two. One, two. One, one, two.

Flames flared and his sword appeared in his hand. A second later, flames licked down his body, and his own training clothes appeared. He began towards her.

She didn't miss a beat as she pulled the sword that was sheathed at her back. That white fire of hers wreathed down its blade, and he sent flames down his own. This would be interesting.

When their blades struck the first time, flames flared. For the longest time, there was only their ragged breathing and clashing of their swords. He felt every emotion in every swing she took, every thrust and block. Rage. *Clang.* Fury. *Clang.* Guilt. *Clang.* More guilt. *Clang.*

Their flames danced with each other, her white flames and shadowfire mingling with his flames of gold and red and orange. Still, she kept swinging. Still, she kept coming at him.

"Scarlett."

She swung again. He met it.

478

Scarlett.

The swords clanged again, sending flames radiating out from them as they met.

Love.

She faltered as two tears trailed down her cheeks, and she dropped the Spirit Sword to the ground. Sorin instantly discarded his own weapon, closing the space between them and pulling her into his arms. She pressed her face into his chest, gripping his back.

"I did not ask for this, Sorin. I did not want this," she said, her voice cracking.

"I know, Love. I know," he replied gently, stroking her hair.

"No matter what decision I make, someone will suffer. I was not raised for this world, for this role," Scarlett said into his chest.

"Perhaps that is precisely why the Fates put you in it."

"The fucking Fates can piss off," she choked through her tears. "What is the point of it all, Sorin?"

"We do not get to know that. We do not get to know the end. We live in the here and the now, and we put one foot in front of the other. The Fates may have shoved you onto a throne you do not want, but you get to decide which stars will shine."

"Despite what Nakoa seems to think, I do recognize all the issues at hand. I do, Sorin."

"I know, Scarlett. I know you do," he answered, continuing with the soothing strokes of her hair.

"Callan needs to return home. His father is already suspicious. Nuri is likely ripping everyone's head off at being so confined. The Syndicate Council is going to filet me alive for leaving like I did. Talwyn is furious and needs me to help her close these rifts. Ashtine just dropped a bomb about these damn shadows, and Juliette and the High Witch gave commands of their own regarding these keys and Cassius. And then there are the orphans and Mikale and Veda to deal with, which honestly is the biggest issue of all of this. They have no idea..." she trailed off.

Sorin couldn't stifle his growl at the man's name on her lips. Before he could say anything, she whispered, "You've been at this for centuries. Tell me what to do."

"No one tells you what to do, Princess, although many have tried," he replied, kissing the top of her head.

"Prick," she muttered.

"I will add that to the list," he murmured back, gently tilting her face up to his. He brushed a kiss to her lips. Then another. "I choose you, Scarlett Semiria. I choose you now and always, and I will follow you to the farthest star and beyond if that is where you wish to go."

"What if I choose wrong? What if I make the wrong choice?" she whispered, her eyes searching his own.

"Then we will deal with it, Scarlett. Together," he said. "Always together."

She was quiet for a long moment, just staring into his eyes, before she whispered, "I love you, Sorin."

"Hearing those words on your lips will never get old, Love. Five hundred years from now, they will still bring me to my knees," he said, leaning down to kiss her once more.

She brought her hands up around his neck, and he deepened the kiss, tasting all of her lavender and citrus and jasmine and embers. He gathered her to him, as if she would disappear in her own shadows. Lifting her off her feet, he stepped through a fire portal into their bedroom.

Then she was lifting her arms as he pulled her shirt from her body. Boots were somehow unlaced and shucked off in between kisses, and he was laying her on their bed. The bed they had shared for weeks now. He kissed and tasted and worshipped every inch of her, making her forget her worries and her responsibilities. His queen. His wife. His twin flame.

When she had found release around his fingers and then again against his mouth, he gripped her knees, tugging her roughly down the bed to him. She let out a surprised squeal as he settled between her legs. He lightly dragged his fingertips up her thighs, along her hips, up her navel.

"Have I told you lately how stunningly beautiful you are?" he asked, taking in all of that bare skin as though he hadn't just feasted on her moments before.

"Mmm," she hummed, stretching her arms above her head and arching her back slightly, her perfect breasts thrusting out. He lowered his mouth to one, sucking in the tip. "Yes, but I never tire of hearing it," she continued, her fingers sliding into his hair.

With a smirk against her skin, he bit down on her nipple at the words, and she hissed, her fingers tightening and yanking hard on his black strands. He chuckled darkly as he slid his lips to her other breast. "So violent," he murmured.

"Says the savage Fae who just *bit* me," she retorted breathlessly.

He swirled his tongue around that peaked point a few times, making her squirm beneath him, before he pulled back and purred, "You like it when I bite, Love." He slowly began dragging his canines up her chest to her throat. She tipped her head back as a small whimper escaped her, and he sucked lightly on her throat before he bit down. She gasped, her hips bucking against him in demand.

He growled with desire as he swiped his tongue against the small hurt before pulling back. He gently took her chin between his thumb and forefinger, her eyes fluttering open. Icy blue orbs with silver and flecks of gold swirling in them met his own. "You, Scarlett Semiria, are a necessity in my life."

Her features softened as her legs came up to wrap around his waist. He let her flip them, rolling onto his back as she settled on top of him. Her hair fell around them like a waterfall of starlight. She leaned in close, bracing her hands on his chest as she said softly, "You, Sorin Aditya, are the brightest star in my darkness."

Her lips met his, and she kissed him deeply, her tongue dancing against his. He felt her icy shadows as they skittered along his skin, and he sent heat into them, wrapping it around their bodies. Scarlett moaned against his mouth at the sensation of their magic mingling, and the sound had him hardening even more. He gripped her hips again, lifting her ass and lining her entrance up with him. Then in one smooth movement, he slammed her down onto him.

She sucked in a sharp breath, her nails digging into his flesh, as he groaned at the feeling of once again being buried deep inside her. It would never be enough. He would never get enough of feeling her tight heat around his cock. He would always want more, always crave another taste, one more time of her writhing beneath him and hearing her noises of pleasure.

She pushed herself up, grinding down and moving her hips in small circles around him. He cursed under his breath then he lifted her hips once more until he was almost completely withdrawn from her before pulling her down once more. The sound that came from her had him smiling in smug satisfaction before she took over the movements. He slid his hands to her thighs, gripping tightly as he watched her ride him, bringing herself closer and closer to her release once more. Her hands slid up her own torso and grasped her breasts as she tilted her head back in clear pleasure, and he brought his thumb to her center, rubbing against that bundle of nerves.

She let out a breathy noise, and he felt her begin to clench around him as she dropped forward, burying her face in his neck. He took once more, one arm sliding around her back and the other hand burying into her hair to hold her to him as he thrust into her again and again. She cried out as he felt her spasm and shudder around him, drawing his own release. He groaned her name as he came, clutching her tightly to his chest.

They were both still panting when he gently shifted her off him and rolled her to the side. She nestled into him, her head on his chest. Sorin stroked her hair in the quiet of their rooms as her breathing evened out, her body relaxed and sated against his own. He savored it. The feel of her against him. The sanctuary of their private chambers. He knew he should ask about the Maraan Lords she had referenced. He knew he should press about the blood magic books Eliza had found. But he knew she would go back to the mortal lands, and what lay in wait for them there would not lend much time for being together, not in this way. So he let her fall asleep in the middle of the afternoon, holding her tightly and not letting her go.

CHAPTER 54

CALLAN

There was a knock on the door that had Callan glancing up from his book. Finn and Sloan had gone down to the training rooms to spar. They had gradually become more comfortable leaving him alone here. He had become rather accustomed to *not* being known here, and while he was growing restless, he was also enjoying not being noticed. He liked that he seemed to blend in with the common folk, that he wasn't something special here.

The knock came again, and he closed the book, rising to answer the door. Lunch wasn't for another two hours, so he wasn't sure who it would be.

He pulled the door open to find Scarlett standing on the threshold. He blinked, wondering if he was seeing things. He looked down the hall in both directions. She was completely alone.

"Hello, Callan," she said quietly. She was dressed in black pants and an emerald green tunic that set her silver hair shimmering against it. A beautiful sword was at her hip, and she had her hands clasped behind her back. "Would you be willing to take a walk with me?" He stood frozen, staring at her, unable to find his voice. She shuffled on her feet. "Unless you are busy? I could come back this afternoon."

"No," he finally managed to get out. "No, now is fine. Let me just put my boots on."

"Sure," was all she said.

"You can come in. While you wait. I will not be long," he said, stepping aside.

"All right." She took a few steps into the room, just enough for him to shut the door behind her. "Where are Finn and Sloan?"

"Sparring. Down in the training rooms," Callan answered, crossing to his bedroom. He grabbed his boots from near the door and slid them on.

"You were reading?" she asked, noting where his book still lay on the sofa near the fireplace.

"I was. I find I have lots of time on my hands here," he answered. Scarlett only nodded her head. Noting she was not wearing a cloak, he did not bother with one either. "Shall we?"

She was silent as she opened the door and started down the hallway.

"You are alone," he said, following her.

"I am."

"They do not even have a guard with you?" he asked. He could not keep the slight bitterness from his tone.

A half smile lifted on her lips. "I assure you, I am scarier than anything that will attempt to accost me in these halls."

"Even Eliza?" he asked with a raise of his brows.

She huffed a laugh. "Valid point, Prince."

"You are back to calling me that," he said quietly. She said nothing, and he suddenly realized they were heading towards the bridges. "I cannot cross the bridges, Scarlett. Not without an escort of the Fire Court."

"You have something better," she replied simply, again with that half smile, as she stepped onto the bridge. He held his breath, waiting for Rayner to step from smoke, and Cyrus and Eliza to come striding from wherever they were, but no one came. She was halfway across the bridge when a fire message appeared near her head. He watched her reach up, plucking the note from the flames. A soft smile crossed her lips. Then she incinerated the note in her palm. "Come, Callan," she said with a nod of her head to the other side of the bridge. "I promise no one will bother us."

Callan sucked in a breath and stepped onto the bridge. True to her word, nothing happened. He bit back his snide remark about her being able to go where she pleased unescorted and followed her across the bridge.

"Your shadows are gone," he remarked as she led him up several sets of stairs.

"They appear when summoned," she answered.

"As panthers?"

Scarlett grimaced slightly. "Sorry. It has been an...emotional couple of days, and I needed some time..."

He forced himself to hold back his retort about Sorin being able to follow her.

They continued in silence up to the highest level of the palace. She led him down a hall and then she pushed through a door. He followed her through and stepped into a large glass greenhouse. Plants and flowers bloomed everywhere. She walked to a bench beside a little pond where various fish swam about. In the center of the pond was a sea star.

Scarlett sat on the bench and patted the spot beside her. "Sit, Callan. There are some things you deserve to know."

He studied her for a moment. A soft, almost sad smile was on her lips as she watched the sea star move along the bottom of the pond. Her hair was partially pulled back, putting her Fae ears fully on display. Her hands were under her thighs as though she were trying to keep them warm, despite the magic that kept the entire palace comfortable and the heat of the greenhouse itself.

Callan crossed the short distance and sat down beside her, watching the fish dart to and fro in the water, and waited.

"I am sorry for missing dinner the other night. I got caught up in some things and wasn't able to send a note," she said.

"In the Witch Kingdoms?"

She cast a side-long glance at him before saying, "We are returning to Baylorin. Tomorrow evening."

He jerked his head to her. "We are going home?"

She winced slightly. "Yes, Callan. It is time for you to return home. We still don't entirely know what Mikale's plans are, but we— *I* have matters to attend to there and have waited long enough to return."

"The orphans?" he asked softly.

"Yes. Among other things." She did not look at him as she spoke, her eyes still fixed on the sea star.

"Have you heard from Cassius? Is everything all right?"

"No. I have not spoken to Cassius since that day weeks ago when Sorin brought him here for me." Silence fell again. "When you return home, you need to stay alert, Callan. Finn and Sloan need to be with you at all times until we have Mikale under control. I will provide them with all the ways I have entered the castle unde- tected. Mikale caught me in one of the tunnels, so I know he knows about them as well."

We. She kept saying we, which meant...

"Who all is returning with us?" he asked slowly.

She closed her eyes, taking a deep breath. "Sorin and his Inner Court."

"All of them?"

"Yes," she replied softly.

"Cyrus, Eliza, *and* Rayner?"

"Yes."

"Why?"

"I need them. To help me with everything."

"I can help you. Finn and Sloan can help. With Cassius and Nuri. We can figure it out, Scarlett," Callan argued. "We will figure this out."

She finally turned to face him. That was indeed a sad smile on her lips. "There is much you do not know, Callan. I need them with me."

"And who will take care of his Court, his people? He will just leave them?" Callan demanded.

Again, Scarlett took a deep breath, seeming to steady herself. "Someone from my Court will be in charge of the Fire Court, as well as his own, until we return."

"Return? You will come back here? You have decided then?" He stilled. The blood in his veins froze. His heart stopped at the words. "You will come back here to be with him?"

"I will," she whispered, her eyes dipping to the ground.

"Look at me, Scarlett Monrhoe," Callan commanded. "Look at me and tell me why."

She brought her eyes back to his. They were full of sorrow, as if she knew that what she was about to say was going to shatter him completely. "He is my twin flame, Callan."

Her twin flame? No. Sorin was her soulmate, not her twin flame. He'd had the Mark since they arrived here. She had not had one. Everything he had read about the Fae twin flame bond came rushing back to him. Everything Eliza had explained to him. "No. There is a Marking and Trials and an Anointing. You have not had time to…"

He trailed off when Scarlett held up her left hand. He had thought she was keeping her hands warm, but she had been hiding it. The black Mark wound and swirled around the back of her hand and down three of her fingers, a stark tattoo against her golden skin, and a gold band with a large diamond and two smaller rubies adorned her finger.

"When?" he whispered.

"We initiated the Trials a few days ago, but we also had a marriage sanctified."

"You are married?" Callan breathed, realization and under-standing slamming into him, one after another. How Sorin was able to find her in the Lairwood House. How he was able to speak to her when she was lost in the thrall of her magic. His overprotectiveness. Her dancing with him and practically glowing. How he had raged when she had been hurt in the Courtyard. Her shadows dimming, disappearing, in his presence. How they were always godsdamned drawn to each other.

"Yes," she answered. "He is my husband. I didn't… I didn't

acknowledge the twin flame bond until a few days ago. Deep down, I've known, but I was such a mess, I couldn't— I wouldn't let myself accept it. Not until his life was in danger, and I realized…"

She brought her eyes back to his and tears glimmered there. One slipped down her cheek, and he clasped his hands together to keep from reaching out and catching it. Someone else's. She was someone else's. He had lost her.

"I loved you, Callan," she whispered. "I did. I do."

"But not enough," he said softly.

"No, Callan," she said, and she gripped his hands in her own. He tried to jerk them back, but she held firm. "I love you enough to know that it would never have worked. That I could never be what you will need when you are king. We come from two very different worlds."

"You never gave me a chance," he argued. "You kept parts of yourself hidden from me."

Shadows suddenly swarmed her, and he lurched to his feet. The shadows mixed with flame and ice, her eyes becoming flames themselves. Another breath and it was gone, snuffed out. "That fear I see in your eyes, that I can *smell* on you, Callan? The parts I keep hidden from you are far worse than what you just witnessed." She stood facing him now. She seemed different, almost regal. "I couldn't be my entire self with you because I didn't *know* my entire self. I did not know I was Fae. I did not know I had magic. I did not know my family name is Semiria, not Monrhoe."

"What?" Callan's eyes snapped to hers. "That is the Fae Queen's last name."

"Indeed," she replied, and a crown of ice and shadows appeared above her head, with a red flame like a sun in the center.

Someone from my Court will be in charge of the Fire Court. The words clanged through him.

"If Sorin's Inner Court is going with you, who shall be left in charge?" Callan asked slowly.

"Briar will be left in charge as he is part of *my* Court. I am the Queen of the Fire and Water Courts. My mother was the Fae

Queen of the Western Courts. My cousin rules the Eastern Courts," Scarlett answered.

"How is that possible?"

"Much was hidden from me as well," she said sadly. "There is still much I am discovering."

"He has not bothered to explain it to you?" Callan snarled bitterly.

"Sorin has explained what he can, but we are learning more each day. I am doing the best I can."

He started at the bitterness in her tone. "You do not wish for this?" he asked slowly.

"Do I wish to be queen? No. I've never lied to you, Callan. I have no desire to be shackled to a throne."

"Then why choose it?"

"Because…" she stared around the greenhouse. "Because while it is my fate, I get to decide how to use it, and so I shall use it to aid my people. Starting with the children in the Black Syndicate. If my crown will allow me to help those who cannot help themselves, then it is a burden I shall endure."

Callan studied the woman, the female, before him. He knew. He had known for quite some time that Sorin was her equal, that he pushed her and challenged her in ways he never could. He knew that Sorin was better for her, could care for her better. None of that eased the pain in his chest. None of that made it easier. None of that lessened his bitterness.

"You could have done that from my side," he ground out.

"No, I could not have," she said simply. "But I will need you, Callan. I will need your alliance. I will need your help, as a prince and as a king, but more than all of that, I will need your friendship."

"Why would you need me when you have him?" he sneered.

"There are battles coming, Callan. There are enemies deeply entrenched in your lands and others. They have been waiting for centuries for this exact moment in time. There are rifts in the world. Beings we are only beginning to recognize. We shall need each other to keep our people safe."

"We will not need you or your Court or your people," he

snarled. He turned on his heel. "I am going back to my rooms. Send word as to when we need to be ready to return to Baylorin."

"Callan," she called after him, taking a few steps towards him. "Let me walk back with you. You do not know the way...and cannot walk through this side of the palace unattended."

Callan gritted his teeth. Of course he couldn't. "Then find me an escort that is not you."

She stepped back as though he had hit her, hurt flitting across her features. She only gave a slight nod of her head, and a moment later, a fire portal appeared. Sorin and Eliza stepped through, Sorin coming to her side.

Callan thought he would vomit at the perfection they were as they stood beside each other, Sorin's hand coming to her lower back. "Tomorrow evening, at sundown, we will depart," Scarlett said, her tone now formal.

"Fine," Callan answered, striding for the door, but he paused, not turning to look at her when she called after him again.

"Almost three years ago, I watched a young prince from a tree branch. He became a friend and so much more. He had a dream that he could make the world a better place for those already in his care. Hope is for the dreamers, Callan." She crossed the space between them, gently grabbing his arm. She pressed a small vial into his hand. The vial looked just like the ones that used to hold her tonic, and he wished she were still taking it. That none of this had happened. That it could all go back. He would take her secrets and shadows over this. Anything over this.

"You will need me, Callan," she said softly. "When you do, I will come. Smash this to the ground, and I will be there in an instant. I will come for you. For my friend."

Callan only jerked his arm from her and headed to Eliza who was now waiting by the door. He stalked past her out into the hall-way. They silently descended the stairs, and he gripped that vial tightly in his fist, resisting the urge not to smash it against the steps of this damn palace.

After the third set of stairs, Eliza spoke. "I tried to prepare you."

"You could have just come out and said it," he spat, not looking at the female leading him down the stairs.

"No, I couldn't have. I swore to my prince I wouldn't say a word, but you were there the day I Marked him. I hoped I had given you enough clues."

"Why did you even bother?" he growled as they approached the bridges.

"Because you seemed as lost as she did when you arrived," Eliza replied, more gently than he had ever heard the female speak.

"And now?" he asked when she stopped at the bridge.

She studied him for a long moment. "I think an obstacle that was preventing you from moving forward has been removed, and you are now free to find your own way."

CHAPTER 55

SCARLETT

"What did you give him?" Sorin asked Scarlett as she stood staring after the prince and general.

"Something to use when I am his only option left," Scarlett replied quietly.

"What will it do?"

She felt him take a few steps towards her. She couldn't turn to him. She knew what was coming. He had let her sleep when she fell asleep beside him late in the afternoon yesterday after all the dramatics of the day. She had slept through the night, not even waking for dinner. He had given her time and space and distraction, but now he had questions and was going to ask them. Was going to push for answers that she had kept so guarded these last weeks... until she had carelessly left that book in the library after her argument with Callan.

"It will summon him help," she said, rubbing her hands along her arms. It wasn't cold in here by any means, but she felt cold inside.

"What kind of help, Scarlett?" She felt him gently touch her elbow.

She took a deep breath and turned to him. "The kind only I can give."

"Tell me what that means." She could see the frustration he was trying hard to keep from his face.

"Why don't you just come out and ask it, Sorin?"

"There are so many things you are keeping hidden, I do not know what to ask first," Sorin retorted.

"Did you finally find your balls?" Scarlett drawled with a smirk.

"What is that supposed to mean?"

She took a few steps away from him, putting space between them. "You've been walking on glass around me for weeks. Afraid to push me. Afraid to ask questions. You've been *afraid* of me."

"Yes! Yes, I have been. Because you put up walls and shut people out as easily as I do. We are one and the same, remember? And there is still a wall up. You put it back up that day we fought, and I have been unable to cross it since," he countered. "What happened to letting each other in, Scarlett? What happened to not shutting each other out?"

"I have answered your questions," she argued.

"Vaguely. You have been half present for weeks, and you have been withholding information."

"Because I haven't figured out how to deal with it all yet," she replied. "I haven't worked out all the details."

"So let me help you. You do not need to do things alone any more."

"Yes, I do! The more people I involve, the more people I endanger, Sorin. It is better this way." She turned and began to walk towards the door.

"No," he snarled. "That is not how this works between you and me." She stilled. "I call you out when you are being particularly vexing. I do not let you win just because you are my queen. You do not get to shut me out."

"Sorin, please," she whispered.

He was before her now, leaning down to look into her eyes. "Why? You have an entire Court who will literally give their lives for you. You will need to learn to trust others, Scarlett. Your Court needs to know you trust them. *I* need to know you trust *me*. Tell me why."

"Because I cannot bear the thought of any of you being put into danger because of me!" Scarlett cried. "Because I know what is coming, and I have not yet figured out how to stop it! How do I explain that to everyone without a clear plan of action?"

"You depend on your Court to help you figure it out, Scarlett. You depend on those of us who have faced such threats before. You depend on *me*." He reached to stroke her cheek, but she stepped back from him.

"I have not depended on anyone so thoroughly since my sisters, and it was used against me, Sorin! It endangered everyone I love!" Sorin's eyes went wide with understanding. "People will *die* because of me! Some of our family may *die* because of my choices and orders. How do I live with that? I barely survived the loss of Juliette. I do not know that I could bear to go through that grief again. I do not think I would survive it a second time."

"Scarlett," Sorin said softly, tenderly. He gently took her hand and led her to the bench she had just sat on with Callan. "Briar did not pledge his loyalty to you simply because you are Eliné's heir. He saw that you were someone worth fighting for. My Court does not blindly serve you because I do or because you are my twin flame. They see a queen fighting for something bigger than herself. You rob them of defending their home and their people that they love by shoving them to the sidelines under the guise of keeping them safe and protected. Give them the choice and freedom to make those decisions."

"Gods," Scarlett sniffed, wiping a stray tear from her cheek, "you really are ancient, aren't you? That's the advice of a wise, ancient sage."

Sorin laughed as he brought his hand to her cheek. "If you do not give yourself permission to depend on others, your time on the throne will be lonely and will feel like the cage you so fear, my Love. Freedom lies in letting others in and letting them share the burden."

"Even though it is mine to bear?"

"Who says? I think you would love to do things your own way, while flipping off the Fates the entire time," Sorin replied with a smirk.

Scarlett snorted, leaning her brow against his, savoring the strength of him. After a long moment of silence, she stood. "Well, let's go then, Prince."

"Where to?" he asked with a raise of his brow.

"To the catacombs beneath your palace."

"The what?" His brows arched higher in surprise as he stood.

Scarlett looped her arm through his. "Really, I do not know how you lot survived without me."

Sorin reached over and flicked her nose, and she batted his hand away as she led him out the door and to the stairs. "But really, as your queen, wife, and twin flame...how old are you?"

Sorin tilted his head back and laughed. "Three hundred sixty-three years old."

Scarlett gaped. She knew he was immortal, but to hear an actual number put on it...

"You are as speechless as you were when I first met you and I told you I wanted your tongue to be my concern," Sorin mused as they descended the stairs. Scarlett muttered a vulgar name under her breath, to which Sorin only replied, "That list just keeps growing."

He pulled open the library door for her, letting her walk through first. She had never been down the secret passageway during the day. It had only been late in the night after dinner with Callan or when she snuck from their rooms, which, astonishingly, Sorin had not yet become suspicious about.

As they made their way down the dark forgotten halls, Sorin asked, "How much do I need to be preparing myself?"

Scarlett gave him a sympathetic smile. "I suppose it is a good thing we delayed our travels. It will give you time to rage over all my plans, try to talk me out of them, and then eventually accept them before we actually enact them."

"When were you planning to tell me about these plans?" he asked when they came to a stop before the ancient bookcase.

Scarlett pursed her lips, debating. "Honestly? Not until I was forced to."

"Scarlett, did we not specifically say no more secrets just last night?" he asked, rubbing his fingers across his brow.

"In all fairness, I did say no more secrets *after* today when we made that deal," she said, crouching before the bookcase. She pulled the trigger book and stood as the bookcase slid into the wall. She stepped onto the passage landing and turned to Sorin. "Shall we?"

He stood completely still, staring at her and the open passageway.

"Sorin?" she asked tentatively.

Without a word, he stepped to her side. She reached behind her to the lever that closed the passage entrance, sealing them in. When the bookcase was back in place, she shaped her flames into a small bird that flew before them, casting a soft glow on their path.

She had gone a few steps when she heard Sorin begin to follow. He spoke quietly, clearly dreading her answer. "When did you find this place, Scarlett?"

"The night you found me sleeping before the bookcase. I didn't come down here that night. I only had a dagger and a small torch…" she trailed off, continuing down the stairs.

Sorin was silent behind her. She summoned her shadow panther and took the book it still held in its massive maw, then sent it ahead of them, feeling for any threats. She flipped the book open, skimming pages as she went. Waiting. He had always waited for her, had always let her sort her thoughts out before speaking. She could do the same for him.

"If you did not come down here that night, then when?" he finally asked.

"The first time was the following week. After I had dinner with Callan and the others," she offered quietly.

"You came down here by yourself?"

"Yes."

"And you have been down here more than once?"

"I've come down here every night after dinner with them, but it wasn't enough, so…" She huffed a sigh. "I've been sneaking from our rooms a few nights a week."

"How?" he ground out through gritted teeth.

She continued to flip through the book as she spoke, unable to look at him. "The nights I come after dinner with Callan, I have clothes stored in a forgotten storage closet. The nights I slip from our room…" She shrugged.

"How have none of my guards seen you?"

"I watched them and studied them, along with the help. I know when the shift changes are. I know which guards are easier to traverse, which routes the help take. I am a Wraith of Death, Sorin. I know how to move about unseen and unheard," she replied.

The rest of the trek down the stairs was quiet. When they finally reached the bottom, she lit the various candles and torches she had hauled down over the past few weeks, illuminating a circular room. The entire perimeter was bookcases save for one spot where a hearth was built into the wall, and in the center of the room was a long wooden table with chairs and benches around it. It was cluttered with the books and all of her own papers she'd been taking notes on.

Scarlett went to the table and set the book Eliza had found among the others. Then she turned and sat on the bench facing Sorin. He was studying her, and she waited. She said nothing as he crossed the room and picked up one of the various books and flipped the pages quickly. She was quiet when he set the book back down and picked up her notes, skimming them and turning pages over. He set her notes down and went to the bookshelves, his hands in his pockets, as he looked at the titles. At last he turned to her and said, "None of these are in the common tongue."

"No, they are not."

"Very few are in the Old Language."

"Yes."

He turned back to the books once more before he came and sat beside her on the bench. "I do not even know where to begin. What to ask you," he admitted, his golden eyes meeting hers.

"Anything. I do trust you, Sorin. I'll share it all, and we can decide together how much to tell the others," she replied, taking his hand in hers.

"How can you read these?" he asked, motioning to the books on the table.

"Some of them I can't. I haven't found a way to translate them, but most of them are written in either this language," she said, pointing to one of the books, "or this one." She held up a second book. "This one is the one I've been able to decipher the most of and what I have spent most of my time down here learning."

"And what language is it?"

She swallowed. There was no going back. Not now. "The Avonleyan language. The other, I think, is the Maraan language, but it is much harder to translate."

"The language that you and Ashtine were talking about?"

"Yes."

"Who are the Maraan Lords?"

Scarlett stood now and walked to an open area of the room. She knelt in the dust and began drawing in it. Sorin stood and watched her as she drew their continent, marking off the various territories. "A few months ago, I thought our continent consisted of these territories," she said, pointing to the three human kingdoms and the Courts. "Then I learned of these other lands." She waved a hand over the makeshift map and various figures appeared, detailing the Shifters, Witches, and Night Children. She took a step to the left and drew another continent a ways away. "I suppose I've always known that Avonleya existed, but it seemed almost like a fairy tale," she said, rising to stand beside Sorin. "Then I learned of the Maraan Lords, but I cannot figure out where they came from. Where is their land? I know there have to be more continents beyond our own, but how did they get here?"

Sorin studied the makeshift map on the floor. "Why do you think they are here?"

"Because according to what I've been able to decipher in these books, Deimas was a Maraan King." Sorin's eyes shot to hers. "You told me no one knows where Deimas' power came from. Well, here it is. He was a completely different race and bloodline."

"Then what were his powers?"

"I haven't been able to find that, but from what I've gathered, their power was similar to an Avonleyan in terms of strength."

"Who are the Maraan Lords?" he asked again. He hadn't moved from where he stood studying her crude map.

"They are the rulers of Maraa, I suppose, with their king gone. There are seven territories, each ruled by a Lord. I imagine they would be comparable to you and the other princes and Ashtine. They are the most powerful now that Deimas is out of play," Scarlett explained.

"And you have faced them?"

She nodded mutely.

"When? How?"

"The first one… He had just arrived here. Was fresh off a ship. I don't think he quite understood how stifled his magic would be in the human lands. He was arrogant and made the comment that he had not believed his kin that were already here."

And she launched into the story of the night when she and Nuri and Juliette had killed a man near the docks. They had suspected he was connected to the missing orphans, but when he had compromised both her and Nuri, Juliette had shoved her sword through his neck.

"How does Mikale know of that night?" Sorin asked when she was finished.

"I don't know how he knows. Some sort of connection maybe that bonds all the Lords?"

Sorin's eyes widened in disbelief. "You think that Mikale is a Maraan Lord?"

"It fits with everything, Sorin. It would explain how he knew about that night. It would explain why he wants me. Why he wants to merge our bloodlines. If I'm as powerful as you think I am, and he is a Maraan Lord, a child would be…" Her voice was barely audible as she trailed off.

The possessive snarl that came out of Sorin made the hair on her neck stand on end. "He cannot have you," he growled. "I am yours, and you are mine."

"I do not think he will care," she replied, going back to the table and sitting once more. She pulled a book to her. The most recent one she'd been so slowly reading and translating. Sorin sat beside her, resting a hand on her thigh. "According to this, there are seven Lords. We beheaded one. I don't know who rose to take his seat, but before we killed him, he told us he was visiting kin here. I suspect there is more than one here, but it can't all be just for me."

"Do you have any idea who the others are?"

"I would venture to guess Lord Tyndell from the way he spoke that day when we left. This plan—" She paused, pushing her hair back out of her face. "They have patiently been waiting, Sorin. This had to have been enacted centuries ago, and they've just been biding their time. Waiting for all the pieces to fall into place."

"But what do they want?"

"I suspect the same thing they wanted during the Great War. Something in Avonleya, which they cannot gain entry to because of the wards so they are trying to find their work around."

"Deimas put the wards up," Sorin countered. "Do these Lords not know how to remove them?"

"That's the thing," Scarlett said. "You told me that Deimas and Esmeray didn't put the wards around the Fae lands, that the Fae did."

"Yes," Sorin said slowly. "You are thinking the Avonleyans did the same?"

"Possibly," she mused, "and if that is indeed the case, they're trying to find a way in."

With a twist of her wrist, her shadow panther appeared once more with another book in its maw. This one she had kept hidden since she found it, not even risking bringing it back to this chamber.

She handed the book to Sorin, and he visibly paled. He slowly opened it. This book had various languages. It was someone's personal spell book. Some of the spells were in the Old Language. Some in Avonleyan or Maraan. Some in languages she could not read nor decipher. But they were all ancient, powerful magic. They were all blood magic.

"It is why you have been asking so many questions about it," he said quietly.

"Yes."

"The cost of a spell that powerful, to overcome an Avonleyan ward, would be horrific," he said tightly.

"Yes. It is."

His eyes lifted from the book, coming to hers. "You found the spell?"

"I found one that would do something similar." She flipped the book to a page she had carefully marked. "It requires the blood of an innocent to be spilled. I can only imagine the spell they're using would need something equally powerful and likely magical..."

"The orphans," Sorin said in astonishment.

"You sound shocked that I figured all of this out," Scarlett said with a pointed look.

"No. I am... I think you are the only one who *could* figure all of this out, Love," he replied, looking over his shoulder at her notes and the books scattered about the table.

"I need to figure out who the other Lords are that are here, but first, I need you to tell me about the meeting the day I saw the Oracle," Scarlett said, gently taking the spell book from Sorin's hands. With a thought, her shadow panther had reappeared and taken it to whatever pocket between the worlds it kept it in. "I saw reports on the table after you had all come back here, and I was still with Talwyn. Ashtine reported the mortals are moving forces around."

"She did, particularly near the borders of the Western Courts," Sorin said grimly.

"How many?"

"She did not know for sure."

Scarlett grew quiet, contemplating.

"How do you plan to figure out who the other Lords are?" Sorin asked as he pored over her notes and translations.

Here we go, Scarlett thought, bracing herself for his reaction.

"I'm going to go and ask Mikale."

CHAPTER 56
SORIN

Sorin could not have possibly heard her right. He stood, looking down at her. "You are going to go and ask Mikale," he repeated.

"Yes," Scarlett said. "Our twin flame Marking will be glamoured in the mortal realm. He won't know of it or know that we are married. I am going to return to him."

Sorin just blinked at her. She bit her bottom lip, holding his stare. She was serious. Completely serious. "No," he said tightly. It was all he could think to say around the rage roaring through his veins.

"It is the only way, Sorin," she started.

"No."

"Sorin—"

"No."

She crossed her arms, leaning back against the table. "I'm going to need you to use more of your big boy words, Prince."

"Fuck no."

She huffed a soft laugh, and the sound of it, along with the sight of the slight smirk that accompanied it, had him fighting every urge to lie her on the floor and bury himself in her right here.

"No," he breathed, not trusting himself to move. "He has nearly destroyed you in so many ways, Scarlett. No. We will find another way."

"If you have a better idea, I am all ears," she retorted, remaining in her seat on the bench. "But he is not going to reveal anything to me if he does not believe I have come to his side. It is just a game that we will resume playing."

"No, it is a game we nearly lost a few months ago," Sorin argued.

She couldn't be serious. Not after everything they had gone through. Not after what he had pulled her out of. Not now that she was finally with him, had claimed him. There was no way he was letting his wife, his *queen*, go into enemy hands. Absolutely none. She would literally have to kill him first.

"Come up with a better plan, Sorin, and we can talk about it, but if not..."

"And what? You just claimed your throne, and now you will do exactly as Nakoa said and abandon your people? What if this goes badly, Scarlett? Because we both know this could go very, very bad, and then your lands, your people, are left with no one," he growled.

He felt something in her shift, but he couldn't quite read it. She didn't meet his gaze as she said softly, "They wouldn't be left with no one, Sorin. If I am a queen, then you are now a king and are far more qualified to lead these people anyway."

Sorin froze. She couldn't mean that. She sounded as if she had planned...

"Scarlett Aditya Semiria, look at me right now and tell me you did not choose a marriage before the Anointing for the purpose of making me a king."

Her eyes snapped to his and something akin to hurt flickered across them. "You know that's not true. How can you even say that to me?"

"Because you have been keeping secrets, Scarlett. Big secrets. And now you drop this bullshit about me being king—"

"It is not bullshit," she shouted, jumping to her feet. "And you are a king. You may be the Fire Prince, but you are also, as of this *marriage,* a godsdamn king of the realm." She spat the word 'marriage' at him like it burned her tongue and held up her left hand. "And if you honestly think that I only accepted the bond to make you a king and avoid my responsibility, then you do not know me at all."

Sorin couldn't tell if the rage he was feeling was his or her own echoed down the bridge. He growled, prowling back to her. She held his gaze the whole way, and he could see the storm in her eyes. A wild storm of ice and rain and wildfire and darkness. A storm his heart skipped a beat at and always made him wonder if he would survive this whirlwind that she was.

"You know," she chided when he stopped directly in front of her, "you're looking at me like you did when we first met."

"Like I want to throttle you?" he ground out.

"Yes," she snapped.

He tugged her to him as he said gruffly, "Travel us up to our room."

"Why?"

"Because there are too many ancient books on this table to shove them to the floor so I can properly fuck you."

"You think that we are going to go from fighting about this to *that* in a matter of seconds?" Her voice was calm, but he scented her. He heard her heart rate pick up.

He smirked at her and whispered into her ear, "Yes, Love, I do because I do in fact know you that well."

With no small amount of satisfaction, he heard her swallow. Her voice was quieter, breathless, when she said, "We cannot Travel or portal into this room. There are some kind of wards or enchantments around it."

"Really?" He hadn't felt them. Not a hint of any type of magic down here at all other than the small amount that Scarlett had displayed.

"Yes. I tried to Travel here earlier, when you were in the bath, and I couldn't get in. You could try to portal, but I don't think it will work."

He did try, and she was right. He ground his teeth together, and grabbing her hand, he began tugging her towards the stairs. "Sorin," she protested, "we need to talk about this." But he smiled as she followed him without any type of resistance.

"We will," he replied as they started climbing the stairs.

"Sorin, we have much to do and prepare for."

"We will," he repeated.

"Sorin—"

But he cut her off. He turned and pushed her against the stairwell wall, his lips crashing onto hers. Surprise sparked across her face, but then she was kissing him back, her tongue tasting his. He pressed himself against her, lining himself up with her, his hand sliding down to her breast. She moaned softly and her hips arched into him, grinding against his hardness. He hissed at the movement and pulled back from the kiss. "Keep that up, Princess, and we'll be doing this right here in the stairwell."

A rough laugh escaped her. "We're almost at the top. I'd hate to fall down these stairs."

He kissed her again, a quick brush of lips, before he turned and began leading her up the steps once more. She pulled the lever to open the passageway door. As soon as the bookcase was back in place behind them, her lips were back on his, and she Traveled them to their room. Had the feel of her body against his not been his sole focus, he would have been impressed at her ability to land them directly on the bed.

Her hands slipped under his jacket, slipping it down his arms. Then she pulled his shirt from him. His hand went up under her tunic, his fingers grazing over her peaked nipple. She groaned at the contact, nipping at his lower lip, as his other hand went down and cupped her over her pants.

She had just reached for the buttons on his own pants when there was a knock on the door. Scarlett froze, her head jerking towards the sound.

"Unless death is on our doorstep, I highly suggest you leave and pretend you were never here," Sorin snarled at the door.

"Well, death may actually be on our doorstep," came Cyrus's voice. "We've been trying to find you two for nearly an hour."

"Apparently, we should have opted for the stairwell," Scarlett grumbled. "A last tumble before death would have been nice."

Sorin growled in frustration as he rolled off of her and stalked to the door. He jerked it open. "What exactly is the issue?"

Cyrus winced as he took in Sorin's bare chest, his eyes flickering to where Scarlett sat on the bed, straightening her tunic.

"What kind of death are we talking about here, Cyrus? Are we dying? Is someone else dying? Am I killing someone? What's happening?" she asked flippantly, rising from the bed.

Cyrus smirked at her while Sorin shrugged his shirt back on. "The borders. There are messengers at the borders. Night Children."

"Both borders?" Sorin questioned as they followed him from the room.

"Yes," Cyrus confirmed. "Sawyer sent word while we were trying to find you. Why couldn't we send fire messages to you?"

Interesting. Apparently that chamber below the library kept out more than just Travelers and portals.

"What do they want?" Scarlett asked.

"To speak with the princes."

"The princes?" Sorin questioned. "Not Talwyn?"

"No," Cyrus answered, his tone grim. "They know you have not turned over their...weapon to Talwyn."

Sorin felt Scarlett still beside him, and he halted his own steps, turning to her. "They're here for me?" she asked.

"It would appear so," Cyrus replied.

"They cannot cross the borders, Scarlett," Sorin said, bringing his hand to her cheek. "You are safe. They cannot touch you."

"That's not... Where are the others?" she asked Cyrus.

"Eliza is at the border with a small unit of soldiers. Rayner is scouting, waiting for orders," he answered, reaching up to tie his shoulder-length hair back with a strap of leather as they continued on down the hall.

"Have we heard from Briar?" Sorin asked.

"Sawyer said he's at his border with Nakoa and Neve monitoring."

"Has anyone told Talwyn?"

"I believe she remains unaware. For how long that remains the case, I don't know," Cyrus replied, and they turned into a council room.

Scarlett had fallen completely silent. Sorin glanced at her, and he knew she was only half here, half listening to what they were discussing. "We should go to the border. See what Eliza has learned," Sorin said, watching Scarlett while she stood before a window, looking out at the mountains.

"Agreed," Cyrus said with a nod. He, too, glanced at the queen and then back to Sorin with a raise of his brows. And he didn't know. He didn't know what to tell his Second. He didn't know what she was thinking through. Was she thinking of Mikale? Had her mind gone to Cassius? Or was it back in that chamber beneath the library and something else she had learned?

"Scarlett," he ventured hesitantly.

"Hmm?" She didn't even turn to them as she bit her bottom lip.

"We are going to go to the border to check in with Eliza."

"Okay." She made no move to come to them, though. Flames were dancing along her fingers and swirling among the shadows she had called forth. He had watched her do so much of the same on the balcony. Lost in her own thoughts and contemplations.

Sorin opened a portal and jerked his chin to Cyrus to go through. He merely nodded once, cast another furtive glance to Scarlett, and went through. Sorin crossed the room. "I would think you would want to go with us," he said when he reached her side.

"What?" She looked at him, her nose scrunching in confusion.

"To the border. I told you we were going to the border to check in with Eliza. I am assuming you would want to come."

"Yes, of course," she said quickly.

Before he could say more, she grabbed his hand, and he felt the familiar sensation of Traveling. Then he was blinking in the midday sunlight in the middle of a small camp on the edge of the border. The way the wards were set up, they could see across to the mortal lands, but they couldn't see in from the other side. It simply looked like a continuous field.

But before them was indeed a small camp of forces, and three Night Children stood on the other side waiting. They clearly knew exactly where the border demarcation line ran. Scarlett let go of his hand, walking right to the edge, and had Sorin reaching out to her before she crossed over.

"Are they the only Night Children here? Just those three?" she asked him. Her shadows were hovering at her shoulders and snaking down her arms. He had gotten used to seeing her without them, and he didn't know if she had summoned them or if they had arisen unbidden this time.

"They are the only ones currently visible, yes," he answered, a hand sliding around her waist.

She tilted her head to the side, studying them. "How can you tell? Other than scent?"

"They do not have physical characteristics like the Fae do," he answered. "They are protected from the sun, though. The others I see have exposed skin."

"Other than that, though, there is no way to tell? If they were all dressed the same, covered, would you be able to tell who was a Night Child and who was mortal if they were standing side-by-side?"

"No."

Her lips pressed into a thin line. "How do you send those fire messages? I want to know how many are at the Water Court border."

"You could summon Briar here," Sorin answered. "Speak with him directly."

"No, he needs to be in his Court until this is resolved," she said, her tone was distant once more. Sorin sent her request though, the fire message flaring before disappearing.

"Do you recognize any of the mortals? Are any from your High Force?" Scarlett asked suddenly.

"No," he answered, scanning the small camp before his border quickly. "No one from the High Force is here."

"What's the plan here, Prince?" Eliza came striding up to them, Cyrus on her heels.

"Has anyone spoken to them?" Sorin asked, watching Scarlett as she began pacing in front of the border, her eyes fixed on the three Night Children. What was she working out?

"No. They have spoken, but no one has responded," Eliza answered.

"What did they say?"

"Only that they wanted to talk to you." Eliza's eyes were now on the queen as well. She had dropped to the ground and begun drawing in the dirt. She drew and wiped the symbols away and drew again. After the third time, Sorin dropped down beside her.

"Love, what are you doing?"

"Did Briar answer? How many are there?" she asked, beginning to draw the symbols again. They were stars and varying shapes and swirls. They were like Marks but sharper, not as elegant.

"We have not heard back from him. Scarlett, what are you doing?"

But she kept working, kept drawing. "You said the mortals were moving forces around. What about the other borders? The Earth Court?"

"I don't know. We are not exactly on friendly terms with the Earth Court," he said slowly, trying to keep the frustration from his voice.

She wiped the symbols away once more as she said, "Do you not have eyes there? Where is Rayner? Doesn't he know?"

Sorin reached out and put his hands over hers. She finally brought her eyes to his, the icy blue paler and nearly silver. "Love, what are you doing?"

"I need… Can you see this Mark on my arm?" she asked suddenly, extending her left forearm to him. Her bare left forearm.

Sorin shook his head. "I see nothing, Scarlett. There is nothing there." She peered down at her arm, her other hand coming up and drawing there now, as if indeed tracing a Mark he could not see. "Is there a Mark there?"

But she said nothing. Her eyes turned back to the three Night Children. "Go talk to them. See what they have to say." She was again extending her hand to him. In her palm lay her Semiria ring. To give him access to his magic across the border.

"You will remain on this side?"

"Yes," she replied, pushing to her feet.

"Why?"

"That would seem obvious, Prince. I'm what they presumably want," she said with a raise of her brow.

"Yes, but I would expect you to taunt and tease them about that, not stay safely behind a magical border like I would prefer."

"If it's what you'd prefer, why are we arguing about it?" Her hands went to her hips.

A flurry of snowflakes appeared at his shoulder, and he reached up to pluck Briar's response to his message. "Briar says there are three."

Her shadows darkened as she shoved her hands in her pockets. "Go talk to them, Sorin," she said with a jerk of her chin. "Take Cyrus and Eliza with you."

"Yes, let's please do something other than stand here," Eliza drawled, practically hopping from foot to foot with bloodlust shining in her eyes.

"Give me a minute and then we will talk to them," Sorin said with a pointed look at his Court. Cyrus and Eliza nodded and went to wait for him. Scarlett's eyes were back on the three vampyres. He reached for her, turning her to face him. When she finally met his gaze, he said softly, "Hey, Love."

He could have sworn grief flashed across her features, but it was gone instantly as she whispered, "Hey, Prince."

"You want to tell me what's going on?"

"Besides the fact that I've been a queen for what? Two days? And I have already brought death to our doorstep?"

"Let's try again," Sorin replied, reaching up and tucking her hair behind her ear. "What have you been figuring out since Cyrus said they are here for you?"

A small smile tugged on the corner of her mouth. Her arms came up and looped around his neck. "That a siren's call draws unexpected power," she murmured, rising up on her tiptoes to kiss him.

"I find your vague answers extremely worrisome," he replied, pulling back from her.

"I find your role of mother hen to be extremely tiresome, but here we are," she drawled. He gave her a pointed look, and she merely kissed him once again before she said, "Go see what those bastards want, then tell them to go to hell."

"Do not think I am going to drop this matter," he answered, nipping at her bottom lip.

"I would expect nothing less."

She dropped her arms and turned to face the border once more, to watch everything from the sidelines. He knew there was more. He knew she was working something out, had figured something out, but Eliza and Cyrus were waiting.

He double checked his weapons and buckles as he walked to his Court, unable to shake his feeling of unease.

"Is she all right?" Cyrus asked.

"No, but I cannot get her to talk to me here," Sorin bit back, taking the bow Eliza extended to him and slinging the quiver over his shoulder. It was fully stocked with black ashwood arrows.

"Let's find out what these pricks want and then you two can go somewhere," Cyrus answered.

Sorin only nodded, casting one last look at Scarlett. She met his eyes and gave him a soft smile. It was one he rarely saw. It was the smile that graced her lips on the rare occasions she spoke of Juliette.

Yes, he'd deal with this, and then he'd take her out to the city. Just the two of them. And he'd coax out whatever was threatening her stars.

CHAPTER 57
SORIN

Sorin stepped across the border, Cyrus and Eliza flanking him on either side. A grin spread across the face of the Night Child standing in the middle, just visible beneath the black hood of his cloak. There was a light dusting of snow on this side of the border, and it crunched beneath his boots.

"You finally answer your door. How courteous of you," the vampyre drawled.

"I do not recall inviting you to dinner, so forgive my tardiness in meeting you," Sorin bit back, sliding his hands into his pockets.

The Night Child snorted in amusement. "We will be feasting soon enough, Fae bastard."

"You can certainly try," Eliza crooned beside him, her sword drawn. The vampyre to the right bared his teeth, fangs out. Eliza merely bared her own canines back at him and purred, "I've got a set, too."

"I'm going to assume you are the Prince of Fire?" the one in the middle cut in smoothly, addressing Sorin once more. Sorin stood silently, unable to identify himself as such in the mortal lands. The vampyre sighed in annoyance. "Where is Lord Lairwood's bride, by the way?" Cyrus's hand clamped down on Sorin's shoulder as a growl emanated from him. The vampyre smirked. "I guess that confirms that. Since I know who you are, allow me to introduce myself. I am Colton, and the Lord has sent me to…check on his weapon."

"He refers to his fiancé as a weapon now?" Sorin sneered.

Colton's smirk turned sinister. "Not that Lord."

"Lord Tyndell then?"

"Very good, Prince. You've figured some things out."

Sorin gave him his own cruel smile. "Their *weapon* figured it out."

Colton chuckled. "Tell me, Prince of Fire, has she recovered from her injury? I wasn't there, but Bowen here tells me she was cut up beautifully," he said with a nod to the vampyre that had bared its fangs at Eliza.

"You were there?" Sorin asked, his eyes going to Bowen.

"I was," he hissed. "I saw Saul slice up her side with his dagger before that bitch encased him in her shadows."

Then he was gurgling at the arrow that was through his throat courtesy of Cyrus who already had another one nocked.

"That was unnecessary," Colton snarled through gritted teeth.

Sorin's dark smile grew. "We have different definitions of what is necessary."

Colton stiffened. "This infernal Court has always been infested with the foulest of you."

"Perhaps that is why Deimas modeled the Black Syndicate after us then," Sorin retorted. "Say what you have come to say before the bloodsucker to your left meets the same fate for wasting my fucking time."

"I already told you. The Lord has sent me to check on his weapon," Colton said with a shrug of his shoulders. "I expected her to be with you based on the little I have heard about her."

"You can tell your *masters* that she is no longer a weapon and is no longer their concern. They cannot have her. They will never have her again," Sorin snarled.

Colton chuckled. "We are not here for her. I think you will find she will return on her own," he mused, his dark eyes glittering. "You will find, Prince of Fire, that shadows always return to the darkness."

"If you are not here for her, then what is your business?" Sorin snapped. He needed to get back to Scarlett. She knew something. This vampyre repeating Mikale's words from a month ago made his unease about her staying on the other side of the border only grow. What was she making of all this? He could feel her pacing on the other side of the border.

Colton's lips curled into a sinister grin, revealing his fangs. "To confirm the Prince of Fire's identity."

"That's it? You brought all these men here for that? Something you have done all on your own?" Eliza demanded from his side.

"No, that's not it," Colton replied. "It was actually more of a bonus to be honest."

"Why are men stationed at the Water Court border?" Cyrus asked now, his arrow still trained on the other Night Child. "And the other two Court borders?"

"Perhaps you should be asking why she did not accompany you to speak with me," Colton countered.

"You are not privy to her reasons," Sorin growled, smoke curling on his tongue. He had kept his hands in his pockets to hide the ring so they would believe him unable to access his magic, but he was becoming increasingly annoyed with the vampyre.

Colton's eyes narrowed coldly. "And you are not privy to that of the Lords."

Thank you for loving me like the stars love the night, Sorin. Thank you for guiding me home.

Her words startled him as they came down that bond, and he froze. He whirled to face the border as realization slammed into him. She had given him that soft smile one other time, aside from when she spoke of Juliette— when she had said goodbye to him to go to Mikale.

He couldn't see across the border. He took a step. To go to her. To make her tell him what she had figured out, but Eliza's warning cry had him turning back. He jerked to the side as a shirastone dagger flew past him, grazing a shallow cut along his shoulder. He didn't have time for this. Something was wrong with his wife.

He growled, stalking forward towards the two remaining vampyres. A circle of flames encased the entire camp of mortals. Cries rang up from the men, and the Night Children hissed as they realized he was wearing Scarlett's ring when Sorin raised his hand before them. As though he were wiping away a stain on a window, flames moved across that small encampment, leaving nothing but ashes in their wake. Tents, flesh, bones. All of it became ashes on the wind. No one was spared. No one was given a chance to beg for mercy.

With a thought, the Night Children had flames encircling their throats and were screeching in protest. He silenced the one who had never spoken by shoving flames down his throat. He collapsed to the ground, never to rise again.

Colton stared at him, hatred glittering in his eyes.

"Tell me what her shadow magic is," Sorin growled at him, that ring of flames squeezing tighter.

But Colton's eyes snagged on his forearm where a Bargain Mark was inked. A flame with three diamonds. His eyes lifted to Sorin's and a slow, cunning smile spread across his face. "You shall learn what her magic is soon enough, Prince of Fire. The Sorceress will see to that," he gasped out around the pressure on his throat.

Sorin only had that noose of flame squeezing tighter and tighter...until his head was disconnected from his body.

"Holy gods, Sorin," Cyrus said in disbelief. "No prisoners to interrogate?"

Sorin said nothing as he turned and raced across the border, crossing at the exact spot she had last been standing.

"Scarlett!" He looked every direction for her, searching for the flash of silver in a sea of black and red and golden hair. But there was nothing. No answer to his call. He could not feel her. He could not find her.

He glanced at his hand where the twin flame Mark stood dark and stark against his tanned skin. The bond was still there. Unbroken.

"What the hell is going on?" Eliza demanded, panting as she came running over the border behind him.

Sorin's blood had drained from his face, though. His eyes had settled not on a queen with silver hair, but on a ring, floating on a shadow. A diamond ring flanked by two rubies. Her marriage ring.

He pulled on that bridge between their souls. He roared her name down it, but he was met with nothing. It was as if there were a wall blocking their connection. He slammed flames against that obstacle. Over and over and over, but nothing cracked it.

Rayner appeared from ashes and stilled at the panic and rage and utter terror written all over his prince's face. His family was frozen as Sorin...just stood there. He couldn't form complete thoughts. He could hardly breathe. She had gone. She had left.

"Sorin?" Cyrus's voice was hesitant. "Where is she?"

But he couldn't form words. They were foreign to him as he stared at that ring floating on a pillow of darkness.

"What is that?" Rayner asked in his quiet voice of cold. He was pointing below the shadow.

To a drawing. The drawing she had been doing in the dirt.

Sorin stumbled towards the ring and the symbol. With a trembling hand, he reached out and took the ring, the shadow immediately dissipating. He closed his fist around that band of metal and precious gems, his chest constricting as if he were gripping his own heart instead. He drew in a breath and jasmine and lavender and citrus and night filled his senses.

"What is it?" Eliza asked.

His Inner Court stood around him now in stunned silence.

Sorin dropped to his knees before that symbol. That Mark.

"What is it?" Eliza demanded again, sharper. Bordering on hysterical.

"It is a Blood Mark," Sorin rasped, finally finding words.

"That's not possible," Cyrus blurted, stooping down to study the Mark.

But it was. It was possible. Because that was blood splattered on the carefully drawn Mark. Her blood. It was possible because she hadn't just been learning about Blood Magic for research purposes these last months while sneaking down to that chamber. She hadn't just been translating the Avonleyan and Maraan languages. She had been learning how to read the Blood Magic spells and Marks.

She had learned how to use them.

She had indeed become a weapon.

A weapon that could start and end a war.

CHAPTER 58

SCARLETT

S carlett crept along the trees of the forest. The camp of mortal soldiers was precisely where she expected they'd be— as close to the southeast corner of the Earth Court as they could be without having to be in Dresden Forest.

The forest ran along the entire eastern border of the Kingdom of Toreall with the Witch Kingdoms on the other side. It was an expansive forest with oak trees so thick you knew they were ancient. Growing up, they'd been told stories of spirits and wicked animals that roamed these woods. Now she suspected such rumors were likely the Witches moving about the forest. And the griffins, she supposed. She still wasn't sure she quite believed Sorin that those creatures were what the Witches flew on. But he did have a good point. Griffins seemed much more fitting for the terrifying females she'd encountered on her brief visits to the territory.

She pushed aside thoughts of the Witches and griffins as she watched the forces before her. There were less here than were camped at the Fire Court border.

Something had not sat right since she had seen those reports in Talwyn's council room a few days ago. Sorin had confirmed that Ashtine had learned that forces were being moved to all the borders, but no one could gather why. No one had any idea as to why the mortals had suddenly decided that they needed to add security along the Fae borders.

Scarlett was beginning to suspect it had nothing to do with the mortals. There were at least two Maraan Lords in Baylorin. What were the odds they were only in Windonelle? The odds were as likely as coincidences had become in her life. Nonexistent.

There had been three Night Children at her own border and three at the Water Court. Their demand had not been for her. The others had assumed that was what they would want, but their demand had been to speak with the princes. When they'd arrived at the border, and she'd discovered only three vampyres present, her suspicions had only grown. If they had been there for her, more than three Night Children would have been there. Lord Tyndell and Mikale knew of her powers. Mikale had seen her since she had fled for the Fire Court. He knew she was working to master her magic. Three Night Children would have hardly been a challenge, even without her magic. No, they were not there for her.

Sorin had thought she was worried about her own safety, but her thoughts had been on anything but her wellbeing. If they weren't moving into place to take her, then what were they doing? Sorin hadn't recognized any of the mortal soldiers stationed near the Fire Court. None of his High Force was there.

The High Force was a small, tight, and impeccably trained unit. One soldier from the High Force was likely equal to ten regular soldiers. They had been learning about the Night Children.

And was likely right in front of her.

Scarlett had watched as Sorin had spoken to the three Night Children. She had watched as they had gone back and forth verbally. She had seen the fury cross Cyrus's face when the one vampyre had spoken of her being stabbed months ago. She'd smiled at the arrow he'd loosed in vengeance for her. She'd listened as the leader had told Sorin they'd expected to see her there. As he'd tried to enrage Sorin enough to tell him her whereabouts. Not because they wanted her, she'd realized, but because they'd wanted to make sure she was, in fact, in the Fire Court.

They were the distraction while something else was going on.

The High Force had not been learning about the Night Children to invade their territory. They had not been training to fight against them, not in the end. They only needed to fight against the ones who wouldn't join their own forces. They only needed to get to the ones who would want to get revenge on Avonleya and feast on the Fae.

She had known then what she needed to do. She'd known Sorin would object, would fight her on it. He would have wanted to meet with Talwyn and Azrael, but there wasn't time. The distraction was staring them in the face, which meant whatever they were up to was happening now. There was not time for meetings and correspondence.

But she also didn't know what she was facing. Nakoa had been right when he'd flung accusations at her. She was a novice who had no fucking idea what she was doing. She was an assassin who hunted down Fae and those who didn't want to be found. She was an expert at taking out one person. She could fight her way out of a crowd. But facing down trained soldiers by herself? A unit that had been trained by Sorin? This could all go very, very badly, and if it did, if she were hauled back to Baylorin, she didn't want it known that she was married. She didn't want Sorin to follow until she knew what she'd be facing. So she'd left her wedding ring behind, and she'd used the Blood Magic she'd been studying in that chamber in the dark hours of the night. She'd used a blocking Mark to create a barrier in their twin flame bond to keep him from sensing her and her from sensing him.

The cost had been having to kiss him and knowing it could very well be the last time. The cost had been having to act completely natural, argue with him, and watch him cross that border without her at his side. The cost had been the trust she very well could have irrevocably broken the second she'd sliced her palm and let her blood drip on that Mark she'd so carefully drawn in the dirt.

She glanced down at her now clear skin. The Mark hidden as a demand of the glamour in the mortal lands. She gritted her teeth, straining to hear the men beyond the trees. How had Sorin lasted three years in these lands with diminished Fae senses?

All the people she'd seen among the small camp were covered head to toe so any of them could be High Force or vampyre. She couldn't scent them this far away, so here she sat, watching and waiting. Something had to happen soon if the Western Courts were currently being distracted.

Sure enough, a few minutes later, all the men began to congregate near the edge of the forest. Scarlett had slunk back farther into the trees as their leader began speaking and giving orders. The leader was the closest to her. The scents of blood and night-kissed wind drifted towards her. A Night Child then. Nine others were hanging on the edges of the group, watching not the leader but the surrounding lands. An escort, she realized. They were an escort of Night Children to lead them through the lands, but they had to cross a small section of the Earth Court first. Prince Azrael would destroy them. Either that or they'd have to cross through a small section of the Witch Kingdoms, which was arguably more terrifying.

This was all assuming they could get past the wards.

Scarlett carefully crept closer.

"Our sole goal when we get into the territory is to find the Contessa," the leader was saying. "We have reason to believe she is not in her palace, but in her private residence. We have someone on the inside close to her who knows where it is. He'll be meeting us as soon as we cross the border. He will fill us in further and tell us how to tell which Night Children to kill and which are on our side."

The Contessa?

Scarlett racked her memories. The Contessa ruled the Night Children. Other than that, she knew little of her. To rule over such a bloodline, though, she had to imagine she was not an easy target and would be incredibly dangerous.

"As soon as the queen arrives and is taken care of, we move," the leader continued.

Scarlett sat up at that. They hadn't moved yet because they were waiting for her? No. They were waiting for Talwyn. Talwyn would kill them all by sucking the air from their lungs. They wouldn't stand a chance against Talwyn.

And they wouldn't stand a chance against her.

Scarlett took a deep breath, calling her shadows forward. They swirled and danced and nearly trembled at being allowed out, waiting to pounce and attack and kill. Then she plunged down deep into that well of magic in her soul. She pushed down and down and down, drawing every ember and drop of water and cold ice to herself. She had summoned her witch-suit and fighting leathers before she'd left the Fire Court.

Drawing the Spirit Sword from her back, she sauntered out of the woods to the waiting forces. They all froze, turning to stare at her as she propped the sword blade on her shoulder, one hand going to her hip.

"If you're waiting for the queen, then here I am," she drawled.

The leader's lip curled back under his hood and his nostrils flared. "You are no queen," he purred. "You are something so much better."

The hand on her hip came dramatically to her chest. "I'm flattered that you think so."

Four of the men guarding the small unit had come to flank the leader. The other five had closed in tighter, herding the men. Not herding them at all really. The High Force was getting into a formation.

"How cute," she smirked. "Practicing those moves that General Renwell spent years teaching you."

"Do not speak to them," the leader hissed, taking a step towards her. "Where is the Fae Queen?"

"Now, now," Scarlett chided. "We just agreed I'm much better. Don't offend me by asking for her when we can play."

A smile curled on the leader's face. "And play we shall, but we cannot make another move until the Fae Queen arrives and is…handled."

"Have you met the Fae Queen? She will destroy you all in a single breath. Literally," Scarlett answered, her tone bored as she flipped her sword hilt in her hand.

"We are well aware of the Fae Queen's gifts," the leader gritted out. "We are prepared for her."

"Pity," Scarlett said with a shrug.

"Why is that a pity?" the leader demanded.

"Because I really like to play," she purred. Flames encircled their entire company, the Night Children hissing back towards the men.

Scarlett stalked forward, her shadows growing thicker with each step creating a shield of darkness locking out all threats. She stopped on the outside of the fire enclosure and gave the leader a simpering smile...as two of the Night Children flanking him froze from the inside out. She sent a whip of her shadows at them, breaking them into chunks of frozen blood and gore.

The leader's eyes dragged back to hers, and she purred, "Let's play a game."

"It appears as though you've already cheated," he hissed, his fangs on full display.

Scarlett winked at him. "I was just leveling the playing field a little bit. You still have way more men on your side than I do on mine."

A snake's smile slowly flitted over the leader's features. "Then let's play a game, Princess." His honey-colored eyes locked onto hers as his voice shifted. It was calm and soft and enticing. Her body went tense and lax all at once. The other Night Children around the men began to move once more. Her gaze flickered to them, but the leader tsked, and in that same voice purred, "Your eyes stay on me, Princess."

Her eyes slid back to his and held. Something in the recesses of her mind thrashed in response, but she quieted it.

"Take down your flames," he ordered smoothly.

Scarlett did so, and as the last of the flames disappeared, the leader came to a stop directly in front of her. He reached up and ran a finger along her jaw. "Everyone desires you. Everyone fears you. Everyone finds you so...uncontrollable. It wasn't really that difficult to leash you."

"What is your name?" she breathed, bringing her own hand up to his cheek, stepping into him further.

His nostrils flared, and he grazed his nose along her throat. "Lennox. Say it," he demanded. "Let me hear it on your lips."

"Lennox," she crooned, her hand sliding across his chest.

One of the other Night Children came up beside Lennox and whispered in his ear. He only nodded, that serpentine smile growing wider as the male stepped back. "It appears I am winning our game, Princess, and our plans have changed."

"What plans?" she asked, her fingers continuing to trail along his chest.

"Our plans to enter the Night Children land, but much more interesting prey has come along," he answered, his hand coming up to cup the back of her head. His fingers gripped her hair, and he gave a sharp tug to jerk her head back and to the side. Again, his nose grazed her neck, a fang sliding along her throat. "The mortals have fallen back to give us room to…work. To contain you."

Scarlett stepped farther into him, all of her pressing against all of him. The vampyre groaned softly. "I'd love for you to contain me," she whispered.

Lennox chuckled. "I bet you would, Princess." A fang scraped again. "If it would not make my death imminent, I'd taste you in more ways than one."

"Pity," she breathed into his ear, "because your death is imminent, anyway."

Her shadows struck, wending around his throat and lifting him off his feet before her. Lennox was kicking his feet in the air, his hands trying to grip the shadows around her neck, but his fingers slid through the darkness as if going through fog. "Interesting fact, Son of Night," she drawled, "entrancing doesn't work on me."

"How?" he gasped out.

"Not entirely sure, and I don't entirely care." With a thought, her shadows threw Lennox to the ground, and she shoved that darkness down his throat into every vein on his body until he stilled.

The remaining eight vampyres descended on her, and flames of white erupted from her hands. Two were dead before they took another step. She dragged up more and more power as she plummeted down into that pool inside herself. A swirling vortex of darkness and starlight, flame and water. She wreathed the spirit sword with those white flames and plunged it deep into the chest of a vampyre that charged at her. Hands snagged her around the waist, but her shadows immediately clamped onto him, prying arms from her. They held him in place until her sword went through his throat.

Two shadow panthers took down two more Night Children, ripping them apart. Arms and legs and chunks of flesh littering the ground. They prowled to her side as she faced the final two vampyres. They were hanging back, fangs bared, circling her.

Two left. She could feel herself lagging, exhaustion seeping into her being. She'd get information from these last two and then Travel back to Sorin. She'd collapse into his arms and apologize for what she'd done and beg him to touch her to get the feel of Lennox's hands off of her.

"What do you want with the Contessa?" she snarled, trying to hide how drained she was.

"The Contessa controls the Night Children," one hissed in response. "Whoever kills the Contessa, takes her place."

And could order the Night Children to aid the mortals and Lords.

The vampyre that had spoken suddenly had a shirastone dagger in its head. Scarlett whirled in the direction it had come from, but blinding pain sparked in the back of her head. Her vision blurred and spots danced. Her shadows flickered as she dropped to her knees.

Another burst of pain...and then blessed darkness.

CHAPTER 59
SCARLETT

"Hurry, baby," Eliné said, gripping Scarlett's hand. "We are almost there."

"Mother, I'm tired," Scarlett complained, rubbing her eyes. "Can't we go to the beach in the morning?"

"You love the beach, Scarlett," her mother said gently. "There is something very important we need to do tonight."

Scarlett fell silent as her little five-year-old legs worked to keep up with her mother's long stride towards the beach. It was so dark, but the sky was clear. The stars glittered and twinkled above them with a full moon reflecting on the sea as they finally came to the beach. Her mother stopped when they neared the water and seemed to breathe in deep, closing her eyes.

"Mother?" Scarlett asked tentatively in her small child's voice.

Eliné stooped down to slide Scarlett's shoes from her feet. "Go feel the sand between your toes, baby. They will be here soon."

Scarlett didn't know who they were waiting for as she ran along the waves gently rolling to the shore. She giggled at the cool water spraying her legs, and she waded out farther, the bottom of her nightgown becoming soaked in the surf. She turned back to make sure her mother was still nearby and found her standing with another. The newcomer was wearing a cloak, the hood up and covering the person's face. The giggles and smile instantly *vanished as she quickly and quietly came to her mother's side, hiding behind her skirts.*

"It is all right, Scarlett. Sybil will be here soon with your Cassius," Eliné said softly, running her fingers through Scarlett's silver hair.

Scarlett nodded mutely, staring at the person standing beside her mother. Cassius was always assigned to watch over her when her mother had to work. He was so strong and always took her to pick pears in the grove. Everything would be better once Cassius got here.

"Her tonic?" the stranger asked. A woman. Her voice was feminine.

"I only gave her half so I could wake her. I will give her the other half when we return," her mother answered. The woman nodded, and although Scarlett couldn't see her face, she knew the woman was watching her.

A moment later, Sybil was indeed coming down the beach with Cassius in tow. Where was Juliette? Nuri? Why hadn't they come?

"This is him?" the woman asked.

"This is Cassius, yes," her mother answered. "This is the one you seek."

"Give me your hand, child," the stranger said, extending her own hand to Cassius. Cassius glanced from Eliné to Sybil, who both nodded to him. He did as they indicated, and in a flash, the stranger had a dagger drawn and had slashed a cut along his palm. Scarlett cried out, but Eliné was already comforting her. "It is all right, baby. Look. Cassius is fine."

Indeed. Cassius had his teeth gritted, but he didn't look scared. He wasn't crying. Brave. He was always so brave. She could be brave, too.

The stranger dipped her finger into the blood pooling in his hand and sniffed it. "Has Ranvir appeared yet?"

"We have not seen him, but we have not seen Shirina yet either," Eliné answered quietly. "I am assuming it is because we are in these lands."

"You have confirmed who sired him, though?"

Sybil eyed the stranger. "Can you not smell it in his blood?"

"I can," the woman answered. "It is just still a wonder to me. He never indicated he would ever take a lover, let alone one with whom to sire a child."

Then the stranger was stooping down before Scarlett. She scooted back farther behind her mother's skirts. Sybil's hands came to Cassius's shoulders to hold him in place as he lurched for her. The woman reached up and pulled back her hood. Her silver hair glinted in the moonlight, and Scarlett's eyes widened. "Your hair is beautiful, Little One," the woman said gently with a soft smile.

Her eyes were silver and glowed in the night. "Tell me, Scarlett, do you like the sun or the moon better?"

"The moon," Scarlett whispered, "but I like the stars best of all."

"Me too," the woman answered. Her throat bobbed, and Scarlett wasn't sure, but she thought the pretty woman might cry. "I have a secret to tell you. Can you keep a secret?"

Scarlett nodded her head, taking a step out from behind her mother, towards the woman. "The world will tell you that the night houses the wicked and cruel, but what they do not know..." And the woman paused as a flame of pure white glittered in her palm, cold as the space between the stars. "Is that the darkness is where the most beautiful things grow."

Scarlett smiled at the woman, and without thinking, reached out to touch the flames in her hand. The woman smiled again, but even at the age of five, Scarlett could tell it was a sad smile. The woman took Scarlett's little hand in her own, the flames vanishing. "I need you to do something for me, Scarlett. I need to make a cut on your hand like I did for Cassius. To keep you..." The woman paused, swallowing thickly again. "It will help keep you safe. Can you be really brave right now, Starfire?"

Despite the nerves in her stomach, Scarlett grinned at the name the woman had given her. "Yes," she said, nodding in emphasis. She turned her palm over in the woman's, extending her fingers.

"So brave," the woman murmured.

Scarlett closed her eyes tight as the woman slashed her palm just as quickly as she had cut Cassius's. A moment later, she was tipping Cassius's palm into Scarlett's, mixing their blood together. The woman swirled it in her palm with her finger. "Turn them," she said to Eliné and Sybil.

The women turned to the children, and Scarlett felt her nightgown being lifted and the woman's finger drawing in the middle of her back. She glanced over as the woman lifted Cassius's tunic and drew on his lower back, too. Two overlapping circles with a line through the middle of them. The red blood flared bright and then turned a pale silvery white against his skin.

There was another flash of bright white flames and a small cup appeared in the woman's hand. She gently tipped Scarlett's palm into it, the blood dripping steadily down until it was half full. "You each need to drink," she said plainly.

"I'm not drinking blood," Cassius quipped, crossing his arms across his already toned chest.

White flames appeared in the eyes of the woman, and Scarlett stepped back. "You will do as you are commanded, young warlord," she ordered. "Drink." She held the cup out to him. Cassius wisely did not argue this time and took a drink from the cup. His lips were bright red when he handed it back to the woman.

The flames were gone from her eyes when they settled upon Scarlett once more. "Can you do one more brave thing for me tonight, Starfire?" The woman extended the cup to her, but Scarlett stepped back into her mother's legs. The woman's features softened. "Can I tell you a story?"

Scarlett nodded, glancing at Cassius. Sybil still held his shoulders. He tried to give her a reassuring smile, but it was tight and forced.

"Once upon a time there was a people who loved the night and the dark. They lived in a beautiful land with snow like diamonds in the mountains and waters as dark as the midnight sky by the beaches. There were special animals that lived in a magical forest there, and some of them chose to protect and serve some of the people."

"What kind of animals?" Scarlett asked.

"Powerful and strong ones," the woman said, and tears really did glimmer in her eyes this time. "A graceful owl. A pair of fierce dragons. A stunning snake. A beautiful panther. To name a few, but there were also people who chose a similar bond. Many times, the people in the kingdom's armies were chosen for these bonds. These people were drawn to each other by fate. It was a sacred bond. A bond that was chosen which made it even more powerful, and it was a bond that was placed above all others, save for one. They became a Guardian of the one they were bonded to. The bond was blessed and honored by Sargon himself. Do you know who Sargon is?"

"The god of war, courage, and bravery," Cassius cut in.

"Exactly right, young warlord," the woman said, glancing at Cassius with a smile. Her eyes came back to Scarlett. "But the bond demanded great and powerful magic and required that the two people become connected by blood. So they mixed their blood and drank. Little Starfire, the Fates brought you and Cassius together so he could be your Guardian just like in that story, but I need you to drink."

"What if he doesn't want to be my Guardian?" Scarlett asked, looking at Cassius once more.

"Don't be stupid, Scarlett," Cassius huffed, shrugging out of Sybil's grip

and puffing out his chest. *"Of course, I want to be your Guardian. I pretty much already am."*

Scarlett stuck her tongue out at him. *"Don't be a jerk,"* she quipped bossily.

Eliné was about to say something, but Cassius stepped forward with a quick glance to her. He knelt down in front of Scarlett and a small smile kicked up on his mouth. "Tell you what, Scarlett, you take a drink of that, and I'll swipe you some extra treacle tart tomorrow."

"I want four pieces," Scarlett demanded, reaching to take the cup from the woman.

"Then four pieces you shall have," Cassius answered. *"Drink up."*

Scarlett took a drink from the small cup and made a face. A coppery metallic taste coated her tongue, and she handed the cup back to the woman. It was warm as it traveled down to her belly, and a link seemed to settle in her that her five-year-old little mind wasn't quite sure what to do with. She gave a questioning look to Cassius, who was watching her carefully, as he always did, scanning her for hurt and discomfort. The women around them were silent, watching them as Cassius reached up and tousled her silver hair. "Good girl, Scarlett."

"Was there a princess in this kingdom?" Scarlett asked, turning to the silver-haired woman.

A sound almost like a cry seemed to come from her, but she quickly cleared her throat. "Yes, Scarlett, there is a princess in this kingdom."

"I bet she's really pretty," Scarlett sighed, looking up at the stars. They seemed even brighter.

"They had a king and queen who loved to dance under the stars among the swirling shadows and blackest nights," the woman said, her eyes going to the night sky as well. *"They had two children, a boy and a girl, who were the prince and princess, and they loved them very much. The princess was as beautiful as the stars, and the prince was as wild as the beasts of the land."*

The two silver-haired persons, one woman and one child, stared at the sky. The others were silent around them. After nearly a minute, the woman brought her hand to Scarlett's hair, winding her fingers through it. Eyes of icy blue met eyes of silver. "Always remember, Starfire, that hope is for the dreamers."

Scarlett groaned at the throbbing in her skull. Had she been knocked unconscious or had she slipped into this state all on her own from expending so much magic?

She pried her eyes open, blinking against the bright sun. Her vision blurred slightly and then came back into focus. Before her lay the destruction of what she'd done. Piles of ashes and bodies. There had been one Night Child left, but there was no one in sight now.

Dirt and grass crusted her cheek as she tried to push up into a sitting position, but her arms trembled and gave out, unable to support her own weight. She collapsed back onto the ground and stifled a cry at the agony that blasted through her head. There was something wet on her lips, though. She brought a hand up and wiped the back of it across her mouth. When she pulled it back, red was smeared across the back. She was bleeding. How or why she couldn't remember.

"She finally wakes."

Scarlett twisted on the ground towards the sound of the voice to find a man sitting atop a rock. He had black hair the color of Prince Azrael's and the same dark golden skin. Something tugged at the recesses of her memory, but her head was pounding too much to focus on much of anything right now. The man was flipping a dagger in his hand as if bored. A shirastone dagger.

Scarlett summoned her shadows, but none appeared. No flame. No ice. No water. Nothing.

The man laughed. "You did not get enough to summon any of your gifts."

Get enough what? Sleep? Sorin had been warning her she was diving too deeply into her magic too quickly without replenishing her reserves. He had been telling her she needed to sleep more, rest more. There just hadn't been time. Everything had been happening so quickly.

Again, she tried to push herself into a sitting position, but she couldn't even get her arms underneath her this time.

The man laughed again. "Hasn't Aditya taught you how to properly pull up your magic safely? You have been with him for months now."

Aditya. He knew who Sorin was.

"Who are you?" she rasped. Her throat was dry and hoarse and a coppery yet almost earthy taste coated her tongue.

The man flipped his dagger again, studying her. "You are not the queen I was expecting to show up here. An unexpected but pleasant surprise."

"You were waiting for Talwyn?"

"The Earth Court is her jurisdiction, is it not? I was not anticipating you leaving the side of your Fire Prince," he answered simply, flipping that damn dagger again. "The Assassin Lord will be quite pleased to have you returned home."

Alaric?

That had her forcing her arms underneath her and pushing up into a sitting position. The world spun before her, but she managed to get upright, pulling her knees to her chest. "You..." she panted. "You know the Assassin Lord?"

"I am wounded, your Majesty," the man said with a fake pout as he leapt down from the rock. "You do not recognize me from the Fellowship?"

"I generally don't remember forgettable wannabe second rate assassins," Scarlett managed to get out around her breathing. She was fairly certain she was going to vomit.

"I have never understood what he finds so endearing about that godsdamn mouth," the man snarled. "Although he did not find it so amusing the last time you were in his presence, did he?"

That was when she'd brought Sorin to the Black Syndicate. He must have been one of the men holding her before Alaric. She swallowed thickly. Gods, she needed some water.

"Who are you?" Scarlett demanded hoarsely again. She couldn't hold her head up any longer. It fell forward, her forehead resting against her knees.

She saw his boots stop in front of her. An earthy smell of forest and soil filled her senses...and power. Some type of magic. She lifted her head and found his pale green eyes watching her. His mouth was tilted up in a cruel, amused smile.

"You are not a Night Child," she ground out, again trying to summon any bit of her own magic to put a shield around herself, but there was nothing. She was completely and utterly drained.

"Don't bother," the man said again with annoyance. "You arrived here without your ring so I cannot access my magic like any other immortal being in the mortal lands."

She sniffed again, taking in his scent once more. She could almost taste it on her tongue. Soil and trees and sand and—

"You are Fae," she murmured. "You have earth magic."

"Very good, your Majesty," he purred.

"You are working with the mortals?"

Her head went back to her knees. Too much. It was too much information. She couldn't process everything with the pain in her head.

"I am working with the Lords," he said coolly.

"The Maraan Lords?"

There was a long pause of silence. "How do you know of the Maraan Lords?"

"My cleverness is why the Assassin Lord puts up with my gods-damn mouth," she mumbled back.

The man chuckled. "And also why he kept you so sequestered for so long, I imagine." He crouched down before her and waited until she lifted her head once more to meet his gaze. "Since you have figured out so much, Majesty, I think it is high time we are introduced. After all, we were almost family."

The confusion must have been evident on her face because the small tilt of his mouth became a full, sneering grin. "I am Tarek. Queen Talwyn's twin flame and rightful heir of the Earth Court."

A NOTE FROM THE AUTHOR

I cannot even begin to describe the emotions that rise up when I think of this book. *Lady of Shadows* was written at a dark time in my life. Scarlett and Sorin and their world became an escape from own darkness and shadows. When I was drowning on dry land, I flung myself into their world, and what came out of those brutal ashes was something truly beautiful.

My husband and I have three wild and beautiful boys. But we also have two sweet girls who did not make it here. We lost two girls in the second trimester of my pregnancies. This series was started shortly after we lost our second little girl, Scarlett Mae. *Lady of Shadows* was being written at the height of grappling with grief and mourning dreams, walking that dark path, and discovering the beauty that grows in the darkness. I can vividly remember specific days of heartache and breaking when I re-read some of these chapters. I remember feeling like I couldn't breathe. I remember not knowing if I would ever find my way out. I remember dear friends climbing down into my pits, not to make it better or to tell me to cheer up, but just to sit with me in my darkness. I remember days of wondering what the hell was wrong with me. I felt everything at once or nothing at all. And I was exhausted.

I still have hard days, and I will be one hundred percent transparent when I say I sometimes re-read certain chapters from this book to remind myself that hard days are okay.

To remind myself that some days, the only thing I need to do is survive.

To remind myself that the stars are always worth fighting for.

I found a deep love for the darkness that broke me. I learned that the darkest nights produce the brightest stars. I walked through a pit of hell, and the person that emerged on the other side of that journey was not the same as the person who went into it.

She's stronger.

She's braver.

She's a dreamer.

So today, my friend, know that it is okay to let yourself be pulled from the river. You only drown if you stay in the water. The stars are always worth fighting for. Hope is for the dreamers.

XX~ Melissa

Scarlett's next book will be out soon, but until then, I want to keep in touch! I get messages from you guys every day, and they fill my cup more than you could ever know. I would love for you to join my little nook on Facebook at Melissa's Nook & Posse. To stay up-to-date on release dates, new series, and more, be sure and sign up for the newsletter, too!

One more thing: your reviews on Amazon and Goodreads are HUGE for me as an author. I'd be forever grateful if you could go over to one (or both!) of them and leave a short review of *Lady of Shadows* to help Scarlett's story reach others. Word of mouth is an author's best friend and much appreciated. Shouts from rooftops are great, too.

ACKNOWLEDGMENTS

Thank you to my readers for falling in love with Scarlett, Sorin, and everyone in their world from the very beginning. Your comments, messages, and excitement for more filled my cup so much. Writing and publishing is hard, and those sweet words would come at the perfect time to remind that it is all worth it in the end.

A big thank you to Megan Visger for being amazing and reading through drafts to catch the things I miss when editing at all hours of the night. You are a gem, my friend, and one I am so incredibly grateful for.

Thank you to my husband for putting up with late nights of editing and for letting me retreat to my happy place when I'm writing and working out story lines and plot issues; and a big thank you to my family and friends who have encouraged me from the very beginning. To the people who stepped out of their normal reading genres and read Lady of Darkness simply because I wrote the dang thing, that kind of love is beautiful, and I'm humbled and grateful to claim you as part of my tribe.

Thank you to the Melissa's Nook and Posse reader's group. Many of you have been with me from the very beginning, long before I started writing a book. You know my history, and have uplifted me through the darkness and the shadows. The support and encouragement you all give me every single day is nothing short of amazing. Thank you.

LADY OF ASHES SNEAK PEEK
BOOK 3 IN THE LADY OF DARKNESS SERIES

Turn the page for a sneak peek at the next chapter in Scarlett's journey! Available now on Kindle Unlimited, Paperback, and Amazon E-Book!

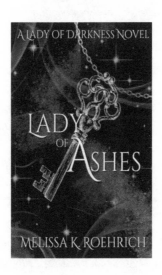

LITTLE WHIRLWIND & THE PRINCE

The girl clapped her hands over her mouth to quiet her breathing. Her knees were drawn into her chest as she huddled under the sofa table in the drawing room. The navy and gold embroidered decorative covering hid her from view. She sniffed the air, scenting him in the room.

"I know you are in here," came his voice. She felt a flicker of power spearing out into the room. She couldn't hear his footsteps even with her Fae hearing, but then again, when a Fae warrior was hunting you, he knew how to move without a sound.

She focused on steadying her breathing like she'd been practicing, willing those winds that flowed around her to calm and keep that covering from moving even an inch. That other power flowed around her, and she felt it scrape a flaming claw down her cheek. She flung her shields up, but it was too late.

"Got you!" The covering was flung up as flames surrounded her, and a male peered under the table at her, his dark hair falling over his forehead into his eyes.

The girl screamed.

The male's laughter filled the room as the girl giggled with delight. "You calmed your wind, but forgot about your shields, Little Whirlwind."

"I know, I know," the girl huffed. "There is so much to remember."

The male's golden eyes twinkled. He gave the girl a wink as he said,

"*Extinguish the flames around you, and I will sneak you some frozen cream before your aunt returns.*" *Then he added,* "*Blowing them out with your breath is cheating.*"

The girl narrowed her jade green eyes at the male. In a whiny voice she said, "*Why can I not just blow them out?*"

"*Because you need to learn to use your power with your mind, not just with your hands and mouth. So either put them out by sucking the air from them, or you will be stuck under there all day while I eat frozen cream by myself,*" *he answered.*

The girl had a pout on her lips, but she closed her eyes. In and out. In and out. She steadied her breathing just like he had taught her to do, pulling from her pool of winds and air.

"*Easy, Talwyn,*" *the male said softly.* "*You control it. It does not control you.*"

"*I know. I know,*" *Talwyn muttered. She reached into that pool of swirling wind, trying to pull up just a small amount of air current, when something else caught her attention. There were flowers and sand and leaves amongst her winds. Where had those come from? The flowers were beautiful. Tiny purple lavender and white dogwood blooms. She reached towards those now, swirling in her whirls of air, and as she touched one—*

A gust of wind blew through the room. The flames around her roared to life. She could feel the heat but knew they would not burn her. Sorin would never let harm come to her.

"*You blew flowers in from the gardens, Little Whirlwind,*" *Sorin said, flicking her nose as he extinguished the flames that surrounded her. Talwyn took his hand, and he helped her from beneath the sofa table. Her turquoise dress swished on the floor as her mahogany brown hair flowed on the phantom winds around her.*

"*Ashtine never does that. She has more control than I do, and she is younger than me,*" *Talwyn complained as Sorin led her to the door.*

"*Lady Ashtine is nine. She is only a year younger than you,*" *Sorin answered with a soft smile.*

"*And she is a Wind Walker. It is not fair,*" *Talwyn said.*

"*What is not fair?*" *came a feminine voice from the hall. Her aunt swept in, graceful and perfect as always. Her dark brown hair was swept into a loose knot at the nape of her neck, and her icy blue eyes were soft when they landed on Talwyn. Talwyn let go of Sorin's hand and ran to her. "Hello, little queen," her aunt said, crouching down to peer into her eyes and stroking her cheek. "Now tell me. What is not fair?"*

Talwyn sighed, blowing a piece of her hair out of her face. "Ashtine has better control over her magic, and she's a Wind Walker."

"You will master your power, Talwyn. You have only just started your magic lessons. Because she is a Wind Walker, her powers emerged sooner. Your magic will grow as you grow," her aunt replied gently. "How did your lesson go today?"

Her aunt had straightened, taking her hand and leading her from the sitting room. Sorin, as always, was to her right as they walked along the corridors of the Black Halls. "It was fine," Talwyn answered. "Except that I blew flowers in from the gardens."

"Did you now?" her aunt said with a laugh. "The violets or the roses?"

"They were little white and purple flowers," Talwyn answered.

Her aunt halted. "We do not have such flowers around the Black Halls."

"She probably blew them in from across the Courts, Eliné. It was quite the gust," Sorin said from beside her.

"Of course," Eliné replied, resuming their walk down the corridor, but something had changed. Talwyn couldn't quite put her finger on it. "Are we off to get frozen cream?"

"She figured out our secret plan again," Sorin said to Talwyn conspiratorially.

Talwyn giggled. "It is not really a secret if we do it every day, Sorin."

Sorin feigned shock. "Shh, Little Whirlwind. She will hear you." Talwyn giggled again as a swirl of leaves appeared beside her aunt's head. Eliné reached up a slender hand and plucked a message from the leaves that disappeared as suddenly as they'd appeared.

Sorin instantly went rigid. "What does Luan want?"

Eliné gave him a pointed look. "Prince Azrael is responding to a question of my own, Sorin." She placed Talwyn's hand into his. "I need to speak with him quickly. I shall meet you both in the kitchens." Tweaking Talwyn's nose, she said, "Leave me a scoop of strawberry frozen cream please."

"I should go with you," Sorin said, his focus on his queen.

"It is a quick inquiry, Sorin," her aunt said, running her hands down her sea blue skirts. "I will be fine."

"Eliné—"

"I will be fine, Sorin," Eliné said, cutting him off. Her eyes flared brightly. Talwyn stood still, looking between her aunt and her closest advisor. She rarely saw them upset with each other.

Sorin was giving her aunt a contemplative look as he said, "Something is wrong." It was a statement, not a question. As if he knew her aunt so well, he could tell such a thing just by looking at her. It was these moments, these glimpses into her aunt's world as queen, that made her pray to the Fates that Sorin would be able to remain her Second when she had to take up her role as Queen of the Eastern Courts.

When her aunt did not reply, Sorin said, "Ten minutes, Eliné. Then I will come to you if you have not returned."

Her aunt sighed. "Someday, Prince of Fire, we need to revisit the chain of command here." She lifted her hand, her palm flat, and blew across it, splashing water into Sorin's face.

Talwyn laughed delightedly, and her aunt threw her a wink before she disappeared into the air. Concern still lined Sorin's face, but when he noticed Talwyn studying him, it morphed into a smile. "Well, Little Whirlwind, what kind of frozen cream shall it be today?"

"Chocolate!" she cried. "It is always chocolate."

"You know you will need to extinguish some flames before it melts into chocolate soup, right?" he asked, rolling small balls of fire between his fingers.

Talwyn groaned. "I bet Ashtine doesn't have to do this."

Sorin smiled, sending one of those flames dancing down her arm. "Lady Ashtine is not going to be a queen someday."

"Do you think I will be as wonderful as my mother was?" she asked while Sorin pushed open the doors to one of the bustling kitchens. One of the cooks saw them and immediately went to the ice boxes.

"Little Whirlwind," Sorin said, lifting her off her feet and setting her onto the counter. "You will be one of the greatest queens this world has ever seen."

Talwyn's heart filled with pride at the look Sorin gave her. So proud. So adoring. "You will be with me, too, right?"

"As long as I am still on this side of the Veil, I will be by your side," he said, giving her long hair an affectionate tug.

"Aunt Eliné doesn't like me sitting on the counters, you know," she said, the cook handing her a bowl of chocolate frozen cream.

"We will call it another one of our little secrets," Sorin said with a wink as he took a bite of his vanilla dessert. "Now hurry, before you are drinking your frozen cream instead."

Talwyn felt her bowl warm in her hands, and she focused on wrapping her icy winds around the bowl to keep her frozen cream from melting.